The
Master
of all
Desires

The Master of all Desires

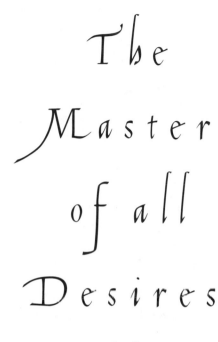

Judith Merkle Riley

VIKING

VIKING
Published by the Penguin Group
Penguin Putnam Inc., 375 Hudson Street,
New York, New York 10014, U.S.A.
Penguin Books Ltd, 27 Wrights Lane, London W8 5TZ, England
Penguin Books Autstralia Ltd, Ringwood, Victoria, Australia
Penguin Books Canada Ltd, 10 Alcorn Avenue,
Toronto, Ontario, LCanada M4V 3B2
Penguin Books (N.Z.) Ltd, 182–190 Wairau Road,
Auckland 10, New Zealand

Penguin Books Ltd, Registered Offices:
Harmondsworth, Middlesex, England

First published in 1999 by Viking Penguin,
a member of Penguin Putnam Inc.

3   5   7   9   10   8   6   4   2

LIBRARY OF CONGRESS CATALOGING IN PUBLICATION DATA
Riley, Judith Merkle.
The master of all desires / Judith Merkle Riley.
p.   cm.
ISBN 0-670-88450-2
1. France—History—Henry II, 1547–1559 Fiction.   2. Catherine de Médicis, Queen,
consort of Henry II, King of France, 1519–1589 Fiction.   3. Nostradamus, 1503–1566
Fiction.   I. Title.
PS3568.I3794M37   1999
813'.54.—dc21   99–29828

This book is printed on acid-free paper.

Printed in the United States of America
Set in Kennerly
Designed by Kathryn Parise

To the memory of my parents

'Guess now who holds thee?'—'Death,' I said.
    But, there,
The silver answer rang . . . 'Not Death, but Love.'
        —ELIZABETH BARRETT BROWNING

Acknowledgments

※

As always, I am grateful for wonderful libraries, in particular, the libraries of the University of California system, the Huntington Library, and the Honnold Library of the Claremont Colleges. I owe special thanks to the librarians of the Interlibrary Loan Desk at the Honnold, who managed, among many other things, to get hold of the more exotic and obscure works of Nostradamus for me. I have also had the blessing of supportive friends and family, the Tea Ladies, Deborah and Susan, my husband, Parkes, my son, Marlow, and my daughter Elizabeth, who read the manuscript with her usual shrewd insight. I am deeply appreciative of the work of my editors, Pam Dorman and Susan Hans O'Connor. And to my agent, Jean Naggar, my awe and gratitude for her astonishing ability to remain serene and reassuring in the face of the manic ups and downs of the writing life.

A Guide to Historical Figures in
The Master of All Desires

✦

THE VALOIS DYNASTY IN 1556

Henri II, King of France. The second son of King Francis I, he became Dauphin after the mysterious poisoning death of his older brother, and king after the death of his father, in 1547.

Catherine de Medici, Queen of France. Great-niece of two Medici Popes.

Their Children:

François, Dauphin, born in 1543. Heir to the throne.

Elisabeth, born in 1545.

Claude, born in 1547.

Louis, born in 1548, died in 1550.

Charles-Maximilien, born in 1550.

Henri, born in 1551. Originally christened Edouard-Alexandre.

Margaret (Margot), born in 1553.

Hercule, born in 1554. Later renamed François.

Victoire and Jeanne, twins, born in 1556. Died in infancy.

THE BOURBON DYNASTY IN 1556

Antoine de Bourbon, King of Navarre.

Charles, Cardinal of Bourbon, his brother.

Louis, Prince de Condé, youngest brother of the King of Navarre.

Jeanne d'Albret, Queen of Navarre, daughter of King Francis's sister Marguerite, and a leader of the Protestant reform.

Henri of Navarre, son of Antoine de Bourbon and Jeanne d'Albret, born in 1553.

FRENCH COURTIERS

Diane de Poitiers, Duchess of Valentinois, the mistress of Henri II, allied to the Guises.

Mary, Queen of Scots, betrothed to the Dauphin François, raised with the royal children since the age of six. Her mother was Mary of Guise, elder sister of the Duc de Guise and the Cardinal of Lorraine.

François, Duc de Guise ("The Scar"). Leader of the powerful Guise family and uncle to Mary, Queen of Scots.

Charles de Guise, Cardinal of Lorraine, his younger brother and co-conspirator.

Anne de Montmorency, Grand Constable of France, and head of the powerful Montmorency family, rivals to the Guises.

Henri de Montmorency, Baron de Damville, second son of the Constable, and Marshall of France.

Gaspard de Coligny, Colonel-General of the Infantry, later Admiral of France, the nephew of Montmorency.

RIVAL ASTROLOGERS AND FORTUNE-TELLERS TO THE QUEEN

Michel de Nostre Dame, known as Nostradamus. The celebrated author of *The Centuries* and other works of prediction and medicine.

Cosmo Ruggieri, head of the numerous Ruggiero clan, traditional astrologers to the Medici.

Lorenzo Ruggieri, his brother.

Gabriel Simeoni, royal astrologer.

Luc Guaric, known as Guaricus. Famous astrologer and mathematician, fortune-teller for various Popes.

FOREIGN MONARCHS

Philip II, King of Spain and Holy Roman Emperor.

Edward VI of England (1537–1553), only son of Henry VIII. Promoted Protestant reform.

Mary I, Queen of England, daughter of Henry VIII and Catherine of
   Aragon. Wife of Philip II, who became King of England with the
   marriage. Pro-Catholic.
Elizabeth I, became Queen of England in 1558, daughter of Henry VIII
   and Anne Boleyn. Pro-Protestant.

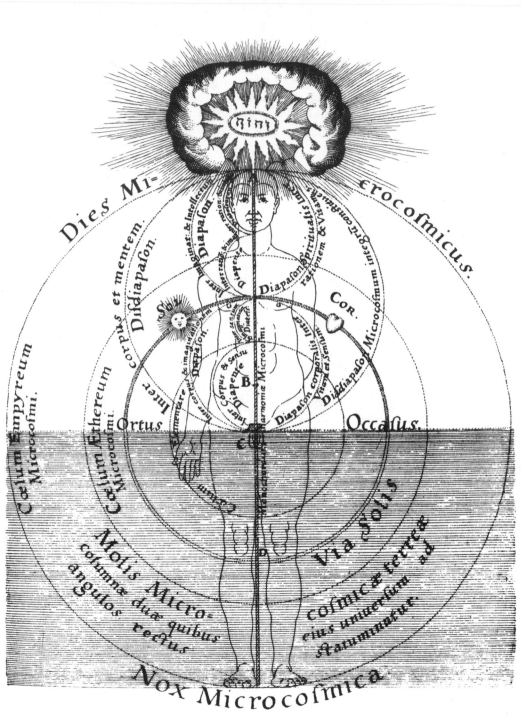

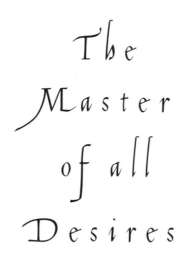

The
Master
of all
Desires

Prologue

ere's the place," said the Queen of France, whispering in Italian. She pointed to an almost invisible seam in the floor of the gilded room. The flickering light of a single candle cast distorted shadows on the walls. The night air of summer was fetid and oppressively hot. The stone halls and bare summer fireplaces reeked of urine, of dankness and mildew, of summer fevers. The court had remained too long at Saint-Germain, and the palace had begun to stink. In another month or two, the king would order the court's removal to another, breezier stronghold. One where the game in the park had not been exhausted by his hunts. One where his nose would not signal for yet another few weeks that it was time once again to move. "I've had the carpenter make two holes in the floor," whispered the queen. "Her bedroom is below. Tonight we'll learn how that old woman does the witchcraft that steals my husband's love from me."

"She is twenty years older than you both. Surely, if you could find someone younger, more beautiful, but utterly obedient to you, you could break her hold, and then ..." the queen's Italian *dame d'honneur* whispered in reply. The alien language seemed to flow like smoke, swirling past the carved satyrs' heads on the fireplace, and clinging in the corners, the sound of foreign conspiracy in the ancient stronghold of the French kings.

1

"Do you think I have not tried that? A moment or two, and then he is back with *her*, flaunting the ancient whore in public, hiding *me* as if I were the mistress. I want to destroy her influence over him forever. I want to be rid of her."

"Madame, you are queen—"

"And my hand must never be seen in anything that happens to her," said the queen. "While he loves her, should ill befall her, he will take revenge on me. But if he ceases to love her . . ."

"Then you must find the witchcraft that holds him," whispered her companion.

"Exactly. And then destroy it with more powerful sorcery." Catherine de Medici, Queen of France, her bulging, heavy-lidded eyes lit deep from within with long-concealed resentment, fingered a magic talisman cast with human blood that hung around her neck. "She has found a powerful spell-caster. But where? Only the Ruggieri have such powers, and they are mine. I swear, if Cosmo has betrayed me—"

"Surely not, Majesty. There are other sorcerers in the realm. Cosmo Ruggieri came with us from Florence. His father served your father— why would *that woman* turn to your servant? He might betray her."

"And he might not. Never underestimate the slyness of the Ruggieri. They are as treacherous as a nest of snakes—I know them well. I will find the magic and make Cosmo remove it, and he and I will both pretend that he never had knowledge of it before. It is time; I have lived long enough under the shadow of that old woman. She turns all my happiness to dust."

"Surely, Majesty, it can only be the ring," whispered her *dame d'honneur*, Lucrèce Cavalcanti, Madame d'Elbène. "All the court whispers that the ring she gave him was cast with the blood of an unbaptized infant. It is the ring that enslaves him. Tonight you will see that that is so." She leaned down and held the candlestick closer to the spot, while Catherine de Medici knelt and scrabbled for the catch that would release the floorboard.

"Blow out the candle," the queen whispered to her. "I don't want them to see the light from above." Only faint starlight illumined the room, as the two women lay on the floor to peer into the brightly lit bedchamber below.

The king's mistress lay stretched naked upon her back on the canopied, heavily draped bed, her arms behind her head, and her graying hair fanned behind her on a jumble of richly embroidered silk pillows. The pallor of her flesh formed a stark contrast to the rich green velvet of the coverlet below her. Her black eyes glittered in the candlelight, and her narrow, painted lips smiled triumphantly, while the king, vigorous, black haired, and twenty years her junior, stripped off his *robe de chambre*. It was almost as if she knew there were witnesses, this night, to her power.

Diane de Poitier's face, taut, seamed with fine lines, the eyes set in sunken, dark circles, held no surprises for the watchers. But at the first sight of the older woman's body the two watching women suppressed a gasp of amazement. It was white, slender, agile, like the body of a twenty-year-old set beneath an old woman's head. With icy discipline, the barren mistress had protected this pallid imitation of a younger woman's form, while the queen, with steel stays and jeweled dresses, could not conceal the shapeless body ravaged by annual pregnancies. Schemer, monster, thought the queen. The Devil has done this for you. When I am rid of you, I will make myself beautiful, too. I'll have masseurs, I'll have potions. Then I will ride at the king's side at his grand entries, with my colors and device displayed at every tourney, instead of being hidden like an ugly secret. Today the sight of me humiliates him. But tomorrow he will love me.

In the gilded bed beneath the peephole, two athletic bodies, one dusted with dark hair, the other whiter than milk, entangled in complex postures completely novel to the watchers above. There in the dark, the queen's eyes widened and she gasped softly. Now they had twisted about, and the old mistress had mounted King Henri the Second. His face was distorted with pleasure. Never had the queen imagined that such curious embraces, such lingering caresses could exist. Why had she not known of such things? Why had he never shown *her* these things? Was she that unworthy of passion, as well as respect? Now the king and his aged mistress had rolled to the side, and the fierce, furious rhythm so shook them that they fell from the bed in a cascade of sheets, completely oblivious, onto the cool, hard tiles of the floor. The king's cry of passion was still resonating in the room below when his wife replaced the floorboard. Tears of rage, invisible in the dark, ran down her podgy face.

"In all the years we have been married," she whispered, "he never once has touched me like that. My hair—it was beautiful—he never stroked it like that—never—ten children, and he never kissed me. He comes in the dark, and leaves without a candle—what am I, that he treats me like a cow, and her like a woman?"

"But, Majesty, you are the true queen. She is, after all, only the king's whore." The dumpy little woman with the chinless, goggle-eyed face wiped her eyes secretly, there in the dark.

"Yes, I am queen," she said. "I *am* queen, and she is not." She straightened herself up, and brushed down her crumpled, dusty skirts. "Can't he see that she is old, old? I was fourteen when I came to him. My uncle the Pope sent me in honor, in a gilded galley with slaves in silver chains. Who was she? A nobody. An old nobody. It has to be the magic ring that's blinded him. The ring she gave him. I don't care what it takes, I'll have that ring from his hand." And then I'll have Cosmo compound me a love potion, she thought. Something strong, something that will bring me more than cold leftovers.

"It's just a matter of waiting for the right moment," said Madam D'Elbène.

"I, of all people, have learned how to wait," said the queen, patting back her tight, artificial curls. "I have waited for many things. Still . . ."

"Yes, majesty?"

"When I was young, they called me beautiful. Why did the king, my husband, never love me like that?"

One

Left Orléans early yesterday. Inn of the Three Kings. My curse upon them. Inn of the Three Robbers would be a more honest sign. Beds despicable. Breakfast, 3 sous. Inedible. Has frozen my bowels. The city itself, highly overrated. Sour people. High prices. An excess of heretics. The Bishop wanted a horoscope. Charged double.

Entered Paris by Porte St.-Jacques. Near the rue de la Bûcherie, annoying swarm of students from the medical faculty blocked my way with some prank. Rudeness when I demanded passage. Insults to my gown, which was not of their faculty. Shouts that I was a foreign spagyric, the loosing of missiles composed of street ordure, accompanied by vulgar offers of a free bloodletting. Paris is always enraged at the sight of the livery of its better, our own medical faculty of Montpellier. Toadies. Lickspittles of the Faculty of Theology. The only things they know how to do are bleed and purge. And they dare to denounce the great Paracelsus! We would never let a graduate of that wretched Paris faculty practice in the south.

Have Léon arrange for the cleansing of my doctoral gown.

Inn of Saint-Michel, Paris. My own name. A good omen for an inn. Linens clean. Dinner, 5 sous. Ragoût passable, wine deserves the name of vinegar.

Find new edition of Scaliger. Try Barbe Renault's. It is doubtless overrated. Morel tells me Simeoni's new prediction of the end of mankind in the *year 1957 is all the rage. Simeoni is an ass. He couldn't predict the end of the month. If he doesn't find a better novelty than that, I predict he will lose royal favor within the next six months. Sent Léon to the Louvre to announce my ar-rival to the queen's household office.*

They seem to want an advance on my bill here. Something about foreign physicians flying by night. See if Morel will lend me fifty nobles.

Curious signs on the road yesterday. A serpent with two heads sunning it-self on a rock. Truly, I am besieged with two-headed creatures. This two-headed kid of Aurons, the two-headed child of Senas. The time of bloody schism draws closer. Later that very day on the road from Orléans, a rustic young lady in mourning traveling in the opposite direction with an ugly hound. Silly, pretentious, headstrong character. But a strange aura. I have the haunt-ing premonition that for some brief while, she will hold the future of France in her hands. What an awful idea. Bad dreams. Check with Anael.

Michel de Nostre-Dame

THE LOST JOURNALS OF NOSTRADAMUS,

A.J. Peters, tr. and ed.,

(Sedona, AZ: Cernunnos Press, 1974)

Vol. 3, Entry 209, August 15, 1556

"You," said the stranger in the foreign doctor's gown and square hat, eyeing me up and down, "you write bad poetry." He had an annoying eye, and one of those long gray beards that catches crumbs. I did not deem him worthy of an answer. It was not clear to me how he had gained knowledge of my little effusions of the spirit, but I would never think to entertain conversation with such a rude personage in a public place. "You tinkle at the lute, write banal études for the virginals, and ir-ritating essays on Nature," he went on. "A dabbler at everything, who can't resist prying into other people's affairs."

"We have not been introduced," I said in my most cutting voice, as I set down my cup of bad-tasting cider beside me on the rustic seat. Above us, the birds twittered in the trees that shaded the outdoor benches. Behind us stood the wayside tavern, a peasant's thatched hut scarcely distinguishable from an overlarge haystack, marked as a place of refreshment only by a broom over the door. It was the summer of the year 1556, the twenty-second year of my life, that time when the last freshness of youth irrevocably gives way to long, lean spinsterhood. The peasant boy who walked at my bridle was at the watering trough with my mare, too far away to summon. Gargantua, my big brindled hound puppy, lay at my feet panting in the heat, with his long pink tongue hanging out. A useless dog, too lazy even to growl. How should I rid myself of this lunatic old man?

"We do not need to be introduced," said the stranger, peering at me from under bushy white eyebrows. "I know you already. I have come to tell you to turn around, return home, and dwell with your family, as a proper woman should. Both you and the kingdom will be better off for it."

"I have absolutely no intention of it," I said. "Besides, it is an impossibility. I must reach Orléans before the gates are closed at sundown."

"You cannot undo what you have done, but you can avoid what is to come: go home, I say." A cold shudder transfixed my physical person. Suppose he wasn't mad? Suppose he was an informer? Had he somehow discovered the reason for my precipitous flight from my father's estate? I stood up suddenly—too suddenly—to flee him, overturning the cup and spilling the last of the cider on the hem of my mourning gown. Hastily, I bent to brush the drops from the dark wool and catch up the cup from the dust. I thought I heard him chuckle.

That's what informers do, before they go to the *bailli,* I thought. They laugh at their victims. I mean, it really wasn't my fault that I'd shot Thibault Villasse. Admittedly, I knew his face well enough, being affianced to him for all those long, dull years, but you must consider that it was dark and and he was masked. Besides, my poetical labors, along with close stitching, have caused a certain shortsightedness to come upon me recently. It really couldn't have been expected that I should do otherwise.

I must admit to a brief spasm of guilt when the smoke cleared and I saw that the face at the windowsill had vanished. Such a dreadful fall, you see, down into the moonlit courtyard, and I am by nature very tenderhearted. Why, I cannot bear to see a fledgling bird fall out of the nest without replacing it. And besides, I had put on mourning for him, which showed the world I was sorry. Clearly, it was not I who had shot off father's arquebus, but Fate. And Fate couldn't be undone.

"You can't change Fate," I said.

"Demoiselle, I have wearied myself traveling all this way to change Fate, and for the good of this realm, I tell you that you must return."

"And for the good of myself, I must go forward. Change Fate another way." The old doctor's face turned crimson, and he sputtered with rage.

"You conceited old maid, do you realize great kings have given me purses of gold for a single word of my advice?" But I am an Artaud of La Roque: insults do not move me. I looked down my nose at him, one of my most successful gestures of scorn, since I am tall above the ordinary.

"Then go away and advise them. I shall do what I shall do." As I turned to go, he seemed so set down, I felt almost sorry for the vainglo- rious old windbag. A southerner, by his accent. They are all boasters, those southerners. Clearly, this doctor had swallowed too many medi- cines of his own compounding. Kings, indeed.

"Stay, wait—" he said, and I paused. He looked me up and down, his gaze assessing. "Even so—yes—it could work out. Just heed my warn- ing: beware the Queen of Swords."

"I have no idea what you mean," I said.

"Oh, yes you do," he said, as his servant brought his mounts to him from the trough. "Old maids always read the *tarocchi*." As the servant came closer, I made out that he was not leading a doctor's mules, but royal post-horses. The strange old man was traveling on business for the crown. Oh, dear, he must be important after all. Had I been too un- civil? Did he know my dreadful secret? As if in answer to my unspoken question, the odd doctor turned back to look at me as he set his foot in the stirrup. "Mourning, pah!" he said. "You should be ashamed." For a moment, my heart stood still.

The proprietress, in slatternly apron and cap, was crossing before me bearing several cups of her odious home-brewed beverage. "Good woman," I said (thus does politeness make liars of us all), "tell me, do you know the name of that elderly fellow with the long beard and the doctor's gown?"

"Him? Indeed I do. From Provence on the queen's business. His man seems to think his name is very important. *Doctor* Michel de Nôtre- Dame, if you please. I've met much greater *here*, I can tell you."

Nostradamus. The talk of every parlor and fashionable *cénacle* since the appearance of his little volume of prophecies in verse. Not a prosecutor's informer, but a prophet who read the future, summoned by the queen, herself. I felt a shiver go through me at the very sound of his name. Fate and I had just met on the Orléans road.

But what had he meant about the kingdom?

Two

It was dawn, the kind of sticky dawn that has brought no relief from the heat, and promises a muggy, unbearable afternoon. Diane de Poitiers was emerging from her cold bath, and two maids stood by with towels to rub her dry. The palace had awakened; in the kitchens, pots were clattering, in the stables horses being brushed and saddled, among them Diane's and the king's. Here and there a late-sleeping roisterer aroused himself, stretched, pissed into the fireplace, and called for drink. In one bedroom, the queen was holding her *levée,* the Duchess of Nevers holding out her shift. In another, the king, his long, morose face oddly contented, was having his points fastened by a valet, as he gave orders to the courtiers that surrounded him. He was pondering a move to Fontainebleau, where the air was fresher, before wintering in Paris at the Louvre. Well, perhaps not just the Louvre. Perhaps Anet, one of the jewel-like châteaux he had given his mistress. She had spoken of planning a splendid entertainment for the entire court during the season of Christmas. A courtier approached him with a message. Ah, what bother—the ambassadors from the Venetian Republic, here so soon? They must wait another day before he could receive them. The council must consider the fresh impudence of the King of Spain. Yes, the Empire grows too great. No, if the heretics do not recant their Lutheranism, they must be executed for the good of the state. There is no excuse for breaking the law.

Diane de Poitiers, La Grande Sénéchale, and Duchesse de Valentinois, holder of the crown jewels, snatcher of estates, and center of patronage and corruption for the entire kingdom, held an audience that morning. Several poets had requested royal allowances in return for works praising her beauty and wisdom; a sculptor had been called for a commission to create a bas-relief depicting Diane, in idealized unclad form, entwined with a stag as Goddess of the Hunt. She in fact did not care for the hunt, but that hardly mattered. When the whole world praises my eternal beauty, she said to herself, how can the king ever dare think otherwise? My artists have made a dull, morose little boy into a legendary lover. What man would willingly refuse such a title? And if he does not see himself as he is, he won't see me as I am. An icy little smile crossed her narrow, heavily made-up face.

After the artists came several distant relatives, desiring offices and church benefices; they did not go away disappointed, although they possessed not a spark of competence among them. Then there was an accountant, bringing her reports of property seized from executed heretics, to which the king, in a fond moment, had given her all the rights. So very little? Surely, heresy must reside in some greater houses. Perhaps there should be more informers, less leniency with great names. And, after all, the entertainment at Anet would be so expensive. . . . Diane was rising to go, when one of her trusted ladies-in-waiting ushered in a humble carpenter. Diane's eyes narrowed with pleasure as she interviewed him.

"Two holes? In the ceiling of my bedchamber? And a secret panel in the floor above, you say? How very good of you to inform me. You shall not leave this room a poor man. Be sure to let me know of any other little surprises you have created for the queen." And as the carpenter left, bowing and walking backward, praising God and the beautiful and gracious duchess, Diane smiled inwardly. It is just as well, she thought, for that pitiful Italian merchant's daughter to be reminded who rules here, and why, and that she has not the slightest hope in the world.

✤

In the city with watery streets, the houses were much taller in this quarter, four or five stories high, crammed in together for want of space,
their rooms low and cramped, the lower floors sunless. Laundry
stretched across the narrow backwater canals, and the fetid stink of the
water mingled with the smell of cheap cooking: garlic, cabbage, and
onions. As the last sunlight gilded the facades of the rich villas on the
Grand Canal, the shadows fell fast and hard in the narrow alleys of
the Ghetto of Venice. In a room at the top floor of one of these ancient
tenements, a young man with limp brown hair was rummaging avidly
through the contents of the shelves in a large, open cupboard on carved
legs. The door behind him opened silently, and an old man entered without making a sound. He had a long white beard, a skullcap, an ankle-
length gown. His face was scarred with deep lines and the marks of old
injuries.

"At last you've come. I've been expecting you." The young man
whirled around to confront him, drawing a wicked knife.

"Don't bother with that," said the old man, pausing to cough. He
pressed a cloth to his mouth, and it came away bloody. "What you're
looking for is in the chest beneath the window." The young man backed
toward the window, reluctant to take his eyes off the old man for fear
of a trick. "The stars told me you would come this evening," said the old
man. There was the slightest hint of an ironic smile on his face. Stars,
thought the younger man. There must be a trick, something magical.
With renewed caution, he looked around the room. It was filled with
alien objects: an astrolabe, an armillary sphere, instruments of brass and
bone, whose use he could not imagine. They'd bring a bit at the pawn-
shop, he thought. Maybe I should do the old fellow in and take the lot.

"Don't try," said the old man. "There is not a dealer in the city who
would not know my mark." The young man started. The vile old man
could read his thoughts. God knows what deception he has in mind.

"No deception," said the old man. He coughed again. "You're welcome to it. Come now, tell me how you got in?"

"From the roof, through the window. You should lock your shutters." He edged toward the chest, and eased the heavy lid open with his
free hand, never dropping the knife.

"It's the silver-gilt box, that one with the engraved signs there, with the thing in the chariot in the center of the lid," said the old man. The young man with the limp hair scooped it up and stared at it, astonished. "Take it away," said the old man. "It will be a great weight off of me to have it gone." He sat down suddenly on a bench by the wall, and bent over to cough again and again, pressing the cloth to his mouth.

"It's—it's very—rich. How can you give it up so easily?" There was something eerie about the box, exquisitely made as it was. Could it be the bizarre image of a snake-footed, rooster-headed deity in a chariot between the sun and moon on its lid? The unreadable letters engraved beneath? The heavy catch, made of a strange kind of steel, that glinted like a Toledo sword blade?

"Believe me, the burden, the temptation ... It has worn me out and used me up. It is done with me now; it has ruined me and knows I am dying. Take it, and what is left of my life, at least, will be free of it. Regret, a vain attempt to make amends—hell on this earth before hell in the next—that is all it has left me with. I warn you though: don't, if you value your soul, look into it."

"How do I know you aren't trying to deceive me with an empty box?"

"You would have a far easier time, I assure you, if it were empty. But it is not. It contains ... the answer to every wish you ever made, and, oh, just God, the most hideous secret of all ... the secret of eternal life. That is the final gift it will offer when it has transformed that very life into agony. Agony unending. That last evil gift, at least, I have refused." The young man noticed that a curious cadaverous smell seemed to surround the old man as he sat. How revolting. When the old man had finished coughing again, he looked up and said, "Since you have left me time to prepare the end of my life, I will reward you with this warning: Do not, if you value your soul, open the box that contains The Master of All Desires." But the old man's face held a curious combination of bitterness, resignation, and malice, as if he knew that no power on earth could keep the younger man from peering into the box sooner or later. The temptation was sooner. The younger man, consumed with curiosity, put down his knife and opened the box. There was a roar, and a flash like lightning in the room.

"Oh, my God, it's vile! I'll see it in my nightmares!" Horrified, he slammed the lid shut again almost as soon as he had opened it.

"My, what a pity. But I *did* warn you. It's all yours now—you won't be able to give it up. Until it's done with you, it will reappear in your life even if you throw it in the deepest ocean. Like a lover you'll be drawn to it over and over again, until in giving you your every desire it has robbed you of everything worth having. Death and doom follow it everywhere. See? Already you are thinking the one you are stealing it for is unworthy to have it. Who paid you for it? What is he, that he deserves such a treasure?"

"Maestro Simeoni," whispered the younger man.

"Simeoni? That third-rate hack? He can't predict a full moon. What a joke! Simeoni wants it!" The old man threw back his head and laughed, but the sound ended in choking and coughing. The laughter seemed to make the younger man's eyes go wild.

"Maestro Simeoni said it would make his fortune. Why should I settle for a piece of a fortune when I can have it all?"

"A fortune? Then it is not Simeoni who wants it after all. He is currying favor with someone greater."

"Why shouldn't he want it? Why shouldn't you want it?"

"Ah, young man, remember I was young and foolish once, too. And remember this from me: Lady Wisdom often charges a cruel price. Oh, yes. And greet her for me, will you?"

"Who?" asked the young man, his voice sarcastic as he tied the box into a bundle on his back. "Lady Wisdom?"

"No," the old man. "She who is willing to pay for that evil box."

But the younger man had swung out of the window onto the rope that dangled beyond, and did not hear these last words.

✦

The thief with the limp brown hair pulled himself onto the high rooftop, coiled up his rope and tied it about his waist, then nimbly made his way across the roofs until he came to an attic window that looked out over the chimney pots. Making his way through a maze of crowded tenement rooms, he climbed down the last three floors of the building via a rickety outside staircase to the lapping water of a canal. There, waiting in the dark on the water, was an unlit gondola with closed curtains.

"Do you have it?" whispered a voice from behind the curtains.

"Yes," whispered the thief.

"Good, get in." There was barely a sound as the gondola slid out into a wider waterway, barely a sound as the dagger slid into the thief's body, and hardly a splash at all, when weighted and tied with his own rope, the still-warm corpse slid into the black water.

The next day, a man with a dark, curling beard and an earring boarded a galley bound for Marseilles. In his baggage was a silver-gilt and ivory box, sewn for the trip into heavy, waterproof canvas, and inscribed with the words, TO MAESTRO COSMO RUGGIERI AT THE HOUSE OF LORENZO RUGGIERI, AT THE SIGN OF THE RED COCKEREL ON THE RUE DE LA TISA-RENDIRIE, PARIS.

Three

 t's all because I'm riding a little brown *roussin,* I thought, instead of a lady's hackney, and I don't have a liveried footman. He took me for some *hoberau's* daughter, who threshes wheat with her father's peasants and hunts rabbits with a bow and arrow. That's why he was rude about my little artistic creations. He doesn't know anything about the Higher Mind. So that shows he doesn't really know about any of those other troubling matters, either. That Nostradamus is just a rude, intrusive charlatan, that's all.

After all, if he could see so much, he'd have seen that my father's escutcheon has sixteen quarterings, and he would have given me the respect that is owed to a person whose bloodline stretches back to before the Crusades. Besides, I was educated for two years at the Convent of Saint-Esprit, where I studied Italian, music, embroidery, letters, and the art of elegant conversation. I am used to associating with the finer sort of cultivated people, not with dreadful, bad-tempered quacks who pretend they know everything. Conversing with more elevated souls has created in me a Higher, or Spiritual, Self that gross-minded persons such as he are incapable of perceiving. He is fortunate that my Higher Self has turned me toward all that is refined and away from the coarser instincts of my Lower, or Sensible, Self, or I might have done something— well, something even more uncivil.

Every turn in the road was an old friend, for each summer of my childhood we would move from our house within the city walls to the farm, and then back again after the harvest. But that time was long gone, and so, too, was my grandfather's rambling old house on the rue de Bourgogne, passed irrevocably out of the family's possession, due to father's improvidence.

The house of my childhood, I thought, I should create a poem to its beloved old vine-covered walls, but as I rode on toward the distant walls and spires of the city, another house rose in my mind's vision, a new and elegant stone mansion in white stone, discreetly tucked behind garden walls. The house of Madame Tournet, my aunt Pauline, just off the cathedral square. And inside—oh, inside I saw again the tapestried room where golden light shone through the windows, catching on the bright silver of a dish sculptured like a seashell. The dish, I know—so clear is the memory—is full of little sweets flavored with fennel.

�֍

"Go ahead, have one," says the aunt of my memory. She looks just like the fairy queen to me. A square linen headdress reveals the coils of her dark brown hair tucked away under a shining green silk net. A high half ruff frames her face, and a loose sleeveless brocade sacque floats over her day-gown. She is beautiful; everything about her rustles, glistens, smells of dried roses and essence of lily of the valley. The crimson satin folds of her wide-hemmed undergown fascinate me—they shine with a different light on the top than in the depths. A magic gown. I reach for the dish and mother shames me with a glance. She is pregnant again, her dress of dark gray wool faded and her oversleeves threadbare at the elbow. I am the oldest, I am six. A maid holds my little sister Laurette, a round-faced baby with pink cheeks and golden ringlets. Mother has Annibal, my four-year-old brother, by the hand. He is still in skirts, and his hair is in long, pale brown curls. His face is distended like a squirrel's, with a candy stuffed in each cheek.

"She shouldn't be spoiled," says mother.

"She doesn't look like the others," says Aunt Pauline.

"She grows more unlike each day," says mother, her voice weary. "Look at her there—she's taught herself to read, she wanders by herself instead of playing like ordinary children—she says she's looking for fairies. What shall I do, Pauline?" The grown-up talk is strange. Big people are so slow, and ponderous, and dull. I think I do not want to ever be one.

"Does he suspect?"

"Not yet ..." Aunt Pauline leans forward in her chair. It has legs carved like a lion's feet. I want to look underneath the chair to see if it is carved like a lion's stomach, but Aunt Pauline's gown is too large.

"Give her to me," says Aunt Pauline, her eyes blazing. "Give her to me. What good is all this wealth? My life is barren. Trade a portion of your wealth for mine."

"But, my husband—Hercule says—"

"I know my brother. He thinks girls are nothing but a burden. You have a son, and a more beautiful baby girl, and he doesn't even like this one—Monsieur Tournet would make it worth his while—"

At home, a storm. One of many. I hide beneath the table.

"I tell you, I will not give Pauline the *satisfaction!*" The sound of blows and sobs comes from above my hiding place. The lid of the kettle that hangs in the kitchen fireplace bubbles and rattles unattended. The blood from a half cut up chicken drips from the tabletop in front of my nose. A pair of heavy boots are standing just beyond the hem of my skirt. "And you, come out, come out, you weasel—I tell you, you grow more abnormal each day—crazy! You'll be a crazy woman, and they'll lock you up forever. *I'll* lock you up! I'll shut you in a trunk, you'll never get out, if you don't quit being crazy!" A big hand is reaching under the table, and I scramble away. "What has my sister given her? I know she's given her something behind my back—" The big hand grabs me and drags me out. My feet aren't touching the ground. "I swear, I'll shake it out of you—" My head wobbles, my neck feels as if it will crack. The gift handkerchief with my initials, all rolled around several sweets, falls from its hiding place in my sleeve, and onto the floor. The heavy boot stamps on it and grinds it into a gooey, filthy mess on the straw-covered tiles of the kitchen floor.

"Father!" I cry, but it seems to be coming from far away, not from me.

"I won't see you corrupted by that woman, I tell you—I'd sooner see you dead!"

"Hercule, no, not your riding crop—she's so little—"

"Never—see—her—again—I—forbid—it." The blows rain down in rhythm with his terrible words. What is wrong with me? Why doesn't father love me?

"I—I'll be good—" I sob, over and over.

✲

But I am grown up now, and I am not good, I thought, as I pondered over the memory to the slow clop, clop of my little mare's hooves. For I was on the road to see Aunt Pauline. And I planned to tell her . . . everything.

✲

There was a time at the convent, shortly after my discovery of my rarified spiritual nature, that I planned to dedicate my entire life to God. But, alas, all idylls must end. Another of my father's financial embarrassments led to my cruel wrenching from the cloistered abode and into the final arrangements for marriage with a neighboring gentleman, Thibault Villasse, Monsieur de La Tourette. Monsieur Villasse had first spoken for me when I was sixteen, but father's fortunes were higher then, and he spurned him for his lack of ancient lineage. Indeed, the man had no quarterings at all, but only a large and dubious fortune made through currying favor with a royal favorite, the Maréchal St.-André, and the purchase of a salt monopoly. His title, in short, was without that sacred validation conferred by tradition, crassly purchased with his estate in the time shortly after my birth.

Monsieur Villasse would never have been my first choice, mind you, being nearly fifty and full of wrinkles, with white already showing in his fading brown hair and rusty beard. There was also a look in his cold green eye, well, perhaps I shall come again to that look later, but it seemed to me the look of a man with inadequate quarterings, peering at the world of noble thoughts and noble deeds as if through a spyhole, an eye that winked and shone with malicious craft and secret desires for revenge. Indeed, the life of a Bride of Christ, limiting as it was, seemed more desirable than union with such a man. But—a woman's opinion is of no importance. A demoiselle must marry where her father wishes. I think it had something to do with a vineyard, left to me by my maternal grandfather, which lay directly on the southern side of Villasse's lands, which possessed no vineyard at all. There was also something about various debts being canceled, and other loans extended, once the vineyard and my personal self (the two being inalienable, much to Monsieur Villasse's frustration) had been transferred into his possession. But I have never pretended to understand about money. It is a subject unfit for a lady, who should never concern herself with it at all.

And yet, money, ever the vulgarian, forces us to think about it, like a drunken man who breaks into an elegant ball to which he has not been invited. For example, imagine my surprise at the time of my leaving my beloved Saint-Esprit, when the mounted valets who had been sent to bring me home turned away from the distant spires of Orléans in the direction of our rustic country seat at La Roque-aux-Bois! "Why are we not going to our town house in this season?" I asked, and thus discovered that our distinguished and commodious family abode within the city walls had been let, partially furnished, to an upthrusting merchant of Italian leather gloves! My grandfather's elegant hôtel, the galleries that had resounded to my mother's childish play, the very rooms in which my infant prattle first resounded, filled with the rattle of alien accents, and the clink of money, and the haggling of purchasers! Why not rent it out for a pawnbroker's, or a bordello? It would be hard to stoop lower.

But the superior mind can always find new possibilities in altered circumstances, even if they involve living year-round on an estate more suited to a pleasant stay during the summer months. I might make a botanical collection and drawings of the local herbs, I said to myself. Or perhaps I should create a cycle of nature poems, matched to the seasons. Rather than regret the reduction of social duties brought on by isolation, I might pick up again the threads of my most elevated, though unfinished project: a work entitled *A Dialogue of the Virtues, in which the superiority of True Temperance, Humble Devotion, and all Excellence of the Christian Belief are Explicated, by a Lady*. In this, my altogether boldest foray into the realms of the mind, the pagan gods debate the Christian saints, to the detriment of the pagan gods. The voice of my Sensible, or Lower, Self I had put in the mouth of Vulcan, a laborious but malformed and unworthy deity. I did not plan, of course, to reveal my name on this manuscript, for a lady of good family must always remain anonymous when setting pen to paper, as Sister Celeste used to admonish us. Nor did I plan anything so vulgar as to put it in actual print. No, the success of a private reading, a rustle of approval in some select *cénacle,* would content me entirely . . .

But, alas, all too soon we rode through the great gates beneath the dovecote tower of our farmhouse. Dismounting in the courtyard of our now year-round residence, I gave thought to how the *cour d'honneur* might be improved by the removal of the chickens and the extension of the paving beyond the entry to the front door of the *logis* at the far side of the dusty court. Entering the front door into the *salle,* which might have benefited greatly from the removal of several hundred pair of deer antlers and their replacement with a few tapestries in good taste, I found myself confronted with father, Monsieur Villasse, and the betrothal documents laid out on the table beneath the far window for my signature. Mother, my sisters, and the household servants were clustered at the back of our hall, silent, looking as if they were attending a funeral.

Villasse appeared somewhat larger than I remembered, his face more seamed, and his cold green eye more calculating. I must confess I had a moment of trepidation: his estate was isolated, and notoriously lacking in those little refinements required for a lady of my delicate and sensitive nature. Besides, there were the rumors about the death of his second wife that I had heard from my second cousin Matheline, who makes up for what she lacks in spiritual disposition by a decidedly worldly affection for gossip and dancing. No, Villasse, though he had acquired the title of Sieur de La Tourette, and was therefore an acceptable match, in spite of lacking in that multiplicity of distinguished antecedents that commands true respect, did not seem to be a man whom one might grow to love.

"Well, what are you waiting for? Sign: here's the pen," said my father, in the brusque tones of a retired *capitaine* of the light horse, accustomed to command. But we women, not having served in the military, are not required to bend our delicate souls to harsh vulgarities.

"It says nothing here about the wedding date," I replied.

"It will be immediately; the banns have already been posted," said my father.

"Oh, that cannot be; I will hardly have time to supervise the furnish-ing of my chamber at La Tourette, to say nothing of those little necessi-ties which a lady of breeding requires."

Villasse's eyes narrowed a bit, but he asked, with great suavity, "And how much time would that be, Demoiselle Sibille?"

"Why, barely a nothing—I hope you will write it in there. Why, even I hate to postpone my moment of joy; but one must think of our future happiness. Preparation is all."

"Preparation? How long a preparation?"

"Well, I must order my trousseau, my gown. And then there are the bed hangings and linens. And I must survey your library in order to send for those volumes of religious consolation required by the female sex. Six months, at least, counting the time to send for the volumes."

"Books of religion?" said Villasse, the creases in his face registering interesting emotions. I glanced at mother, stiff, pale and silent. I thought I saw her eyes glint.

"I told you she was educated," said my father.

"A mistake. Luckily one you have not repeated with your other daughters."

"It was a fancy of my sister's. She seemed better suited to the con-vent." This, of course, was my father's habitual way of remarking that he considered me too plain to marry off. And, of course, when the old-est cannot marry, the younger cannot move ahead of her. When my aunt Pauline, who is also my godmother, offered to pay for my educa-tion, father jumped at the chance to be rid of me. I felt the rosy tint warm my maidenly visage. Just because the Giver of All Good Gifts felt that an excess of boldly creative spirit might compensate in my case for a certain lack of physical charm does not mean it should be commented upon on such a significant day in my life.

It is true that certain of my old schoolmates made sport of my height and boniness; but I note that they were those of bad complexion and ill figure, and count them as simply jealous of my excellent clear skin and large dark eyes, my plenitude of richly curling black hair, and above all of my melodious singing voice, which surpassed theirs. Besides, I was certainly handsome enough to be the third bride of Thibault Villasse, who, as I have said, was not only lacking in youth and physical beauty, but also in spiritual development.

"So, you are refusing to sign?" said my father, rather menacing this time. I thought I heard my sister Laurette suck in her breath, but could not see where she stood in the shadow of the immense, carved sideboard beyond the table. Dinners of bread and water, imprisonment in a remote chamber, nightly beatings—these are not things I wish to make part of my life. Therefore I am always agreeable to father.

"Oh, never in the world. I yearn only to make you happy and hasten the joyful occasion of my wedding. But I know that Monsieur Villasse craves to make me welcome in a way that befits his nobility, just as I crave only to serve the happiness of his home and person." My father's eyes rolled, as if he were saying, now what the hell does *that* mean, and I smiled, a small but contented smile.

Villasse, seeing that smile, beamed upon me and said, in a purring voice, "Why, we'll have the notary here make an addendum, with the condition that you can decide to hasten the day of our union at any time, if you so desire."

"You're giving in to her? Stubborn girls should be shown the whip, I say. And none come stubborner or flightier than Sibille. You are starting ill, Monsieur Villasse."

"My bride shall have nothing but respect. Demoiselle, when the volumes of religion arrive, perhaps you will be able to read them to me in my easy hours, and instruct me further." Father looked shocked. Villasse beamed upon him. The notary scratched. I signed. "Wine, to celebrate our union," said my betrothed, in his silky-smooth voice, and mother nodded and smiled a wan smile. As I sipped and they toasted, my Spiritual Self began to think that perhaps I might civilize him after all. A delay so that he might value me the more, then the nightly reading of Uplifting Works aloud, perhaps regular attendance at mass. These things have been known to soften a man's soul, my Higher Mind assured me. Or perhaps, if you can put it off long enough, something might happen to get you out of it, whispered my Lower Self.

✤

An infinitude of intervening possibilities can occur in six months, I thought, as I set my card book, the *Giardino di Pensieri*, out on the big canopied bed I shared with my sisters. Ah, would that I, like Penelope, had an infinite tapestry to unravel by night, I sighed to myself as I laid out the cards. Why, I thought, let's see—May is almost gone, but there's June, July, August, September, October. That's practically forever. Besides, not only was my botanical collection coming on well, but I had begun a series of drawings of the wingbones of various birds, hoping to discover the secrets of flight.

"Ah, there you are, Laurette. The four of deniers—that's money after a wait, I'm sure. We don't even have to look it up—I remember that one from the book." Beneath the bed there was a contented munching and groaning sound. Gargantua, large of body but small of brain, was consuming an ox bone. Useless in the hunt, useless on the watch, he was born the size of a large lapdog, and since then had done nothing but eat and grow. No one knew when he would quit. But he was a devoted creature, so mother wouldn't let father get rid of him.

"Oh, how wonderful to be educated," sighed Françoise, who had just turned ten that summer.

"Did the nuns teach you to read cards?" asked Isabelle, who was twelve and disliked sums.

"Oh, no, nuns don't believe in cards. They're strictly forbidden. But then, they don't know everything, do they? Cakes and pet kittens and cards, they do find their way in." I picked up the card book and leafed through it. "Dominique gave me her deck when she renounced the world. And Cousin Matheline gave me her book last year when she left to be married. Her husband hates fortune-telling."

"I saw her going to the cathedral two days before we moved," announced Laurette, who at eighteen was the beauty of our family. "She was riding a gorgeous white hackney, behind a groom in silk livery. She greeted me. They say she is very rich, now that she is married."

"Ladies never discuss money," I said. "It is a lower taste."

"Honestly, sister, you have no sense at all," Laurette answered. "One can't do anything without money, even sit all day and daydream and scribble, the way you do. As for me, I'll take the lower and let the higher take care of itself. Now, lay out some more cards for me. Tell me

I'll be rich, and mistress of a great house, and attend at least two—no, three balls a week, and have gowns and jewels and horses all of my own." I sighed. Not only do I not look like my sisters, I don't even want the same things.

It is difficult to describe the burdens of a civilized soul born into entirely the wrong family, by some mischance of a jesting God. It's not as if the Almighty might not with profit have placed me in a more genteel and congenial setting. Willingly I would have sacrificed my place as eldest, vineyard and all, for, perhaps, birth as the only daughter of a Gentleman Philosopher or a well-born Doctor of Theology, rather than one of the overstock of a patriotic warrior's excessive family. Indeed, on my father's side, so numerous were the cousins that the family estates had been subdivided into crumbs, so to speak. Poverty is the curse of ancient but numerous lineage. Of that whole side of the family, only Aunt Pauline had money, and she had married it, by sacrificing rank to fortune. Father regarded her as one dead, though her offerings from the tomb, as it were, were not scorned as greatly as her person.

It was mother who had been the heiress, bringing my father several farms, a vineyard with a spring and a ruined tower, and my grandparents' town home. But all of her rich inheritance except for La Roque-aux-Bois had fallen to father's extravagance, the requirements of his position, the need to purchase for our brother Annibal a commission in the fashionable company of Monsieur de Damville.

It was only thanks to grandfather's foresight, the vineyard had been left to me, while I lay in my mother's womb. And before he died, he had set the little inheritance so thickly about with legal entanglements that it could not be separated from my person. A strange gift, one that had resulted not in my good fortune, but in my betrothal to a gross being of purchased title who wished to extend the boundaries of his estate.

But the cries of strangers and the sound of horses in the courtyard broke into my Contemplation of Fate. Even reverie and speculation must be sacrificed in a household of barbarians.

"Look, look, who's in the courtyard!"

"Annibal! He's back, and he's brought people with him!"

"The horses, Sibille. They are splendid! Just come look!"

Clustered in the upstairs window, we looked down on a grand sight.

Six armed foot soldiers were escorting an immense dappled gray de-strier, led by two grooms holding his silver-trimmed bridle. His ears were trimmed down in the military style, and his mane shaved, and his immense shoulders stood a good three hands above those of any of the other mounts in the party. Behind the destrier trailed a mounted groom, his trainer, and ahead of him rode two officers: Annibal, our brother, in his short, embroidered cloak, flat plumed hat, and high boots, and a stranger, even better mounted and more grandly fitted out than Annibal.

"Annibal, Annibal!" cried Françoise and baby Renée, and he looked up and waved. The stranger looked up, too. He was splendid: eagle-eyed, dark mustachioed, and commanding. He rode with an easy arro-gance and surveyed the world as if he owned it.

"Oh, who *is* he?" sighed Isabelle.

"I swear, I'm half in love already," said Laurette.

For myself, I was a betrothed woman, so I did not allow myself to think anything.

❧

"So, when Monsieur de Damville heard that Le Vaillant was for sale, he entrusted us with the purchase, on behalf of his father, the Constable." Annibal put his knife into the pigeon pie and cut another piece. "Ah, this is wonderful; home cooking is always best."

"Annibal, why did you never tell me your sisters are all beauties?" said the stranger, raising his wine cup and glancing knowingly at Lau-rette, who blushed.

"Monsieur d'Estouville, if you will only stay a few more days, you will find the hunting around here admirable." The remains of empty platters sat all around father, who was feeling mellow.

"Annibal, do stay a bit longer," said mother. "We see so little of you nowadays."

"Annibal, never refuse a mother's plea," said the stranger, smiling first at mother, then at father. "That's a beautiful piece you have on the wall there. Italian, isn't it?"

"Battle of Landriano. Took it from a Spaniard."

"Those were great times, they say. It has the new wheel-lock firing.

A great improvement. My father used to tell me how the arquebusiers would plant the guns on their stands, light the fuses, and then turn their backs for fear they might explode, rather than fire at the enemy."

"A good mechanism, but tricky. One can't risk leaving it uncleaned for a month, especially in damp weather, and I can't trust it to a valet."

Guns, hunting. The boring occupations of the barbarian mind, I thought. The only thing that remains to be discussed is dogs or falcons.

"Your mastiff there—he's the biggest I've ever seen. Have you tried him on bear?"

"Gargantua, at a bear hunt? He's the most useless creature God ever made. Does nothing but eat and grow. I tell you, he'd flee a rabbit, let alone a bear. I'd have drowned him long before now, but my daughters would howl and fuss."

"Oh, we couldn't have these delightful demoiselles unhappy for even a moment," said the charming stranger, flashing us an ingratiating smile.

"We really cannot overstay—" Annibal was saying.

"I have a new peregrine I want to try at ducks. Do you like falconry, Monsieur d'Estouville?"

"I am tempted. After all, we can't weary Monsieur de Damville's new prize stud with forced marches, now, can we? A day more—tell me, what lure do you use in this part of the country?"

"For hawking at the brook? Mallard wings, and only mallard wings—so did my father and grandfather before him."

"The wisest course—the weight of them is more satisfactory. So, Annibal, your father has tempted me to stay another day. The ducks—and this wonderful wine, here. Where did you say it was from?"

"From a vineyard I have south of Orléans—not so far from Blois, actually. Perfect soil."

"Ah, you can always tell the soil."

"And the sun. The weather, this year, perfect for grapes. So tell me, M. d'Estouville, which bird would you find more profitable to train, one with a good conformation and bad plumage, or a bad conformation and good plumage?"

"There are those who'd be fooled by the plumage, but I'd take the bird with good conformation—it will have more staying power—"

"I had one once, that simply refused ducks. Not that good-looking,

either. I sold it to a neighbor who fancied it and thought he could train
it. The first time it perched; the second time it raked off and was never
found. Monsieur de La Tourette it was; have you heard of him?"

"La Tourette? Is that in the duchy? What is his family name?"

"Villasse."

"Villasse. Ah, I see . . ." His voice dripped scorn.

But my ever-busy imagination had been set to dreaming about the little peregrine, circling, circling above Villasse while he sat on his horse,
first summoning the bird with his glove, then shouting in rage, as she realized that nothing held her, and she flew blithely to freedom. I never
heard the rest until Annibal said, "Sibille, Sibille—you will go with us,
won't you?"

"What? Oh, yes," I answered, without even thinking.

"How splendid to have the ladies join us," said the gorgeous Philippe
d'Estouville, flashing his absolutely charming smile at me. I did not sleep
all that night.

✤

We were away when the letter from Villasse was delivered to mother. I
imagined her putting her hand to her heart when she received it, and
turning a little pale. But we were splashing into the reeds by the pond at
full canter, sending the ducks scrambling into the air, where the falcons,
already loosed, were waiting, flying in circles until the game should be
sent up to them. Bright silver water flew in every direction, Laurette
laughed and turned pink, and Annibal pointed up into the bright azure
above.

"Look, she's got one!" Father's peregrine dove suddenly, catching a
mallard in her claws, the force of her dive sending her into the water
with the flapping, screeching duck.

"I told you she's a bold one," said father, riding into the water to save
the peregrine, as it clutched tenaciously to the still-living duck. With a
thrust of his finger, he broke the skin of the duck and pulled out its
heart as it convulsed in its death agony, feeding it to the falcon. Sunlight
glistened on the leaves of the trees at the far side of the reedy pond. Already the ducks were returning to the water there, far from our horses,
where the peregrines did not dare to pursue them. As if in a dream, I

saw Annibal retrieve his bird, which had brought a mallard to earth in a flurry of feathers and hard-beating wings, as the mallard fought back with all its strength.

"There's a sweet little bird," said the stranger, riding up beside me, his eyes catching me with a knowing, sideways glance. Somehow, it didn't seem to me that he was talking about birds. I lowered my eyes suddenly, and my face felt hot. Something inside me was trembling all over.

"My brother is a wonderful falconer," I said.

"So am I," he said in that voice of his, which gave it a double meaning. He flicked his gaze over me, then spurred his horse forward to congratulate Annibal. In a flash, I was hating myself, thinking, oh, Sibille, how could you, with your natural delicacy of expression and intelligence of spirit, have failed so miserably to say something witty, something light and charming that would keep him by your side for a moment more of conversation? On paper, your words flow in a sparkling torrent; in life, you are as dumb as a stick.

"A perfect day, my friend," I heard him say to Annibal as we rode home past the green stalks of growing wheat, the swaying poplars, the peasant huts with their little vegetable gardens toward the pointed gables of the farm. My brother's reply was lost in the breeze. But as we clattered through our courtyard gates, I heard him say, "You are a fortunate fellow, Annibal, to be pampered by all these good-looking sisters." Again, Philippe d'Estouville flashed that delicious, knowing smile. How dazzling the glance of his amber eyes! How bold and charming and, God help me, young and vibrant, he seemed, compared to Thibault Villasse. But between us stood rank and favor, the demands of family, reputation, and honor. If only I dared . . .

He had spurred his horse forward, and now was riding beside Laurette, telling her a joke, and she was laughing. I saw him glance at the pretty ankles she managed to let her riding habit reveal, mounted sideways as she was, her dainty little feet placed like a pair of jewels on the brightly painted board buckled to the left-hand side of her saddle. I saw she had worn her best pair of green stockings. And how on earth had she got them to stretch so tight? I looked down at my own big, bony feet where they sat beside each other. Betrayers, I thought. No one wants to see *your* legs in stockings, no matter how high your skirts get hiked. Maybe Villasse was all I deserved.

You must imagine the mournful state to which I had descended, in complete contradiction to the glorious red of the setting sun, by the time mother greeted us at the door, with the unwelcome letter reminding me of my impending fate. Villasse had written that he had acquired, from a printer at Lyons, an entire stock of religious works, with hand-illuminated capitals, and ordered the new curtains for our wedding bed. Since there was now nothing lacking for my personal and spiritual comfort, there was no need to delay the joyous occasion of our nuptials any longer.

"He's enclosed a list of the books, Sibille. They seem quite numerous," said mother, handing me the letter. Oh, dear, there they all were, pious sermons, works of the church fathers, a missal, a book of hours. I thought they'd take longer to find than that. He must have sent his clerk directly there.

"B-but I haven't finished embroidering my wedding linens yet," I stammered. Too soon, much too soon.

That evening we played tric-trac after supper, and then sang harmonies about the table. But the vast dejection of spirit I was experiencing weighed down my heart and spoiled my voice. So downcast was I that I did not even offer to read the first pages of my *Dialogue*, although they had been received so successfully at the last artistic afternoon I had attended at my cousin Matheline's. Somehow, it was all the worse watching the dashing stranger dote upon Laurette, who wound her golden curls about one finger while she sang, looking up from beneath her eyelashes at him. How fascinated she seemed with every word that Philippe d'Estouville said: about life at court, the politics and favoritism in M. de Damville's company, and blow-by-blow descriptions of every one of his twelve celebrated duels, in which he had never failed to kill his man.

"I have such a difficulty at court, you see—so many ladies are attracted to me—their husbands, so jealous, but with each affair of honor, the ladies flock in even greater numbers. So my blade brings on more of what it would end—"

"Of course, oh, it is a trial, suffering such people," said Laurette, as he glanced at her with burning eyes to gauge the effect of his speech. Ah, Misery, were I to portray you in verse most symbolic, you would be more than wrapped in dark vestments of sorrow: you would have large feet.

The following day, when Monsieur de Damville's new stallion, sleek and rested, was led out the courtyard gate with his retinue of grooms, his trainer, and his military escort, we stood at the front steps waving, then ran to the tower room to catch the last sight of the procession, of Annibal's bright cloak, of the stranger's elegant form, until they vanished out of sight on the dusty road.

"Sibille, take out your cards and tell me about *Philippe,*" sighed Laurette when they had disappeared.

"He's due to inherit estates in Picardy and Normandy, and is out of your reach," I said, rather cruelly. "You don't need the cards for that."

"But I *know* he likes me," she answered. "Why should you be jealous? You have a husband already."

"I'm just pointing out the truth. A man of his standing does not marry where there's no dowry."

"Do you think you can set yourself up, just because grandfather left you property? He might have done the same for me, if I'd been born before he died. And when Aunt Pauline dies and father inherits her fortune, we'll all have dowry enough. Philippe said I had wonderful eyes. Beauty does count for something, you know."

"So you count on Auntie dying? How do you know she won't leave everything to the church?"

"Oh! You are unspeakable!" said Laurette, and she flounced off in a rage down the tower stair. "I have better things to do ..." I heard her voice fade off as she vanished. And I have worse, I thought, and put my head down on the windowsill and wept.

Now it was not too much time later, as I recall, only a week or so, when I was in the midst of gathering up my poor nerves to write Villasse a letter explaining that my trousseau was not yet complete and the material ordered in Orléans for my wedding dress had been delayed in shipment, that something most unusual happened. I was in the *salle* at father's big desk—my grandfather's really, inlaid in six woods and too valuable to be left in the house that had been rented to the glove merchant—struggling with my response, when a valet in livery arrived at the courtyard gate.

"But, Sibille," Isabelle was saying, as she leaned over my shoulder to read what I was writing, "you're not ordering material from Orléans. You know you're making over mother's wedding dress." Mother, seated at her embroidery frame, pretended not to hear, but her mouth was tight with disapproval.

"It's almost the same. Making over a dress takes a long time. A very long time. Longer than ordering, really, because remaking is much harder than sewing fresh. Besides, you wouldn't want him to think we wouldn't honor him enough to have an entirely new gown made, would you?" I was just admiring the effect that powerfully reasoned arguments of logic have on twelve-year-old girls who are driven by an unholy and Pandora-like curiosity to read other people's writing over their shoulders, when Françoise came running in.

"Sibille, Sibille! Auntie has sent her very own footman with a wedding gift! Oh, you should see how beautiful his livery is! He has a silk doublet in her colors!" Mother looked up, half rising from her seat.

"So, let's all see what that crazy old woman has taken it into her head to send you this time," said father, who had found the valet would not deliver over his charge except into my own hands.

"There is also a letter from Madame Tournet," said the valet, skillfully evading father's grasp. Mother stood, coming closer to see the letter.

"Well then, read it, read it," said father. "Let's hope she sent you money, and not another daft book of poetry."

" 'My dear Goddaughter,' " I read aloud. " 'The cards told me that you are soon destined to leave home. Last week, on my way to Mass, I saw Monsieur Villasse in the street near your old home, and learned from a servant that he is at last to wed you, and that the date is not far. How like my brother not to tell me—' " At this, father snarled, "Do you think I have to let her in on all my business?"

"But Father, surely, you could invite—"

"I told you I don't want you ever seeing her, and the same is true for all of you! Don't any of you have anything to do with her! She wants nothing better than to drag you into the gutter with her! Sister indeed! My sister is dead!"

"But Father," said Isabelle, "she doesn't live in the gutter at all. Her house is very large, and in the best part of town."

"And I would love to see what's in it," said Laurette.

"I forbid you to ever set foot in that house. The name Tournet must not cross your lips in public." But I read on:

" 'Although I have not been allowed to see your face since you were a little thing, through Annibal, I have learned that you have grown as I thought you might.' "

"Why is Annibal allowed to see her, if she is my godmother?" I asked. Suddenly curious, I looked up from the letter. My father's face was as hard as stone.

"Annibal is a man," said father. "Read the rest."

"Auntie bought him that bay hackney he was riding. He told me so," piped up Françoise.

"Shh!" said mother, putting her hand over Françoise's mouth. I read on:

" 'My gift is one that you must keep about your person always, for your own consolation in your new married life. *Read it in solitude.* It will bring you much solace. Take my blessings with you, whatever comes. I remain always, your affectionate, Auntie.' "

I unwrapped the oiled silk from the packet the valet proffered. It was a plain book bound in calfskin, curiously heavy for its small size. I opened it at random and saw a beautiful engraving of Our Lord, surrounded by men in armor, being kissed by an unpleasant-looking fellow whose malignant eye had an unpleasant resemblance to that of my intended. "*Passio domini nostri iesu xpi secundum Johannem,*" it said beneath, in red letters. A book of hours, most singularly appropriate and in good taste, if not as lavish a gift as I had hoped.

"A *prayer* book. What greater hypocrisy is that woman capable of?" said father, and I knew suddenly he had been anticipating money, or wedding jewelry, which he might well have caused to be transferred into his own hands for some useful purpose of his own contriving. And handsomely made as the book was, the plain calfskin binding, slightly stained with some brownish stuff, reduced the value. Yet there was the matter of the weight. I turned it over in my hands, inspecting it again. This talk of solitude, I thought; it may be more than a tribute to my sensitivity of spirit. When I'm alone, I'll look inside the spine. Aunt Pauline doubtless knows father even better than I, and may have hidden a little money in the book for my own use. On further contemplation of the matter, it seemed that a book of hours, even though printed in two colors, if it had no hand painting on the plates, was a bit too plain for a wedding gift. Definitely, there must be more to the book than appeared on the face of it.

But there was a stir and a cry. Mother, who had pressed in close again to see what the gift was, had fainted.

Four

It was suppertime, and the gentleman led the Sieur de Bernage into a beautiful room draped with magnificent tapestries. When the food was brought onto the table, he saw emerge from behind the tapestry the most beautiful woman it was ever possible to behold . . . except that her face was very pale and her expression very sad. When she had eaten a little, she asked for something to drink, and a servant of the house brought her a most remarkable drinking cup made of a skull, the apertures of which were filled in with silver. The lord of the house explained to Bernage that the lady was his wife, and the skull that of the lover he had murdered on the way to her bed, from which he had made her drink for all the years since to remind her of her sin.

"Ladies [said Oisille] if all the women who behaved like this one were to drink from cups like hers, I fear that many a golden goblet would be replaced by a skull! . . ."

"I find the punishment extremely reasonable," said Parlamente. "For just as the crime was worse than death, so the punishment was worse than death."

"I don't agree," said Ennasuite. "I would far rather be shut up in my room with the bones of all my lovers for the rest of my days than die with them, since there's no sin one can't make amends for while one is alive, but after death, there's no making amends."

Marguerite of Navarre
THE HEPTAMERON, 1512

35

Now what with the stir over mother fainting, and the fetching of water, and the fanning, and the shouting, it was a while until I got the book alone. A short inspection revealed that it contained ten gold florins, newly minted and not clipped, wrapped in an embroidered handkerchief and stuffed into the spine of the book, much as I had imagined. I sewed these into my petticoat as a precaution, since even a lady may occasionally have need of money of her own, just for some emergency, you understand, and not for any reckless or unsuitable female plans. And as for mother fainting, she said it was the air, and took to her bed for a long stay, where she lived on broth and coughed up blood.

But within a few weeks, father grew bored with her illness and rode off to Orléans on our best saddle horse, with his steward on the second-best horse, ostensibly to collect the rent from the glove maker—or was it glove seller? Whatever it was, it was entirely too commercial for respectable gentlefolk to deal with and may possibly have involved foolish expenditures it would have depressed me to know about.

And then, too, there was something melancholy and compelling about the little prayer book with the stained cover, that caused me to carry it about, and pause in my little nature rambles not to admire the wild roses by the meadow or the flash of blackbirds' wings, but to draw it out, and wonder where it had come from, why it was stained, and what the strange house that had held it was really like inside. This new brooding brought on nightmares, and several times I awoke in a fright, not knowing what was wrong, and thinking I heard cries and the clash of steel. And then, one night, I woke, or dreamed I woke, and saw a man, really almost a boy, perhaps seventeen or eighteen and younger than I, standing by the bed and staring down at me. He was wearing an old-fashioned doublet and student's gown, and his heavy, dark, curling hair escaped from his flat cap in an unruly mass. But it was his eyes, so deep and sorrowful, that terrified me. They made me think of death. I sat up so quickly I annoyed Isabelle, who said in her sleep, "Sibille, quit all this rolling around at night—you've taken the covers again." But by then, the figure, or the dream, had vanished.

The following day, high clouds began to pile up in the sky, and then a thunderstorm kept me from my walk, which made me even more nervous and fretful. But at last the weather cleared, and it was then that we saw Vincent the steward coming around the bend in the road, riding through the puddles alone.

"Vincent, where is my husband?" asked mother. The smell of damp wool mingled with the muggy heat in the kitchen as the old servant hung his still-damp cloak by the fire. He was covered in mud from the long walk. Mother had risen from her sickbed to supervise the skinning and cleaning of a brace of hares for the supper pot. She had a big apron, spotted with blood, over her gown. In the long silence that followed, the sound of the kettle lids rattling on the boiling pots sounded like an entire battery of snare drums. At last Vincent drew a long breath, and then spoke.

"Madame, he has been taken by the *bailli,* and is being held in prison."

"For what, dear God?"

"For bein' a Lutheran and a heretic."

"A heretic?" I said. "That's ridiculous! Why on earth should they think that?"

"That glove merchant, Dumoulin, who was rentin' the house. He was one of 'em—a Lutheran for sure, which was bound to cast suspicion on Monsieur. I told him, Madame, I told him—but you know how set he gets when it's about money."

"But, surely—"

"The neighbors saw people goin' in at the same time almost every week, then comin' out late. Somebody—nobody knows who—denounced Dumoulin for the crawlin' snake he was, so the authorities waited one night and pounced on 'em all. Sure enough, it was one of those damned devil's assemblies they call a '*prêche.*' There they all were, orgyin' and worshipin' Satan, with Dumoulin leadin' them all! Dancin' naked, they said they was, around a chalice with human blood, in a mockery of the Lord's supper! Heretical tracts from Geneva were stuffed into every cupboard, and I hear tell there was a whole trunkful of infant skeletons left over from their bloody sacrifices. I heard it all at the Moor's Head tavern while I was waitin' for Monsieur, but no, he wouldn't listen to nothin' and when he went for his rent, they took him in. Me, I was lucky enough just to get away when I spied the *bailli.*"

"Orgies! Infant sacrifices! In my father's house! I can hardly breathe for the shame of it," said mother, sitting down suddenly on a stool, and beginning to cough again.

"But why would they arrest father? They know who we are. We are good Catholics. Father was deceived," I said.

"That sly ol' demon, Dumoulin, said under torture that Monsieur de La Roque knew about it when he rented them the house, so they think Monsieur is one of them."

"But, Vincent, you should have stayed and told them the truth," said mother.

"Oh, Madame, I'd have stayed a hundred times if it would have done a bit of good. But when I told the boys at the Moor's Head, they explained to me there's no way I'd be knowin', since lords that are Lutherans all keep themselfs hid, with the Devil's aid. You can't tell it from the outside. Even a wife can't tell a secret Lutheran. You have to pry it out from the inside. They'll be burning the glove merchant and the lot of 'em next week. The whole city's plannin' to go."

Vincent's eyes slid sideways in a way that aroused a certain suspicion within me. Surely, a man who had been offered such trust, such position in a family of distinction, should have remained bravely with his master to defend him against the evil slanders of a treacherous, heretical seller of gloves! But to the circumstances of Vincent's birth I must attribute many of his flaws of character, especially a certain cowardly self-seeking and a greasy mercenary streak. He was, after all, only a bastard of father's on a peasant woman, and not a real member of the family. But father had been excessively fond of Vincent's mother while she lived, and this weakness had led him to place greater trust in her son than I would consider appropriate.

"Suppose he did know the man was a heretic? Suppose he did?" whispered mother to herself. "Ah, God, then we are ruined at last. Everything we own will be forfeit. Reduced to beggary, oh, thank God my father never lived to see this day! My babies, my poor babies."

"Mother, everybody knows who we are in the city. I'm sure that when father explains that he goes to mass every year and would never dream of associating with heretics, they'll let him go."

"I'm afraid it don't work that way, Demoiselle Sibille," said Vincent. "They can't risk lettin' one of 'em go. Besides, I been thinkin' he might 'a known. Not because he was one of 'em, mind you. He might 'a just done it for more rent. Not knowing where it would lead, you understand . . ." I felt a distinctly heavy sensation in the region of my heart. Such behavior would not be unknown to your father, my Sensible Self whispered in a malign little hiss. Nonsense, replied my Higher Self, think of it this way: he could very well have been totally deceived, being the sort of person for whom the complexities of the spiritual dimension of life were an entirely closed mystery. Why yes, I thought, that was doubtless the explanation. My heart lightened, then gave a bound as my Higher, Poetic Self suddenly presented my mind with a noble image of great inspiration.

"Mother, I have heard about these cases. I heard of a gentlewoman who took a petition to the Bishop for her son."

"A petition? Who can write us such a thing? How could we summon a notary in time? How could it be taken there before—? The strappado— surely they wouldn't use that on a gentleman born—heresy—who knows what they do there? Oh, God, God, if only Annibal were here." With all the commotion and bad news, my sisters and several household servants had crowded into the kitchen, their eyes wide, their faces solemn.

"Maman," said Françoise, tugging on mother's skirts for attention. "Maman, Sibille is very clever."

"Oh, my mind's a fog. I don't know what to do. I must have Annibal, we have to send for him . . ."

The gold pieces sewn into my petticoats seemed heavier and heavier, and I could almost feel them burning there. You can do anything, they whispered. You can hire an *avocat* to search out the law, and prove that father is entirely innocent of conspiring with heretics. You can travel to the city; you can see the Bishop. He won't deny you an audience; after all, didn't he himself baptize you, long ago when he was still only a priest? In my mind, I could see myself, dressed tragically in black, my eyes delicately tear-stained behind a silken veil, presenting him with a petition so elegantly and movingly written as to bring tears to the eyes even as it moved the reader to deep admiration of its composer. Oh, moving and profound Word, what can not you accomplish in the hands of an inspired soul?

"Sibille, you must write that petition and save father," said Isabelle.

"Annibal is too far away. Only you can do it." With her words, my Higher Self swept all doubt away in a veritable torrent of exalted feeling. If I were the one who saved father, he would never again remark on the size of my feet, or the boniness of my person. Liberated from the cruel prison and the shadow of the gibbet, he would embrace my feet, generously sized as they were, weeping in gratitude. So beautiful was the very thought of it that my Sensible Self, that squalid little voice, was entirely drowned in the floods of exquisite anticipation.

"I know just how to do it," I said. "I've read about it in a book. You take your petition, and you just fling yourself on the Bishop's feet and weep and then he grants your request."

"Was it a book about Bishops?" asked Laurette, whose narrow mind and insensitive nature often lead her to suspicion of those inspired by higher sentiments.

"Not exactly, more about petitions."

"What kind? The heresy kind?" At that moment her little blue eyes looked especially like enameled beads of the more common, inexpensive variety.

"No, the traitor kind, which is almost exactly the same. How the Duchess of Valentinois rescued her old father from a traitor's death by flinging herself at the feet of King Francis."

"Sibille! That's a dreadful, scandalous tale!" said mother, suddenly distracted from her grief. She looked at me suddenly with red-rimmed eyes, and put her hand on her bosom. "Where did you find such a filthy thing?"

"Matheline had it. We girls had a *significant* discussion of it."

"In a *convent*?" said mother, scandalized.

"Oh, but it's a moral principle you see. I mean, we didn't discuss the book directly, but we'd all read it. Matheline said it was all right, because it was important to know whether it was better to be disobedient to do the right thing, or to be obedient and see wickedness triumph. The Duchess's father blessed her for what she had done."

"And so that dreadful Matheline passed her wicked book around in secret. What else did she show you? Matheline is a wolf in sheep's clothing!"

"But, Mother," I said, suddenly struck by something, "how do you know so much about what's in that book?"

"I was young once," answered mother, her voice icy. "And I paid. I had hoped you would do better."

"Who else will go to plead for father, if I don't?"

"I'll send Vincent at dawn tomorrow to carry the news to Annibal. He must use his influence with the Montmorencys; he must go and plead with the Constable himself for his father."

"And suppose he doesn't get there in time?"

"Oh, Annibal, Annibal, if only you hadn't left so soon!" Mother wrung her hands, then doubled over, in another one of her coughing spells. Blood seeped between her fingers. But she was a creature of steel. Eyes half-closed, propped up sitting on father's big chair, she gave orders to send a boy north on our second-best horse to find Annibal at Compiègne, and tell him to carry her request that his commanding officer, the Baron de Damville, and Damville's father, the great Constable Montmorency, intervene in Father's case, for the sake of his ancient service to the crown. "Daughters," she said, as we carried her, half-fainting to her room, "there is nothing to do now but pray."

✣

It was very nearly midnight. My brain aflame with a thousand worries, I sat in my nightgown at the very table where I had signed away my liberty and grandfather's vineyard, writing, writing in secret while the household slept. An almost spent candle stood before me, casting its feeble glow over an ocean of crumpled sheets of paper. I set down my pen to inspect my last and best effort. How could all those noble and poetical touches look so contrived, so silly, so inadequate? Was it just the dark, the summer heat, that made the sweat drip off my face and dampen my palms? Perhaps something on a more classical model, more austere, fewer adjectives. I took up the pen and surveyed. "O harken to the distressed and pitiful cry of miserable and helpless orphans, great Christian, generous, discerning lord—" Firmly, I scratched out "orphans" and substituted "faithful and obedient daughters of the Church." Orphans might imply that father was guilty, after all. But somehow the new addition didn't look right either. I crumpled up the paper and took out a new sheet to start over. Somewhere, somewhere, I thought, there must be a Muse of Official Documents, dried up as a prune, dressed up in a drab robe ornamented with sealing wax. Sitting somewhere on a throne of files and folders, she is mocking me now. Oh, why was I such a boaster, so sure of the powers of my passionately flaming pen?

In the shadows that stretched above me, the wall bristled with the antlers of dead stags. They were boasters, too, whispered my Sensible Self, and now their pride ornaments their enemy's hall. Above the mantel, the dim light gleamed on engraved steel, the long barrel of father's military trophy, the powder flask and ornate key that hung beneath it. Some Spaniard's antlers, that's what that thing was, the thought came to me. This room is a record of failed pride. Above the arquebus, lost in the dark, was the grim and disapproving portrait of my maternal grandfather, stiff in the court dress of old King Francis's time. Somehow, I imagined that his eyes were staring at me in the dark.

It was at that very moment that I heard the softest sound in the world in the courtyard, outside the closed shutters of the hall. It sounded like horses' hooves, well muffled. Impossible, I thought. Our farm buildings, manor house, servants' houses, stables, and granary form a continuous, high-walled square around the courtyard. Surrounding the house are the still waters of an old moat, planted about with poplars. Whoever enters must come by the gate or by the wicket beneath the gatekeeper's house, where Vincent lives. And the last thing at night that Vincent does is bar the great gates and the wicket, and turn the mastiffs into the court. No one could be there. Even poor old Gargantua, the most useless creature in the world, who wants only to sleep beneath our bed, had been put out into the summer dark that night for stealing a new plucked capon from beneath the cook's very eyes. Who could pass by Gargantua without a noisy greeting? It must be my nerves, I thought.

Silently, I stood up and crossed to the closed shutters, to listen more closely. Then I was sure of it. Directly outside the shutters, almost next to me, I heard men's quiet footsteps, and something being laid against the wall with a soft *thump.* Why hadn't the dogs barked? I heard a whispered command. There was no doubt. Strangers were in the courtyard, and they were laying a ladder against the wall to the upstairs bedroom above the hall, where my sisters lay sleeping in the big bed we all shared.

Now, despite my general delicacy of feeling, I have the fiery blood of heroes in my veins. I am not the daughter of a military hero who served under the late King Francis at Pavia for nothing. Thieves were climbing to my upstairs bedroom! Bold and immediate action was required! With fierce joy my Poetic and Higher Self struck down the withered gray Muse of Official Documents, and my Flaming and Inspired Heart stirred as if at the sound of a military trumpet! My mind, illumined as if by brilliant lightning, went quick as a flash to father's wheel lock, which had only the disadvantage that I had never shot it off. But after all, my brain sang boldly, I have seen it done dozens of times, and nothing could be simpler! Why, women could shoot off muskets all the time if they wanted to, were it not that it detracts from the feminine allure. But what had I to lose of feminine charm, me, deprived of these gifts by a forgetful Deity, who managed only to make the feet double sized?

With a sudden burst of lion-like, or possibly lioness-like, courage, I took the heavy old thing down, nearly staggering under the weight, upended it, poured the powder into the open end, and smashed the wadding down with that long rod that is attached to it. Then I poured a dab more powder into the little pan on top, just the way I'd seen father do. I grabbed the winding key from its hook and crept upstairs in the dark, as silently as a viper, lugging my dangerous sting, as it were, on my back.

The arm of the arquebus made a click, as I lowered it to brace the gun on a low chest of drawers, pointing it toward the shutters in the dark. There I lurked, like the dangerous spotted panther of the Indies hiding in a tree to spring on unwary natives.

"You've taken the covers again," muttered Laurette in her sleep, feeling for me. "Sibille? Sibille? Where are you?" she said, coming half awake as she felt the empty spot.

"Shush, for God's sake!" I whispered fiercely, for I was feeling for the spot where you put the key to wind up the firing mechanism.

"What are you doing?" she said, and I could hear her sitting up in bed.

"This," I said, winding up the wheel with a clatter of the mechanism. "Stay where you are."

Then everything seemed to happen all at once.

Someone slipped a long, thin knife through the crack between the shutters and slid up the catch. Moonlight flooded into the room, showing a masked man climbing over the sill, almost exactly in front of the muzzle of my mighty weapon. Laurette screamed and leapt up, waking the others. At the very same time, I pulled the trigger, and there was a hiss of powder, sparks flew from the wheel, and there was a huge *boom!* Too late I recalled the stories of gunners blown up by their own weapons, and as I was thrown to the floor I was sure that I would awaken in the other world. If the screaming had not awakened the household, the explosion would have. The room was full of the stink of gunpowder. As people poured into the room, I realized I was still in this world and stood up. The face at the window was gone. Vengefully, I lunged toward the open window and pushed the ladder over onto the huddled figures below. For in that very split second before I had pulled the trigger, I had recognized the greasy collar of the leather hunting coat and the narrow, malignant mouth beneath the mask. It was Thibault Villasse.

"Thieves, thieves! Downstairs! Catch them!" was the cry. I watched from the bedroom window as servants poured out into the moonlit courtyard. But the men below the ladder had gathered up their burden, flung him across a waiting horse, and shouted dreadful vengeance as they vanished at a gallop through the open courtyard gate into the dark. I watched from above as the bobbing torches moved hither and thither in the dark, held by the servants searching the courtyard. One by one the lights illumined the corpses of the mastiffs lying dead in the dust, poisoned.

"It's Nero, dead." I heard the voices below. "What a crime. There'll never be another like him."

"Oh, no, not Belle, too."

"Look," came another voice, "one of them's still moving."

"It's the most useless of the lot. Gargantua, the greedy gut. He ate so much of the poison bait, he threw it all up."

"Vincent, where is Vincent?" asked mother. We helped her downstairs. There she sat, bolt upright in father's big chair, a Turkey shawl on her shoulders over her nightgown, her nightcap close over her gray-ing blond hair. Sick, unclad, her fine features somehow stronger in the candlelight, it was clear who was in command. Power radiated from her steel spine, her suddenly fierce eyes.

"Madame, he appears to have fled with them," said a valet.

"Traitor," she said. "My father would never have retained such a false steward. He poisoned the dogs so they would not give the alarm, then opened the gates to them. I see it all clearly."

"Mother—Mother," I stammered. "I—I know who it was. The man in the mask. I'm sure it was Thibault Villasse."

"I'm not surprised," she said, her voice calm. "But you must get away before dawn, before they think to send anyone for you—if they dare."

"B-but, why? Why did he do it?"

"Why? If your father is found guilty, all our property will be seized by the church, and he will lose his vineyard. If he had succeeded in car-rying you off by force and marrying you before the verdict, he would keep his claim. I am not surprised that he would try such a thing. He has official connections, you know, and I suspect he may have heard how the verdict will go with your father. It is a bad sign, his haste—it means a person of great power covets our estate, and intends to make sure your father is found guilty in order to take possession of our property."

"I shot him, Mother. I killed him."

"It is hardly regrettable. I never cared for him," she said. "But of course, you have no proof of who he was."

"B-but, I'm sure—"

"Nonsense. You just imagined who it was. Your mind was disor-dered. Such worries. They lead a girl to fantasy. The men who came were robbers, and the authorities should pursue them and hang them. Imagine, trying to attack innocent young virgins in their own bedroom! No doubt they heard the lord of the house was away, and hoped to steal our silver plate. Have all of you heard that? That is what I wish you to say if anyone comes to question any of you." Mother's commanding eye swept the family and servants that crowded into the hall. "Not that I imagine they will," she added, her face cold and hard.

"Mother," I said, "you act so—so *experienced,*" I said.

"I am not unacquainted with the aftereffects of murders," she said, her voice with that even and distant tone that means one can never ask why. "Sometimes things come around in a circle. But it seems that the circle never ends in quite the same place, now, does it?" She looked about her, as if she were in some sort of strange reverie, to the desk, to the front door still open, where the faint starlight showed the outline of a boy pulling the dead dogs away by their feet. "I see the stars fleeing the dawn out the front door, my daughter. You must dress and go."

"But where? What shall I do?"

"Where? Why, to Pauline, of course," said mother.

"Father would never forgive me—"

"Your father? He will not be able to forgive anyone unless he is more fortunate than I imagine. But I see you were writing a letter on the desk. Your candle is quite burned down. It is a great waste to write by candle-light. You know we must economize."

"Yes, Mother."

"I imagine you had conceived a plan of writing to the Bishop, whether or not I wished it. Am I right?"

"Yes, Mother."

"Then take the letter with you. It will explain to the world why you have left so suddenly. It might even do some good. Pauline will know what to do. I have not been permitted the pleasure of seeing her for many years, but I trust her implicitly. Now, help me back to bed. I am very weary."

Within the hour, I had put on my mourning gown and departed my father's house on the little packhorse, with an armed valet at the bridle. But once over the bridge and past the trees, as I turned to say a last farewell to home and family, I saw a lolloping hound, nearly as big as a calf, running in pursuit. His tongue was hanging out, and his great, ugly, spotted face was frozen in an expression of foolish eagerness and utter adoration. It was Gargantua.

Five

My wife will lose her best shawl two days before next Michaelmas. It will be taken by a new maid hired next month after Marie elopes with that tinsmith who has been insinuating his way into the kitchen with his pots and pans. Remind Anne not to hire any maids missing a front tooth. I told her we did not need the laundry boiler mended. But when do women ever listen?

✤

Last Tuesday completed my son César's natal chart. What truth to the saying "the shoemaker's children go bare"! The boy is almost a year old. What promise! He will become a distinguished historian, looking backward in time as I have looked forward. Perhaps his will be the safer path—no, tyrants and patrons want their pasts as tailored to their desires and fancies as they desire their futures. Ah, God! Only saints do not want this kind of flattery—and saints do not patronize either historians or fortune-tellers. I plan to dedicate my great work, The Centuries, to him, if the All Bountiful spares me the time to complete it.

✤

Ordered a face cream compounded for Madame de Peyrès. Told that wretched apothecary I would take my business elsewhere if he did not make better speed. Madame's son does better from his catarrhus, after anointing his head with

*my balm of oil of lilies, rue, dill, and almonds, and the employment of a clyster
of my own secret composition, which I did send to expell the hurtful humors.
Ha! And all this after that false physician from the Faculty of Paris ordered
blood to be taken from the liver vein! Had he read my book instead of adher-
ing to the so-called wisdom of his wretched masters, he would have known it is
a cure only for the pleurisy, which the fool could not tell from a winter rheum.
Having failed in the cure, he has crept back to his kennel by the Seine. I say,
bleed them with their own lancets, dose them with their own false remedies until they cry mercy to heaven for their sins.*

❧

*Myself—a long, unpleasant journey to the north, at royal command, in two
year's time. A man of my age gets tired of being sent for like some dressmaker.
I see little profit and much irritation in this trip. Must consult again with
Anael.*

Entry no. 126, vol. II.
THE SECRET JOURNAL OF NOSTRADAMUS

Nostradamus had not planned to be on the Paris-Orléans road that golden-dusty day in August when he met the solitary lady in black at the wayside watering spot. Indeed, the good doctor had intended to re-main at his comfortable house in Salon de Provence, surrounded by his numerous and agreeable family, from whence he conducted a prosper-ous mail-order fortune-telling business, in addition to publishing a lucra-tive series of farmers' almanacs and various self-help medical books. He disliked travel; with his gray beard had come gout, and commuting to meet the needs of his rich local patrons and the requirements of his chair on the Faculty of Medicine at the University of Montpellier was as much as he desired these days. Once it had been different; stunned by the death of his first wife and children, his practice in ruins, he had wandered across the face of Europe and Asia in search of the Secret of Life. He studied at the feet of magicians, philosophers, mystics. What he found was—well, whatever it was, it led him to return home to his own sunny land, marry a wealthy and good-tempered woman, and settle into a cozy house increasingly populated with offspring.

But it was the product of that old journeying which caused Fate to send him on this most recent trip. He had seen it two years previous, with some irritation, in the engraved brazen water bowl that sat in a tall wooden tripod in his secret study. "Damn!" he said, as he saw the image of himself on horseback, looking for a decent inn. The Spirit of Past and Future History, whose name was Anael, leaned over his shoulder and chuckled.

"Serves you right, for bothering me at these odd hours," he said. It was a blustery midnight in March of 1554, two years before his long and trying journey to the north. Wind rattled the shutters and made eerie whistling sounds, and the house timbers groaned.

"I *asked* you for a vision of the End of Time, and you sent me this." Outside, rain-filled clouds scudded across the pallid face of the moon. A perfect night for calling spirits, if a bit chilly.

"It can't be helped," said Anael. "I keep everything in a jumble. It's you folk who organize history into tidy categories after it's happened. Then you write it all up, and it makes sense to you, but not to me. You keep history your way, and I'll keep it mine. So there." Rain began to batter on the roof above them, and blow in gusts against the attic shutters. Against the midnight cold and damp, the master of the occult wore a fur-lined bathrobe under his sacred white linen diviner's robe. Furry slippers and his doctor's four-cornered hat, silk-lined and horsehair stiffened, with button, completed the outfit. The latter was for authority. Spirits need to be kept in their place.

Nostradamus took out his little green notebook, the secret one he saved for predictions about himself and his family, and wrote, "a long, unpleasant journey to the north—"

"—at royal command," prompted Anael, putting a translucent finger, dark blue and swirling like smoke, at the place in the book where the old doctor's pen had paused.

"Royal command? Then maybe I'll make some money on it," said the doctor, visibly cheering up.

"Don't count on it," said Anael.

"Vile and disobedient spirit," intoned Nostradamus, sprinkling a bit of water from the brazen bowl in the direction of Anael, "bend unto my will, I conjure thee by the Four Words which God uttered with his mouth unto his servant Moses, Josata, Ablati, Agla, Caila—"

"Ve-ry well, if that's how you want it," said the spirit, drawing him-self up to his full height, which just brushed the ceiling of the study, and folding his arms. Anael was a very attractive spirit, as supernatural phe-nomena go. For some reason known only to a jesting God, he was not only the keeper of past and future history, but also of the planet Venus, in all her epicycles and influences. In appearance, he had the figure of a young man, quite bare, with long, unruly hair. He was completely translucent, of a dark midnight blue color with little twinkly things in-side that swirled about when he was annoyed, as he was now. An im-mense pair of wings, raven black, iridescent with blue and purplish lights, folded about him like a cloak. His eyes, strange, yellow, and some-what terrifying, seemed to penetrate to the beginning and end of time. He also possessed a charming, sarcastic smile and a rather perverse sense of humor, as the course of both history and love have repeatedly shown us.

"Reveal unto me, o spirit, a vision of the End of Time," said Nos-tradamus, putting away the little green notebook, and taking out the big, brown, embossed leather one. It was full of the predictive visions the spirit had sent him: wars, deaths, conquests. It was going to be his masterwork, the almanac of almanacs, suited to guide the monarchy of France until the Second Coming and the world triumph of the Catholic faith. It required only a rousing vision of The End to complete it before it could go to press. When he first explained it to the spirit, Anael had laughed wickedly. Then the spirit had stirred the waters and shown him a vision of a pallid little fat man getting his head cut off in some sort of machine in front of a large, bad-mannered and vulgar crowd. Michel de Nostre-Dame had grown several new white streaks in his beard that night, upon which his wife commented, suggesting that he give up his hair-raising hobby of calling infernal spirits at night.

"Nonsense, my dear. It's bread and butter on the table. Besides, I want to see how it comes out," is what he had told her. She sighed. Such a splendid man, so wise, so dignified and good-looking, such a good father. I suppose this magic thing is better than a mistress, she thought. Mother always told me that the best of husbands has a flaw. That evening she made him his favorite dish, and told him that she only wanted to see him happy. The spirit did good work that time, when it showed me which woman I should marry, thought the old doctor as he reminisced, waiting to see what answer the spirit would give him this time.

But Anael's upper half had vanished. There were thumping and clattering sounds, as if he were rummaging in some large, untidy armoire. "Seem to have mislaid it," came a voice floating out of nowhere. "Would you like an Antichrist?"

"What do you mean, *an* Antichrist?" said Nostradamus, his flesh beginning to creep.

"Oh, and here's another you might like . . ." Suddenly, the old man felt weary.

"Just serve them up. It's late, and I have to attend the baptism of the son of the Sieur de Granville tomorrow. His brother's ordered up a horoscope as a gift, and I still have to finish copying it out." The upper half of the spirit reappeared, his arms folded, his face impenetrable, his glowing yellow eyes inscrutible. Nostradamus stirred the waters in the brazen vessel, then stared into them a long time. Slowly, colors and forms coalesced in the waters as they stilled.

A vision of a crowded hall, filled with men and women in rich, alien robes. The Pope, in full regalia. He is placing the most curious crown, not a royal one, but one like the golden laurel wreaths of the ancient Roman emperors, on the head of a short little man with a shrewd, hard-bitten face and penetrating eyes. Suddenly, the man reaches up, taking the crown from the Pontiff's trembling hands. He crowns himself.

"An usurper," whispered Nostradamus. "He has compelled the Pope himself. What else has he done?"

A voice like a sigh breathes into the old man's ear. With the caution born of a brief brush with the Inquisition, Nostradamus encoded the syllables, mixing them up. Let who will decode them when the time comes: "Pau, Nay, Loron." Napoleon.

"Will the One True Church conquer before the end?" asked the old prophet.

"Always, you ask the wrong questions," said the spirit softly.

"How many Antichrists are there?"

"As you define them, three," whispered the spirit.

"When will you reveal them to me?"

"Never mind, they'll turn up. They're in there *somewhere*. I'm really very careful, you know. Never lost anything yet. Things are just a little mixed together. Don't you want to see the other image I've found?"

The vision vanished from the waters. There was no sound in the room but the scratching of the prophet's quill in the brown book. Then the old man paused, puts his hands over his eyes for a while to rest them. The candles in the seven-branched candelabram on his work-table flared suddenly, and the old man started, opening his eyes. A fine tremor ran through his whole body. As he touched the water with his wand, he saw his hand was shaking. The image began to form beneath the ripples, and he realized he could recognize the faces, the costumes. This one is close in time, he thought. And I can hear everything that's going on clearly. And—yes—they're speaking French. Can I not be spared the sound, at least, o spirit?

A vision of a burning barn, surrounded by mounted troops. Men, women, and children dressed in plain, dark clothing are fleeing through the open door. Horsemen swoop down on them, slashing them to the ground. Shouts, hoof-beats, the dreadful scrape of steel, screams of horror. Children's bodies, lying dis-membered and bleeding, women trampled to death over the bodies of infants. Books, dropped by the dying, lie smashed into the mud and gore. The barn is a heap of smoldering timbers now. Two men on horseback ride up to inspect the damage, the bodies. The commanders. The old doctor knows their faces. Two brothers, with similar narrow, pointed faces and hard eyes. The Guise brothers. The oldest has a huge, depressed scar in one cheek, the bone smashed in from an old wound. François, the Duc de Guise, called Le Balafre—The Scar. The younger, his clerical garb sacrificed to half-armor, is the Cardinal of Lorraine, the Grand Inquisitor of France.

"That's one more nest of heretic devil-worshipers gone," says The Scar. This time, there is smell, too, Nostradamus notices. A penalty of the closeness in time. He smells horse sweat, and blood, and the Duke, who has not washed in some time.

"Hand me that book of Satan worship," says the Cardinal of Lorraine to a foot soldier, pointing to where a lone volume lies in a puddle of blood, its pages fluttering forlornly in the wind. His eyebrows go up in surprise as he leafs through the fat little volume. "Why, it's a Bible."

"*A false bible of devils,*" says The Scar.

"*No,*" says Lorraine, his voice sounding curious. "*It's exactly the one we use. The word of Christ.*"

"*Nonsense!*" roars The Scar. "*Christ has been dead for over a thousand years! He can't do any writing. That proves it's a forgery! Heretic lies!*"

"*What kind of simpleton are you?*" says the Cardinal, turning in rage to his older brother. Nostradamus sighs, and his breath ripples the water by accident.

The vision in the water changes, and at the sight of it, the old man watching draws a deep breath, almost like a sob. *Now there is smoke, climbing to the sky above city walls. Familiar walls. Closer, yes, it is Orléans itself, the city of princes and treasures, and there is the great cathedral that dominates the skyline. It is burning, the timbers for the foundation of the great cathedral bell tower undermined. Armed men in plain, dark clothing swarm like ants, looters flee the great doors ahead of the flames.*

"*Take down the tower of Satan.*"

"*Revenge! Destroy the idol worshipers! Today their cathedral of abominations, tomorrow, The Great Antichrist of Rome!*" *There is a creaking, groaning sound, as the timbers give way, then an explosion as the powder charges rolled under the foundation are at last ignited. The immense, ancient spire crumbles, and the crowd around the cathedral cheers.*

"A civil war," said Nostradamus, his voice shaky. "A bloody civil war of religion. And soon. Anael, you always raise more questions than you answer. Who is the victor in this war? The True Religion?"

"Hmm. I seem to have lost that part, under this stack of South American presidents," said Anael, his upper half vanishing again.

"You tempting, wretched Devil," said Nostradamus.

"Please, I'm an angel."

"A fallen one."

"Only semi-fallen. Besides, it was your idea to summon me up. It's not as if I volunteered. Secrets of the Ages you wanted. Now you get them. You people are never content." Anael yawned and stretched his raven wings. The twinkly things quit swirling and gradually settled out in little spiral patterns. "I'm going now; I'm tired and don't want to answer any more questions."

"Just a little one," said Nostradamus. "What is a South Armorican precedent?"

But the spirit had vanished.

✤

In the chateau of Fontainebleau, the unpacking process was still under way. Certain heavy carts for furniture had been delayed on the muddy, rutted roads, and only now had arrived in the courtyard, where they were being unloaded with much confusion. Maids scurried through the corridors with armloads of linens, teams of lackeys carried heavy chests, while servants unrolled the last of the rugs and hung the arras in the king's reception chamber. The court was full of small households, all busy: the king's, the queen's, the resident ladies- and gentlemen-in-waiting, the great captains and nobles who followed the court when not on their estates, and the children's household, when not away at Blois to avoid infection. Even the queen's dwarves had their governors, laundresses, attendants, and household pets. In the midst of this turmoil, the queen, attended by only two of her *dames d'honneur*, strode rapidly, looking neither left nor right.

The ladies who accompanied the queen today were the most trusted of the trusted; Italians from allied Florentine families, married to French gentlemen. They descended a wide stair, another narrow one, and passed through chambers unfashionable in their location, until at last they reached a low door. Here the queen rapped abruptly, and when it opened, she gestured her companions to keep watch outside. The room she entered was ill-lit and dusty, its contents only half unpacked. Worktables stood empty before her; in a corner, an athanor, its fires not yet kindled, stood cold and empty of vessels. In the back, a figure clad in black leather scuttled among barrels and boxes of glassware like some sinister crab.

"Send your boy off, Cosmo, I want to talk with you alone," she said abruptly, looking at the shabby waif who had opened the door. Without a second word, the boy vanished, and Cosmo Ruggieri, the queen's hereditary family sorcerer, came and bowed before his mistress.

"Most beautiful, most serene highness—"

"Enough, Cosmo. I want use of your powers to divine for me what magic the Duchess of Valentinois uses to hold the king's love."

"At last, you have come to me, poor loyal Cosmo, instead of those dreadful charlatans who besiege you." The queen's magician had switched the conversation to Italian, as if speaking in her natal language might soften his patroness's heart.

"As if I hadn't been here before! What haven't you promised me? I've poured gold down on you, hired your relatives, and put up with scheming that would shame a snake!"

"Cosmo has labored, labored to make you queen, to give you heirs—"

"Are you still resentful of the payments the king has made to Doctor Fernel? That is not something I can help."

"If you let the king see my powers—"

"The king does not believe in your powers, you disloyal rogue. It should be sufficient for you that I believe in them. And I believe that the duchess has got possession of a magic ring. And what is more, only you could have made it."

"My queen, knowing your desires, I was preparing it for you."

"You liar, you cast it for her. Your father would not have lived a day longer if he had treated my father so."

"My father was more greatly held in honor; he attended court on great occasions, and I, shunned, hidden away, so poor, so many relatives in need—"

"I swear, this time I'll have you killed, Cosmo. Pulled in tiny pieces alive, then gathered up and burned, for the edification of all treacherous magicians."

"Oh, Majesty, what a pity that would be. You know the stars have said that you will outlive me by only three days."

"You low, conniving liar—"

"Try me, Majesty. Oh, much as I would sorrow at my own death, it would be a far greater pity for France to lose such a queen."

"I'll send you away."

"Oh, pity, Majesty. Away from your beautiful and august presence, I'd poison myself out of pure grief."

"You are a devil, Cosmo. You know that."

"Alas, Madame, only a Florentine, no different than yourself."

"Of all the souvenirs I brought away from home, you are the one I'd most happily part with; do you know that, Cosmo?"

"Ah, Majesty, it is only the bitterness of the moment that makes you speak like that to your most loyal servant. My heart is moved by your grief. Oh, how I regret that wicked duchess's vile and seductive lies! But out of pure devotion, I would offer you a suggestion: in exactly three weeks, Saturn will come to govern the king's house, and his old disease of the joints will return, with a fever that will lay him low. Take advantage of the confusion in his sickroom, and when the Duchess of Valentinois is away from the bedside, order the ring removed."

"Cosmo, if I get that ring back, you are returned to favor."

"Favor only? My youngest nephew's baptism, the gifts, you understand, the feast, so expensive—"

But the Queen of France had slammed the door behind her.

✤

Puddles glistened on the cobblestones and drops of silvery water still hung on the trees when Michel de Nostre-Dame, the seer of Salon, came to his front door to greet the town dignitaries who were making up the party on the way to the baptism of the son of the Sieur de Granville. It was one of those fresh, southern March days that comes after the rain, when the wind blows away the clouds and the pallid winter sun sits in the blue sky in chill imitation of May. But Nostradamus had been up too late to appreciate the day; his head hurt from breathing too much smoke from his braziers of strange herbs, and his mind was heavy with the sorrowful knowledge he had gleaned from his midnight researches. Now he saw that milling around his doorway, between him and the boy with his mule, was a crowd of townsfolk and a half-dozen peasants, sent from the country estate of the Sieur de Chasteauneuf, holding a monster in a basket.

"Maistre Nostredame, Maistre Nostredame," the cry went up from the crowd.

Lord, not another. Every freak within a hundred leagues gets brought to my doorstep. Carefully, he stepped down to meet them, with the aid of his silver-headed malacca cane. The chill of the night before had not helped his gout. All these mysteries, he thought, and did I once have the sense to discover the mystery of gout? Perhaps Anael is right, and I should give it up.

His dark, intelligent eyes swept the crowd. Around each figure he could see a dancing, shimmering motion in the air, not unlike the waves of heat that rise from a wheat field in summer. Each aura gave him a sense of fate: here, accidental death; there, good fortune and hearty old age; and in another place, a mortal disease gnawing invisibly. It was another gift he had developed during his long exile, and now he regretted it. In ordinary conversation, he always had to behave as if the aura wasn't there, shouting the person's secrets at him. Otherwise, one risked a black eye or a broken nose, or worse, a course of the strappado such as had crippled one of his teachers, the great Guy Lauric, who had foolishly told the truth to the tyrant of Bologna.

My curse, he thought. I was young, foolish, filled with a passionate desire to see the future. I knew it was wrong, but who could have resisted that Agent of the Tempter, himself? A just fate decreed my punishment at the very moment that vile, supernatural thing granted me the powers I begged for: now I can see, but never tell. A lifetime of agonized silence is my punishment. Cassandra was at least granted the boon of telling her prophecies, but not being believed. Me, they believe, but if I don't want to be hanging in pieces outside the city gates, I can never tell. God of ironies, I set out in search of the secret of eternity, and you set me to writing almanacs for farmers to plant by.

"Well, well," said Nostradamus, stroking his beard in a sage fashion, "what have we here? Ah, I see, a two-headed kid." Behind the horn buds, one of the heads had an extra pair of ears, small and misshapen. It bleated at him. "Hmm," he said, "I fear this is an evil omen."

"Master, master, tell us what it means." The crowd was pushing around him now. Nostradamus pondered the safest of several dangerous answers.

"It means," he said slowly, "that the kingdom of France will be divided in two, but that its body and soul are ultimately one, and the right will prevail." The misshapen head bleated again. The head with only two normal ears looked asleep.

"Ha! The ugly one's Lutheran!" shouted a wag.

"The right-thinking head's asleep. Wake up, wake up! The saints are in danger!" shouted someone else.

Nostradamus shook his head. How these fools rush into an endless maze of sorrow and blood, he thought. Just as each individual had an aura, so did the crowd. It was filled with flickering black spots. Death and madness. But when? A chain of murders, prevarications, and treachery lay between France and this agony. If he published his *Centuries* now, would his predictions lead just one person to change his actions, abort one step of the dreadful descent into destruction? At night, sometimes he awakened and sensed the aura of France. It made his blood run cold.

Six

MENANDER of Corinth, also known as Menander the Magus, B.C. 239–?
Little is known of the historical Menander, who supposedly founded a dissi-
dent sect devoted to the worship of Apollo that featured orgiastic worship ceremonies and ritual magic. The Menander legend of medieval alchemists may
have been a later creation with no relation to the actual life of the celebrated
magus. Said to have bargained his soul to the Devil in exchange for the secret
of eternal life, Menander incurred a terrible revenge when the Lord of the Infernal discovered that he had been tricked, and the fulfillment of the wish
made it impossible to collect the clever magus's soul. The Devil "so filled the
spirit of the King of Persia with envy and fear lest the Magus should serve another" that he struck off his head, which nevertheless retained its eternal life.
The Devil's revenge was to condemn the magus to serve the desires of any person who possessed the coffer in which his head resided, in exchange for the
possessor's soul.

The search for the head of The Master of All Desires is one of the darkest
secrets of occult lore of the late medieval and early Renaissance periods. Various persons are rumored to have possessed the head at one time or another, including the Empress Theodora, Michael VIII Palaeologue, and Catherine de
Medici.

ENCYCLOPEDIA OF THE SUPERNATURAL

Vol. 6, L–N, p. 216.

"I am sorry, Madame, he does not want to see you." The valet at the king's sickroom door was firm. The Duchess of Valentinois, her slender form clad in black velvet with white satin trim, was holding a bottle of cordial, made by her own hands. Aside from a slight tightening of the jaw, no sign outside revealed the furious rage that boiled within.

"There is a mistake," she said. "Only this morning he asked for this cordial." Through the half-open door, she could see the king, feverish, propped up on several pillows in his great bed, his eyes closed, mumbling something. Several physicians in long gowns were present, supervising a surgeon who was opening a vein on the king's wrist. Blood, almost black, dripped slowly into the basin, and each of the physicians in turn bowed over it, inspected it, and nodded as if in agreement.

"You are barred from the room. Those are his majesty's orders."

The king fumbled at the bedcovers with his long, pale fingers. Rapidly, carefully, Diane de Poitiers inspected his hands. Where was her ring? That damned, treacherous Italian astrologer, she thought. He has betrayed me to her. Doubtless he'll come crawling back to me with some story or other. I swear, I'd have him meet with an accident, if he hadn't predicted that the date of my death would be the week of his own....

One of the physicians handed some small object she couldn't see to a valet, who bowed and turned to leave the room.

"See here, boy," she said as he came through the door. "What were you given there?"

"A ring that the king promised to send to the queen, as a sign of his favor."

"May I see it?" she asked. Remembering the king's habit of taking revenge on all who crossed the duchess, and sure of his eventual recovery, the valet showed her the ring.

"My, it's lovely," she said, admiring it. Suddenly he feared she would take it. What would he say? What would he do? But then she handed it back to him.

"I think they have made a mistake. This is a ring I gave him, and he swore never to part with it. It is the ruby ring on the other hand that was meant. Return this to the king's hand and take the other one in its place." Contentedly, the king's mistress watched as the valet conferred with the physicians, the physicians conferred with one another, and the valet placed the ring back on the king's left hand, taking the ruby one from the same finger on the right. The king, eyes still half closed, appeared to be saying something. One of the physicians leaned close to his head to hear him.

"What is it?" she heard another of the physicians ask.

"Has the Duchess of Valentinois brought the cordial she promised? He's asking for it. He says only with her presence will he recover."

"Well, then, why is she late? Send a page to go summon her."

"Oh, don't bother," said the valet holding the ruby ring. "She's waiting outside. I'll send her right in."

There was triumph in the duchess's cold eyes, as she swept through the door, her silk petticoats rustling, triumph as she knelt by the bedside, murmuring endearments, triumph as she stroked the hand adorned by the curious little gold ring.

⚘

Up and down the queen paced along the long gallery between the state apartments and the oval court at Fontainebleau. Rain rattled against the tall windows and outside the rumble of receding thunder grew more distant. Behind her trailed several little white lapdogs and two dwarves in Moorish costume, who attempted to distract her with bad jokes. For days, she had complained of a headache and the confinement caused by bad weather, but those who studied her eyes knew that she was consumed with some secret rage. Not only had Diane de Poitiers's reign continued without the slightest sign that it would ever end, but in celebration of the king's recovery, she had invited the entire court to her sumptuous château at Anet for an extravagant Christmas celebration the following winter, so sure was she of her continued dominance. The devious astrologer, Cosmo Ruggieri, had conveniently disappeared to Lyons on an "errand" where he could not be found, and the queen had dispatched a half dozen of her guard to locate him and drag him back. Now, suddenly, the little dogs began to bark and clamor, the dwarves gave up their joking, and the queen smiled a vindictive little smile: two guards stood at the far end of the gilded, heavily ornamented gallery, and between them was a familiar, beetle-like figure in black leather, slightly the worse for wear. Cosmo burst forward and flung himself on her shoe, bathing it in tears as he exclaimed in melodramatic self-abasement. With difficulty, the Florentine queen restrained a powerful urge to kick him.

For several weeks now, she had played the role of humble and contented wife while Diane thwarted her at every turn. There was a little property she had wanted for the husband of one of her ladies of honor; Diane claimed it from the king. The Queen of Scots, that ungrateful little fourteen-year-old chit, had become ill, and when Catherine hurried to her bedside with a list of infallible home remedies, she was turned away from the sickroom, for Diane was already there with two celebrated physicians and a surgeon who had done not one, but two bloodlettings. Having drawn up a list of subjects essential to the Dauphin's education, she found that Diane had already sent instructions to M. d'Humières that the Dauphin should study less and take more exercise in order to strengthen his constitution.

And all the while the poets praised Diane, a thousand annoyances had gathered around the queen like a swarm of flies. How dare the latest pamphlets from Paris call her sons degenerate! A sickly heir conceived during the queen's menses, because of the advice of a quack fertility specialist, they said. What nonsense! All her children were perfect! The pamphleteers should be found and executed! The only problem with her boy, François, the Dauphin, was that his betrothed, the Queen of Scotland, was a year older and so much taller. Spoiled, that girl, and pushy. She doesn't set him off. A few colds, that's all that's wrong with him. Part of his age. Growth, a better tailor, a little more Latin instruction will do everything necessary to make him the very figure of a king. Besides, a group of Italian players doing knockabout comedy, her favorite, had come to court. . . .

And now, her devious magician, reminding her of all that had gone wrong. "Ten thousand, a hundred thousand apologies, my great, my merciful queen," said the worm at her feet.

"Cosmo, you're staining my shoe. Get off. You know she got the ring back. You deserve to be hanged." The dwarves and the dogs prudently withdrew.

"Oh, my beloved queen, do not withdraw the sunshine of your presence." The rain was letting up outside. A thin ray of sun shone across the parquet floor on which the leather-clad figure lay. "Tell me how your humble Cosmo can atone. For what mighty deed do you wish my humble services?" Now he was attempting to kiss the hem of her gown, but the queen withdrew it.

"I have asked the Duc de Nemours to throw vitriol in her face. An eyeless, faceless monster will not please the king, no matter how many rings he wears. I want you to do a reading of the stars for the proper date."

"A poor idea, most noble Majesty. I need no stars to tell me that. Even if the Duc de Nemours flees instantly, your connection to him will be found out."

"But his family is a known enemy of the Guises, her relatives."

"And he is a known friend of yours. Believe me, Madame, the walls in this place have ears. They even have little eyeholes."

"Cosmo—" the queen's voice was menacing.

"Oh, pardon, Majesty, I would never suggest for a moment—but, remember, if the king discovers you, his great love for her will make him take vengeance on you. He would not be the first King of France who had locked away a wife forever. Or he could cause your death. And I would hate that, Majesty, since it would seal my own doom. So you see, I speak only for your own good, since our interests are the same, in the end."

"I cannot describe the disgrace of being tied to you in this despicable way, you toad."

"Oh, indeed, it's a pity, but it can't be helped. It's the stars that did it. Oh, curses on the day I made that ring!"

"Curses indeed. Quit wearying me with your oceans of false tears. You did it all to cause me to increase your allowance."

"Me? Do that? You must think me greedy. It's my cousin's oldest son, his little girl needs a dowry, my sister is feeling poorly, she needs to go take the waters, my poor little godson—you see, I'm like a father to so many. The responsibilities, they're crushing—"

"I'm telling you here and now, Cosmo, I want my husband freed of that woman's power. I want his love, his respect. I want the honor I am due as Queen of France. I never want to hear the phrase 'Italian shop-keeper's daughter' out of that woman's mouth again. Do it, Cosmo, or I'll lock you up out of the sun until you wish you were dead, but haven't got the means for it."

"My queen, my queen, how could you have so little faith in me? I had hesitated to tell you, but now—well, now, I must reveal a secret of power and terror to you." At this, the queen looked interested. She cocked her head to one side, as if thinking, and Cosmo swore he could see her tongue run out at the corner of her lip. Good, safe again, he thought. How clever I was to discover Simeoni's plan to displace me. The fool can't even predict the coming of Saturday, and if he'd managed to keep The Master of All Desires—ah, Asmodeus! Don't think of it—how fortunate that my servant got hold of it before it ever came into his hands. "Yes. I have come to acquire a diabolical object of profound magic, which is capable of granting all human desires but one."

"But one? Why not all?"

"That one is redemption, which is not in Satan's power to grant."

"Ah, indeed. I understand all now. I would sell my soul for the power to get rid of that woman. Just what is it you've got hold of?"

"Well, ahem, will shortly get hold of. Have you ever, in your occult readings, seen reference to The Master of All Desires?"

"The Master of All Desires? Well, perhaps I have. Say on, you toad." She hasn't, he thought. I shall dazzle her.

"Surely, you recall the legend of Menander the Magus?"

"Who is said to have discovered the Secret of Eternal Life?"

"That is what they say. Nearly two thousand years old, he'd be today."

"Eternal life—eternal life," mused the queen. "Then there is no hell, is there? One is free of God's judgment—to do—anything—anything one likes—"

"But the legend says he got infernal power by selling his soul to the Devil—"

"Who couldn't collect, because he was immortal. Yes, I remember that story. But what has it to do with your latest discovery?"

"Great and magnanimous mistress, most high and puissant queen, the legend does not end there. The King of Persia found some fault in Menander, and for this, had him beheaded. My father once knew an astrologer who offered to sell him one of Menander's very finger bones—"

"So this is all foolishness on your part? Don't play with me, Cosmo, I punish people who make sport of my worries."

"My queen, my queen, trust your poor old servant, your humble, weeping servant—"

"Come to the point, Cosmo. What, and how much?"

"My queen, Menander's head was severed from its body, but *it lived on.* Thus Satan had his revenge for the trick he had been played. It is this living, severed head, its magical powers and secret wisdom entirely intact, which I have acquired for you."

"To be my slave?"

"To grant your every wish, great queen. His powers, which are diabolical, know no limit, and his living head is condemned to serve whoever possesses it."

"Cosmo, if you knew about this all along, why did you never get it for me before?"

"Your highest and most glorious Majesty, the Undying Head of Menander the Magus may grant your every wish, but from all accounts, it is not a happy object to possess."

"I am not a happy woman, Cosmo. Curses, damnation, or Satan, I want you to get me that head."

When the door had closed behind the backward bowing sorcerer, a thought occurred to the queen. If that despicable man ever gets possession of that thing, he'll get his wishes first. Then he'll ration out my wishes, and charge me for every one of them. That undying head is clearly not here, or he'd be boasting of having it. He must be having it sent from somewhere. I think I'll just have him followed, and have it intercepted before it gets to him. Why, if it's as good as he says, I'll just wish my way free of his treachery, after I've dealt with the duchess.

Seven

"It is time, my lords, to join the ladies." Henri II, King of France, tall and grave, led his courtiers to the queen's chambers. The king was a man of great courtesy and permanent gloom. A childhood spent as a hostage in a Spanish prison had left him forever joyless. Around him spun the farces, practical jokes, and intrigues of a pleasure-bent court, but he never took notice. High wit and low humor had no hold on him. Music, drink, ribaldry all passed him by. He diverted himself with hunting, combat, and his aged mistress, who reminded him vaguely of his long-dead mother. He scheduled his days like a clock wound up by duty. No one had ever seen him laugh.

On his left hand, slightly behind him, strode his chief advisor, the Old Constable, Anne de Montmorency, Grand Master and Constable of France, who held in addition, either within his own hands or those of his family, the Colonelcy of the French Infantry, the Admiralship of France, and the four great Governorships of Provence, Languedoc, Picardy, and the Isle of France. Square-set and gray haired, the Constable walked with the confidence of one who had known King Henri in the cradle, who had been advisor and friend to his father the great King Francis, and to whom no human treachery was surprising.

On the king's right walked the Old Constable's chief rival, the Duc de Guise, head of the second great family of the realm. Tall, hard-eyed, elegant and remote, one side of his face had been smashed in by a lance, causing him to be known as "The Scar." His permanent favor in the royal court was assured by his alliance through marriage to the king's mistress, Diane de Poitiers, as well as by his link to the Dauphin himself through the boy's betrothal to his niece Mary, who had inherited the crown of Scotland in her infancy. Behind The Scar walked his younger brother, Charles, the Cardinal of Lorraine, in the full red silk robes and pectoral cross of a cardinal of the Church of Rome. The Guise brothers had a great enterprise in the making: the unification of the Kingdoms of France, Scotland, and England under their power, to be followed by the purging of the Protestant heresy from all of these realms by fire, sword, and the noose.

The cards were already in play: Mary, the girl-queen of Scots, was, through her mother, the eldest sister of the Duke and the Cardinal, a Guise. But through her dead royal father, the King of Scots, Mary was a direct descendant from Henry VII of England. This made her the last legitimate Catholic heir to the throne of England once Edward, the sickly son of Henry VIII, and Mary, the childless daughter of Henry VIII's first, Catholic queen, were dead. The English Princess Elizabeth, daughter of Anne Boleyn and Henry VIII, was the darling of the English Protestant faction. But to the Catholic faction she was a bastard who had no claim, since Henry VIII's divorce and remarriage to Mistress Boleyn had no standing in the Catholic Church. To the French then, the Guises' Mary was the legitimate heiress, born to bring England back to the Catholic fold. Her uncles, the Guise brothers, dazzled the king with her claims, and the possibility that his oldest son, the Dauphin, through marriage to their niece, could be king of three realms.

But the actual moment of the Queen of Scots's marriage to the Dauphin would seal the Guises' supreme power permanently. For this reason, the shrewd Old Constable, Montmorency, was doing his best to delay or undermine the wedding, for the sake of his own family.

The Guises were patient and brilliant; they did not play for short-term gains. They had smuggled little Mary out of Scotland at six, and seen to it that for all these years she was raised with the Dauphin, and trained by Diane de Poitiers in the graces that would charm the king and control his sickly, simpleminded son. The girl herself was encouraged in uselessness, vanity, and feminine frivolity, and to turn for any serious advice to her dear uncles, the Duc and the Cardinal. Their puppets were almost in place. Someday, through Mary, they would rule. She would be queen of beauty, and they, in all but the crown, kings of France, of Scotland, and of England.

Behind these scheming rivals and supports of the throne came a throng of courtiers, the highest lords and military commanders and land-holders in the realm, dressed in satin and gold-embroidered velvet, tight silk hose with shining garters, codpieces as puffed and embroidered as their padded doublets. The Dauphin, ill-grown and bad tempered, also accompanied his father. Shorter, with goggle eyes, bulbous nose, and a receding chin that resembled his mother's, his face was marred with great patches of angry red, and his mouth hung slightly open with adenoids. He had none of dignity of the king, whose somber, long-nosed profile gave him an air of great seriousness and gravity of purpose. Still, parents must work with what they have, and the king, now at the height of his powers, intended for his son, someday, to be an even greater king than he had been.

"Ah, the garden of delights," breathed the King of Navarre, first of the princes of the blood, as the courtiers entered the queen's tapestried reception chamber. Musicians were playing in a gallery, games and food were laid out here and there on little tables. The queen herself sat on a low, cushioned chair, with a slightly grander and higher one empty at her side. The colored tile floor was covered with rare carpets and soft, embroidered silk cushions, on which the gloriously dressed ladies of the court sat around her on the floor, their bright skirts spread about them. After making their formal greetings to the queen, the gentlemen joined the little groups of women to play cards, tell stories, and hear the latest gossip and songs. The evenings with the queen were something no gentleman would willingly miss: there one could carry on flirtations, make assignations, and trade an old mistress for a new. Harmless diversion, they thought, as they looked over the ladies of honor assigned to the duchess's and the queen's households. Women, so light-headed, so delicious, so easy.

But these women were pledged in loyalty either to the queen or the royal mistress, who clothed them, financed them, and ruled their lives like a pair of generals. They assigned them their lovers, controlled their affairs, and required the reporting of their pillow talk. Yet so subtle and perfumed was this rule that the gentlemen of the court never understood that they were in the hands of two rival espionage services, deployed with all the brilliance of two military commanders in the field.

The king, with a half dozen of his lords standing behind him, joined the queen, making polite conversation with her. "My lord," she said, trying to find a place where their disparate interests might join, "have you read this strange new book of prophecies by this Doctor Nostradamus? There are many curiosities there, about the future of the realm."

"I do not take political advice from soothsayers," said the king. "That was sufficient for the pagan emperors of Rome, and led them into misery. We are fortunate to be a Christian kingdom."

"Still, I have here the book, and it might be considered a curiosity," she said, showing him an open page. Slowly, the king read the verse to which she had pointed.

> *"Le lion jeune le vieux surmontera*
> *En champ bellique par singulier duel:*
> *Dans cage d'or les yeux lui crèvera:*
> *Deux classes une, puis mourir, mort cruelle."*

Behind him, the courtiers shifted. "The young lion will overcome the old in single combat—" The lion was a king, no doubt of that. Books of prophecy were quite the vogue these days, and this one was something of a scandal. There were those on the street who said this very verse prophesied the death of Henri II. Yet wasn't prophesying a king's death treason? "This doesn't mean anything," said the king. "If a man's going to be a prophet, he should say it straight out. Look at these verses. Mixed up Latin and French, with anagrams and dialect stirred in for good measure. He just wants to be cryptic so he can claim he was right after the fact. And who can say no? Nobody can figure out a word he's said."

"My Cosmo says it prophesies danger which you must avoid."

"Your Cosmo?" said the king, his voice scornful. "That ghastly quack magician you brought with you?"

"The Ruggieri have served the Medici well for generations," said the queen.

"Ever since they took up pawnbroking and peddling," whispered Diane de Poitiers to her little protégée, the Queen of Scots, who snickered. Catherine heard, but the only sign was a brief flicker of her eyes sideways toward the source of the comment.

"Still, how does he propose to interpret this verse? It is far too cryptic for *me,*" said the Old Constable, an ally of Queen Catherine's in the secret struggle against the Guise, trying to smooth over the situation.

"He says that the king bears great danger of being killed in single combat. My lord, this verse has troubled me so much that I sent to the celebrated Guaricus in Rome to inspect your horoscope." The king sighed. Horoscopes, diviners, cards, anything foolish and superstitious diverted his wife. That and those horrible Italian comedies everybody else laughed at. Didn't she have any normal interests?

"Very well, did he inspect it thoroughly?"

"He sent this letter, which M. de l'Aubespine has put from Latin into French. He says in particular to 'avoid all single combat in enclosed spaces, particularly around the forty-first year, because in this epoch of the king's life, he is threatened with a head wound that will lead rapidly to blindness or death.'" The queen handed the king the translation of the letter from Italy, and the monarch's somber gaze rested a moment on the offending passage. He was silent for a long time before he spoke, not to the queen, but with a turn of his head to the Old Constable.

"Well, just see that, my friend, how they all predict my death," said the king. It was said in a sardonic tone, but the Old Constable smelled the despair that lay beneath. The king did not need to be encouraged in his natural gloom and pessimism.

"Ah, sire! Do you want to believe these boasting, lying quacks? Throw that stupid letter in the fire."

"My old friend," said the king, his voice weary, "sometimes these folks tell the truth." The King Who Never Laughed shrugged his shoulders and spoke again. "I don't mind one kind of death more than another; but I'd prefer, no matter at whose hand I die, that the man be brave and valiant, and that the glory would be mine."

Oh, that damned Diane de Poitiers, thought the queen. She's poisoned his mind with all that romantic swill from old ballads. A king should be more practical. The purpose of a good fortune is to evade danger. Why, if my cousin Ippolito had listened to his fortune-teller, he would never have been poisoned by my cousin Alessandro. And in a great court, enemies are everywhere. And look how my husband rose to the throne when his own brother, who didn't even keep an astrologer, was poisoned! For the good of his subjects, a king should struggle against the hand of Fate by keeping many magicians, as I do. Aloud, and well aware of her audience, she said, "Sire, you are king of a mighty realm. For the sake of your people and in thought of the youth of your son, to say nothing of myself and your other children who are devoted to you, I beg you to take care of yourself in your forty-first year. It is not such a long time, and after that the prophecy of Luc Gauric does not hold."

The king looked at her as if she were the stupidest creature God had ever invented, and said, "Gauricus is only one of the doomsayers. Look at this other, this Nostradamus. Does he give a date? What is to keep these fortune-tellers from manufacturing another prophecy, and yet another, just to keep me from my glory, and your gold flowing into their purses?"

"Nostradamus, sire, is much more than a common fortune-teller. This book marks him as a great prophet, who sees farther than the others. Let me send for him, to clarify these words he has written, and read the future for the royal house. Then your mind will be put at ease."

God, how the woman pushes, thought the king. What a stupid, ugly busybody. Still, it is best her hobbies keep her busy. Diane has said to encourage her preoccupations; it will leave us more time together. Distantly, soberly, the king nodded his assent. The following day, a royal messenger set out with dispatches for the Governor and Grand Seneschal of Provence. Among them was a royal command that Doctor Michel de Nostre Dame appear at court as soon as possible. It was June of 1556, almost two years and a half after Nostradamus had noted the unpleasant conversation with the Spirit of History in his little green notebook.

✤

"I knew it," said Nostradamus, when the Seneschal's servant dismounted at his doorway. He shaded his eyes with a hand against the midsummer southern sun, which was so fierce the very stones of the road seemed to shriek with the heat. July 1556, almost a year from the time the printer in Lyons had first taken the manuscript of the *Centuries* from his hand. As obvious as a boulder rolling downhill, one thing had followed another, exactly as predicted. Now this official messenger, trudging up his front steps. "It's that damned royal command, arrived at last," he addressed the dusty fellow with the high leather boots, who looked taken aback. "Paris indeed! With my gout? That's more than a month away, even with royal post-horses!" Annoyed, Nostradamus did not invite the fellow in out of the sun, but stood in the doorway and opened the seals. "Never mind," he said. "My bags are already packed. I knew this was coming." The messenger turned pale.

"You are to leave as soon as possible," he said.

"And what kind of a prophet would I be if I couldn't prophesy that I'd have to shut down my practice for a month? I've already got someone to cover for me; just tell the Seneschal I'll be off tomorrow for St.-Esprit. By the way, did he advance any funds for the trip?" Sheepishly, the messenger extracted a little purse from his pocket.

"Good," said Nostradamus. "Never try to fool anybody with supernatural powers. Hmm. Light, this purse. It won't even get me halfway there. What do they expect? That I'll travel at my own expense?" Grumbling, he re-entered his shady house, malacca cane tapping on the tiled entry, while the messenger fled in superstitious terror.

Following the route of the royal posts, and taking care to travel, when possible, in a company of merchants or the train of an illustrious nobleman for the sake of safety, Nostradamus and his servant made unusually good time, finding themselves traveling from Orléans to Paris by mid-August. All the way, Nostradamus grumbled to himself that he would have made even better time without Léon, and it was all his wife's fault for being so nervous about him. After all, hadn't he traveled alone all through the known world in his youth? I mean, should a man be reduced to dragging along a *valet* like some dandy who changes his clothes three times a day just because his *wife* gets nervous?

"At least he'll write to me to let me know how you are," she'd said, "and you know you always get too busy for things like that."

"*Write?*" answered the old man. "The fellow can't even hold a pen."

"But he was with my father for twenty years before he came to us, and he's absolutely devoted, and he knows how to hire a public letter writer as well as anyone. Besides, Léon is very practical. You need look-ing after." So Léon came, and he wasn't so bad after all, being very prac-tical, but still, if you considered the added expense of another mouth and the fact that it was an insult when a man had traveled to the heart of Arabia by himself and escaped the clutches of the Great Sultan in Constantinople and studied the secrets of the Cabbala among the Magi of the Holy Land, and never needed a baby-sitter of a servant to follow him about. . . .

He was grumpily considering this problem at a particularly debased watering place that kept its custom only by monopoly of location, when he noticed something odd. Or rather, somebody odd. A girl out of place, unaccompanied except by the biggest, ugliest hound puppy he had ever seen. The gangling thing lolloped around her in circles, smelling every-thing, and she addressed it as Gargantua. This made the old man perk up. Literary. Hmm. Genteel, too genteel to be without a duenna. One footman, if you can call a peasant boy without livery a footman. Dressed in a made-over mourning gown too short in the hem, but not in the least sad. The aura—guilty about not being guilty—she's just done something outrageous. Very preoccupied with some unusual task. And here was the queer thing. Most auras the old prophet saw clung about the person like a limp cloak, readable but unremarkable. Once, however, he had seen a shepherd with an immense one that radiated nearly twenty feet. He had bowed to him and addressed him as a future Pope. But this demoiselle, how curious. Her aura *hiccuped*. First it would swirl close, then pop out, here, there, only to be sucked back in again. Something was going on. She was changing. From what into what?

Curiosity overcame him, and he looked closer. With her delicate aquiline profile, olive skin, and heavy, curling dark hair, she looked more like a southerner, but taller than the women of the south. And she had a regal posture, but heavens! The most angular of elbows, the boniest of ankles, and the largest feet! Different, somehow. People might call her handsome, beautiful even, but never pretty. He addressed her; she answered in the local accent, but looked long at him with a pair of dark, assessing eyes not unlike his own. Yes, something southern.

Generously, he gave her fortune without charge, at which she was insulted and turned her back on him. Her horse was tied in the shade. A little brown *roussin,* heavily overburdened with a gaudily tooled and painted lady's sidesaddle. Nostradamus scratched at his temple, where it felt as if a gnat were walking. No, not a gnat. It was his hidden sense, telling him that this pretentious, irritating creature was part of the problem he was mulling over. Somehow *she* was connected to the fate of France. Something would happen within the next twenty-four hours, something that involved her.

Eight

Au feu, au feu, meurent les Lutheriens! Death to all heretics!" A
fierce mob was crowding beneath the heavy portcullis at the
city gate of Orléans, and spilling out onto the road beyond. The
coarsest soul could not fail to shudder at their grim chant; gooseflesh
rose all over my body, and my heart grew as heavy as a stone. For there
in the midst of them was a man in his shirt, his knobby knees bleeding
from a previous fall, carrying a heavy bundle of kindling on his back. A
heretic being led out to be burned alive. Who? I didn't recognize him.
Perhaps even the glove merchant himself. And what of Father? The boy
at my bridle shrank from the unruly crowd, while I was all the more
anxious to make haste to pass through the crowded gates.

"Demoiselle, you'll find it hard going to enter while the world wishes
to press out," I heard a man's voice say, and I looked down to see a
heavy, rough sort of fellow, pressing through the crowd toward me. He
looked like an artilleryman on the way to join his company: he had
his powder charges strung around his neck, and he was carrying a
bundle on his back. At his side was a short sword, and on his head a
battered hat with the scrap of a plume. What was it that looked wrong
about him?

"Where is your arquebus?" I asked.

"Ah, Demoiselle, there is the story—it's left for security with a pawn-broker on the rue Sainte-Anne within the walls, and I can't rejoin my company without it. Put my bundle behind your saddle and I'll help your boy clear the way." Still in shock at the sight before me, I nodded silently. Gargantua sniffed at the bundle as he tied it on, as if it contained something delicious, like a ham, but then, Gargantua thinks old shoes are appetizing. "Make way, make way, for the demoiselle who is called to her grandmother's deathbed," cried the soldier, and this plus his bulky and warlike person pushed us all the way to the gate.

"Gillier, you old salt-smuggler, halt where you are," cried one of the guards at the gate, and two others rushed out to grab him before he could unsheath his sword.

"Halt? I'll have you know I'm a reformed fellow, in the service of this lady here," he said. Now people were stopping to look at our little drama, and despite my facade of cool and ladylike elegance, I was all in a panic to hurry on before someone recognized me as the daughter of the man who had rented the heretic his house.

"I'm visiting my sick aunt, Madame Tournet, who lives near the cathedral square," I said by way of explanation. The guards were searching the soldier, and I intended to give them his bundle, but then the thought of Villasse's purchased salt monopoly rose in my gorge, and I saw no reason to be of assistance, even posthumously. Why hand over the evidence, whispered my Sensible Self. It will just involve you and slow you down. Very good, said my Higher Self, for once we agree. If the package is salt it ought to be free anyway, since it was created in great plenitude by God for the use of all men. That despicable Villasse would have tried to charge for air, if it had been possible. Then it occurred to me that it was all his own fault he'd been murdered, because God obviously had wished him to perish for his greed, so that I was merely a Divine Instrument, and therefore hardly to blame at all.

In the midst of these cogitations, I felt a sudden nervousness that certain earthly authorities, currently engaged in executing the glove merchant, might not fully understand my role as Divine Instrument quite correctly. The soldier, or perhaps salt-smuggler, cast me a frightened glance, as if to say, don't give my bundle to them. It then came to me that questioning about my possession of an illicit package might well lead to the uncovering of the unfortunate accident to Monsieur Villasse. My brilliant mind responded at once. "My aunt said I must not delay. I've a letter to her from my mother," I said, my voice high and snobbish. As I watched them squint at the address, I realized they couldn't read.

"Good enough, pass through," said the guard. "But your servant is going to the *bailli*." He'll soon enough be let out, I thought, since they have no evidence, and we are both as free as birds. Once again, the higher mind triumphs over the artifices of the uncouth. As my boy and I passed through the gate, a curious dark man with an earring moved to speed in behind us. If I had been less modest, I would have thought he was trying to follow me.

"Not you, fellow," I could hear the guards say behind me. "You look like a foreigner. If you can't show business within the walls, you can't enter. This city is no place for aliens and masterless men." Entirely proper, I thought. One cannot be too careful what sort of criminal riffraff one admits within city walls.

✤

All moral literature informs us that it is the fate of criminals to sink ever lower in social standing until their final meeting with Ultimate Justice, which hurls them into the pit. It struck me as I leaned from my horse to lift the bronze knocker on Aunt Pauline's courtyard gate that perhaps I was more criminal than I had supposed. The house looked untended and the gate was not new as I remembered it, but unpainted, with rusting hinges. The walls on either side of it were crumbling and vine-covered. Perhaps fleeing to this decayed place was my first step Downward.

Again I knocked, this time louder. Still, there was no answer. Suppose Aunt Pauline had died unexpectedly, or moved away, and we had never been told? An unpruned plum tree from some hidden garden within had dropped spoiled fruit over the wall, and the sweet stink mingled with the filthy odors of the street. When Monsieur Tournet had lived, his wealth had made him welcome in all the more raffish circles, though we had never been allowed to enter his house.

"Filthy money," my father would say. "She sold our family honor to a nobody for cash." Sometimes I would hear the older women talking with mother, "Of course, we cannot *receive* her, you understand. That husband she married is quite without distinction. What on earth pos-sessed your husband's parents to allow such a mismatch?" And mother would remain silent, or perhaps say, "Madame Tournet remains a rela-tive, no matter whom she married," and that would be the end of it. Once, in a weak moment, she said to me, "And how do you think your grandparents remained in possession of their estate, without Jean Tour-net's loans? He was good enough to finance and equip fleets for the king, but not good enough for them. And they consider it beneath their rank ever to repay him." It gave me a moment's glimpse of a hidden side of her, a stranger who put justice before rank. What other secret thoughts, so different from my father's, did she harbor? But the hidden window on her thoughts closed as abruptly as it had opened, and she had sailed away, blank-faced, elegant, the image of good breeding and propriety. And then Monsieur Tournet had died, and with him his loans, and our prosperity.

Again I banged on the gate, this time loudest of all. With that a face appeared at a grilled opening in the gate, took my name, and vanished. Then, after another interminable wait, the gate swung open with a dreadful creaking. While I stood and stared at the unpainted, vine-invaded, almost abandoned-looking manor within the courtyard walls, a morose servant led my footman and my horse away without saying a word. The face at the grille, belonging to an old valet with a wooden leg, inspected me silently from head to toe. Still wordless, he led me across the cobblestoned inner court to the front door, which swung open from inside to reveal the shadowy interior of the reception hall.

"Come in, come in, Goddaughter," said a woman's voice from deep within the dark, luxurious room. "The cards told me you would be ar-riving here today." The eerie house, the voice in the semi-dark, made me suddenly timid. A few candles stood on an inlaid table made of different rare woods that shone and glittered in the feeble light. Dark, heavy, carved furniture, chairs, benches, chests, seemed to lurk about the walls and in the corners. Here and there the candlelight caught the shine of satin cushions and silk tapestries. An immense, complexly patterned dark rug shone like the color of old blood at the center of the room, then receded into the shapeless darkness by the wall. I caught a glimpse of another darkened chamber, vast, rich, with shrouded furniture. The smell of mice and decay rose from the floorboards, the tapestries, the very walls of the place. "Oh, you've brought a dog. Señor Alonzo will not like that."

"I'm sorry, Madame Tournet. He ran away from home and followed me here, and now he won't leave me."

"Madame Tournet? Sibille, my goddaughter, call me your Auntie, *ma tante*. I *am* your aunt, after all. Come closer, come closer. I have not seen you since you were six years old, and I wish to see how you have grown." Auntie sat at the table, a spread of cards laid out before her. Face cards, the atous, the suits; the entire deck of the *tarocchi* was in play. A pattern I didn't recognize. She laid out a six of deniers onto her spread, then set the rest of the pack aside.

"I've brought a letter from my mother," I said, extending the letter. Auntie had father's nose; the rest was herself. She had grown plump with the years, and required quite a wide chair. Her hair was the shiny and alien black that can be achieved only through the dyer's art. Her eyes were intelligent, a knowing amber, surrounded by lines earned through some secret, hard knowledge. Her mouth was painted, and cir- cles of rouge sat on her cheeks. She had a hint of a mustache, but her skin was soft and white and curiously unwrinkled for her age. From her face, the way she moved her hands, her posture, it was clear that memory had not played me false, and she had once been a great beauty. A cane with a strange silver head in the shape of a monkey lay against the side of her chair. Gargantua, sniffing about the unfamiliar room, knocked it over. When she took the letter, I retrieved her cane for her.

"Ah, thank you, my dear. My gout, you know. Sometimes it's hard to get about. The seals are broken on this letter. Did you read it, Sibille, my insatiably curious goddaughter?"

"The whole world has read it, Auntie. They wouldn't let me pass in the city gates so close to sunset alone, so I had to show them mother's letter."

"How unpleasant for you, to be taken for a woman of ill fame. They must have been very rude." What was it about Auntie's strange house, and her even stranger person, that stripped away my Higher Self and left some inner being, raw and naked, aching to tell my carefully hidden secrets?

"I am worse than a woman of ill fame, Auntie. I'm a murderess, even though it's not my fault—entirely not—and I had to, but it was all a mis-understanding, just a mistake, you see. And if father can't be freed, I'm a beggar, too. Will you turn me away now?" She looked at me with those amber eyes, whose centers were great black wells in the semi-dark.

"A murderess? My, how discreet your mother was in this letter. Whom did you murder?" Auntie was quite calm.

"My fiancé, Thibault Villasse. Entirely by accident, though," I has-tened to add. At this, the old woman let out a sound somewhat between a series of snorts and a cackle. When she regained her composure, she said:

"Pull up a chair, my dear. I want to hear all about it. You may rely on me to keep your secret. After that, a little supper." She rang a little silver bell. "Arnaud," she said, "lay a third place at the table. My goddaughter has come to stay for a while."

I had scarcely got through the story of Thibault's sudden and unex-pected embrace of religious literature when it was time to transfer the conversation to the supper table.

"My goodness, dear," she said as she helped herself to the dozens of rich dishes that came one after another, "you're hardly eating anything. No wonder you're so thin."

"Auntie, I'm hungry and not hungry all at once. I'm so worried about father, my stomach hurts." At the mention of father, she gave an almost imperceptible little sniff, then served herself the breast of a duck pre-pared with candied orange peels and a strange spice I could hardly bear to smell. How curious her table was, I thought, as I watched her chew. Just the two of us, and an empty place, set with a half-size silver goblet and plate. The chair before it was high, narrow, and cushioned.

"Never mind about *him* for tonight," she said. "It's more important that you eat and rest right now. You've had a terrible shock, I'm sure. Villasse. Heh, heh, heh." She wiped her lips on her napkin, then helped herself to a ragoût of beef that lay in a large silver dish. "What a pity Señor Alonzo hasn't seen fit to join us. See here? I've his favorite can-died pears tonight. He'll be sorry, the ungrateful wretch. I'm afraid, my dear, he is jealous because you have come. He grows more spoiled every year." So, that was Señor Alonzo's chair, not a child's. He must be a dwarf. Rich ladies all have dwarves and jesters. They make the time pass in between cards, gossip, and hunting. I didn't imagine Auntie to be fond of hunting.

"Who—?"

"Now, you must tell me exactly how you caused Villasse's demise. I want to enjoy the details." Auntie was a strange audience. Where I expected her to frown, she laughed that peculiar laugh of hers. Where I expected horror, she showed bright-eyed concern, where interest, disapproval. Sometimes her mind just wandered off and she spoke of something else entirely, even though all the while she was still thinking over what I had said. I had never encountered anyone like her. She seemed completely unaware of what was proper in life. And all the while she spoke and listened, she consumed the most astonishing array of foods. I was quite in awe of her.

"You collect stones?" she said, when I told her of Monsieur Villasse's gory death. "What sort? Oh, how interesting. But you haven't a bezoar. I have several. I suppose they're too costly for a girl's collection. But you do seem to know a great deal of natural history. And you draw bones? I'd love to see that some day. That Villasse, he deserved it. But if you free your father, be assured, Villasse's family will never dare speak of it. Tell me, do you have an interest in the stars? I prefer night to daytime. The stars are guides; the sun merely spoils the complexion. Throw open the curtains, Sibille. It is quite dark now, and I want to see the moonrise."

"He must have bribed the steward—"

"Oh, it happens. It happens all the time. Here within the walls, we have them, too, these abductions, despite the city watch. Villasse always was impetuous. A bad trait, don't you think? Now, look, isn't the moon splendid? Help me up; I want to lean out the window and speak to them. To whom? The stars, of course. There, see the North Star? That is my guide. A sure harbor, said my late husband. Let the others move; that one is constant. I have never forgotten you, Sibille, though they would have liked me to. Some things are right, some are wrong. The North Star is always right. Villasse, my dear, bores me already. He was evil. He will be buried in the great tomb of secrets already hidden beneath this city. How very appropriate that a murder has brought you back to me. Someday you may understand why." All of a sudden, a pang of conscience shot through me. She noticed it and said, "What's wrong, dear, have I said something to shock you? I'm afraid I've grown used to shocking people over the years."

"No, not that, Auntie. I've something on my conscience. I've a sack full of salt that's not mine, and I don't know how to find the owner, who was so helpful to me. But if I throw it out, I'll feel guilty."

"Let me call Arnaud," she said, having heard my story. "The whole thing sounds rather suspicious to me. From what you tell me, this man sounds like a sly fellow bent on some scheme to get his sack into the city without inspection. You could very well have been arrested your-self. You are a bit of a goose, my dear, to be so trusting of strangers." She rang, and the peg-legged valet returned with another bottle of wine, filling both our cups. "Arnaud, fetch me the sack that was with my god-daughter's chest; I want to see what's in it. I'll be very surprised if it's salt." She had me repeat the story. Arnaud listened silently. "It is my opinion that he may be back for it," she said.

"It is also mine, Madame," said her servant. "I will notify the house-hold," he said, stumping off to return with the sack for Aunt Pauline's inspection.

But as he opened it, there on the table, the candlelight caught on the sharp glitter of metal, and we sucked in our breath as one person. It was a heavy leather case, sealed with the arms of the Queen of France.

"Sibille, my dear, I fear this is worse than I thought. Your stranger has robbed a royal courier."

"A royal courier would rather die than give up his charge," remarked Arnaud. "I fear there's murder in this somewhere."

"That is my thought as well," said Auntie, wiping grease off her little mustache with her napkin. "The question is whether we should bury the case, or whether we should send it to the *bailli* in the morning, say-ing it was found on the road. Luckily, the seals are intact, so I think we can risk the *bailli*. Word will get around, and the robbers will not return here to find their prize. Arnaud?"

"It shall be done, Madame."

"Excellent. Put it back in the armoire where you found it. We'll get rid of it tomorrow. And a little more of that sweet wine over there. It does help me to sleep."

Hours later, tipsy with godmother's wine, I followed the discreet valet with the wooden leg back to my room. The stolen case, the murder I had done all began to work on my mind and fill it with fears, which swarmed and grew in the alien, mildew-smelling house. The light of the candle Arnaud carried through the winding corridors and rooms ahead of me illuminated bizarre foreign objects roosting between the tapestries of saints and the statues of nymphs. Here were painted leather shields, the spears and clubs of savages, long tubes with clusters of sharp arrows arrayed beside them. Hideous masks leered down from the walls. As we entered the high-ceilinged room where I was to stay, I, the woman who had shot off a musket without flinching, had begun to shiver. At that very moment, Gargantua began to growl, then bark and leap about. Suddenly, with a strange cry, something hairy, smelly, and clawed leapt on my back and seemed to entangle itself in my hair. I shrieked, and tried to fling the hairy thing off me. It vanished into the dark, and I heard the sound of scuffling, climbing, as the dog barked at the bed canopy as if it had treed a cat. A strange chattering sound came from near the ceiling, and the candle showed the canopy dipping and swaying as if something were on it.

"What is that awful thing?" I cried, trembling all over.

"Ah, so there you are, Señor Alonzo, you jealous devil," said the valet, speaking for the first time. "Madame has been missing you. Come down, come down." He set down the candle, made a chirruping noise, and reached into a pocket for something; it looked like a piece of cake. There was a sort of blurring rush, and the thing leapt from the canopy to the valet's shoulder. Brown and hairy, long-tailed, wearing an embroidered velvet jacket. As it stuffed the cake into its mouth, it looked at me with beady black eyes out of a face that seemed indescribably old and forlorn.

"A monkey," I said, recovering myself. "What's a monkey doing here?"

"This is not just any monkey. This is Señor Alonzo, my second in command," said the valet. "We once sailed together, him and me." At this, the monkey on his shoulder grimaced, showing sharp little eye-teeth. "We keeps things in order for Madame, doesn't we, Alonzo?" Gargantua was snuffling and whining among a mound of petticoats on the floor.

"Oh, my things! They're all undone!" I said, rushing to pick them up. What a disaster! The armoire doors stood open. Petticoats and manu-script pages were crumpled and scattered all together, a bottle of scent poured over the lot, and the whole thing trod together as if the monkey had danced on them in a rage.

"Sorry, Mademoiselle. The Señor must have smelled the dog on them. And he's angry at you for staying here and keeping Madame com-pany. I'll put things to rights for you. Say, this is a beautiful box you've brought. What an odd design." As he picked up the silver-gilt coffer and set it on top of a tall chest of drawers, the monkey began to chatter, and jumped to the top of the huge, ornately carved armoire.

"It's not mine—I've never seen—oh, no—" On the floor lay the leath-er case, wide open. The monkey, in his orgy of destruction, had opened the seals and undone the buckles. "The box," I said. "That was what was inside the dispatch case."

"Well, well," said the wooden-legged valet. "I think this finishes the plan of handing it over to the *bailli*. They'll ask too many questions that you are not prepared to answer. I will consult with Madame. But it seems to me the best course of action is to put it back in the case and drop it on the road outside of the gate tomorrow morning, and let fate do what it will. Either that, or drop it down a well." My insides cringed at the thought of my naïveté, at getting my own godmother entangled in such a dangerous mess. The sooner I was rid of it, the better.

That night, I couldn't sleep. Dreadful dreams kept awakening me. I saw again the vicious mob, and heard their sinister chant, only this time it was father in his shirt, carrying the faggots. But when I looked at the scaffold, I didn't see him there, but a different execution, someone to be beheaded. "Oh," said the passersby, "a woman who slew her betrothed. Dreadful. Unnatural." The block, dripping with blood . . . and through it all, a sly little voice seemed to say, "I can give you anything you wish. Just open, speak the words engraved above the lock, and your greatest dreams will be yours." Who could be saying that? I'd wake up and stare into the dark, hearing nothing but Gargantua breathing. Again and again it happened. Then I became aware of something else breathing. Breathing very, very softly, almost not a breath at all. That awful monkey, I thought, he's sneaking back. But no, the door was closed. Then a soft sound, like whispering, coming from the top of the chest of drawers. It *is* the monkey, I thought, and he's afraid to come down, because Gargantua's here. I pulled the covers over my head, as if that would keep him from me, and turned over and tried to sleep again.

At last, as the silver light that leaks from beneath the rosy curtain of dawn penetrated my chamber (ah, that's very good, Sibille, you must save it for your next poem), I pulled the covers from my head and saw the monkey wasn't there. Pen and paper, I thought, I need to put down that curtain of dawn before I forget it. Poetry, once my splendor, now you will be my consolation. . . . Barefoot and in my nightgown, I began to rustle around the strange bedroom. It was then that I heard the whisper more urgently than ever:

"You conceited female, aren't you in the least curious? Open the box, and you will find inside a secret that will make you the greatest poetess in the world."

Without even thinking, I answered back, "What good is that? There are hardly any women Truly Dedicated to the Muses anyway. Being the greatest poetess, that's like being the Emperor of the Antipodes." At the sound of my voice, Gargantua awoke.

"Poet then, poet. Author of all authors, divinely worshiped, quoted everywhere by lovers—" The whisper was hurried. Yes, definitely—it was coming from the top of the chest of drawers. I stiffened. There was something, something awful in that box. And it was whispering my fondest dreams to me. My skin prickled. I was also humiliated, hearing my secrets all repeated in that vulgar, insinuating whisper. I resolved never to open that box. The sooner at the bottom of some well, the better.

"Your dreams, at the bottom of a well? How could you do such a thing?" Gargantua growled, as if he could hear it, too.

Now when things are utterly illogical, it is best to meet them with logic. So instead of running mad through the corridors of the strange house, I merely addressed the top of the chest of drawers, and said, "I listened to that stranger, and brought down nothing but trouble. I'm not listening to you. Whatever you are, ghost or demon, I've had enough of tempters. Today is the day you go back into the pit. I've half a mind to have you exorcised." An eerie wail came from the box. Definitely, a demon, or the threat of holy water wouldn't have distressed it so. I almost felt sorry for it.

"Oh, that's it. I'm a poor, pitiful thing, trapped in here. You'd find me darling, tender, so soft and lovely—"

"Liar," I said. Lord, how clever it was, molding itself to every momentary desire. They say that's how the devil works.

"Oh, not clever at all—a sorrowful, wretched little thing, only wanting a pure maiden to liberate it and turn it back into a handsome prince with a kiss—" At this notion of myself as a romance-infected, weak-minded dreamer, filled with inflated ideas of her own sensitivity, I became furious.

"That does it!" I shouted, and I pulled the box off the top of the chest of drawers and slammed it into the heavy leather dispatch case. As I prepared to buckle it in, it whispered one last thing:

"Aren't you even interested in what I am, that the Queen of France wants me so desperately?" Then it fell silent.

Maybe I've killed it, slamming it around like that, I thought. It's awfully quiet. I wonder what it is. If it's dead, it can't hurt me. It can't be so harmful, if the queen herself wants it. I mean, it's probably sealed up in a bottle or something. I didn't hear any glass break, so it won't be loose. A little magic thing sealed in a bottle. An imp or a fairy. One little peek wouldn't hurt. Especially now that it's dead or unconscious. I could close the box up quickly, and it would be as if I'd never looked. All these thoughts, and no whispering. Just silence. Unearthly silence. Definitely, it was at least unconscious. I pulled the ornate, silver-gilt box out of the case. There was not a sound, not even of breathing. If I've killed it, I really ought to know, I thought. Just a peek, no more. When I picked up the box, Gargantua whined, then vanished under the bed.

There was a lot of engraved writing on the box, in letters I couldn't read because I had never seen anything like them before. The designs were alien and eerie. There was a thing in a chariot with snaky legs and the head of a rooster. Above the lock was a plaque set over the designs, with nonsense words written in the Roman alphabet. I shook the box. Nothing rattled. I smelled it, and didn't smell anything unusual. I set it on the nightstand, and opened the catch, planning to peer in just a little.

There was a sudden roar, and the pink dawn's light darkened suddenly to midnight, and the box lid flew open in something like a wind that tore at my nightgown and made the bedclothes fly across the room. As the light returned, I saw something unspeakably old and evil sitting on a rotting crimson silk cushion inside the box. It was a mummified head, shriveled, dark brown, covered with peeling, parchment-like skin.

"Ah, God!" I cried aloud, as I crossed myself.

"Too late," I heard the insinuating voice say. The dried, peeling lips barely moved. "You peeked. Now I'm yours." One sunken rotting eyelid opened, and a shining, living eye peered out at me. The monstrous thing winked, and its parchment lips seemed to stretch out in a smirking grin. With a scream, I slammed the lid shut.

Then there was terrible confusion, as Gargantua emerged, barking, servants came running in, and at last, Auntie, in a dressing gown and ruffled cap, leaning on her walking stick, came puffing into the room.

"Now what is it? What's this commotion? Has your dog caught a rat? Surely, Sibille, you are stronger minded than that."

"Auntie, Auntie, there's a horrible, dried up dead man's head inside that box."

"Hmm," she said, "then we can't throw it down the well after all. It might poison it. Let's see. A head by courier. It could very well be the head of someone distinguished, being retrieved after an execution—"

"There are probably people hunting for it right now. Maybe several sets of people. These things have sentimental value, you know," said her valet, Arnaud.

"Then we'll bury it in the cellar, and throw the box down the well," announced Auntie. At this, an eerie cry rose from the box.

"Auntie, it's—it's alive—it—talks—horrible, horrible things—" I said, almost suffocated with the thought of that living, leering eye. The thing in the box made a sinister sound, so that even Arnaud crossed himself.

"Shut up, you, I'm thinking," said Auntie, and gave the box several sound raps with her walking stick. She was so engrossed in her thoughts, she never noticed how she had dented and scuffed the lid of the rich metal coffer.

"Don't damage my box," said the thing inside. As I watched in horror, the dent and the scuff marks from Auntie's stick slowly vanished, and the coffer was exactly as it was. Auntie didn't seem to notice.

"A talking box," she said. "These things are worth money. Doubtless going to court as a curiosity. No wonder it got stolen. Tell me, in there, are you good for anything else besides chattering?" There was a long silence. I had the distinct feeling the thing in the box was sulking. "I say, wake up!" said Auntie, giving the box another couple of whacks. There was a low, sinister whine from within. At last a voice spoke, faint, irritated.

"In all the seventeen centuries since I was put to death, I have never encountered a more monstrous female. You, woman, are an abomination above all abominations."

"I would hope so," said Auntie. "I've learned a few things since I married my late husband for his money. And one of them is never to put up with bad-mannered spiritual phenomena. Tell me—are you good for anything? Otherwise, into the cellar with you. Deep. And don't think to curse the house. It's absolutely crowded with walking spirits and cursed objects already. They followed my husband home from his work. There's hardly room for you as it is."

"Recite the words above the lock, and look into my face, and I can grant you your heart's desire," the words came floating out. But they sounded a bit lackluster.

"Now *there's* a foolish thing. Most people, having given it far too little thought, would be horrified if they received what they say is their heart's desire."

"Exactly," said the voice, sounding happy. "Why are you the first person I have ever encountered who knew that *before* they were tempted to enter my power?"

"Very simple," said Auntie. "I wanted money more than anything. Along came Monsieur Tournet, sprinkling money wherever he walked.

It's not getting what you want, it's the baggage that comes with it that makes the trouble."

"Ah, ve-ry good. Almost as if I'd done it myself." At this gloating tone of voice, Auntie paused.

"You *are* a malignant little thing," she said. "Sibille, it's time to dump this creature. Half the world will be wanting it, but I want it out of my house. There just isn't room for another curiosity."

"Too late," gloated the thing in the box. "The young woman who fancies herself a poetess has already seen my face. Since my last posses-sor has already been murdered, that means I'm hers until she dies or condemns herself to eternal damnation by her continual wishing. She'll be drawn to me, drawn as if to a lover, hating herself more each time she sees my face. Then she'll make a wish—just a tiny, tiny, one. But such troubles it will bring, she'll soon need another. Oh, I give people exactly what they want, and they mend, and mend, and mend, and get deeper and deeper—"

"Not *my* goddaughter you won't bother that way. Arnaud, take it out and dump it in the river. We'll burn the dispatch case. Sibille, quit snif-fling and get dressed. You've errands today, not that your father de-serves your devotion. My devoted brother, ha! He hasn't spoken to me in years, except to ask for money." As I watched Arnaud taking out the box, I could hear it saying:

"Not the river, oh, think, how I have suffered. You above all, who has lived without a leg, can understand a man who has to live without a body—I could give you your heart's desire—wouldn't you like a lovely, strong leg back again—"

"You old quack, why don't you give yourself your body back, then—" But the rest of the conversation was lost down the corridor. I looked at Auntie, my eyebrows raised in the unspoken question.

"Oh, don't worry. He won't be tempted. Arnaud knows the face of evil quite well. And make no mistake about it, that box is pure evil."

"But—but it sounds rather pitiful. I mean, it knows it's ugly—"

"Sibille, don't let yourself be taken in. Evildoers always sound pitiful when you get close to them. They are as full of excuses as a dog is fleas. The whole world is to blame but them. Ah yes, find me a righteous man who claims he was mistreated and is only getting his own back, and I will show you a true villain. I'm sure if we could question a black-hearted creature like Nero about his crimes, we'd find he claimed he was pitiful, too."

On the best of days, I would find this a difficult thought, and this was not the best of days. But still, even with my nerves utterly exhausted, I asked politely, "Auntie, how do you know so much about such things?" I was really thinking of her cold-blooded and fearless approach to what I regarded as a shattering and abnormal experience. I mean, there she was, in her dressing gown and walking stick, smacking down diabolical objects before she had even had breakfast.

"About evil?" she answered. "Sibille, my dear, perhaps some day I will tell you how Monsieur Tournet made his money—"

Nine

I envy you, brother, this pleasant home, a nice little city practice. You have no idea of how difficult and demanding it is, serving a single patroness, and she all-powerful. No, it is your good fortune to run your own business, free of the queen's insatiable demands." Cosmo Ruggieri gestured about him to the narrow confines of his brother Lorenzo's best room, part of an upper-floor apartment in the rue de la Tisarendirie. His black leather boots were propped up on the only footstool, and his black cloak was hanging on one of a row of pegs driven into the wall. Above them, several star charts had been nailed beside the red-painted sigil of Asmodeus, the Ruggiero family's patron demon. After all, sorcery and fortune-telling were a family business.

Cosmo's brother's wife, a pleasant little woman in housedress, white cap and apron, bustled in to refill his wineglass. In the next room, children could be heard reciting their lessons for the youngest of the Ruggiero brothers, who was also their tutor until his paintings might bring him sufficient funds for a separate household.

"Well, Cosmo, that is your blessing and your curse—being the eldest. You inherited the family patron. Beatrice, are there any more of those little cakes for my honored brother? And what fortune! What stars! Our father always said our Duchessina was destined to be Queen of France. And look at us here, all prosperous, because of her good fortune, and yours! I tell you, Cosmo, you are just nervous. You should get married; it will do you a world of good. My wife has a cousin in the old country they say is so beautiful she makes the clock in the church tower stop every time she passes—"

"I can't do it, brother. Domestic harmony would spoil my mystery as surely as if I wore any other color but black. Professional demands— father always warned me—and now, the Great Lady is at me nearly every day like a harpy. Entirely thankless that it was I who made her queen! What chance did *she* ever have, the wife of a second son? I tell you, my life's in jeopardy if I can't satisfy her this time."

"Again? What happened to gratitude? Here she was childless, about to be abandoned, and thanks to you and the spell we had from our fa- ther, she had ten children."

"That puffed up, self-congratulating Doctor Fernel claims the credit. So does the surgeon who performed the operation on the king, as does that meddlesome Gondi woman, who sent away for some quack charm or other, and besides that the Old Constable, Montmorency, who col- lected foreign remedies on his travels, and a crowd of everyone else who wants her favor. You just can't expect laypersons to understand good, sound, diabolical principles."

"The curse of our profession, isn't it, brother? Father was right. Every amateur thinks they understand sorcery, and we are reduced to over- awing them with puffs of smoke and mysterious robes to keep them in their place. Parlor tricks! Maybe Roger was right to take up painting. Sorcery's a demanding business."

"To say the least. Ah, these little cakes—your wife certainly knows how to cook ..." Cosmo Ruggieri brushed the crumbs off his sinister black leather doublet as he spoke. "The queen won't rest content until she prys the Duchess of Valentinois out of her husband's bed. She's taken up amateur spell-casting, and getting it wrong—"

"—they always do that—"

"—then she threatened to send for that meddlesome old Michel de Nostre-Dame to take my place—"

"Not sound, that man. And a bad poet, too. *The Centuries.* Cheap self-advertising—"

"And Simeoni was breathing down my neck—"

"Simeoni? He's no good—"

"But he heard some Venetian astrologer had discovered the legendary Master of All Desires, and thought it would get him ahead of me in royal favor, so he sent off an agent to get it for him." Cosmo's brother sat down hard on a little cushioned stool, and struck at his own forehead.

"The Master of—you mean the Undying Head of Menander the Magus? That awful thing! Didn't Guaricus have it?"

"No, that's rumor. He's too wise to ever touch it. It was Josephus Magister. So I sent Giovanni to steal it from Simeoni's agent—"

"That thing—that despicable, filthy thing—even father wouldn't touch it when it was offered to him. Cosmo—it's a mistake—"

"I had to do something, the queen was growing impatient. So I told her I was obtaining it—then one of her ladies came by for a love potion and told me in strictest secrecy that the queen had dispatched two royal messengers to intercept it—"

"It's working already. A trail of misery follows that thing—"

"—and that the Duchess of Valentinois wants it now, too, so that the queen can't have the powers it grants. Knowing her, I can't believe she hasn't dispatched her own agents to get hold of it."

"Ugh, a tangle of women. There's nothing worse. Beatrice, my dear, open that bottle we've been saving under the bed. Cosmo, you will stay for supper, won't you?" Silently, Cosmo, his face flushed with wine, nodded his assent, then wiped the beads of sweat from his forehead with a black silk handkerchief that he pulled from his sleeve.

"That's a nice touch," said his brother admiringly, looking at the expensive little trinket.

"Gift from the queen—ah, brother, brother, when you walk higher, you can fall farther—at this moment, I'd give it all up for a nice little city practice like yours—rich ladies who want astrological charts for their lapdogs, lovesick young men in for a potion or two, some amateur diabolists who want a seance with their favorite demon—no threats of the rack or the *poire d'angoisse*. Ah, Asmodeus, how I suffer!"

But wonderful smells of garlic and rosemary, warm bread and roasting lamb were penetrating the room, and the inviting clink of metal goblets and knives being set on the table called the queen's chief sorcerer from his melancholy musings. As they went into the next room, the younger man put his arm around his older brother's shoulders.

"A wife, that's what you need—and a cozy little household you could keep in secret. The old lady who lives downstairs isn't going to last long, and my wife would love the company—" But Cosmo Ruggieri was still absorbed in his own thoughts.

"Turning the Undying Head of Menander the Magus loose in the royal family. A dreadful idea—still, it wasn't mine. In a way, it serves her right, all that amateur meddling with things she doesn't understand. And if I don't control that ghastly old thing, then he might work against me. A sealed niche, protected with the Seven Sacred Signs—meetings in the dark of the moon. I must somehow get her to open the box first. I certainly don't want it attached to *me*. Nobody who's owned it has escaped an early and ugly death—"

❧

"I'm sure this is very intelligent," said Auntie, as she squinted at my petition. "The words are long. Long words show intelligence, and you are quite as full of them as a sausage is full of garlic. And what devotion! My brother doesn't deserve a daughter like you. Why aren't the others here? Don't answer, I always knew it would be you—headlong courage, passionate loyalty—" She paused, and shook her head over some secret thought. "The mind. It's in the blood. I knew it would be."

Auntie put down the reading glass and closed the curtain so that the tiny sliver of sunlight that illumined her ornate desk was strangled into nothingness. "Sun," she said, spying the look on my face. "Nothing is worse for the complexion. See mine? Not a wrinkle. And you've already turned brown. Too much sun, once you moved to the country. Soon lines, then folds and sags, and after that, you'll look no better than that dried up old head in the box we've just thrown out. Oh, don't look so horrified. It's not too late. You must simply begin a *regimen* of beauty. This afternoon, when you've returned from the Bishop's palace, we'll burn those awful dresses you brought, and you will lie down for an hour with a facial treatment I have devised of cucumbers and cream." she rang her little bell. Taken aback, I looked down at my dress. In her rich and rather decadent house, it suddenly looked pitiful, countrified, and too short in the hem, having no train at all.

"Do I look wrong? My dress—"

"Surely, you weren't thinking of wearing *that,* were you? Important people are never impressed by sincere poverty. That is a fantasy of the poor. Black silk, I have just the thing from my slender days—I had Amalie lower the hem for you last night." With an assessing look she regarded my pedal extremities. "Those feet, my dear, they must be your little secret ..." Then she cocked her head on one side, as if thinking. "The hair, it does shine, even if it is a common color—the dearest little soupçon of a veil. . . . You'll warm his heart before you've said a word. Oh, yes, and do me a favor. Wear this ring. It will bring you good luck." She rustled in her desk drawer and came up with a strange old ring in red gold, heavily engraved with a floral design in which the letters "P" and "M" were engraved. Tiny brilliants spangled waving vines about the letters. It was a woman's ring, just the size for a narrow little finger.

"Oh, it's too pretty, I couldn't—"

"Just for today, my dear," she said, as she slipped it onto my finger, where it looked far too grand for my bony brown hand. "It's a bit of a keepsake. But today, it will make you lucky. Oh, there you are, Arnaud. Have Georges put her sidesaddle on Flora. The velvet-trimmed blanket with the gold embroidery, the one I used to use on Sundays, back when I could still sit a horse. Remember this, Sibille—a lady never sets her foot on the ground, not even to walk across the cathedral square. And only a bumpkin would ever consider traveling on that fool packhorse of your father's. Even *he* wouldn't ride it into town. I have caught you just in time, before you were beyond reform."

✢

I must have cut a mysterious figure, a veiled woman on a richly decked out gray hackney, with two liveried footmen at her bridle. Sweating passersby, a laundress with her basket, two clerks in conversation, idling boys, and even the beggars in the shadow of the cathedral porch, glanced up briefly, then turned away as if the heat made even staring too great an effort. Over and over I rehearsed my speech, finding it worse

each time I said it to myself. My petition made me cringe with shame.
The work of a fool, a know-nothing. If only it were Latin, drawn up by
a clever notary. . . .

As one of auntie's lackeys held my horse in the courtyard of the
Bishop's palace, the other helped me to dismount. Again, servants
slowed on their errands to stare, a priest paused to sniff his disapproval,
and two ponderous, well-dressed older men in heavy silk gowns and
gold chains, who had just been shown out through the great double
doors, paused on the top of the stair to inspect my person. Rich merchants, by their clothes, not gentlemen. Leaving the door behind them
by several paces, as if accompanying them but not wishing to be seen
with them, trailed a tall, olive-skinned young man with an aquiline profile and observant eyes. I watched as he glanced dismissively, one by
one, at the petitioners that were already crowding the courtyard. His
dress looked alien to him, as if he had been waylaid and forced into it on
pain of death, and, somehow, out of pure truculence, it was busy undo-
ing itself. A loose point dangled from beneath his doublet, his short
gown sat askew, and his ruff lay, limp and unhappy, like an overheated
dog, around his neck. Hmp, I thought, he looks as if the wind blew him
in. He must be a relative. No clerk could dress like that and keep his
place.

But he was very good-looking, in a tallish sort of way, and I found
myself wishing him not to find anything to scorn about *me,* even as I
was scorning him. I set my chin high, and prepared to sweep past, but
not failing to take note of the changing tilt of his black eyebrows and
the new expression in his dark eyes. They brightened as they spied me,
and followed me even as he pretended they weren't. Aha, I thought, I've
won the duel of the eyes, no doubt thanks to my new, costly silk gown.
That's the sort of thing that impresses people like that. Now to pass on
quickly, I thought, before I forget my hard-memorized speech.

But one of the older men suddenly turned to address me. Surely I
didn't know such, oh dear, yes, he had trimmed his beard a new way
and it had grown grayer—It was my gossipy cousin Matheline's husband, that vulgar rich banker, M. Bonneuil.

"Why, indeed, it's Matheline's cousin Sibille!" he said, moving
closer, his companion still at his elbow. "Sibille, you have grown quite

elegant in the time since we last met. Allow me to present a dear friend, Monsieur Montvert of the House of Fabris et Montvert, and this is his son—" I hardly heard the rest, so concerned was I that the last of my speech would vanish in the interruption. Besides, I had never heard of Montvert, whatever that was. Some new estate with a purchased title, no doubt, or a banking firm of slippery Italians. "—Demoiselle Sibille is a poetess of note in our city, and her *Dialogue of the Virtues* was received with great admiration at my wife's *cénacle* Michaelmas before last—"

My speech, it's going—it's vanished—I'll fail—and all because a grand silk dress has attracted that upthrusting, uncouth husband of Matheline's, I thought. Then I noticed that the strangers were all looking at my feet. Oh, God, my shoes—such a contrast with the borrowed dress and veil—and so big—the hem—not low enough—I could feel my face growing red beneath the veil. I could hear the strange older man say something about the Muse, and I stammered something back, but mainly all I heard was my heart beating, thumping out of pure humiliation.

"It's a pity about your father's trouble," said Matheline's merciless husband. "I'm afraid you'll find most doors barred to you, even ours, my dear, should he be burnt—heresy, you know—one really can't risk, these days—but you're right to come to the Bishop. I hear all the bankers' gossip, and the word is that M. D'Apchon, that creature of Marshall St.-André's, has had his eye on your grandfather's house for a long time. They say he borrowed a considerable sum not only to refurnish it, but to bribe the *bailli*—the confession of a commoner under torture—hardly enough to accuse a gentleman under ordinary circumstances."

"Annibal is coming, with a letter from Constable Montmorency—" I stammered, "b-but we were afraid he'd be too late."

"Listen, my dear cousin, you must be sure to stress your family's connection with the Constable. He stands above St.-André in favor at court, and even M. D'Apchon will not want to anger him. Innocence and guilt are not the issues in this case—remember that." With a few polite words, they excused themselves and passed on leaving me certain that my doom had been sealed by their interruption. The speech, once so moving and elegantly worded, had now entirely vanished, and in its place was pure panic.

The panic redoubled when I saw the hard benches in the long *salle* outside the Bishop's audience chamber. They appeared to be crammed with pallid, weary petitioners more or less exactly like myself, though considerably less well clad. They could have been here for days, I thought. Maybe he'll never see me. But then auntie's footman escorted me to the attendant at the sealed inner door, and motioned me to re-move my right glove. "Take a look at my mistress's ring," he said, "and tell your master that Madame Tournet's niece wishes an audience." This seemed to be the exact right thing to say, and we were shown directly into the Bishop's audience chamber, where priests and secretaries hur-ried in and out on important-seeming errands.

The chamber itself was of a wealth that rivaled the finest rooms and rarest furnishings of Auntie's sumptuous, if decayed, mansion. Rich ar-ras hung on every wall, and between the gilded arches that supported the ceiling, scenes depicting Christ enthroned in heaven, all surrounded by angels and saints, had been painted by some cunning artisan. Beneath the heavenly canopy, however, an entirely secular conversation seemed to be in the finishing stages, something to do with church property and the income from some estate whose title was in question. How odd: I al-ways thought that Bishops spent all their spare time in prayer, but even in the very shadow of the temple of God I was hearing more money-talk and seeing bankers and other people with calculating eyes go in and out. But then my guide showed me across the floor and presented me, and I was allowed to kneel and kiss the Bishop's ring.

The Bishop's face, smooth, well-fed, and worldly, showed signs that he had once been a handsome man. He brightened as he looked at me, then glanced at the ring on my hand. Something in his eyes flickered, and I knew the curious object had done some secret work. "Well, well," he said when I rose, surveying me up and down, "this is the third favor in a quarter of a century. Let me see this petition." He smiled ironically as he opened it up and looked over my writing. "You clearly wrote this yourself." My well-controlled panic began to rise again. "What an inter-esting defense of your father." My heart began to pound harder. What will I say, what will I say? "Are you the daughter who is Madame Tour-net's goddaughter?" he asked. I nodded with what I hoped was great dignity, but not a sound would come out of my mouth. Oh, a thousand curses on those wretches in the courtyard. "Was this your idea?" he asked. Oh, it was hours between each question, and I could tell he expected me to say something.

"I—it's all just terrible, just a plot to seize my grandfather's house—my father would never read a book by M. Calvin, let alone own one—he—he—hardly ever even reads at all—he thinks theology is for priests—and Annibal is too far away to come soon because the Constable is so far in the north just now, even though mother has sent for him—"

"Your brother knows the Sieur Anne de Montmorency, Constable of France?" said the Bishop, his tone newly respectful.

"Yes, the Sieur Montmorency himself. My brother is an *enseigne* in his son's company of light horse and M. de Damville relies on him utterly—the Constable himself said my brother was very promising—why, Annibal hardly ever gets home anymore—" Where was my speech? "—surely, in your goodness and noble mercy, your discerning powers, you will see the innocence of my father and intervene for the sake of divine justice—"

"I don't think either D'Apchon or St.-André suspected your family was so well connected—" A strange, ironic smile flitted across the Bishop's worldly face. What stupidity made the low gossip I'd just heard tumble out of my mouth?

"Our family has owned that house ever since Gaston de La Roque built it in the reign of King Charles VII. M. D'Apchon is a vile conspirator and even his patron Monsieur de St.-André will disown him if he offends the Constable, who is personally very concerned if a brave soul like my brother had to leave the service of his family because of a false plot to steal his father's estate." I burst into tears of pure rage. Oh, what was going on? Why hadn't I done it all smoothly, elegantly, the way I'd imagined? And what was that sound I heard? Oh, God the Bishop had put his hand over his mouth. That sound. I'm doomed, I thought. The Bishop, I'm sure of it, had snorted.

"Well," he said softly to himself, "it seems once again Pauline has done me a favor." He looked at me curiously. "Who would have thought that you, of all the family, would be the one to come to me? You appear devoted to your father."

"My—my father is a great man. And innocent—" I said.

"I'll see what I can do," said the Bishop. "The evidence is very scanty."

"It's forged, all forged—" I said, wiping my eyes beneath that horrid soupçon of a veil, so that I could take my leave, at least, with some decent dignity.

✤

"Well?" said Auntie, as I gave her back her ring. "Did you get in to see him?"

"I did, but I was just too nervous to say anything right. I just know I've failed, Auntie, I was so stupid, and the words didn't come out right, and now we'll lose everything. What will we do? How will we live?" We were in Auntie's great gilt-decorated, shadowy, reception hall, where she sat on her cushioned chair, the velvet curtains pulled against the dangerous midday sun. Outside, in the light, I could hear the faint cry of vendors in the street beyond the courtyard gate. Life and air seemed very distant. I felt as if I were smothering. Father. Everything gone. On the table beside her sat a book, *On the Discernment of Spirits,* with her embossed leather marker sitting halfway into it.

"A pity," she said. "I thought his memory would be a little better. Age takes us all, I suppose." She sighed, and shrugged her shoulders. "I imagine you might live here," she said. "And your mother—she was my best friend before she married my brother, did you know that? I'd enjoy her company now. But your sisters—I fear they couldn't tolerate the place. Too frail, too nervous." For a minute I was irritated. I mean, *I* am the sensitive one, and *much* more frail than *they.* The sensitivity of brilliance is ever so much more sensitive than just being droopy and feminine.

"What do you mean by that?" I asked.

"See that over there?" she said, picking up the walking stick that lay against the desk, and pointing it in the direction of the curtain. A light breeze was swaying it, and there was a sort of blurring, almost like a mist, in its upper-right-hand corner, near the ceiling.

"Why, yes," I said. "The curtain's moving. Is the window open?"

"That's what I mean. Even Annibal would shudder when he saw that curtain move, much as he needed the cash for that little mare he wanted. And your sisters—my! They certainly wouldn't last long around *here*. But you, you just ask if the window is open. No, it's not. That's Doña Vargas y Rodriguez. I let her stay because I enjoy her company. Very genteel, excellent conversation of an evening, even if her French is bad." She looked up and addressed the moving curtain. "It's all right, Dolores, this is a relative. You can come out. Sibille, let me introduce you. Doña Dolores is too polite to manifest without a formal introduction." Auntie then proceded to introduce me to the air, and made the air acquainted with me. It was all too curious.

But as I watched the spot she addressed, the misty form of a slender young woman in a heavy Spanish silk gown took shape in front of the curtain. Her heavy, peaked, pearl-encrusted headdress clung close about her hair, her dark eyebrows were mobile and expressive, her eyes and mouth like hidden pools. And her throat was cut from ear to ear. The black shadow of ghostly blood soaked her gown all the way to the hem. I couldn't help shuddering. But the spirit, for that's what she obviously was, seemed embarrassed by my reaction, and pulled a light scarf around her ruined neck with an apologetic smile.

"You see? What a lady! She's my very favorite. There's not many of them so considerate." The misty lady's mouth moved. She appeared to be talking. "Do you hear her?" asked Auntie. "No? Well, you will in time. It just takes practice. She's telling you her story. She always has to do that, before we sit down to a good ladies' gossip. I have had some excellent recipes from her."

"But her story?" The ghost had clearly reached a very dramatic part of her narration, where she flung aside the scarf and revealed the wounds that had killed her.

"She was newly wed, on a galleon headed for New Spain to join her husband, when Captain Tournet murdered her for her wedding jewels and trousseau. After, I am afraid, various insults to her person which should not be repeated before an innocent young woman such as yourself."

"But your husband—?"

"My dear, with all the insults that your family has no doubt showered on me, did they never tell you how Monsieur Tournet made his fortune?"

"Only that he was not socially acceptable."

"Ha! How like Hélène. Not a rude word ever passed her lips, the whole time we were best friends. She deals in euphemisms, your mother! Sibille, dear, my husband was, to put it bluntly, a pirate. Or rather—shall we be genteel about it?—a licenced privateer, sailing under royal commission. The notorious Captain Jean Tournet, who organized many a private fleet for his majesty out of La Rochelle. Had he an older escutcheon he would have been respectable enough, once rich. And you'd think, of all those who use crimes to gain estate, there would be nothing special to single him out—" Auntie sighed, shrugged, and spread out her plump, white hands before her. "But *they* pursued him, the shades of the slain. From the sea inland, from place to place. We once owned two great houses at the oceanside, and an estate in the north, and this little one here, in the land of my own ancestors, which he bought to please me. All of them were stuffed full of ghosts. What respectable folk would pay a visit to a house where *they* inhabited? He never mentioned his murders, you understand, but the spirits, they sit in the walls and whisper."

Oh, I thought. That explains the strange rustling sound I sometimes heard in the wall. I thought it was mice. Spirits, I do not find shocking. But the thought that Monsieur Tournet might have been a man of no birth whatsoever—why, I had always taken father for a snob, an exaggerator— "Auntie, how—?"

"My marriage? Arranged, dear, for his money. What did you think? And my despicable brother Hercule was loudest of all in his promises of gratitude, if only I would sign the papers."

I must have looked rather taken aback at this new view of my father. Auntie's smile was cynical. "This house, this fortune, like so many others, is entirely built on blood. Oh, don't be shocked. Where do you think money in this world comes from? Work? No, it's theft. The New World has made the Spanish king rich, and us, too, indirectly, thanks to our king's commission. Monsieur Tournet retired, far from the sea, and tried to become a gentleman. You know how it is; marry into a good family, buy a bankrupt estate, build a large house, give money to charity. It didn't work for him. His houses were too full of ghosts. Most of them moved in here when I sold the other places after his death. The jewelry, the gold, the pitiful things for which they died, they cling to them. See those candlesticks over there?" She pointed to a pair of huge, gold torchères that stood on the floor. Behind I could just make out a row of stolid-faced, alien men in feather cloaks. "The gold was melted down from some heathen idol of theirs from across the sea, I'm sure," she said. "We didn't do it—the Spaniards did. You'd think they'd go haunt the churches in Toledo and Madrid where their treasures were made into church ornaments. But no, they have to cram in here with the rest of the spooks. Maybe it's because I'm too hospitable." She sighed.

"I don't know why we should be the ones to have them, when so many others deserve them. Oh, well. They keep me company. If they're quiet, I don't have them exorcised—it's very expensive, you know, and it disturbs everything. But your family, yes—they wouldn't be as bold as you. And I really am not rich enough to set them up in a separate establishment. All those dowries—no, it can't be done. Hercule couldn't do it, and I don't see why I have to. Especially when he was perfectly content to take Monsieur Tournet's tainted money when he was alive, and never even spoke once to me, his own sister. It's a judgment on him, what's happened to him, even if it is based on a lie." At this, the ghost nodded happily in agreement, but I felt stunned. No help from the Bishop, no help from Aunt Pauline. What could Annibal do? By the time he got here, it would be too late. The burnings are scheduled right after the completion of the interrogation. Even I knew that much. Could the interrogations be stretched out? Could I take another petition, a better, improved one, to the Cardinal in Paris? How would I ever get an audience?

"You look pale, my dear. It's that dreadful dress. You need a brighter color to set off your complexion. And dinner. Dinner always mends everything. And you can see," she said, gesturing to her generous figure, "that I have had a lot of mending to do." I followed her as she puffed up the stairs to her own room, which was crammed full of furniture: a huge bed with carved cupids holding up the canopy, chairs, chests, silver and gold candlesticks, plates, basins, and ewers of fine porcelain, all decorated with bright gold and enamel patterns, and figures of the gods and goddesses of Greek mythology, and several armoires stuffed to bursting with rich silk and velvet court gowns in an array of styles and sizes.

"I wore all of these at one time," she said. "I know you won't believe it, but when I was young, I was as slender as you are now—but without the height, of course. Let's see—a dressing gown—day-dress, yes, the blue is nice—and this one. Something for evening—can't do a thing about shoes—your feet are not your best feature, dear. They are much too large. You will have to minimize them. Longer hems, perhaps, but no ruffles—plain, keep the decoration high, to distract the eye . . ."

I know it was all well meant, but as she rummaged in her armoires and talked to herself, I began to feel myself gradually transforming into a bony oaf with huge, galumphing feet, in need of strenuous efforts at mending and concealing, instead of the delicate and poetic creature of nature that I preferred to think of myself as. This I found more upsetting than the ghosts. That is, until I noticed what was happening to her dressing table.

"Auntie, look at your dressing table," I said, and she pulled her head out of the squat green and gold armoire in the corner. On the ivory and lapis inlaid surface of the table, something translucent was shining. Auntie's eyes narrowed and she took up her walking stick.

"You again! I told you to be off! Now, scat, or I'll have you thrown right back into the river!"

"I'm warning you, you old cow, don't you dare dent my box, or there'll be hell to pay." The shining thing had finished forming up. A bit of river slime dripped from its corners. It radiated the scent of damp, decayed flesh. It was the ornate silver-gilt box of the dreadful head.

"My lovely, foolish Sibille. I told you I'd never leave you," said the thing in the box. And at that moment, in the midst of horror, I felt a great temptation. It grew like blind desire, like a living thing. I craved to open up the box. I wanted—I wanted to wish for smaller feet. "Feel it? Feel the desire? Oh, just open up my box, and say the word, and you'll have your heart's desire."

"Don't listen to that thing," said Auntie. "It'll send you straight to hell. I know evil when I see it."

"Vulture," said the thing in the box. "You're next."

❧

Cosmo Ruggieri was seated in his tower workshop, wearing a new black leather jerkin with leather-paned trunk hose puffed out with black wool panels that made him resemble an unpleasant and overlarge beetle. Kneeling before him was his servant Giovanni, the man with the earring, who had stolen the Master of All Desires from Simeoni's courier in Venice.

"Great wizard, your mightiness, it was not my fault—the theft from Simeoni's agent went perfectly—consider my travels, the hardship—"

"Then why do you not have it for me here now?"

"Maestro, I was robbed of it in Marseilles by two ruffians who left me for dead—"

"A remarkable recovery," observed Ruggieri.

"But I recovered myself through a miracle, and questioning the kitchen wench at their inn, discovered they were agents of the Queen of France herself—"

"Quiet, enough," said the queen's magician, while he fumed inside at having been double-crossed by his own patroness.

"I followed, I followed—I stuck to them like a leech, all the way to Lyons, where a dismal sly fellow dressed as a soldier drugged their wine in a tavern and made off with it in great haste—"

"Excuses, excuses." Ruggieri tapped a finger impatiently on a stiff black leather panel of his trunk hose. "Did you discover who this one was working for?"

"I knew his face, Maestro. A notorious criminal—he has done work for the Duchess of Valentinois. He saw me behind him, the city gates of Orléans ahead of him, and passed it to a lady who took it into the city for him. Just as well, for he was arrested at the gate for some other crime, and it would have been seized and kept from us forever—"

"A woman confederate, eh? The duchess, she is full of surprises. Did you find out who the mystery woman was?"

"I questioned the guards at the gate. She was a tall, dark-haired woman, easy to remember. She had showed them a letter to her aunt, a widow Tournet, who lives within the city walls. A wealthy eccentric old woman, but I found her house locked up and well guarded. She rarely goes out. I was unable to break in."

"Well then, we shall have to use other methods. What did you say this dark woman's name was?"

"Sibille, Demoiselle de La Roque."

"Of the great de La Roques?"

"No, the name comes from some pretentious little *hoberau's* so-called estate near the forest off the Paris-Orléans road, known as La Roque-aux-Bois."

"Hmm," said Ruggieri. "A plan is beginning to come to me."

"Thank you, thank you, Maestro. Send me wherever you desire. I am your hands, I am your eyes."

"And my dagger," added Ruggieri, smiling benignly at his groveling servant.

✢

"Get out of bed, Cosmo. Fernel says you're faking. Fever, indeed! I don't see even a bit of a sweat on you." The dumpy little Medici queen had invaded her astrologer's bedroom in one of the attics of the Louvre—beneath the long chambers where the servants slept three to a bed, but much tinier and more remote than the chambers of the upper palace staff—and stood at the foot of his bed like an avenging spirit, her toad-like little pop eyes blazing with fury. Her rapid, angry Italian rattled like hailstones against the stone walls. At the far door of the little room, which was actually constructed like a sort of swollen segment of a cor-ridor, with doors at both ends, his Italian apprentice, who was also a cousin, set down the jug of barley water he had just brought, and fled. "You're hiding. Hiding from me, in spite of my orders to appear. You've stolen my magic head and sold it to the Duchess of Valentinois. I saw it all in a dream. And my dreams are infallible. Infallible, do you hear me? They show me where traitors are lurking." At the near door, another woman was standing, arms folded and dark eyes flashing, her mouth tight with disapproval. Madame Gondi, the banker's wife, known now as Madame Peron, *dame d'honneur* and the queen's companion in the supernatural.

"My great and glorious queen, oh, pardon, that I am too weak to rise and greet you. I am eternally grateful that you sent your own personal physician to me, but my illness was beyond his powers."

"He says your urine's as healthy as horse piss. How dare you attempt to threaten me by pretending to be mortally ill?"

"It is more than an illness of the body, great Majesty. It is an illness of the soul—the slightest shock might send me off." At this, the queen paused, then the faintest of smiles crossed her ugly, chinless round face.

"Oh, I'll take very good care of *you*. But, Cosmo, my friend, I hear your brother is dabbling in sorcery along with his little astrological business. I'd hate to have the good doctors of the Sorbonne discover that." Cosmo drew a deep, shaky breath, and closed his eyes briefly. "Ah, good," said the queen. "At last we understand each other. Now, where is my magic head that you promised me?" Ruggieri turned down the sheet and wiggled himself into a sitting position in bed. The queen noted that even his nightshirt was black. It seemed a good sign of his devotion to his primary task. Of all the fortune-tellers she'd ever supported, only Cosmo Ruggieri seemed a perfect sorcerer, from top to toe.

"The Duchess of Valentinois does not have it, although she has attempted to gain possession of it—" Ruggieri paused, playing for time, while his brain spun with alternative plans. "She—she has as an agent a woman sorceress, who drugged my messenger—the woman—possibly the agent of some foreign power—has kept the head for her own advantage—"

"You're lying, Cosmo. You have it yourself. Someone poisoned my messengers in Lyons, and there wasn't a woman in sight. It bears all the signs of your work." The queen had seated herself on the stool beside the bed, and was drumming her fingers impatiently on her knee. She was wearing an attractive day-dress of dark green silk embroidered with pearls, and detachable, puffed sleeves, slashed in salmon color. The stiff, translucent linen ruff at her neck still trembled slightly with her concealed indignation.

"Great, mighty Majesty, this is the truth. The woman has it."

"And what is her name, this so-called sorceress?"

"The Demoiselle Sibille de La Roque."

"Ah," said the queen, while she thought a bit. "The La Roques. I'd never suspected them of harboring an adept. Such a dull family. And here I'd imagined she was someone more—disreputable. This changes things. I will bring her into my own service. How sly of her to capture the head for her own advancement. Yes, the plan is easy." She conferred briefly with Madame Gondi, who immediately became consumed with envy. *She* after all, had only obtained the queen's favor by presenting her with a rare and unusual lapdog. How much more could a woman get if she gave her the immortal head of Menander the Magus?

"I'll dangle a court appointment before her eyes," said the queen, thinking aloud. "Perhaps hint at finding a suitable husband. Her relatives will apply pressure. —No, she must stay alive—someone else, some *man* potentially less tractable, might get possession of the head if she perishes—" The queen cast a knowing glance about her, and Cosmo did not miss the look. "But she mustn't know how much I know. I will remind her that with a single signature, she could disappear forever. How much happier she could be living as one of my pensioners. Yes, there she'll be, serving me in some other capacity, and no one need know—So obvious, so simple—" At this point, Ruggieri's gut heaved with a spasm of furious jealousy. He knew the queen. Not only would she get her magic head from someone who wasn't him, after all his trouble to get hold of it, but she'd give credit to anyone crafty enough to outwit him. The Medici queen respected self-interest. It made people predictable in her eyes. A thousand devils, thought Ruggieri. I hate this unknown woman. But how can I get the head away from her without having her wish me into oblivion?

Ten

ow, you see, Sibille? It doesn't show at all, where we took out the fullness of the underskirt, and put the plain band on it to lengthen it in front. Now, turn around. Yes, the shoes are practically invisible." For a week, seamstresses had labored to make over the dresses Auntie had chosen from her voluminous and many-sized wardrobe. The colors she had chosen seemed a little bright, and the design— well, I can't pretend to understand fashion, since I have spent my life dedicated to higher spiritual pursuits—but they didn't seem to look like other people's clothes. Even less so, once she had had them altered. Still, they were rich, exquisite silks and velvets, and the textures and glitter of them had a sensual beauty all their own. I had never dreamed of wearing such things. It made me think that perhaps a more mannered, decorative style would improve my poetry, particularly my epic, which might involve pirates. Every afternoon, I lay down for an hour with my face covered in a concoction of ground-up fruits and vegetables and various slimy things that was guaranteed to whiten and refine the complexion. But nothing could be done about the feet, except to order plain, dark shoes, to cause them to recede in interest, as Auntie said.

"If you can say boats are invisible," said Menander the Undying from the top of the dresser.

"If you don't quit being nasty, I'll shut your box again," I said. For days, the box had followed me about the house, materializing in the bed-room to offer criticism of my hygiene, in the reception room, to critique my cardplaying with Auntie, in the garden, to spoil my communion with Nature. The thing inside made irritating noises to get me to open it up, so it could see what was going on. So there is was, all dried up and ugly, rolling its weird, living eyes beneath its drooping, parchment eyelids, of-fering its interfering comments. It's amazing what you can get used to, if you see it every day.

"Being nasty is my nature," said the immortal head. "You're lucky I don't drive you mad. I've driven a number of my possessors stark, rav-ing, lunatic. Do you know what happens to a person who doesn't get any sleep?"

"They get rapped on the box so they don't get any sleep, either," said Auntie Pauline calmly. "Sibille, do try the sky blue silk. It does such lovely things to your complexion. And I want to see how that lengthen-ing with the band of velvet at the top of the skirt, just below the bodice, came out."

"You could have just wished the dresses longer," sulked the thing in the box.

"And miss the fun of alteration? Really, you are an ignorant thing. This is even more entertaining than moving the furniture," said Auntie. By this time, I had stripped down to my petticoat and stays. Needless to say, with that ridiculous head following me about, we couldn't keep a lady's maid for a single minute in the same room.

"What a bony figure," said the head. "You should just quit trying, and content yourself with the knowledge that you're a freak." I glared at the head and moved toward the dresser to shut the box. But the head, which was really rather subtle, made a distracting comment to interrupt my purpose. "Really," it said, rolling one lurid eye at my underwear, "why do you squash yourself flat with that stiff thing, and then put on the puffiest clothes I've ever seen? I've seen tumors with better shapes than some of those padded sleeves you put on. Women used to look beautiful when I was young, with lovely, loose draped gowns that showed their darling little bosoms."

"You are entirely ignorant of ladies' fashion," said Auntie. "How long has it been since you saw any?" She held up the beautiful sky blue silk to drop it over my head.

"About a thousand years. But it was better then."

"Old people always say that," observed Auntie, as she helped me do up the buttons.

"You've been around more than a thousand years, and you never noticed what women were wearing?" I asked.

"Not my fault," grumped the head. "Shut up with magicians most of the time. Same bat-wing decor, same mystic robes, same wands and star charts. And busy. I was very busy. It is not the easiest thing, designing the ways to use people's own desires to suck them down to their well-deserved doom. It takes a brilliant, never-resting mind."

"Piffle," said Auntie. "They'd do it by themselves if you weren't around."

"*That*," said the head, "is a great insult. I remember things like that. Don't ever expect mercy from *me*." Auntie laughed.

"As if I ever did. Sibille, dear, just look at yourself in the mirror. Admit you're quite transformed."

The dress, made over from a Spanish gown, had a split skirt of dark blue and silver brocade that opened to reveal a sky blue silk underskirt. Laced to a matching bodice with puffed sleeve caps, separate sleeves of the same silk, slashed, had been lengthened with ruffles to cover my long arms and bony wrists. Above a stiff, boned collar, a tightly folded little ruff extended almost to my ears. It was fashion beyond fashion, the most elegant garment I had ever beheld.

"Your head looks as if it were on a platter," said the thing in the box.

"Is it all right? I asked.

"The very latest fashion, set by the Duchess of Valentinois herself. My tailor told me so last month," said Auntie. "Don't let that old mummy put you off."

"I've seen calves' heads served exactly that way," said the immortal head.

Auntie picked up her walking stick and swished it through the air with a single swift gesture, shutting the lid of the box. "That's enough of *that*," she said, as the thing was reduced to muffled squeaks of indignation. "And now that you are elegant, Sibille, let us go play cards in the reception room. I've had a message from—an old friend, and I'm expecting a visitor today, though I'm not sure of the hour. Friday. Yes, it is Friday, isn't it? Julian said he'd have him out of prison by Friday morning." Julian? My goodness, did she know the Bishop personally? Who— who was coming? I began to tremble inside. Auntie heaved herself up from her chair, and began to move heavily toward the door, her walking stick tapping with each step.

"Why yes, it's Friday, of course, Auntie. Who's coming?"

"That, my dear, is a surprise. Now tell me, why do you always remove the *atous* and lay out only the deniers when you read the cards?" We were walking toward the reception room in the front of the house now, through a series of richly furnished little chambers that ran together in place of a corridor. Every so often, Auntie would pause, and take down a particularly egregious cobweb with her walking stick. All that luxury, and uninhabited.

"That's how the *Giardino di Pensieri* says to do it. It's only a game, Auntie. Cousin Matheline showed me how when she gave me the book."

"That Matheline! An amateur at everything! You must use all four suits, my dear, and all the face cards. It is from the *atous* that you will receive the secret wisdom. I'll show you. The cards never lie to me. They said you would be coming, and you did. Now they tell me I'll be traveling. At my age! I have no intention of it. So you must cast them and read them for me. I need a second opinion."

"I don't like the *atous*, Auntie. They give me odd feelings when I look at them." A beetle scuttled from under a carpet. Auntie squashed it with the hard tip of her walking stick. In this room, the curtains had been left open by accident, but it made no difference. The windows were veiled in green vines, and only the palest living light could penetrate them.

"Odd feelings? Don't be frightened of them. I think, my dear, you may be a natural card-reader. You should quit letting your nerves bother you. After all, you've never minded that strange, feathered fellow in the back bedroom. Why should you be frightened of painted pictures on cardboard?"

We passed the better part of the afternoon in agreeable conversation and the study of the cards. The head, sulking, remained in the cupboard and did not materialize his box near us for some good time.

"Now, lay them out again, Sibille, the second crossing the first—See here, this time we've got the Popess. That's a favorite of mine—"

"What's that you're up to? Some new fad?" Menander's box had begun to shimmer and solidify on a carved cedarwood side table. His voice had that deceptive sound that made me think he was anticipating something, and had come for the view. "In my day, a good ram's liver was enough to tell fortunes. Open my box." But there wasn't time to answer. Without even waiting to be announced, someone had thrown open the front door so hard that it thumped against the wall. Auntie never looked up from the cards. There was the sound of a scuffle, as the visitor pushed aside Auntie's valet.

"Cut the cards, Sibille," said Auntie, never looking up. A voice reverberated, loud in the silence of her empty, ghost-filled house.

"So there you are, you avaricious old woman! And what are *you* doing there, Sibille, all dolled up in silk like a rich man's mistress? I tell you, I'll tear that trash off of you. I knew it, I knew I'd find you here. I told you never to set foot in this house. Go get your own clothes on at once! I'm taking you home right now!"

It was father.

Now this was not exactly the sort of reunion I had envisioned, which had been altogether more touching in my imagination, involving as it did both gratitude and sentimentality. I thought, perhaps, he would weep at seeing my face after he had been so near to death, and then embrace me and praise me for my bravery in petitioning the Bishop, and say he had never truly appreciated me before, but now he understood everything in that flash of insight that comes when one has faced the end. That was more or less as I had planned it, but I suppose Fate, which had spoiled my speech and filled me with humiliation, had arranged this unpleasant practical joke as a final blow to my damaged pride.

"Well, well, Hercule. Ungrateful as ever. You have not even greeted me. And here I've even ordered up a little collation in expectation of your arrival." Auntie never even looked up from the cards, but dealt herself two more.

"Pauline, you know what you are. I have forbidden Sibille ever to enter this house. And now I find her here playing cards, dressed in a gown not hers, and indulging in God knows what other debaucheries."

Father looked quite dreadful, quite in need of washing, with his hair askew. Auntie took him in with a cold eye.

"Why, Hercule, I remember in our father's house, when you knelt before me, and begged me to accept Captain Tournet, for the sake of family. You swore on your honor you would never abandon me. Honor, ha! You don't know the word."

"You don't expect—why, who would ever marry my daughters, if they knew they associated with—my reputation—" Father huffed, stopped short in his dash across the Turkish carpet to grab me by the ear.

"The daughters of an executed heretic? Sibille, the most dutiful of your children, braved the road alone to present the Bishop with a petition of her own composition, arguing most cogently for your innocence."

"Nonsense. Quit spinning moonshine. I never gave in. My will was iron, even when they showed me the instruments. They were so impressed with my loyalty, the Bishop himself came to question me. Then they allowed me to recant. Recant! Me! Do you know what it means, to sign their slimy, deceiving paper? And what gratitude do I get, saving my family—my *daughter*—from ruin by giving in to them?" Father, hollow-eyed and bitter, fairly spat out the words.

"Your daughter deserves your thanks," said Aunt Pauline, her voice cold. "Not everyone is allowed to recant—especially if their property is wanted by a royal favorite." Father's eyes narrowed as he looked at me.

"She deserves nothing. It is I who deserve thanks, for striving to see her established in an honorable way of life."

"The blue is pretty on her, don't you think? It sets off her lovely olive skin. And the headdress with the pearls—her eyes are very expressive and intelligent, wouldn't you say?" Something about what she had said set him off. His eyes blazing with fury, he reached out to grab me, and I leapt up so fast I nearly overturned the table. At that same moment, Auntie's stick flicked out faster that a snake's tongue, and cracked him right on the funny bone. With a howl, he grabbed his elbow, as several servants hurried toward him to hustle him to the door. "Always so violent, brother," observed Auntie. "Sit down in that chair over there. If it was you that freed yourself, pray how did I know to reserve this chair especially for your appearance this very Friday? Arnaud, pour M. de La Roque a cup of that excellent wine I've been saving for him. I have a business proposition to make, Hercule, and I want you to hear me out."

"With you, it's probably poisoned," grumbled father, as the wine was poured. "Tarting up Sibille, inflating her already inflated head. She needs humility. Humility and hard work, not silk dresses."

"What is it to you if it pleases me to see her attractive?" asked Auntie. "After all, it's my money. *All* my money, Hercule, and just mine." Watching the two of them glaring at each other, it was as if there were two conversations going on, one with words, and the other without, having to do with deep secrets long buried, of which I had no clue. "And unlike my late husband, I have no need to try to buy my way into your favor, in some vain hope of gaining respectability."

"How like you, Pauline, to so excuse your stinginess, your turning your back on your own blood relations."

"It's not my back that was turned, Hercule."

"If you have anything to say, speak up. I don't want to waste any more time here."

"Good, then I'll be blunt. I've enjoyed having Sibille here. She's clever, and having cultivated herself, she has a thousand lively topics of conversation. She doesn't mind the infestation of my house—"

"And what's it infested with? Rats? How like her. She probably wants to study their bones, or breed them to see if she can get them all one color. Ugh. I always knew you were a bad housekeeper, Pauline. Or is it insects?"

"Never mind. Something like that," said Auntie. "Let's get back to the subject." I could see Doña Dolores had formed up behind father, and was listening with great interest. Why didn't he even feel her? I suppose there are some people who aren't bothered by ghosts. Maybe M. Tournet wasn't, either. It must be a necessary qualification for the profession of arms. Auntie leaned toward father and put her fist, which was decorated with heavy rings on every finger, on the table. "Hercule," she said, "I want you to give me Sibille."

"Never," said father. "We've been through this before."

"Yes, but then your estate was not so encumbered with debt."

"Sibille, you've been talking again. Will you never learn to shut your mouth?" My eyes widened. It was entirely unfair. I'd never said a thing.

"What reason have you to keep her, except to spite me?" said Aunt Pauline. "You know God has never favored me with children. I want a daughter, and you're too stingy to even marry her off."

"And just how much are you proposing to offer this time?"

What did he mean, this time? Were they just bargaining over me, like you would for a pig at the market, or did my father really love me, and refuse as a matter of honor to sell me off as a companion? And was my indulgent, ever-kindly godmother in reality just a cold mercenary who thought money could get her anything? I was horror-struck. I mean, not only was it a question of my delicacy of feeling, but also I was beginning to doubt my powers of perception of human character, as the two of them seemed to shift shape before my very eyes.

But they were negotiating fiercely now, father's face red with wine, and Auntie's pallid and doughy, her eyes burning bright, with huge pupils in the semi-dark.

"You offered more when she was six."

"I was younger then. She would have lightened my sorrows for many years. I could have seen her grow up."

"You could have spoiled her to the bone, you mean. She needed to learn her place."

"You only kept her because you knew I wanted her."

"Pauline, you don't *deserve* children, have you ever thought of that?"

"And you don't deserve a sou of my money. Everything will go to the church when I die."

"Or to Sibille as your heir if I give her to you. Why should I set her up like that, to lord it above her sisters and her brother?"

"I said, I'll pay off your debts if you give me Sibille. Otherwise, you'll never see a penny—no, not you nor yours either, now or after my death. Snap! Cut off! The church will be all the richer, and you the poorer. Think carefully about my generous offer, and how little you deserve it, before you refuse, you cold-hearted excuse for a brother."

"It's you who's the monster, Pauline. I've raised her honorably. I've done well by her. I even arranged a decent marriage for her, which is more than she deserves."

"Slavery to an oaf? You call that decent? I call that the coldest of concealed cruelties. And what if her grandfather hadn't left her that vineyard? Villasse! And what dishonesty did you plot with *him?*—Ha! I'd almost forgotten! You have to leave her here, brother, whether I pay you off or not! Too bad, watch my money fly out of your grasp!"

"What in the devil are you talking about, you madwoman?"

"Villasse is as dead as a herring, and Sibille is the cause. She's fled the scandal, brother. You can't keep her at home anymore, without threatening the *reputation* of your whole wretched family."

"She drove him to suicide? I never thought it of him. My God, the disgrace!"

"More than that, brother, and if I were you I'd never mention it again. You don't want it to get around."

"The loans—he was to make me another loan—What about my debts?"

"I thought that might move you. Consider me Villasse's replacement in your life, and sign this paper, if you please, brother. I no more trust you than the wise kid trusts the old wolf. I've had it drawn up. A legal guardianship. I don't want you to reclaim your paternal rights when she comes to visit her mother, and decide to throw her into a convent."

"This is an old paper—"

"I've had it a long time, but it's just as good as the day it was written. See that line? 'Valid in perpetuity' it says. I'm no fool."

"Then take her and be damned. It's good to be rid of her. She's never given anything but trouble, and now she's overage and unmarriageable. I wish you the joy of her—"

"But, but, Father—" The tears were welling up in my eyes.

"I want a cash deposit," said father.

"Never fear, Hercule, you'll have it. Don't cry, Sibille, this is for your own good—" But I had already fled the room. Reaching my own bed-chamber, I took off the beautiful silk dress and the high linen ruff and the pearl headdress, all more beautiful than anything I had ever even touched before, and threw myself on the bed and wept.

"You could always wish that they truly loved you," said the insinuating voice of the thing in the box.

Eleven

Last night ate at the table of Monsieur de Biragues. The chicken had pin-feathers and the sauce aroused my dyspepsia. How do the great survive their tables? Have Léon fetch some senna from that wretched apothecary in the rue de St.-Jacques as fortification for my next invitation into the realm of these iron-stomached lords.

※

Note: a dream, doubtless caused by the sauce. Or at least I hope caused by the sauce. I was in the darkened chamber of some wizard well after midnight, and saw from behind a woman in widow's black enter and kneel down before a table dressed as an altar, with black candles. Before her on the table was a coffer, which, when she opened it, caused the candles to go out as if in a fearful whirlwind. But before the room went dark, I swear I caught a glimpse of something I had hoped never to see again on earth. I awoke with the sound of hideous laughter ringing in my ears, and a voice that said, "Michel de Nostre-Dame, I have come at last into France to try you. Stop me this time if you can." Took a cup of barley water that stood by my bedside and said divers prayers. It is my hope that this dream is not prophetic. For I swear what I saw was the head of Menander the Undying, destroyer of kingdoms, robber of souls, the Devil's own gate into Hell, as I first saw him in the treasury of the mighty Suleiman *the Magnificent. Oh, God, for my sins, the memory of this monstrous object haunts me with dread and fearful desire.*

THE SECRET JOURNALS OF NOSTRADAMUS
Vol. VI, Entry #439, September 8, 1556

Still smoldering after the unfortunate accident to his gown caused by the mud-flinging ignoramuses in the rue St.-Jacques, Nostradamus was not far from the Pont St.-Michel when he looked up to see the half-timbered second story of an inn from which swung a signboard depicting Saint Michael, his own namesake. There was something fortunate look-ing about the crimson-gowned archangel, who, with wings unfurled, was triumphantly brandishing a fiery sword at a crowd of demons not unlike those charlatans from the Paris Faculty of Medicine. "An excellent sign, Léon; we shall stop here for luck," said Michel de Nostre-Dame, and even as their horses were being led away in the inn courtyard, Léon arranged to send a messenger to St.-Germain to let them know that the great prophet Nostradamus had made his appearance in Paris.

Unfortunately, he was overheard, and before Nostradamus had even settled in, a crowd of housemaids, stable boys, two cooks, a saddler, and a spurmaker had besieged his room, all clamoring to know their for-tunes. The more he tried to get rid of the growing crowds, the more seemed to squash in, battering on his door, waiting in lines in the hall outside, trying to shout in his window. At last he gave in: it was clearly a Sign that while he waited for the queen's reply, he was meant to re-plenish the funds he had expended in travel. The third evening after his arrival, he had barely cleared out a horse breeder, a chandler, and three old ladies and their lackey, when two officers of the light horse, still in spurs and riding boots, forced their way into the room. As the dark one flung a handful of silver on the table, Nostradamus narrowed his eyes. Ambitious, arrogant, money-hungry little puppies, thought the old prophet. Besides, my supper is getting cold. He was about to demand that they take their money and leave when an image came to his mind; the image of the tall, bony girl on the little brown horse, her nose in the air and her aura knotted with well-concealed fear, headed off in the di-rection of the spires of Orléans.

"Does either of you have anything to do with a tall, bony young woman who writes poetry and possesses an extremely large, brindled hound called Gargantua?" he said.

"My sister!" exclaimed the round-faced, blond *enseigne*. "But how did you know?" Then he thought a moment, and drew back, wide-eyed, in awe.

"I have a warning for you. Bottle up your greed. The fortune your sister is destined to inherit was never yours—it will go to a convent if anything happens to her, so I suggest you cultivate her good will—"

"*Her* good will? But she's stolen my inheritance—"

Nostradamus shrugged.

"As it stands, it is not her blood family, but the man who marries her who will be rich. Now, get out, the both of you, my supper's getting cold, and you didn't have an invitation."

"How dare you dismiss me like that," said the other young officer, the one with the narrow-boned face and dark mustache. "When Philippe d'Estouville favors a commoner with his presence, he is not sent away like a servant." His hand went to his sword.

"Touch a hair of my head, and you will answer to the King of France," said Nostradamus, never raising his voice. "Besides, you would have been happier if you'd left without hearing what I have to say about you. You are not destined to inherit your uncle's estate. And you will lose your thirteenth duel." The dark-haired cavalryman turned pale, and his hand dropped from his sword hilt.

"Don't believe him, Philippe," said the blond officer.

"I don't. But still, Annibal, I'd rather die gallantly by the sword than shriveled up with poxy old age."

As they swept out of the room, the old prophet said after them, "I didn't say *that*." But only Annibal heard it.

As the door shut behind them, Nostradamus got up and bolted it to stop the inflow of petitioners. Enough of these vulgar devils, he thought. I'm not in Paris for my health, but until I see the queen, I'm out of cash. As he rummaged around getting out the cash box and putting away this latest payment, he thought, now where did that dish of mine go? But then he saw that Léon was heating it over a candle flame, and he was happy. He poured his cup full of a really excellent red wine, and let the delight of anticipation trickle through him. That was one of the greatest secrets he had learned in his travels, though he was still working on perfecting it; to enjoy the moment as it is. Especially when the moment is supper, thought the old prophet happily.

✢

"It's not *fair,* it's just not *fair!*" Weeping so hard that she began to choke and gag, Laurette threw herself down on the bed, convulsing with rage and grief. Her little sisters stood about the huge, sagging four-poster, stiff and silent with amazement and awe at this volcanic eruption of emotion. The sound of her wailing echoed through the upstairs rooms, drawing curious serving maids, and at last her mother, fresh from the kitchen, her sleeves rolled up, and a big white apron over her woolen day-dress.

"Laurette, Laurette—"

"Go away! You just don't understand! You *can't* understand!"

"I understand more than you think," said her mother.

"She's ugly! She's stuck up! She gets *everything!*"

Madame Artaud de La Roque noticed a piece of crumpled paper on the tile floor, and stooped to pick it up. Smoothing it out, she said:

"Annibal's letter was to the entire family, Laurette. You had no right to take it away and crumple it up like this. I keep all his letters in my box, and now you've spoiled this one."

"It should be *burned!*" shrieked Laurette, rising from her pillow to confront her mother.

"He says nothing in here but pleasantries, and tells us of his successes. His letters will be a family treasure someday. What right have you to steal this pleasure from me, from our descendants?"

"From the children of Sibille and *Philippe,* you mean! It's *me* who should be courted and petted. It's *me* who should be Madame d'Estouville! Didn't you see that part where he says that 'M. d'Estouville takes great pleasure in Sibille's conversation these days. What a fortunate connection this would be for our family—'?"

"Laurette, my dear, dear girl. A glance, even a flirtation, does not amount to a marriage. A family alliance of that degree must be based not only on lineage, but on the bride's dowry. Your aunt has doubtless let it be known that she will be generous—"

"She's *my* aunt, too! Sibille already has a vineyard! It's *me* who should have had that dowry! Aunt would have given it to *me* if Sibille hadn't gone to her house like some beggar! Why didn't you send *me* to live with Aunt Pauline? I *deserved* to be rich!"

"Laurette, my darling, my child, you know why—"

"I know Sibille had a husband and she *shot* him, all because she wanted *Philippe* for herself, that's why! Philippe liked me better anyway, I know it! I'm far prettier! Aunt should have taken *me!* And now Sibille wears silk and Philippe sits at her feet while she reads those horrible poems of hers—" Laurette, having raised herself up on one elbow, now sat up, her face burning and bitter.

"The letter says none of this, Laurette—"

"It might as well—you know that's what's happening at this very minute." Madame Artaud sat down on the bed beside her furious off-spring, and began to stroke her back.

"Laurette, my daughter, listen to me. In marriage, facts are facts. You have no dowry. It is only by God's grace that your father escaped that evil glove merchant's accusations of heresy, and we were not thrown into the charity hospital. If your sister makes an advantageous alliance, as she is raised in the esteem of the world, so will your brother be, and through him, your chances of a substantial marriage, a marriage of comfort—" Madame Artaud's face was drawn and pallid, a white tomb-stone for some secret grief.

"An old man, an ugly man, a poor man, some leftover—that's what's for me. You might as well say it out."

"My dear, my love—as it stands now, there is nothing at all for you. Do you want to live as a pensioner in someone else's house?"

"In *Sibille's* house, you mean! I tell you, it will never be! I won't sit in her house, minding her children, watching Philippe chuck her under the chin and call her 'darling' while she gets that smug, conceited look she gets when she smiles!"

"Oh, Laurette, my beautiful, beautiful girl—if you only knew how I pray for you—"

"Prayers! What good are they? Sibille has silks and satins and dowry money gushing like a waterfall, and I have prayers? If God were just, Sibille would be hanged, and *I* would be Madame d'Estouville."

"Shh. Shh. Never say it. Laurette, my dear, my precious. Listen to my advice. Do not let your emotions rule you. If you wish to marry accord-ing to the place your blood deserves, then you must rule yourself with an iron hand, as I have learned to do—come, girls, I need assistance, and your sister must be left in quiet." Laurette's mother rose to return to her work. But as she left the room with Françoise and Isabelle following be-hind, Laurette, her face pinched and bitter, whispered softly;

"If you ruled yourself so well, why did it not bring you a higher mar-riage than father?"

✣

It was the Old Constable himself who came to escort Nostradamus to the current royal residence at St-Germain-en-Laye. He made quite a stir at the inn, with his elegant horses and military escort in half-armor. In the Constable's entourage, Nostradamus recognized the two young men who had consulted him, handsomely mounted. The Old Constable was the natural one to send on this mission; during the queen's long barren-ness, he had collected recipes, the advice of wizards, and fertility charms from all of his foreign travels for her. They kept up a lively correspon-dence while her husband was on campaign, for the king never told her any of the news; he confided only in his mistress. The queen called the Old Constable her "gossip," signed herself *"vostre bonne coumère et amye,"* and counted on him to tell her what her husband did abroad; he thought she was his friend. He was so old, a remnant from the court of King Francis the First, and she so much younger, of such greater rank, and so terribly plain, that no one ever suspected any gallantry. And in terms of social climbing, until she had had the children, she had been a bad bet; those more anxious for preferment clustered around the mistress, not the wife.

But there was another reason that Anne de Montmorency, Grand Constable of France, wanted to escort Nostradamus from Paris to the palace that lay a few miles off, on a bluff overlooking the Seine. He wanted to pick the prophet's brains on the ride. He wanted a secret consultation, not on the future of France, but the future of himself in regard to the throne.

Montmorency saw himself as the power behind the throne, and he had rivals. In his mind, he counted them up: first, the Guise brothers, with their little niece, Mary Queen of Scots. They had only to sit and wait, and they could become puppet-masters of France when she married the Dauphin. Then the Old Constable would be thrown onto the scrap heap. Next, there were the Princes of the Blood, the Bourbon brothers, the closest natural rivals to the Guises. But if they ever came to power, they'd pitch out Montmorency and the Guises, too.

How to balance off these two rival families and preserve himself? Neither faction contained a reliable ally. Both awful, but in their own way. The Guises—coldly brilliant, fanatically Catholic; the Bourbons, three brothers, feckless, changeable, and useless. Damn!

First I need to break up the marriage plans of the Guises, thought the Old Constable, as he rode into Paris. Delay the wedding date with a thousand excuses, then locate a better-connected bride for the Dauphin that they simply can't pass up. Let's see, who will help me? I'll need allies in this—hmm, it has to be the Bourbons—they'll lose out if the guises take power. Perhaps Antoine de Bourbon, the King of Navarre, can be convinced—but all he ever thinks of is how to get Spanish Navarre back into his hands again. So I'll tell him it will regain his kingdom—if only he weren't such a fool! The only *man* in his family is his wife— For a moment, the image of Antoine's starchy, no-nonsense Protestant wife came to the Old Constable. Jeanne d'Albret, the daughter of old King Francis's clever sister. Now if I could make an alliance with *her*—

I'll just have this Nostradamus tell me how it all will come out, he thought. Then I'll know and can plan accordingly. Seated like a pillar of iron on his gray stud-horse, his face impassive, his dreams invisible, he stared straight ahead. Those who saw the old warrior pass by thought he was thinking of battle.

✤

"Maistre Nostredame," said the Grand Constable of France, condescending to lean down slightly from his big horse to speak to the old man on the pacing mare who rode beside him, "the queen is much taken by your *Centuries*. Tell me, why do you write them in such cryptic language? There are many arguments about their meaning."

"You mean to say, my lord Constable, that they think I conceal my ignorance and chicanery behind difficult language. Let them continue to think that. The visions that have been granted to me are not for the ignorant to know. Unintelligent people make bad use of everything, including knowledge of the future."

As they clattered over the bridge past the moated city wall and into countryside beyond, the Constable replied, "Why, of course, of course—I myself believe in your gift. Yes, absolutely. But why set them out in such disorder? I have such difficulties. If I could but divine the date—" A flock of squawking chickens scattered from in front of the horses. In the distance, windmills turned slowly in the warm breeze.

Nostradamus shifted in the saddle, trying to find a more comfortable arrangement for his complaining spine, and said in an irritated, cryptic fashion, "It is as the Spirit dictates. I have nothing to do with that." Or with his terrible housekeeping, he added in his mind. My fate to become connected with a spirit who keeps everything in a jumble. Noting the Constable's superstitious shudder, he hastened to add, "The stars shape fate, but they do not control it. Were I to set out the visions in plain language, by date, no one would struggle to change anything, and mankind would be weighed under an iron yoke more terrible than the rule of the Antichrist. It is God's will that those who are capable of understanding make choices that will escape the chains of history in order to demonstrate His grace." There, that ought to settle you, thought Nostradamus, sensing a demand for a free personal reading in the offing.

"Understanding, yes, I see it all," said the Old Constable, and fell silent, wanting to number himself among the elect, and not among the unintelligent who demanded everything be spelled out because they were incapable of mastering their fate. Nostradamus rode on in silence, well content. He had not eluded the Inquisition all these years through good fortune alone, and he was always pleased when one of his stock of philosophic arguments produced exactly the response it was supposed to. The Old Constable would carry it through the court and it would simplify the prophet's life considerably.

By the time they had reached the staircase of the *cour d'honneur* of St.-Germain-en-Laye, the old doctor was grateful for the Constable's armed guard. He was surrounded by a swelling, noisy crowd as he progressed toward the queen's reception chamber. "Nostredame, Nostredame!" they cried, jostling up against him and risking his balance and his gout. "He's here! The diviner! The prophet! The queen herself has sent for him." Women tried to touch him and strangers pulled at his clothes. Desperate folk shouted questions about lost lovers or absent sons, wags banged against his walking stick and pelted him with joke questions about their mistresses and hunting dogs. Soldiers, pages, servants, aristocratic loungers all squashed together, filling the corridors, to get a glimpse of him.

"Away, all of you!" shouted the Grand Constable. "Make way for the queen's astrologer!" At the back of the crowd, a dark, bearded Italian-looking fellow, clad entirely in black leather, scowled and muttered. Why does everybody make a fuss over someone just because he's published a book? thought Cosmo Ruggieri. It's common, some sort of gutter impulse to seek out the praise of nobodies. My thoughts are much too subtle to commit to something as vulgar as print. You have to be a person of discernment to understand my wisdom. You'd think that wretched woman would appreciate my long service, my brilliance. That Nostradamus just drools to get the worship of the mindless masses. Look at those idiots trying to get his attention! There's no *substance* to the man. He's a deceiver, and no one but me can see through him. I have a duty to mankind. . . .

In the crowd, Nostradamus could feel an aura of pure hate, but when he glanced up to find the source, it had vanished. Cosmo Ruggieri had gone home to cast a death-spell on the old doctor.

❖

The queen's aura was devious and slippery in a manner that Michel de Nostre-Dame had found quite common on his travels among the princes of the earth. What was uncommon was not the saccharine smile with which she masked her calculations, nor yet the host of petty snobberies with which she shored up her weak position in a court that admired only beauty in women. What flamed up from the aura, unique and powerful, was Will, pure Will, fueled by a bright flame of rage, carefully concealed beneath a veil of caution.

"I see a long life," said Nostradamus, having gazed at the lines in her palm, the freckles of her lower arms, and the balance of features on her pop-eyed, homely face. They sat alone, her attendants banished to an outer chamber.

"But my lord and husband, the king—" but then the queen hesitated, afraid to ask the critical question, the dangerous one, directly. "His life— is the prediction about the two lions in your book about him?" Nostradamus answered with great care and tact.

"The king your husband will live to an age of sixty-nine years, and be known as the greatest ruler since the Caesars. There is only one precaution: he must never duel in single combat with a man whose coat of arms contains a lion."

"But the king is unlike any other; he cannot be challenged to a duel—" Nostradamus had taken in at a glance the cabalistic rings, the chain to some hidden medallion or charm, the dozens of signs that the queen believed herself in command of dark powers.

"With your powers," he said, "you will know the time. It is up to you to dissuade him. Thus will you save the kingdom." The pop eyes widened, and the chinless, round face nodded solemnly in agreement.

"Will he, will he—come to love me ever?" she asked.

"He will come to appreciate you," said the old prophet. "More than that, I cannot tell."

"That will never happen while he is under the spell of that old whore of his," she burst out suddenly, her voice bitter. "How I yearn to be rid of her! Give me something to cause her to lose her influence over him! Tell me I'll be free of her!"

"Your Highness, dabbling in sorcery would cause me to lose my powers of foresight," said the old doctor, who had never hesitated to dabble in sorcery for his own benefit, but had given it up when he found it messy, inaccurate, and trying. "But I guarantee the time will come when you'll be free of her." A safe enough prediction, given the difference in their ages, he thought. But the queen assumed he was being tactful, and telling her, sorcerer to sorcerer, that her own magic would soon do the trick. Her heart surged with joy, and after a pleasant exchange on the subject of a special ointment that Nostradamus had in-vented, which would preserve her complexion in beauty forever, thus eventually making her more beautiful than all her rivals at court (since the old prophet assured her that a fine complexion and good character withstood the ravages of time far better than mere surface beauty), she asked him to go to the children's household at Blois, to cast their horo-scopes. "I want them all to achieve thrones," she said.

"Why, of course," said Nostradamus. Upon being escorted out of the queen's audience chamber, he found he had received an offer of accomo-dation at one of the more luxurious mansions of Paris: the Hôtel de Sens, home of Charles, Cardinal de Bourbon and Archbishop of Sens. This splendid building, one of a collection belonging to the old royal en-clave known as the Hôtel de Saint-Pol, was well located across the way from Les Tournelles, not far from the Bastille. An excellent location for a little temporary side business, thought the old doctor, although it was a bit far from the bookstores of the Left Bank.

Well, well, I lack only an invitation from the Guises now, he thought contentedly. There is nothing like factionalism to improve business. Sig-naling to his escort to pause, he stopped on a terrace to take in the splendid moment: the Seine lay in a shining arc below, winding into the distance between emerald banks. He took a deep breath, listening to a distant birdsong, the crow of a cock, the wind whipping the banners on the castle wall above him. His mind filled with joyful thoughts of home.

But the pleasant imagining of the nice little additions he would be able to make to his study, the repair of the garden wall, the new Christ-mas dress for his wife, was interrupted by renewed twinges of his gout. Damn, he thought, I could be in bed for days with another attack. The twinges got worse, and turned into sharp pains. By the time he had re-turned from St.-Germain to Paris, he had to be carried up the steps into the Archbishop's palace. His joints felt exactly as if someone had thrust huge pins through them. Even when Léon was sent for and brought his opium, sleep fled before the agony.

Twelve

 o man could be more astonished than I to receive your letter, but since it was your father who gave it to me, I can only assume we have his permission to meet alone, this way." A cloud crossed the sun, and its cold shadow made Laurette shiver and draw her shawl closer. She stood in the apple orchard, not far from the farmhouse, within sight of her father's cold eye, which peered from an upstairs window at the clandestine meeting.

"My father and I are of a like mind," said Laurette. "Sibille has disgraced us, flaunting herself in public, behaving like a hussy, dragging our good name in the mud." The smell of rotten apples rose from around her feet, the last remainder of the harvest past. Pigs had been turned into the orchard, and the sound of their grunting, accompanied by the cry of a distant cockerel, broke the still autumn air.

"She has done far more than disgrace me," said Thibault Villasse. Black powder exploded at close range had permanently stained his face with a dark shadow; a black leather patch covered his sightless right eye.

"I grieve for your wound, Monsieur de La Tourette," said Laurette, making her blue eyes huge and sympathetic. Her simple blue wool dress set them off, she knew. She had braided the coils of her thick, golden hair into a crown and pinched her cheeks to make them rosy in preparation for this important meeting. Show interest, her father had said, and you may yet wed, my girl. A man puts his money where there's attraction. I've seen his eyes when you're in the room. My father's a fool, thought Laurette, but I am not. I'll take this chance to have what I want.

"Your sister is a devil incarnate," said Villasse. "I only live because she is an idiot about firearms." He was wearing heavy hunting boots, his old deerskin jerkin, and a broad-brimmed hat pulled low over his long, stringy, graying hair. His big bay mare was tethered behind him, still sweating from the long ride.

"I despise her," said Laurette. "She is no sister of mine. She has stolen the dowry my aunt would have given me."

"As well as the inheritance your father expected from his sister. The old woman had no children, after all—he was a fool to have given her Sibille—"

"But you see," said Laurette, "if Sibille cannot marry, through some dreadful accident, of course, then my aunt will surely be generous with me—after all, I am her niece, too."

"An accident? You mean, kill—?"

"Oh, no, that would be—I mean, that's a sin—but revenge, the same amount, that's fair, and no sin, you see—"

"What have you in mind?"

"Men swarm after her these days, you know. She lives at ease, gloating at the harm she's done you. It's no crime to get even, and really, it would work out better for both of us—"

"How?" said Villasse, leaning forward, his voice suddenly demanding.

"If she were hideous, blind, perhaps, the way she almost blinded you, then she could never marry. Why, she couldn't even be seen in public. She wouldn't be amusing anymore. My aunt would doubtless arrange for her to live in a convent—Sibille always said that's what she wanted anyway, you know—then aunt would want *me* for a companion."

"Exactly what do you have in mind?"

"Oil of vitriol—I've heard all about it. It can't be washed off. It burns away the flesh to the bone. Just a splash, you see, but in the right place—she'd have to go into hiding forever—and couldn't identify the attacker, either. And so many women who live as she does have rivals—why, it's common—anyone could have done it—"

"And I am to arrange it?"

"I can't leave here. Besides, I don't know how to get it. But *you*, you can go where you wish. Throw oil of vitriol in her face, and we both have our revenge. It is entirely fair and just. And I will have what is mine."

"What a brilliant plan," said Villasse softly, almost to himself. "Only a woman could think of a plan like that." He looked down at Laurette. She was so charming, so innocent, so much prettier than her bony, ugly, witch-like big sister. It was almost as if they weren't of the same blood. Here was a real beauty.

"I would love the man who brought me justice," said Laurette, looking up through her pretty eyelashes.

"So you'd displace your father in his inheritance?" said Villasse, his voice condescending and amused.

"He's displaced already," said Laurette. "Aunt Pauline told him that if she didn't leave her fortune to Sibille, she'd leave it to a convent. But when Sibille's gone, she's bound to get lonely—"

"It's perfect," said Villasse.

"Old ladies,—you know how weak-minded they are. After a few weeks it will make no difference to her at all who reads aloud and plays cards with her, except that it's much, much, more fair—for us both, you see," she hastened to add.

As she watched Villasse ride into the distance, Laurette heard a rustle in the dead leaves behind her.

"Well, Laurette, did you speak to him of my debts?" She turned at the sound of her father's voice.

"Of course I did, Father, exactly as you asked," she answered.

"I'm sure your pretty little face will gain his sympathy," said the Sieur de La Roque.

"I'm sure it did," said Laurette. It's a pity you're such a fool, Father, she thought, but I'm not going to let that ruin *my* chances.

Ah, Laurette, how useful that pretty, brainless little head of yours is, thought her father, as he escorted her back to the farm gate. Once Villasse is thoroughly attracted, he'll realize he can have vengeance, the vineyard, and you, all with one stroke. What does it matter to me if Sibille's dead, as long as I didn't do it? Once he's done the deed, then the vineyard passes to Laurette and Villasse gets it and a prettier bride.

Sibille, that snobbish little sneak. She went too far when she wormed her way between me and my sister's inheritance. What gave that girl the right to steal the fortune I'm owed? I swear, I always knew she'd come to bad—and once she's out of the way, it won't be hard to regain the inheritance my sister is hoarding from me. . . .

❖

Far away from the isolated farmstead, in Paris, on the rue de Bailleul, there is a substantial stone house whose peaked slate roof is orna-mented with a dozen little turrets and equally as many chimneys. In a niche over the wide front door is a pretty Italian virgin and child, brightly painted, with real gilding on her crown and the stars that line her midnight blue perch. It is the house of Montvert the Italian banker, advisor to kings, to dukes, to anyone who needs a loan for a war, a new estate, or a fashionable mistress. From its glazed windows to its well-stocked cellars, it gives off an air of prosperity, new money, recent Frenchification, and a certain smug content. All of these things are a source of infinite humiliation to the only son of the house, who would sacrifice every stone of the place to have been born an impoverished French aristocrat of ancient pedigree, whose sole support was his ready rapier and sardonic wit. At the very moment that Laurette was in the apple orchard, Nicolas Montvert was deep in disagreement with his sin-gularly thickheaded father.

"—and at the very least, if you were going to change it from Mon-teverdi, you could have made it *de* Montvert—"

"That would have been false—"

"So is Montvert—"

"Don't change the subject on me, Nicolas, I told you you're not going with me to Orléans, and that's final. Your mother needs you here—"

"No more than I need to be there—"

"For what? You have failed to ingratiate yourself with M. Bonneuil, as well as all the other important connections I've made for you. Why would you suddenly want to—aha! I can tell by the look in your eye—"

"My eye looks just as it usually does."

"Oh, no, it does not. You've fallen in love again. Were you hoping to droop after that skinny cousin of Madame Bonneuil's? Hang under her window playing the mandura, or maybe set me up for a cash payment to get rid of her? That's it, I know it, I see it all in your eye. Sibille Artaud—stay away from her. The whole family are nothing but a crowd of blue-blooded, money-sucking wastrels—"

"She's different, Father, I can tell—"

"After *one* chance meeting? You can't even tell which side of the bed to get up on. You mooncalf! *If* you ever become responsible, and *if* you ever make a respectable place for yourself in society, your mother and I will send to your cousins at home to find you a good Italian girl, a pure girl of some substantial banking family, to be your wife. Until then, stay away from women of ill fame. I won't pay a sou—"

"She's not—how dare you—she has a noble bearing—she—"

"And *I* have heard from Gondi that she's been invited to attend the queen at court, and you know what *that* means—affairs, fortune hunting, perhaps a lover chosen by the queen herself for some purpose of high politics—stay away, Nicolas. You are not of that rank—or that level of depravity. You will be gobbled up in an instant."

"I will *not*—"

"I'm telling you, if I find you hanging around a woman like that, I'll sign the papers to put you in the Bastille as a wayward son of dissolute life—"

But, alas, Scipion Montvert had, in his fury and indignation, selected the one argument that would cloak the unknown woman in a permanent air of desirability, the glamorous fascination of forbidden fruit. In that very moment, Nicolas's wayward eye, so easily intrigued by the glimpse of a remote-looking, elegant young woman, was now permanently affixed to the polestar. Sibille Artaud de La Roque. Tall, slender, aristocratic-looking in black, concealing a secret tragedy in her eyes, a woman of wit and learning, of ancient name, and best of all, appropriately impoverished. Only he, Nicolas the hero, with his bold sword and dauntless spirit, could save her from the evil cesspool of court life, to which she had doubtless been driven by the cruelest necessity. She was all he wanted on this earth.

"—and what is more, by the time I return, I expect you to have mastered the calculation of compound interest ..." His father's voice resounded up the staircase as he vanished in the direction of the stable.

God didn't mean me for a bookkeeper, thought Nicolas. I am meant to rescue the tragically beautiful Sibille from the intrigues of a sinister and decadent court, we are destined to be one....

✤

I distinctly remember that it was a Tuesday when the royal messenger came, bearing a letter laden with seals. Auntie was already aflutter with the preparations for the weekly visit of her second cousin once removed, the Abbé Dufour, who came as regular as clockwork each Tuesday at midafternoon to devour sweets and play checkers while discussing the newest discoveries in the sciences and the occult. He was a man of small stature and great wisdom, invited to many uplifting afternoons, where he would read the latest selections from his monumental work-in-progress, *On the Life and Habits of the Tortoise, with Additional Notes on the Waterways of the Île de France by the Author.*

"Five kinds of preserves, three cakes, and candied cherries, too! Auntie, you've outdone yourself today."

"The Abbé loves my candied cherries almost as much as the *jeu de dames.* Don't forget to put out the board over there, on the little table— Arnaud, I hear my cousin—show him in, show him in! I must tell him about the new pain I have, right here, and the strange ache over the liver, have his opinion about which waters will do it the most good."

Once a year, the Abbé escorted Auntie, along with another elderly maiden cousin and his old mother, to take the cure at Plombières, at Enghien-les-Bains, at Évian or some other spot where the waters were guaranteed to cure rheumatism, gout, headache, pallor, wasting, consumption, palpitations, dropsy, paralysis, nervous afflictions, overbalancing of the humors, or a thousand other diseases, all of which they assumed they had, and some of which they actually did have. Part of what made him such a valued guest and confidant was his fondness for discussing the symptoms of rare and exotic diseases, preferably apparently mysteriously harmless at first, the awful deaths they occasioned, the randomness of Fate, Godly ends, and Miraculous Cures. I had learned much on these Tuesdays, and as these were new topics to me, and not about hunting, I did not mind them.

But it was not the Abbé who was shown in. Instead, we saw a dusty man in the queen's livery, who waited for a reply.

"Read it for me, I'm so excited I can hardly make out the lines—no, give it back! See here, how splendid, how amazing—yes, it truly says it: 'summoned to appear before the Queen,' right there, written as plain as day—and to read a selection of your poetic and artistic works! Oh, my heart!" Auntie sat down and placed one hand on her heart, and with the other, fanned herself with the letter she was still holding. "Yes, yes, tell the queen we are most honored to accept—"

"The queen has charged me to inform you that she has a collection of rare and ancient boxes, and hear that you have a coffer worthy of her collection. Were you to present it to her, she might consider even greater favor—an entirely new position attached to her household—that of poetess—purely ceremonial, you understand—"

"A coffer? Nothing could give us more pleasure," said Auntie, still beaming from her seat and clutching the letter.

"But—but my writings," I said to her when the messenger had left. "How could the queen know?"

"How could she know about the box? Queens have their ways. But the honor, the distinction! To read your works! We'll have a splendid presentation copy made up by hand—ha! They'll *crawl* in this dreadful little town when they hear *we* are going to court! Not good enough for them, was I? And the Abbé will be thrilled when he hears that he can escort us to Saint-Germain! Sibille, that wretched mummy in the box has brought you good fortune without you having to wish for a single thing! That just goes to show that Virtue always wins in the end! But—yes, Arnaud, that's him at the door at last. Hurry, hurry, I have such news!"

But the next visitor Arnaud showed in was not the Abbé either. One glance at the richly dressed visitor's painted smile and bright, beady blue eyes, from which no detail ever escaped—

"Cousin Matheline!" I exclaimed. Why should she, of all people, suddenly take it into her head to visit a house shunned for years by the respectable ladies of Orléans? "What brings you here?" Cousin Matheline seemed very conscious of being clad in the latest style; she had the new farthingale, which made her several petticoats and skirt stand out far beyond anyone else's, the narrow ruff that peeped from above her high, silk collar was real lace, and at her narrow, corseted waist, hung a dear little embroidered velvet purse and a fan of painted silk and carved ivory.

"Oh, my dear, my dear cousin Sibille, and dear Madame Tournet—I am paying a too-long overdue courtesy call. I have been so busy—so *overwhelmed* by the duties of marriage. But at long last, you are here in town and we can converse once again about your beautiful poetry."

"B-but, my letters—"

"Letter?" said Matheline, her voice bland, her eyebrows raised. "You sent letters? Oh, how cruel, I never received them. I would have loved to have had your letters. We were always such *close* friends—" Without invitation, still standing, she began to consume the candied cherries, neatly seizing on them one at a time, with little white fingers as swift and sure as a peregrine's beak.

"Do have a few cherries, Madame Bonneuil," said Aunt Pauline, her voice a study in suppressed sarcasm.

"Oh, they are lovely. I do hope you received my little note of thanks for your wedding gift—I have intended to call for ever so long—" But her gaze traveled back to me. "You look so *well*, Sibille—my goodness, an invitation to court! And to think, soon the queen herself will listen to the very words that first were heard in my simple little provincial *céna-cle*. My dear Monsieur Bonneuil was so impressed when he heard. Just think, poetry, he said. She was invited for her *poetry*. Why yes, I said, poetry gives us wings!"

"Why yes, it's very impressive what literary talent will do," said Aunt Pauline, in the exact same tone in which she had offered the cherries. "And how rapidly the word spreads about worthy works of art."

"Bankers, my dear, they know everyone—it's their *business* to have the very latest news from court. That *was* the royal messenger I saw leaving just now, wasn't it? Official letters take so long—"

"Why yes, indeed, they seem to be behind everyone else," said Auntie. But Cousin Matheline shook her finger at me in mock displeasure.

"And I know," she said, "*I* know you have been conquering hearts. Why, *dear* Monsieur Montvert, who is ever so wealthy, even if his family is only recently French—his investments, you know, he is really terribly clever—was asking after you at supper only yesterday evening. He pretended indifference, but I just *know* he's interested in you! His wife, they say, is sickly—expect a go-between at any time, my dear! That's how these affairs are arranged at court, you know. His house in Paris, very lavish—connections everywhere. He was the first to hear of your good fortune. Oh, I can't even describe the joy I felt for you, Sibille, when I heard the news from him. And such questions he had! Why, I said to him, my darling Sibille and I were at Saint-Esprit together—she has an absolutely *impeccable* lineage—though she had to leave after only two years, you can see it left her very *cultivated*—" Aunt Pauline, who was out of her line of vision, made a dangerous noise.

"So she had no vocation? he asked, and I said, well of course her family had arranged a betrothal to Thibault Villasse, a very *substantial* landholder—So she is engaged, but going to attend the court? he asked, and I assured him, Villasse couldn't make any objections, because he was so desperately ill he has not left his bedchamber all this time, thought of what I don't know, but some say he had a hunting accident and shot himself through his own clumsiness and is trying to keep it a secret—" Both Auntie and I sucked in our breath at the same time.

"'Thibault—is—still—ah—well, I—hmm, hope?" I asked.

"Well, I should think so, though of course nearly dead of shame I should imagine. But Montvert just said, 'How convenient for her,' ever so discreetly, so I am just *sure* you will be hearing from him soon, and I know for a fact he hasn't a mistress, and they say he's terribly generous, charities, you know—and that worthless son of his, he's just *poured* money into him. Study here, study there, and he never finishes! My husband says that Nicolas Montvert is a born wastrel. What tolerance his father has for him! Too, too saintly. My husband says that any son of *his* who lived like that should go straight to the Bastille. So you see, Monsieur Montvert has a naturally generous, forbearing character. That's just perfect for a lady who, well— And you must admit that although he is a bit old, he is *far* more distinguished-looking than Villasse, and away at court, well, a lady should have a gallant, but, I mean, maybe you'll meet someone of better rank there, and in the meanwhile—and you see, he wouldn't be hard to get rid of, once you did better—"

"Dear Matheline," Aunt Pauline said, her voice dripping honey, "would you care to stay and meet my cousin, Abbé Dufour, who is coming to accept a contribution I am making to his Leprosarium?"

"His—ah—what?"

"Surely you've heard of it, his little hospital—Saint-Lazare? He is a very holy man, I'm sure you'll find his conversation quite edifying. He washes the leper's sores himself."

"Why, why, that's splendid—so charitable, so worthy. I do hope I'll be able to meet him another time—it's been so long since I have conversed with a truly *sanctified* person—so many these days are shallow— oh, Sibille, we must embrace, I have missed you so." So Cousin Matheline, having never seated herself, clasped me to her stiffly corseted velvet bosom and we kissed, and she departed, leaving a cloud of lilac-water scent behind her.

"She's eaten all the cherries," said Aunt Pauline, who had never risen from her seat by the table.

"Oh, Auntie, he's not dead after all! What shall I do? It was easier being a murderess," I wailed.

"Do? Play *dames,* of course. You are better at it than I. And I will comment over your shoulder, which is even better than playing, because then I will not lose. And after that, the Abbé shall advise us of a good lawyer. And I do believe I hear his footstep at the door this very moment."

✤

Now the Abbé Dufour would never have conceived of washing a leper, because it would have interrupted his studies of the life cycles of rare and curious plants, his search for the hidden Will of God in the *lusus naturae,* his readings of the church fathers on the nature of the afterlife, and most especially his work on his massive monograph on the life of the tortoise, which was going to astonish the world of scientific philosophy. Besides, in the matter of leprosy, only the theory of leprosy would have ever held any importance for him, the mere possessors of it being too common for consideration. A tiny little man, curled of spine and pale of complexion, he charmed the ladies with his witty talk and utter neglect of all practical matters, which he left to them. Only in the matter of his own personal bodily comfort did he display precise, applicable knowledge. Thanks to this quality, when we at last departed on our grand and fateful journey, he knew of an ideal monastery for our overnight stay on the road, where the cook was a personal friend, and an excellent place to stay in Paris, an inn on the Left Bank in close proximity to several bookstores that he favored.

He was a perfect traveling companion, not minding the slow pace of Aunt Pauline's ornate, curtained litter, which was slung between her two big grays, Flora and Capitaine. Every so often he would call down into the closed curtains that Auntie should risk the sun to take in this or that or the other interesting sight upon the road. And when the rays of the Evil Disc were aslant in the correct direction, Auntie would raise the curtains on the shady side, and he would regale us with amusing tales of famous robbers taken on this very knoll, or among the trees of that distant wood, or hairy monsters found later to be human just there, beyond those little houses near the hill—

"Théophile, why are we stopping? Have we reached the inn?" We had only briefly let in the sun as we paused to pass within the city wall of Paris by the Porte St.-Jacques. Now, all around us, in the joggling, dusty, dark of the litter, the entrancing sounds of a strange city came to our ears: the cries of street vendors, the calling of women out of the upper stories of their houses, the shouts of children at play. It was a great relief when Auntie opened the curtains and called out to the Abbé, where he rode beside us on his rangy sorrel mule.

"It's much farther, my dear cousin," he said, leaning down from his mount to the level of the open litter curtains. "This is some dreadful student imbroglio blocking the way, I fear. Youth is never quiescent in this district."

"Are we in Paris yet? Open my box, I want to see the place," came a muffled voice from the box beneath our cushions.

"Absolutely not," said Auntie, dropping the curtain and addressing the space behind her ample bottom. "It's bad enough having to bring you along at all. I certainly don't have to take you touring."

"You'll be sorry," grumped the thing in the box. "I'm used to being treated with much more reverence."

"We will simply have to go by another way," came a voice from outside the curtains. "They are prying up the paving stones—oof, there goes one—definitely, by another way—Madame my cousin, we must turn; kindly order your valets to back the horses into this alley."

Aunt Pauline gave the thing beneath the cushions a rap with one white, jeweled hand, while she lifted the curtain with the other and called out, "Arnaud, Pierre, have them back the horses according to my cousin's instructions, and do look out for dear little Señor Alonzo, that he doesn't become frightened with this dreadful racket." What with the screeching of the monkey in his special silk-padded traveling box, the clatter and bang of Aunt Pauline's armed valets shifting the litter-horses, and Gargantua's barking, the complaining of the thing beneath the cushions went unnoticed. Good, I thought. So far we have suc-ceeded in keeping it secret even from the good Abbé. As soon as we've given it away, my life will be my own again.

In the shadowy alley, we opened the curtains to peer out.

"Oh, look, *ma tante,* across the way—'At the King David'—a book-store." A group of students rushed past toward the sound of the trou-ble, carrying an effigy stuffed with straw and wearing some sort of academic gown. Some well-hated professor, no doubt, about to have in-dignities rained upon him in absentia.

"There's a better one we shall see tomorrow—'At the Four Elements'—it has far more curiosities," said the Abbé, but Aunt Pauline, looking at the hurrying students sniffed.

"So little *fashion.* How drab they all look! We certainly can't do any shopping *here.* Lower the curtain Sibille, I see the way is clear enough for us to proceed." But as we pushed through the narrow streets away from the sound of rioting, I couldn't resist peeking out. "Of course," Auntie was saying, "you simply have to have a few more things—"

"But, *ma tante,* I have so many dresses already—"

"Don't contradict me, Sibille, I feel a shopping urge coming on. Why, that little place, the goldsmith's there, doesn't look half bad, even if this *is* the less fashionable section—my, hold up the curtain a little higher, dear—see that place over there—yes, it is beginning to sweep over me like a fever—"

"But, *ma tante,* you said—"

"Never mind what I said! See there! A glovemaker's! It's not the dressmakers we need to see—it's the *shoes!* The *gloves!* You know your hands and feet are simply too large for anything of mine. We *must* shop! You can't see the queen without *gloves!*"

"B-but, I have a pair of gloves, you got them just—"

"Nonsense, I hear my money calling out to me. Would you deny a poor old lady her one pleasure? Why, I can feel my heart palpitate! Don't stop me now, you wouldn't want to be responsible for my death, would you?"

I tell you, it was like releasing a tiger from a cage. "A *fan!*" she cried, as she spied a lady with a fan on her wrist, mounted pillion behind her valet. "Did you see the one your dreadful cousin Matheline had? You must have one much better! Ah! Over there! Just *look* at that shop with the darling embroidered slippers! I must have some. Théophile, my cousin, halt everything! Baptiste, stop, stop here, and run in and get the shopkeeper! I want him to bring out those silk ones embroidered with roses that I see on the shelf in there behind the worktable!" She turned to me, her eyes glittering with shopping madness. "Sibille, you must learn never to lose an opportunity when you are shopping. If you pass something by, you may never see it again. Then you'll dream about it. So it's best just to buy it at once."

Embarrassed as I was, still I couldn't help feeling sympathy for Auntie. That is, when a shopping sort of lady has been immured for many years, it seems natural that she should go a little wild when finally getting to the biggest city in the kingdom. Ever since the queen's messenger had arrived with the letter, she had been awhirl with joy, planning the trip, packing and unpacking jewelry, veils, headdresses, and exulting over how father, having given up all claims on me, wouldn't get to share in the glory. She'd even sent him a crowing letter that she wasn't good enough for him, but was good enough for *royalty,* so there.

The shopkeeper had come out into the street and bowed before her, carrying the coveted slippers. Auntie took one, and, behind a half-closed curtain, slipped it on her gouty foot and pronounced it perfect.

"I'll have them. Do you have anything like them but *really large?*" she asked. I could feel myself blushing again.

"We could make something up," offered the shoemaker. "You could come in and see our lasts, and perhaps you'd find something suitable."

"Madame my cousin, the delay—we are almost at the inn—perhaps later—"

"Théophile, my dear, dear cousin, could you be an angel and run ahead and make the arrangements? Baptiste, you stay here—I'm going to stop at this master cobbler's establishment for a while and order a few little things." Oblivious to the little crowd that had gathered to stare as she was heaved out of the litter, she sailed into the shop ahead of me, a footman and Gargantua bringing up the rear of our procession.

"Look at that *dog,* will you!"

"It's only a pup."

"That's what I mean. It's already a big as a full-grown wolfhound. What will it be when it's grown up?"

"The paws, you can tell by the paws."

"Haw, they're as big a that woman's feet—"

"Wonder how big *she'll* be—?"

"I think she heard you, Georges—"

Ah, God, I thought, if only I were a satirist with a vicious tongue, instead of a sweet and delicate soul of poetic nature. How I would stab them with a vicious cut! But instead I just wished the ground would open and swallow me up, large feet and all. Worst of all, a little voice in the back of my mind told me I had better get used to it, that life in the future would be a series of embarrassments, or, as my mother used to say when father was drunk in public, "These things a lady must learn to deal with graciously."

Mother's dictum was tested again at the inn, when poor Baptiste, laden with packages, ran directly into a provincial-looking valet coming out of our room, similarly laden. As they scrambled to pick things up, it became clear that the previous tenant had not yet fully departed, and his servant was engaged in transporting his things to the Hôtel de Sens.

"So sorry, so sorry," said the valet, "my master has taken ill, and I've been in such a hurry."

"Ill, eh?" said Auntie, blocking the valet with her large bulk, and poking her walking stick at him, just for effect. "Is it catching? I don't want to stay in a room where someone has come down with a catching illness. Where is my cousin? How could he have done this? Without me to guide him, he doesn't take even the most rudimentary precautions! And just like an innkeeper! Why, they can put you in a room where they've just taken a dead body out! Shameless ruffians! You there, tell me what your master has."

The valet, pulling himself up in a dignified way, said, "My master, the *great* Nostradamus, does not have a catching disease!"

"And how does *he* know?" said Auntie, as I shriveled up and prayed that no one else would see this interchange.

"Madame, my master is the greatest plague doctor in the whole world. If *he* says he hasn't got a catching illness, then he hasn't. Now, let me pass, if you please." Yes, I thought I'd recognized the valet. Now I was sure. The servant who'd held the horse for the interfering old doctor I'd met on the road to Orléans.

"Auntie," I whispered, "it really is the servant of Maistre Nostredame, the great seer."

"I don't care if he's the archangel Gabriel. I want to know his symptoms, before I stay in this room."

"It is a return of my master's old complaint, the gout. He has pains like hot irons through every joint. Now, Madame, let me pass."

"Hot irons, eh," said Auntie, never lowering her walking stick, with which she was prodding the unfortunate servant in the chest. "No, it shouldn't feel like hot irons—that's something else."

"I vow to you, Madame, it is the gout."

"No, it's not. It sounds like a hex. But hexes aren't catching. You may go, boy, but if your master wants the hex removed, I am something of an expert. Have him send word to me. We'll be here the next two days, and after that, at *Saint-Germain*. We have an audience with the *queen*."

"Auntie," I said, my voice low, "it's *Nostradamus,* he knows everything, he sees the future." And here she is offering advice on hexes, as if he were a nobody who didn't know anything about the supernatural. I was completely mortified.

"I know who Nostradamus is, Sibille, and I know he's a man. Men don't know anything about removing hexes." With that, she put her walking stick back on the floor and leaned heavily on it as she walked suspiciously into the room, sniffing at the walls, lifting up the bedclothes and peering at them. "These sheets have not been changed," she announced. "Sibille, go tell that valet on his way to—oh, there you are back again. Have you thought again about the hex?"

"Madame, I need to check the armoire, I think he left—oh, my God—" As he pulled the heavy doors open, we all saw what he was seeing. That wretched box was forming up on an interior shelf.

"You damned busybodies," said the thing inside, "haven't you anything better to do than go shopping all day? First you bore me to tears, and then you leave me in the litter down in the *stable.* I tell you, I expect more *respect.*"

At the sound of the voice from the box, the strange valet fainted.

"Baptiste, fetch some water," said Auntie. "We seem to be in a pickle. I wonder what it will take to buy his silence? We certainly can't let him go without an explanation. That thing is an intolerable social burden. Whatever possessed you, Sibille, to open it up in the first place?"

❧

"A talking box, you say, Léon? What did it look like?" Nostradamus, groggy with opium, lay in a vast, ornate bed in one of the guest rooms of the winding old medieval hôtel that was the Paris home of the Cardinal Bourbon. The covers were turned back from his painful leg joints, and his bare, swollen feet stuck out on the heavy tapestry bedcover. They were gradually taking on a dusky blue hue.

"Silver-gilt, quite ornate, with letters written over the catch. Something like Agaba, Orthnet—"

"Don't repeat them, Lèon, if it is what I think it is, it would be . . . most unwise." He spoke slowly and carefully, as if he were afraid he might slur words, but it was clear to his servant that even in a fog his mind was keener than any ordinary man's.

"And I swear, I recognized the younger one. The girl on the Orléans road, only dressed up so's you'd hardly recognize her in a dark blue traveling gown with slashed sleeves and silk trim. She acted embarrassed."

"As well she might—if she was silly enough to open that box. It will follow her until it kills her, Léon. I knew there was something—ouch— significant about her. Didn't I tell you? She holds the key. Somehow, she has wandered into the center of one of Anael's historical knots. That wretched angel, why doesn't he keep his cupboard in better order? Then I'd know what the alternatives are. That horrible coffer—it's the gate straight into hell. It is fully capable of sucking down the whole country. No wonder I have been having all these horrible visions lately. How can I—uff—save France? I wonder where she found it—ugh, ow, this pain. Entirely unlike gout. I swear, my feet feel as if they were being held in the fire, and yet they're turning as blue as if they were frozen. Ugh. Now it's my heart. My chest is being crushed. The covers—take them off my heart—This is nothing—nothing I've ever seen before. Perhaps that old harpy was right. I'm willing to try anything at this point. Get her for me right away, Léon. New dresses, trips to the queen—it's clear to me they've already begun wishing themselves to perdition. If that ghastly box succeeds in doing what it always does, it will pass on to someone else quite soon, and earth won't be seeing those two women again. Ah, God, the pain. Where's my opium?" Léon rearranged the covers, and holding up his master's head from the pillow, spooned another does of tincture of opium down him, the last in the bottle. Then he hurried away to the inn at the sign of Saint-Michel.

✦

Across town, the two Ruggieri brothers had barred the door to Lorenzo's little workshop room. A wax doll with a scrap of cloth wound around its middle, and with pins thrust through its limbs lay on a table next to a dish of water and a burning candle.

"It's working, Lorenzo. The queen herself complained to me that Nostradamus is pretending to have gout, so that he won't have to go to Blois right away. She suspects him of wanting to linger in Paris to see clients. Now, let's give him the sensation of drowning. She'll be sure he's malingering."

"Just finish him off, Cosmo. The longer he stays in Paris, the poorer my business will be."

"No. Discredit first. I'm tired of her saying, 'Nostradamus this, Nostradamus that,' as if he were the oracle of the age. That's how she repays my faithful service! Flying to every new charlatan she hears of, looking for a guarantee of good fortune! No, I intend to go slowly. Keep him in bed, then every day a little something. Then hold the head above the flame, slowly, so the brains melt bit by bit. By the time I'm done with him, no one will ever dream of usurping my place again."

❧

"Humph," said Auntie, inspecting the blue feet. "Definitely not gout. It's a hex. I can feel it all around you. Are you missing anything personal? A hair? A fingernail clipping?" But the old prophet was incoherent, choking and spluttering as if he were being held underwater.

"You see how it is. Hurry, Madame, if you can do anything to help," said his horrified servant.

"Baptiste, hand me my hex powder. I never travel without my hex powder. Sibille, beat on that little drum I gave you." Baptiste reached into a wooden box full of little stoppered bottles and gave her one that was half full of a poisonous-looking greenish-brown powder. She took a little pinch and sprinkled it about, the way you'd salt an overlarge cauldron of soup.

"Stop that infernal racket," said the great Nostradamus, opening his eyes, spluttering, and wiping his face as if it were wet.

"Ha!" said Auntie. "It works every time."

"What about the drumming?" I asked, for my hands were getting tired. It was a little drum, barely bigger than a little goblet, all made of some dark metal, with barbaric designs etched out in gold on its surface. The drumhead, stretched tight, was a very sinister brownish stained color. My fingers were beginning to feel bruised, from striking the rim. The noise was so irritating that even faithful Gargantua had given up lying at my feet and with a doleful howl, had fled and hidden beneath the bed. I began to drum more gingerly.

"Keep it up, Sibille. Don't flag now. I'm going after the pins next."

"Léon, this is your fault. Where on earth did this horrible woman come from? Can't a man have any rest? My God, what a headache! My head feels as if it were melting. Get her out of here."

❧

"I don't understand it, Lorenzo. Look, I'm holding the head directly in the flame, and the wax doesn't melt."

"Cosmo, look at the pins!" said his brother. As Cosmo Ruggieri pushed the head of the wax figurine deeper into the flames, the pins thrust through the figurine's right leg began to move, first slowly, then with greater speed. Then one of them fell to the table with a *plink!* sound.

"Put that back, will you, brother."

"I can't! The wax is as hard as iron!"

"I'll fix that," said Cosmo Ruggieri, and ruthlessly ran the candle flame up and down the entire body of the little wax mannikin. But instead of melting the wax, the heat made the cloth wrapped around the figure burst into flames. With a cry, the sorcerer dropped the red-hot figurine to the table, where the flames suddenly flared up hugely, threatening to set fire to his wiry black beard and beetling eyebrows. He leapt back.

"The curtains, brother, the curtains. Beat it out before it spreads!" Thinking quickly, his brother upended the bowl of water on the flaming figure, which entirely vanished with a sputtering sound as the flames were doused.

"That damned old man—" said Cosmo Ruggieri.

"I've never seen anything like it. He's got a way of countermanding the death-spell. I'd give anything to know what it is."

"I doubt that he'll tell you, after this," said his older brother with a sigh. "It looks as if I can't get rid of him this way. I'll just have to think of something else."

"You've never failed yet, brother. No one can outthink a Ruggiero."

❊

I could have sworn it was gout," said Nostradamus, sitting up in bed and rubbing his bare, pink ankle. He had quite bony feet, I noticed, and didn't trim his toenails very carefully.

"I can't do a thing about gout," said Auntie, who, without invitation, was sitting on the foot of the bed. "If I could, I wouldn't have it myself. But I'm outstanding on hexes."

"May I ask who taught you this—unusual technique?" inquired the old man, his eyes roving up and down the huge, silk-brocade-covered mountain of flesh, unconfined by corseting, and taking in the little mustache, the strange, mushroom-like pallor, and the vast arrangement of glossy dyed black hair beneath the complicated and eccentric head-dress of her own devising.

"An African sorcerer. Sibille, remember the old black fellow with the crocodile tooth necklace? That was his drum. Works every time." She beamed at the bedridden prophet. "The powder's his recipe, too. Took me absolutely forever to get the ingredients, and one of them's just hen-bane picked at the new moon, which had to substitute for some plant he kept insisting on, but I simply couldn't find—"

"You have both traveled in Africa?" said Nostradamus, his voice tinged with respect. "I have traveled only in Egypt. I studied the secrets of mummies, and the mysteries of Osiris and Eternal Life. But beyond that—"

Auntie's face was envious. "I've always wanted to travel," she said. "But Monsieur Tournet said he'd done enough traveling for the both of us. I never set foot out of the house. Spas. I've been as far as Balaruc and Montpellier, but only before I married."

"But the sorcerer?"

"He came to me. On the drum. A slave ship, you know—when my husband pursued, they lightened the load by throwing them all over-board in their chains. The drum was a souvenir the captain kept in his cabin. Convenient, don't you think? Easy to pack."

"Then I take it you were instructed by—"

"By a ghost. Of course. My house is infested with them. It's all the fault of my late husband's business. Insensitive, that man. He never even noticed them."

"But, Auntie, how could the African fellow speak French to tell you the recipe?"

"He doesn't. Just a bit of Portuguese. And I know a bit, too, so we've managed. He started by throwing the furniture around, but just as I was about to call in the exorcist, he called a truce. I offered to pray weekly for those pool souls at the bottom on the ocean, and we've got on well ever since."

"You pray for heathens?" Nostradamus's servant, who had been lis-tening intently, could not help exclaiming in surprise.

"So what if I do?" answered Auntie. I saw the light of interest, and a

kind of deep understanding kindle in Doctor Nostradamus's eyes. Auntie seemed to fascinate him, like a whale, or a volcano, or some other
very large manifestation of nature. I could feel his gaze gently probing,
like an insect's feelers. First her, then me. We were clearly a phenomenon. My face was getting hot again, and I wished I could shrivel away
and vanish through the half-open door.

"Madame," said the old doctor, his voice courteous and concerned,
"is there some return I can make you for this—singular—ah, service?"
Auntie's face looked concerned, and she picked her walking stick up
from where it was resting against the foot of the bed and pointed it in
my direction, where I was trying to shrink myself into the floor.

"Over there, my goddaughter. I knew it was heaven sent when I
heard you were hexed. The Great Nostradamus himself. I *seized* the opportunity, you may imagine."

"Yes, I do imagine," he said, his voice prim, as he put his bony pink
foot back under the covers and motioned for his robe.

"I find myself simply *flying* since I left my house full of ghosts. Op-
portunities present themselves at every corner. And I take them! Life!
Splendor! All around me! The rose-embroidered slippers, for example. I
bought two pair. And then, of course, you."

"Ranking only slightly behind shoes. I am honored, Madame."

"Think nothing of it," said Auntie, waving her hand as if shooing
flies. I wanted to die. "My Sibille is being followed by an obnoxious
mummified head in a vulgar silver-gilt box. See? There it is, forming up
on your nightstand." Nostradamus looked alarmed, and I distinctly saw
him shudder. "Since you know the Secrets of the Ages, I thought you
might know how to get rid of it. It wakes her up at night with its gib-
bering, and keeps offering to grant us our heart's desire. It also comments rather rudely on my housekeeping. I've tried throwing it in the
river, but it always comes back."

"Madame Tournet, I have seen that thing once before, in the possession of an old friend, now deceased. It is the quintessence of evil. I take
it that she opened the box and looked it in the face?"

"Exactly what happened."

"It must have been ownerless at the time. It attaches itself like a
leech to the first person who opens the box, and offers to give him his

heart's desire. But each wish it grants leads to another, every one with worse consequences than the first. The horrified victim becomes en-meshed in a web of evil deeds, wishing and mending, sleepless at night, sick with remorse, yearning for death. But the box won't pause in giving its victims their innermost desires until, through their continual wishing and the damage it has done, it has sucked them into the grave and eter-nal damnation."

"Worse than I thought," said Auntie. The box made an evil, whistling sound. "You in there, shut up! I'm consulting the wisest man in the world! Have a little respect, will you!" She gave the box several sharp raps with her walking stick.

"I *told* you not to do that," said the thing in the box.

"I wouldn't do that if I were you," said Nostradamus, his voice mild, but his eyes full of a kind of admiration mixed with shock.

"You out there. It's Michel de Nostre Dame, isn't it? That French puppy who thinks he knows everything. The only worse one is that fool, Scalinger. Are you still hanging about him, Michel, you dotard? Has your beard gone gray since we first met? I imagine you're getting old. Wouldn't you like a few more years for your studies? Just think of the good you could do. Michel de Nostre Dame, savior of France— no, savior of the human race! It could be you, Michel. But it all takes time, you know. I can offer you the Secret of Eternal Life. It's authentic. Egyptian."

"Scalinger and I have parted company, Menander. And as for wishing for anything from you again, I wouldn't even consider it. I've tasted the bitterness of the cup you offer. And I heard what you did to Josephus."

"Bitterness? I gave you exactly what you said you wanted. You must not have thought things out right. The art of divining the true future, right? And didn't you get it? And then you were so low as to cheat me in the bargain. But for you, an old friend, I could give you another wish, and you could get it better next time. Next time—well, just think, if you lived forever, you could see if your prophecies in the *Centuries* come out."

"Again, you are in error. Fortunately for myself, when I at last dis-covered the Secrets of the Ages, I opted to study the Secret of Happi-ness first, and from that I found not only how to escape *you*, but that I do not need to live forever. Just look at yourself, crammed into that box, no longer master of your fate, and doomed to repeat forever and ever the mistake you yourself made, when you asked for immortality and didn't specify the conditions."

"I didn't make any mistake at all. And I'm very happy whenever someone repeats the words, and I give them their heart's desire."

"And that desire is filled with poison, the twisting agony of regret, and of grief unending."

"I told you it made me happy," said the thing, and fell silent.

"Just plain malicious," said Auntie.

"You haven't made any wishes, have you?" asked the great prophet.

"Not a one. Neither of us. I suppose that's why it follows us around, instead of staying at home, decently, on the shelf."

"That's how it kills, you know. One's desires are never perfectly expressed. And it is very cunning and literal. You wish for money, a beloved relative dies and leaves it to you. You wish for love, it is the cloying adoration of some lout you are soon dreaming only of getting rid of. You wish to mend the wish, and it gets worse. The victim is overtaken by despair and horror, sinking gradually, knowingly, into damnation. Sometimes they go mad and throw themselves off high places, set themselves on fire. Eternal torment, first in this world, and then the next. It is a dreadful way to go."

"Oh, dear," said Auntie. "It's more or less as I thought. And Sibille and I were having such fun shopping."

"The Greeks, the Romans, the Egyptians. It has left a trail of wreckage through the centuries," said Nostradamus. "For a while, it disappeared in the sack of Rome—"

"That was one of my best jobs," said the repulsive object in the box. "I combined six contradictory wishes into one—it took a lot of thought—"

"Then, when I saw it, it was in Constantinople. After that, I heard that it had gone to Venice in the possession of Josephus Magister. I was hoping it would never find its way to France."

"I tried the hex powder on it," said Auntie.

"With what result?" asked the seer.

"I told you, don't ever try *that* again," said the thing in the box.

"It made him sneeze," I said.

"Have you any idea what it is like to sneeze in a box?" said Menander the Undying. "Open this thing up, I want to see what the great Nostradamus is looking like these days. Older, I imagine." I started for the box, but the old man said:

"Young lady, you are in the greatest danger. It is willing to lie in wait for you for years. It will prey on your weakest spot, which in your case is not greed, or lust for power, but sympathy. You pride yourself on it, don't you?" Silently, I nodded. "Then that is the avenue through which it can tempt you. You'll feel sorry for it, or for someone else, and that is when it will offer you the bargain you will be too weak to refuse. One little wish, the best-meant wish in the world, and hell's gates will open and you will be sucked down in agony, bit by bit, and all through your own doing. After all these centuries of satisfying the greedy, the envious, and the vengeful, it will doubtless be amused at the novelty."

"Shut up, Michel," said the thing.

"But—but I can't help it. I'm just naturally sensitive and sympathetic. My poetic muse, you see—" There was a wicked chuckle from the thing in the box. Old Nostradamus just shook his head.

"Harden your heart," he said.

"But how do we get rid of it?" asked Aunt Pauline.

"You might try giving it away. Preferably to someone you don't like, who is going on a long sea journey. No one knows how far it can travel on its own—" Nostradamus paused, and sighed. "But mind you, I have never heard of anyone able to give it away, either. It seduces its owners like a lover; they can't resist the powers it offers. But you have resisted it so far. Give it away, get someone else to look directly at its face, and you may succeed in scraping it off. That's the only thing I can suggest."

A vast sigh, a regular mistral, swept through Aunt Pauline's body. "Who is their right mind would want an accursed, mummified head in a box?" she said.

"You'd be surprised," said the head.

"Get me my slippers, Léon, I am feeling much better, thanks to this good woman's efforts, and would like to escort my guests to the door," said the old prophet.

"Oh, no," said Léon, as he searched under the bed. "Look—" he pulled out one well-chewed sole and held it up tragically.

"Mademoiselle, your hound has eaten my slippers," said Nostradamus, his face a study in irritation as he inspected the sad remains. Gargantua, with that sense that all dogs have when they are being talked about, looked pleased with himself, and then rolled on his back and made that huffing sound he does when he wants his stomach scratched. Absentmindedly, I began to scratch his big, freckled stomach with one hand, but stopped suddenly when I saw the warning look on Nostradamus's face.

"We'll go immediately and get another pair. Sibille, shall we send for that dear man with the cobbler shop where we stopped to come and take Doctor Nostradame's measure? No, that will take too long. We need something already made up—let's see, there's a place I recall seeing yesterday with the best bargains in morocco leather—"

"No embroidery," said the prophet. "I am a plain man, with simple tastes."

 osmo Ruggieri had borrowed a somewhat paint-spotted brown velvet doublet with threadbare sleeves from his younger brother the painter, by way of a disguise, and set off for the Hôtel de Sens to try to discover for himself just what had gone wrong with the victim of his death-spell. But at the main gate to the residence, he found himself nearly elbowed to death by a crowd of people all clamoring to be admitted to see Nostradamus and have their fortunes told.

"No more today," shouted the guard. "He's having a nap to restore his powers."

"Tell him Madame de Bellièvre wants him to read her horoscope." A royal page, frantic and dusty, pushed his way through the crowd at the door.

"Admit me at once, I am a page for the king."

"I have an appointment," said Ruggieri, hoping to trail in behind the king's page.

"He has no consultations scheduled for today." Blessings on my brother's old clothes, thought Ruggieri. "My appointment is not for a horoscope," said the devious sorcerer, "it is to take his portrait at the queen's command." Glancing at the spotty doublet, the tattered plumes set in his cheap, gaudy hat, and the worn cloak of made-over green wool, the guard took Ruggieri's little case of poisons and spell-casting equipment for a painter's box, and let him pass in the wake of the king's page.

Slinking through long corridors and oozing through doorways to un-familiar rooms, he at last came to the chamber where Nostradamus had taken up residence, only to find that the dusty page who had come in ahead of him was still hammering on the door. The door half-opened, and the figure of a servant blocked the way in. Ruggieri could hear the prophet's voice from within.

"What's the matter, king's page? You are making a lot of noise over a lost dog. Go and look on the road to Orléans, and you will find it there, being led on a leash." I swear, thought Ruggieri, he never even looked at the boy, or heard what his business was. No, it can't be—it's all a parlor trick. As the awed page turned to go and look for the valuable dog from the king's kennel that he had lost, the voice came again. "Quit lurking outside my door, Cosmo Ruggieri the Younger. The spirit told me you would come and pester me today. Either leave, or come in and introduce yourself properly and sit down. I believe you want to know why your death-spell didn't work."

"I can't imagine what you mean, Maestro," said the sorcerer, accept-ing the invitation.

"Ah, so that's how you got past the guard," said Nostradamus, eyeing Ruggieri's tatty disguise. "It was very impolite of you to cast a death-spell before you had even paid a courtesy visit." The old doctor was seated in a high-backed chair beside a table littered with natal charts and divining equipment. His gouty foot was propped up on a cushioned stool.

"How did you know it was me?" asked Ruggieri.

"My clairvoyant powers," said Nostradamus calmly. "You'd be hard to mistake—you look a good bit like your father did at your age. And it's you who would be displaced should I become the queen's official astrologer—so who else would wish me dead?"

"That wretch Simeoni," said Ruggieri hastily. "You have no idea how envious he is."

"Simeoni can't predict rain when the sky is cloudy. Did you ever hear the story of how he got the Duke of Milan's moon in Jupiter be-cause of an ink blot?"

"Ha! That's Simeoni, all right," said Ruggieri, all the while thinking, draw him out. Get him talking. He'll boast and give away the secret. They always do. "An infant could best him—but me, no one beats me in prediction—or in sorcery—" Ruggieri could see Nostradamus eyeing him, measuring him. Now he'll tell, thought the cunning Italian sorcerer, he won't be able to resist.

"I'm afraid I have bested you. But of course it was simple—I had the help of Menander the Deathless." Nostradamus smiled a secretive smile calculated to drive Ruggieri wild.

"You have it—you have the box. It's—it's mine. I sent for it. Give it to me."

"I'm afraid I haven't got it," said the old doctor. "It's in the possession of a young woman who doesn't know what she has."

"Has she opened it?"

"Of course not; she can't get the catch open. She brought it here to me to find out what was inside with my clairvoyant powers, and I told her she needn't bother, it was valueless." Looking at the ceiling, as if musing, the cunning old doctor said, "You know—I imagine she'd sell it to you, if you asked. She's staying at a rather expensive inn, at the sign of Saint-Michel, and I'm sure at the rate she's shopping, she'll soon be out of money." As Ruggieri scurried away without even saying thank you, Nostradamus said to his servant:

"Léon, hurry over to Madame Tournet's and tell them to leave that box out in plain sight somewhere, and hide their jewelry. The queen's astrologer will be over to steal it shortly."

"I thought you said, Master, that he could buy it."

"If he is anything as stingy and crafty as his father, he wouldn't think of it. It would undermine his pride to do it the simple way. No, I have no doubt he'll climb in the window at night, or lure them out on a ruse. Anything to save a sou, that man. Hurry now, I don't want them surprised or harmed." As Léon hastened away, shutting the door behind him, a figure composed of dark blue, filled with twinkling little whirly shiny things, stepped from its hiding place in the shadows.

"Well, Anael, let's get back to work; that's my good deed for today," observed Nostradamus, picking up his wand from the table. "With one stroke, I have relieved those silly ladies of temptation for a while, given Ruggieri a means by which to wish himself into a well-deserved oblivion, and, with any luck, aborted the demoiselle's writing career, thus saving France from some measure of the increasing burden of bad poetry that spews forth daily from the printing presses of Paris and Lyons."

"Quite neatly done," observed the Spirit of History.

"You wouldn't happen to know how it comes out, would you?" asked the old prophet.

"I thought I'd found it the other day, and I was saving it for you, but now I've gone and misplaced it," said the spirit, ruffling his dark wings.

✣

On the Pont-au-Change, not far from the high-towered stone gate that separates the bridge full of shops from the Cité, passersby stopped to behold a curious sight. A gaudy, curtained litter, slung between two handsome gray hackneys, had paused before a goldsmith's shop. A woman's hand, covered with rings, gestured from behind closed curtains, and a footman in livery, one of a half dozen accompanying the litter, hurried to assist someone out into the doorway of the shop.

A tall, dark, sharp-featured young man in a black velvet doublet with two buttons undone and one missing paused to join the onlookers. There's no crest on the litter, he thought. The mistress of some great courtier, out shopping. A hand emerged, an arm in a slashed silk sleeve, then a foot—rather large, and quickly covered with a discreet velvet-trimmed hem, and the man saw the tall, regal figure of a slender young woman step onto the paving stones. Suddenly his heart stopped. It's her, he thought. I'd know her anywhere. My tragic, aristocratic beauty, driven into a sinful alliance with some corrupt, ancient nobleman by a harsh world.

All around was noise and bustle: a peddler of old shoes and boots, pushing a cart, a woman selling eel pies, and beneath it all, the hard rush of water between the piers, and the continual rumble and vibration of the mill wheels beneath the the bridge, grinding the grain for the bakeries of Paris. But to the man, a curious golden stillness surrounded the moment. The young woman seemed, for a second, to be surrounded by something that glowed, some trick of the light that made her appear luminous. God strike me for a sinner, he thought, she's even more lovely, more desirable than the first time I saw her that time in the courtyard of the Bishop's residence at Orléans. Look at her there, her aquiline profile set off against her black velvet hood—an eagle, a falcon—her posture, so noble, her walk—a doe at sunrise— A queen, no, an empress. Nothing is good enough for her—and yet, oh, unspeakable, she's settled for dishonor and a courtly connection. Then curiosity grew in him like some huge, overpowering vine that can cover houses and barns in a night. I have to know who is keeping her, he thought. I'll follow her. I have to know who she settled for. I can't be content giving her up until I know her reasons.

But just as an astonishing hatred for the vile, putrid roué who had stolen her youth was beginning to grapple his heart in iron claws, his mood was broken by an astonishing sight: the hugest woman in the world was being levered out of the litter by four grunting footmen. Astonishing! thought young lounger, as his eye was overwhelmed by the very vastness of the woman, surrounded by an even vaster array of petticoats and a dazzlingly ornamented skirt made even larger with the swaying wooden hoops of a Spanish farthingale. Then there was the amazing powdered and rouged complexion, that had clearly never seen a ray of sun, the immense, fantastically shaped yellow silk headdress, sparkling with beads, the crinkle and rustle and glitter that accompanied every step. What an astonishing duenna, thought the man, this is the oddest and most mismatched pair of ladies I've ever seen. He could feel the itch to spy on them redoubling itself. Walking very slowly, peering at shop sights and pretending to survey the passersby, he paused several times before the window of the jeweler's establishment, catching glimpses of the transaction within. It was curious—the older woman, the duenna, seemed to be the one selecting things, not the younger. As they left the store, chattering together happily, he caught the phrase "—Señor Alonzo's crucifix couldn't be set off better with that chain— you really have to display it to advantage, dear—" Señor Alonzo. A *foreigner's* mistress. What's worse, a *Spaniard*. Rapidly, he envisioned some ambassador's aide's little pied-a-terre, a heart paid for and broken—for the honor of France, I must find him and call him out, thought the man.

I'll disgrace him on the field of honor and send him packing back to his kennel beyond the Pyrenees. An intoxicating sense of mission overcame him, erasing all lingering feelings that spying out a lady's movements might be a bit disreputable.

By late afternoon he had discovered what glovemaker they preferred, three shoemakers that they favored, a draper's, a fanmaker, and two pâtissiers. He had also found that the young lady had the curious habit of reading natural history, and planned for that purpose to return to The Sign of the Four Elements on the rue St.-Jacques on Monday afternoon in two week's time to see if her order of *Historia Animalium* had arrived. She is too good for that Spaniard, he thought morosely, as he walked back to his father's house on the rue de Bailleul. She had a decent enough family, except for that rattle-brained Matheline. What led her to it? A man can't marry a Spaniard's ex-mistress, even if he kills him. What good is a duel after all? She's ruined. It's over. Put her out of your mind, he told himself. But the more he put her out, the more he saw her, all shining and outlined in the sun.

✤

"Auntie, don't you think mother will just love the pretty bracelet we picked out? And the silver rattle, it's just right for the baby—" The tall young woman's face was glowing with unaccustomed happiness as she set down her purchases on the bed. The extraordinarily rotund, fantastical, dyed and painted old lady who had followed her in sighed as she lowered herself into the chair by the little table.

"Ah! My feet! Oh, Sibille, how like the old days! Your mother and I had so much fun together when we were young! How I wish she were here now! We would spy out the best-looking young men in the street together, and dream about how someday we would each live in a castle, and pay each other visits. But my brother is such a tyrant he won't even let her out of the house—I really don't understand why you insisted on getting him a present, too, he really doesn't deserve anything—oh! Look at the table! That horrible box is gone!"

"And the window open!" said the younger woman, crossing the room to peer out. "Look at that! He climbed right up from the balcony

and stole it! That Nostradamus is the greatest prophet in the world!"
She closed the window and did a little dance in the middle of the room,
out of pure joy, while the old woman smiled indulgently.

"There's only one thing I don't understand," said Aunt Pauline,
propping up her bad foot on the footstool.

"What's that, Auntie?"

"We sent notice to Saint-Germain three days ago that we were here,
and ready to come for your reading. We should have heard back by
now. We need to know when your audience is so that the Abbé can go
ahead to find rooms in the town. I'm beginning to feel suspicious about
this whole thing. Maybe the queen has changed her mind."

"We have the letter, *ma tante,* and it does say she has heard much of
my poetry and desires to read it for herself and meet the authoress."

"Yes, but the messenger said it would not go amiss if we brought a
certain box the queen was interested in, and we'd know which one.
Now who did that fellow Léon say was coming to steal it? Maistre
Cosme, the queen's astrologer. I think we might be in the middle of a
tangle, Sibille, and not because of your poetry."

"Surely, the queen does not commission thieves when we would
have gladly given her Menander ourselves."

"Yes, but perhaps more people than the queen knew we had him. I
did tell you to keep it a secret. Are you sure your gossipy cousin Matheline didn't hear about it?"

"Absolutely certain. I've never told a soul. I'm just mortified at the
thought that my Art may come to its justified public acclaim only because I came into the accidental possession of a mummified head."

"Well then, *something's* going on—I wonder how many people at
court know you have it? I certainly hope they don't find out what it will
take to get it from you—"

"You mean, if it's truly stolen, my invitation will be rescinded, and
we creep back home in disgrace with the presentation copies, and if it
comes back, my life is in danger—"

"More or less like that."

"Honestly, Auntie, I can't decide which is worse. Do you know how
my father will mock me? When I think about it, I'd rather be dead."

"Myself, I'd rather be neither. I'll just have to think of something. I'll consult Maistre Nostredame again. He seems to know a great deal about Menander's habits."

✦

"Back again so soon?" said the proprietor of the Four Elements. "The book's not here yet, so neither is she." The shop bell tinkled again as two alchemists, deep in conversation, pushed through the door. The shop window, which let down like a shelf beside the door, was open, letting in both light and air, and allowing the tempting array of books on the shelf behind the counter to be visible to the students and learned doctors of the Left Bank.

"I—I'm looking for a fencing treatise—Marozzo's *Opera Nova*," said Nicolas Montvert.

"To buy, or to thumb through?" said Maître Lenormand.

"To buy, as soon as my father advances the funds," announced Nicolas. The bookseller snorted in derision. "Don't be so haughty," said Nicolas. "I'm expecting a payment from Achille any time now—I may just take my custom elsewhere."

"After all the credit I've extended you? I've half a mind to tell your father you are partnering young dandies in an illegal fencing school for money—"

"Then he'll sign the orders for the Bastille, and I'll *never* buy any more books from you," said Nicolas.

"Now, now, don't get so testy," said the old man. "You know I'm not that hard-hearted."

"You ought to be currying my favor," said Nicolas, reaching down the coveted work on the new Italian fencing techniques from the shelf and thumbing through it. "I have every intention of becoming celebrated some day. People will flock to this very spot, all because I once read Marozzo here—"

"Put that back, you're wearing it out—"

"See here? Marozzo is completely wrong when he describes the defense in low ward. My book will be much better than this—you'll sell dozens of copies."

"Your book doesn't exist yet, you puppy. And you think to outdo the celebrated Marozzo? How far are you from finished, anyway? Have you found a printer yet?"

"Why—I'm not far from done at all—not at all—almost there, in fact—and I'm sure any good printer would just jump at the chance to publish an important new text on fencing like mine is going to be—"

"Nicolas, Nicolas, take an old man's advice. Learn the trade your father wants for you. Apply yourself to your studies, make him happy. He's not a bad fellow, and he wants the best for you. The way you carry on, hanging out with those bad fellows, you'll wind up dead in an alley and break his heart. Enter his trade, Nicolas. You can't be in another place than the one you were born in, no matter how much you wish for it."

"Be a banker? But then—then I couldn't even dare look at her. She's so far above me, Maître. I can't live in the mud if I want to reach for the stars. I need to become famous, right away. Famous and rich—"

"Notorious and dead is more like it," growled the old bookseller, as he watched Nicolas walk out into the busy, narrow street, then turned and put the book back on the shelf.

❧

Once again, Madame Gondi stood watch outside Ruggieri's little attic chamber, while the Queen of France conferred with her astrologer inside. Behind the sealed door, the sorcerer whisked a silk cloth off something that stood on a long, bottle-filled table beneath the eaves. Even at noon, the little room was dark, and smelled of dust and long dessicated rats, poisoned and dead beneath the floorboards. Several astrological charts were pinned haphazardly to the wall, and the sigil of Asmodeus was written in red over the fireplace, which contained a redbrick athanor, whose chimney disappeared up the larger chimney of the fireplace.

"My queen," he said, "I have spared nothing to acquire this treasure for you." Concealing her avidity, Catherine de Medici glanced at the silver-gilt box with the strange designs, then at her sorcerer's malicious, triumphant face. A tiny smile, almost invisible, pulled up one corner of her mouth.

"You mean, you have stolen it from the sorceress. Ingenious, Cosmo, ingenious. She must not have any powers worth my knowing about, if you could so easily best her. So her bid for my favor fails, and you remain triumphant."

"Majesty, I can conceal nothing from you. You remain the most brilliant and insightful woman in the kingdom."

"But now I shall be the best loved. Open the box for me, Cosmo."

"Your Majesty must open it herself, for it to work," said the sorcerer, averting his eyes as she fumbled with the catch.

"Great Jesus, it's moving! It's alive! Oh! My God! What a ghastly, ugly thing!" exclaimed the queen. The peeling, parchment lips of the mummified head moved, revealing decayed, yellow teeth. One shriveled eyelid moved, and a glittering, evil eye, alive and shining, could be seen in the depths of the rotten, bony socket.

"You're not exactly so attractive, yourself," said the head of Menander the Deathless.

"C—Cosmo, tell it what I want," said Catherine de Medici, who at this stage in her life was not yet far enough gone in magic to be unshakable in the face of horror. An eerie, sucking, pulsating sound seemed to resonate all around her, as if Hell itself were tugging at the hem of her dress, her long, glittering sleeves, her heart.

"Majesty, you yourself must tell it, reciting first the words engraved over the catch of the box."

"I don't want to *kill* the duchess, Cosmo, I want her alive to see me triumph. I want—" But the box had begun to shimmer; now it was translucent; it was in the very act of vanishing. "My coffer! Where's my magic head going?" cried the queen.

"I would love to oblige," said the head, beginning to fade from sight, "but they're missing me back where I belong—"

"Where's that?" cried the queen's sorcerer, aghast at the mysterious fading of his treasure.

"Sibille de La Roque owns me, at least for now—" said the head in a thin whisper as it and the box vanished from sight.

"Well, Cosmo, it turns out you aren't very clever after all. I should have known when you told me to put off receiving her that you were just jealous. She's mightier in sorcery than you are, and you just didn't want me to know. She's probably forseen your every move, and let you steal the treasure just to show you up in exactly this way." Cosmo Rug-gieri paled. What would he do? His enemies—he had so many. Without the queen's protection and patronage he was a dead man. And it was all the queen's fault. For whose sake had he made those enemies? He could have been cultivating a pleasant little society practice, but no, he must be the victim of ingratitude. Oh, the ingratitude of the great. How they disposed of faithful servants just for a moment of novelty, some stupid parlor trick like a mummified head that talked. It probably didn't grant wishes anyway. It was all a deception mounted by the mysterious sorceress. . . .

"Don't even *imagine* trying to poison her, Cosmo. If she's tractable, I am going to arrange to keep her near, so that the head will always be at my disposal and not fall into the wrong hands. That way she will take the danger of keeping it, and no one but I will have the advantage of wishing on it. I want her, I want my magic head back, and if you kill her it might very well fly away forever—" Oh, dear, thought Cosmo, I hadn't thought of *that*. I'd have to be right on the spot, when I killed her, and that could be so messy—

"Look me in the eye, Cosmo, you worm. I can see your thoughts, did you know that? Don't play any tricks on me. I want that head, or I'll have yours, and just *see* how valid that prediction about my death is. I can get other sorcerers to change that, you know. Why, maybe I'll just wish that prediction away on my lovely new magic coffer. Then see where you are— Now behave, or I'll lock you up and keep you so near starvation you'll wish you *were* dead."

"Great, merciful Majesty, pardon your wretched servant," he said, bursting into crocodile tears and falling upon the floor to kiss the hem of her fashionable mauve taffeta and velvet dress. "I sought only to please you, oh, see my great distress and suffering, and pardon, pardon!"

"There'll be no pardon for you if you stain the hem of my gown, Cosmo. Cheap tears; I see better in the theater."

"Then you do pardon me; you are amused—yes, I, Ruggiero the Younger, have been the wretched object of your amusement—what joy that my pitiful state has brought even a moment of pleasure to the great queen, some brief distraction from her weighty cares—"

"Stop that and quit groveling on the floor, Cosmo. I know what you're thinking, and I don't like it. Just understand me; I expect you to be civil to that new sorceress I'm consulting, and not sprinkle any powders about—oh, yes, and no death-spells, either."

"Can't do that anyway," he grumped. "The head puts 'em off."

"My goodness, it does? What a treasure! More powerful than my bezoar stones. Yes, I'll send my guard for her at once, and have one of my most trustworthy ladies escort her. Oh, I can hardly wait—"

Ingratitude, thought Ruggieri as he watched the stiff, dumpy little form sweep from the attic chamber, you are a bitter payment for all my loyalty, my infinite devotion. . . .

❧

A tall, bulky, figure with greasy long hair, an eye patch, and a bristling gray and white beard stood in the doorway of the little apartment on the rue de la Tisarendirie. Even Beatrice, so used to seeing menacing-looking folk of all varieties, felt somewhat nervous at the sight of the sinister one-eyed man. Hidden violence seemed to roll off him in waves, like heat off a wheat field.

"Your husband, I have heard of him. Is he at home?" said the man.

"Why not just this moment, h—have you business with him?" said Beatrice, suddenly thinking the man could be a hired assassin.

"I hear a man inside," said Villasse.

"M—my husband's brother. The painter. The court painter, you know."

"I didn't know. Let me in and I'll wait. I've business with your husband. I hear he sells something I wish to buy." Oh, what a relief. He's going to assassinate someone else, thought Beatrice, as he pushed past her and seated himself in the best chair in their tiny front room.

"Would you like a glass of wine while you wait?" she asked.

"Not here," said Villasse, with a malignant chuckle. He had scarcely begun to inspect the room, and wonder whose demonic sigil that was over the fireplace, when Lorenzo returned with his arms full of packages.

"Maestro," said Villasse as Lorenzo put down his load on the table and turned to his customer. "Maestro, I hear you will sell me oil of vitriol." The sound of a baby crying came from the back room.

"That, and a dozen other things. I take it you want revenge on a woman?"

"How did you know?"

"Simple. They always want vitriol for that job. A woman's face—it's all she has, isn't it? Tell me, do you plan to throw it yourself? If you do, you must be sure to check the direction of the wind first—get in close and don't let any splash on you. Water alone won't wash it off."

"I don't plan on doing it myself. Suppose there are witnesses? I intend to hire someone. Perhaps you might suggest a name."

"I know several fellows, but they are expensive. If you wish to be a bit more thrifty, you can try at the sign of the Black Bull, down by the river. There's ex-soldiers there, ready for anything. Just don't pay the man you get all at once. Offer him half, then the other half when the job's done."

"An excellent idea, Maestro. I can see I've come to the right place."

"I always try to give the best quality to my clients," said Maestro Lorenzo, taking a little brown bottle of oil of vitriol from a locked cupboard at the back of the room. "Remember, if you decide to throw it yourself, be sure to wear gloves."

❧

A languid summer breeze, carrying some mysterious hint of the autumn to come, stirred the tops of the trees. Beyond the garden terrace of St.-Germain, the panorama of the river and the hazy, far distant walls and church spires of Paris stretched out beyond them. The tall young lady paused. "Oh, it's all just so wonderful," she said. She walked on the arm of her brother, a bold, cheerful young man of medium height, dressed in the boots, puffed baggy breeches, and doublet of a soldier. A crimson cloak was thrown over his shoulder, and he had, since she had last seen him, grown a mustache more grandiose in its conception than in its execution.

At her left strode an extraordinarily dashing young officer with flashing eyes and a much more successful mustache: Philippe d'Estouville, fellow officer in the service of Monsieur Damville, professional charmer and celebrated duelist. His seal-brown hair was combed quite flat beneath his narrow, plumed hat; his high-necked doublet opened to give way to a stylishly narrow ruff that sat just below his ears. An Italian rapier in the latest fashion hung at his side, its elaborately cast and gilded basket hilt advertising its owner's wealth as well as his daring.

"—poetry, Sibille—who'd have ever thought it would get you a royal audience?" laughed her brother.

"I am certain I should esteem your sister's poetry at first sight almost as much as I esteemed her person," said the smooth-tongued young officer. Sibille blushed with pleasure.

"I have only a poor copy, besides the presentation copy, and that will be gone tomorrow."

"—and what a coincidence, finding you here at Saint-Germain, exactly when we were required to escort the Constable and M. de Damville here from Ecouen. You could be a great success at court here, you know, perhaps even get a royal allowance. Who'd have ever thought your scribbling would bring so much? When I got the letter from Laurette, I did laugh. You could almost hear her scream of rage all the way from the farm! Of course, *I* never wished you anything but well—but you can't blame Laurette for being jealous when Aunt Pauline wanted you for a companion instead of her."

"I'm glad, Annibal, that it didn't change anything between us. You're the only one who seems to rejoice in my good fortune."

"And I," added Philippe d'Estouville, his voice agreeably flattering. "Never was good fortune better deserved."

"How goes Villasse?" asked Annibal. "Laurette says a hunting accident has put him at death's door."

"Well, Auntie is determined to sever the engagement, whether he is well or ill. She's found a lawyer who can prove that he's related to grandfather through a distant cousin. Kin can't marry, you know, so that invalidates everything. She says she can't stand the thought of him having the least chance of trying to put a claim on her estate." So engaged was she in talking to the charming officer on her left that she did not notice the slight hesitation in her brother's walk, or the way he suddenly stared off into the distance at the word "estate."

"I've met the man once. He's too ill-favored for a beautiful young lady—Annibal tells me he's greedy, too."

"For a vineyard that's my dowry," said Sibille.

"And only for a vineyard—what a petty man," sniffed d'Estouville. Sibille's eyes froze for an instant. D'Estouville quickly added, "What I mean to say is that a man should only choose beauty, for the sake of true love. Don't you agree?"

"Oh, yes, of course," answered Sibille, sounding relieved.

That evening, there was a knock at the door of the rooms that the Abbé had rented in the little town that lay beneath the castle. A little page said, "For the Demoiselle de La Roque," and thrust a sealed letter into the astonished Abbé's hand.

"So what is in it?" he said, as Auntie tried to read over Sibille's shoulder.

"It's a rondeau—from Monsieur d'Estouville—and it's dedicated to me," answered Sibille, her olive complexion growing pinker and her eyes shining with the pleasure of one who sees a secret dream unexpectedly fulfilled.

"I never heard he wrote poetry," said Aunt Pauline.

"But he does, because here it is, and it's very nice, too. Just hear this: 'Rose, thy blush is envy at my Sibille's shining eyes—' "

"He probably paid to have it written," sniffed Aunt Pauline.

"Nicely put, the line balances well," said the Abbé.

"The interest seems rather sudden," said the old lady.

"He's been away with Annibal. Besides, it's only natural to make new friends at court," replies Sibille.

"Exactly so," said a muffled, sarcastic voice from the box on the end table. "And of course, he doesn't think at all about how much money you may come into." But Sibille was so happy, she didn't even hear it.

❧

It was the wife of Catherine's Italian maître d'hotel, Madame d'Alamanni, who introduced the tall young lady to the queen as she sat in the midst of the ladies of the court. On a chair near the center of the room, she recognized the Duchess of Valentinois by her signature black-and-white gown; her face no longer young, but pinched and distinctly preserved looking, she was deeply engaged in conversation with one of her ladies-in-waiting. Apart from her, only the two queens present had chairs, the redheaded girl who was Queen of Scots, and the Queen of France, who sat in a carved, cushioned armchair next to an ornate table with several attractive volumes on it. Well coached, the Demoiselle de La Roque approached and curtseied deeply, then offered the Queen of France first two thin, bound quarto volumes, in beautifully tooled-leather covers, and after that an exquisite silver-gilt box of antique design.

Those who sat nearby, on the velvet cushions spread out on the colorful oriental carpet, heard snatches of conversation, but nothing unusual enough to distract them from the main business of the afternoon; the flirtations, the music, the cards, and in the corner, a neglected poet reading from a work in praise of the fourteen-year-old Queen of Scots's goddess-like beauty. The teenager in the chair was a tall girl—taller than many a Frenchman and still growing; the court poets had lately abandoned sprites and fairies when praising her, and taken up the larger sorts of deities. Several of the Italian wives of Catherine's court favorites were chatting together in Italian—the subject was infant teething fevers—and at the far-right-hand edge of the carpet, a young courtier, urged on by his friends, was quietly insinuating his hand beneath the skirts of a young demoiselle engaged in animated conversation with two of her cousins newly arrived from the country.

"—I am honored to offer it to Your Majesty—" said Sibille, and the queen nodded, her mouth pursed up in a small, but definitely triumphant smile.

"—he turned quite red, and screamed all night, and I gave orders to the nurse—" one of the Italian ladies was saying.

"—you say it has a problem? Nothing serious, I hope—" The queen's voice could be heard over the babble.

"—teeth that gleam like pearls of orient—" came the faded voice of the poet from the corner.

"—it fades out; it seems to follow me about. I hope that the honor of being possessed by a person of your rank will cause it to remain with you—" The queen leaned forward, her shrewd eyes sizing up the young woman before her.

"—ha! Queen of Cups! I win! My prize, Demoiselle!"

"—well then, if it returns to you, then we must just arrange for you to follow the court. An appointment, perhaps, a suitable and pliant husband—you said this second volume is not poetry?"

"—only a very little work, entitled *A Dialogue of the Virtues.*"

"—I said, only one! Just because you won the game doesn't give you the right to more than one kiss—"

"—as your patroness. A reading here, and a publisher—" the Queen's voice was indulgent.

"—cold compresses for the fever—"

"Your Majesty, I—I am overwhelmed with the honor—"

"—luminous as a young Athena, she makes her way among her worshipers, who drown in her radiance—" the poet read on, ignored in the chatter.

"Gratitude and silence. Our own little confidence—" murmured the Queen of France. There was a scream from the far-right-hand edge of the carpet, and the demoiselle who had been seated too close to the courtier stood up suddenly, her face crimson, crying with rage and embarrassment.

"How dare you, in my presence," said the queen, shooting a hard glance. "From this moment, both of you are banished from court."

"But, but *he* did it—" sniffed the woman.

"You should be whipped," said the queen to the little lady-in-waiting, and then turned back to the tall, dark-haired petitioner. "And now, oh yes, your *Dialogue of the Virtues.* Exactly the sort of thing I wish to encourage. How unusual, a woman, to write such an ambitious work. You have studied the classics?"

"A bit. And also natural history."

"Ah, yes," said the queen, her voice knowing. The occult. How charmingly she disguises it under an innocuous term. "Yes, unusual studies. I may want to consult you from time to time on your *natural history.*" As the young lady withdrew, to be joined by her duenna, a very large, gaudy woman, the queen turned to Madame Gondi, and said in Italian, "I never thought it would be so easy. Of course, she is concealing a great deal, but it is clear that she sensed my own spiritual powers. We who command The Beyond know each other. It is a feeling—a sort of *tingling* one cannot mistake. And how simple; she just wanted a place at court and a patron for her poetry. That's why she plays tricks with my lovely new coffer. A writer. Who would have thought that? Writers are always so vain, so easy to win over. A bit of praise; a purse or a medal every so often; the whip concealed—they crave praise the way infants crave sweets. So uncomplicated to control." She sighed, thinking of Cosmo Ruggieri. Now if only *he* wrote poetry, she'd have him firmly on the leash.

"Just think, Maddalena, not only do I have my coffer, Cosmo will be considerably more pliable, now that he knows she is its keeper, and the powers of this strange creation will always be at my service." Sitting on a low table next to a jeweled reliquary, an ivory statue of the Virgin and Child, and a bound copy of a manuscript on the sanctity of marriage, all of which had been offered to the queen that day, the silver-gilt box looked right at home. No one was seated close enough to feel the odd pulsating, sucking sensation, or to hear the vague humming sound coming from inside the box, the sound of a malicious mind, unbound by considerations of mortality or human ties, happily anticipating deeds of pure evil.

❧

Cosmo Ruggieri labored up the third flight of the outside staircase to his brother's rooms, following his nine-year-old nephew. In the leather wallet at his waist was a distillation of aconite, quick acting and guaranteed to be fatal. The thunder was rumbling at lengthier intervals as the storm receded, but still the last of the rain soaked into the black leather of his doublet, and he was growing out of breath.

"Father says, go in the back way, the man will be coming in the front any time now." The boy scratched softly at the back door, and Lorenzo's wife, in cap and apron, stealthily let her brother-in-law into the kitchen. The room was stifling, smelling of damp laundry and sausages. Beatrice offered Cosmo a seat, then put her finger across her lips as she pointed to the open door beyond one of the lines of diapers hanging to dry. The voices in the room beyond were clearly audible.

"She is still coy, in spite of everything you told me to do." Philippe d'Estouville's voice sounded irritated.

"Did you hire the poet I recommended?"

"I have sent her a rondeau, three sonnets, and a villanella, all very costly, I might add, and she refuses to meet me alone."

"Did you cast the spell under the full moon that I gave you?" Lorenzo's voice came from beyond the curtain of diapers. Stealthily, Cosmo took the little brown bottle of poison from his wallet and handed it to Beatrice.

"Put *this* in one of *those*," he whispered, pointing to several empty green glass vials on the table. All of them were engraved with the legend LOVE POTION in large, square letters. "But be careful not to touch it." Beatrice nodded quietly.

"I'll need a funnel," she whispered, and taking the brown bottle and one of the green bottles, she vanished beneath a sagging line of undershirts and children's stockings hung up to dry.

"Once under the full moon, and once under the new moon, for good measure," came the voice of the visitor from the other room.

"Oh, dear, then they've canceled each other out. Are you sure there's no other way to get her to marry you?" Lorenzo sounded brusque, professional. Beatrice reappeared from behind the line of shirts and stockings, and silently handed Cosmo the refilled bottle, nodding conspiratorially. As Cosmo inspected the little green bottle labeled LOVE POTION the shadow of a smile crossed his face.

"I need to be married quickly; we're going on campaign and I need a new breastplate and helmet in keeping with my rank. Monsieur d'Andelot is demanding my gambling debts. My tailor is even holding back on the delivery of my new velvet-paned trunk hose. I swore I'd have him horsewhipped if he held back any longer. You have no idea of the troubles that beset me! Her guardian is a fountain of money. If I can send her wild with love, and compromise her, she'll beg me to marry her, the quicker the better. I need that love potion. Have you mixed it up yet?"

"I think I have—let me check in the back room. But first, I do require payment in advance. Have you the cash?"

"I do indeed; what do you think of me?"

"Only that you are a gentleman, but that I am a poor commoner, and cannot live on promises the way men of rank do." Cosmo could hear the man jingle a purse, and then his brother appeared, ducking beneath the diapers.

"Do you have it?" he whispered.

"Here," whispered Cosmo, handing him the deadly little dose of highly purified aconite which Beatrice had decanted into the Love Potion bottle. It was of his own manufacture, a specialty of his, guaranteed to bring death in seconds. His brother nodded, Cosmo nodded, and Lorenzo disappeared behind the diapers again. Voices floated through the doorway.

"This will cause whoever drinks it to fall instantly and violently in love with the first person they see after waking up."

"Waking up? They fall asleep?"

"In a deadly faint. The main thing is to guarantee you're the one they see when they open their eyes again."

"I see, I see—but it might be difficult to manage. Her guardian is a ferocious old soul, and might lock her away from me if she faints."

"Oh, I see, you have to administer it in company—that will be difficult," said Lorenzo. "Usually a lover—well—administers it alone—and then nature takes its course, if you know what I mean. Then, you see, you've had your will of her, and she awakens full of love."

"It's a problem, but not an insoluble one; I must get an invitation to dinner, that's all, and sit next to her."

"That's it, that's it. Good luck, my cavalier. Soon you will be rich."

Beautiful, thought Cosmo, from his perch on the stool in the kitchen. She'll die, and he'll take the blame. It amused him to think of the noble Philippe d'Estouville fanning and mooning over a corpse in the hopes she would revive with love. He had only to find out when the dinner invitation was, and he could seize the box the very instant she was dead. A tiny twinge of conscience made a brief appearance when he thought that his brother might be discovered and suffer for his role in the poisoning. No bother, he thought. When I have The Master of All Desires, I'll just wish that Lorenzo won't be found out. And, after all, what's a brother for?

Fourteen

While Nostradamus was in bed tending his gout in the palace of the Cardinal de Bourbon, King Henri II was sitting in council at St.-Germain-en-Laye, and the question was war. The past summer's famine and the shaky peace treaty with Philip II of Spain had kept the armies of France quiescent. But now King Philip's battle chief, the Duke of Alba, had invaded the Papal States and the Pope had appealed to France to make good its pledges to him, break the treaty of peace, and send an army into Italy in his defense. But to honor France's pledge and break the treaty with Spain meant war with Philip, who was not only King of Spain, but Holy Roman Emperor and King of England through marriage. France would enter the war outnumbered and entirely surrounded.

Grave and polite, the king leaned forward in his tall, ornate chair that sat on a dais at the head of the council table. "My lord Constable, you have read the new report on the events in the Papal States, how do you counsel us to respond to the Holy Father's appeal?"

The Old Constable, that cunning old gray head, lord among lords, battle chief of two great kings, and a father with a not-so-secret need to get a Papal dispensation to wed his warrior son to Diane de Poitier's daughter, spoke slowly and with consideration, offering a clever compromise. "If the Duke of Alba's actions have broken the Truce of Vaucelles, then the honor of France requires that we send assistance. This will, however, throw us into a great war with Spain at a time of bad harvests and poor levies. But if Your Majesty declares that the Duke of Alba's actions do not constitute a violation of the treaty, then we are not obligated to go to war with the Emperor. This is the wisest course; we can then maintain the peace while sending the Holy Father financial aid to raise his own armies."

But the Guise brothers, the powerful Duke François and the Cardinal of Lorraine, whitened with fury at this suggestion. The great scar that ran across the Duke's collapsed cheekbone grew livid against the pallor, and with a flaming glance at his brother, he signaled silently that one of them must speak.

"Majesty," said Lorraine, his voice sly and politic, his narrow face impassive, "your honor requires that you mount an immediate expedition in response to the request of the Holy Father." So speaks the church, thought Montmorency, but he is first of all a Guise. Beneath a corner of the wide sleeves of the Cardinal's scarlet robe, the Old Constable caught a glimpse of a fist tightly clenched.

"If Alba does not withdraw immediately, Your Majesty must declare war or lose all honor in the eyes of the Holy Father, and of the world," said The Scar.

"Our honor is also pledged to keep the truce," said the Old Constable. "While we must aid the Pope, we must do it in a way that does not violate the treaty. We must send funds, not armies. Otherwise the Empire will make war on our northern frontier as well as the south. A two-front war, after a time of famine—"

"We must send an army," urged the Duke of Brissac. "The English Queen Mary is an old woman, her kingdom shriveled and wasted. She will not dare to offer much aid to her husband, King Philip. Then what can he do in the north? Nothing."

Constable Montmorency watched the king's face closely as the debate raged, and sensed the shifting of his opinion from the droop in the monarch's heavy-lidded eyes as he stared at his old counselor. I have lost, thought the Old Constable, who could feel his influence waning as if it were wine draining from a broken cask.

How long, how cleverly, had he held the reins of government by shielding the king from the baneful influences in his council. How slyly had he suggested to the king that he might be getting fat, and should let others make policy while he took exercise! But the council must meet, and the Guises, with their golden tongues and sly plots were two, while Montmorency was alone. Bitterly, Montmorency surveyed the weak-lings and egoists that sat at the council table. That wretched Antoine de Bourbon, lounging inattentively unless the war involved the retrieval of the Spanish half of his Kingdom of Navarre. Look at him, nodding and agreeing with everyone, stroking that miserable, thin little goatee in his fat, self-congratulatory face! Look at them all, the blind fools!

"It is my decision to send an army," said the king, "and since I am merely going to the aid of the Pope, I am not violating the truce with Spain. The Duke of Guise, our loyal servant, will command the expedi-tion into Italy. We must increase the levies, regardless of the famine." Guise. He has won the glory of command, the Old Constable thought bitterly. France will lose, but Guise will not.

"Majesty, blood cannot be squeezed from a stone, or taxes from the starving. We must approach the bankers of Lyons—the Italian bankers," said the Old Constable.

"And who has said so, my wife?" said the king.

"Majesty, we must ask their aid, and she is the best intermediary. Her counsel is not without value."

"I tell you, I do not want that woman interfering in matters of state! Do you not understand that wherever she gets the slightest opening, she *pushes in*? I will not hear of her involvement in any business of this kingdom. The throne of France finances its own wars. We will com-mand the city of Paris to provide more money—"

"Majesty, Parlement may oppose—"

"Parlement!" hissed the Cardinal of Lorraine, who was also, by order of the Pope, Grand Inquisitor for the Kingdom of France. "A nest of heretics! Every one a traitor! Would that I could hang every one of them—"

It is slipping beyond control, thought Montmorency. War, war on two fronts, and, if Lorraine is set loose on Parlement to batter the money out of them, perhaps even revolution and civil war, a war of reli-gion. And through it all, the Guises, rising like demons through the smoke; their house, their influence. It must not happen. I will outflank them; I will seize chaos for my own. My son has become a great captain, and once allied to Diane de Poitiers. . . .

As the Guises swept from the council chamber together, Montmorency, walking alone, heard behind him the Comte de Saint-Pol saying to the King of Navarre:

"Did you hear what I said? The king nodded in my direction. It is my advice that he listens to. A telling blow, I say—" And the voice of that self-centered flutterhead, Navarre, floated to him, saying, "Sound, sound. Your ideas have promise. Now, should war with Spain come, after our victory I will negotiate for nothing less than the return of Spanish Navarre to my throne—"

"The Empire, what are they? In battle, it would take a dozen of those decadent Spanish to be compared to one brave French gentleman—"

If the Spanish declare war, thought the Old Constable, I can undermine the Guises when peace is negotiated by arranging a marriage with a Spanish princess for the Dauphin in place of his marriage to that Guise girl, the Queen of Scots—no, all is not lost, not yet. It is I who will be master of the coming chaos. . . .

✤

In the dark, two heavily armed men were making their way through the narrow, muddy streets of Paris by the light of torches. The flickering light illuminated here an archway, there the painted and timbered fronts of buildings, their heavy shutters tightly sealed. It was the time of foxes and wolves in human clothing, the cutthroats, the burglars, the sellers of dead men's clothes and ruined women's virtue. But none approached the two men. The second, a burly old soldier, was a well-known *escrimeur* from the most vicious fencing school in the city. The first—well, he was not without reputation, either, and besides he had a mandolin on his back. There was clearly no profit in the pair.

"Here's the street. She lives around the bend, near the end," whispered the taller of the two.

"A very nice neighborhood," said the burly man.

"I told you; Alonzo is rich."

"When she opens the window, what then?"

"I'll throw her the note."

"But what if she doesn't open the window?"

"She has to, she must. What other hope does she have to escape from him?"

"But I hear something—look there, beyond the bend—all those people. Lanterns. And music—another serenader's got here before you, Nicolas—"

"Three viols, a lute, two hautbois, and a trumpet—and her window's opening! What an awful racket! I'll see to them! I'll drive every one of them into the river! By God, they offend the night with that caterwauling!"

"Nicolas, you're outnumbered—don't be a fool—they're all armed, and look, there in the shadows—you're not the first rival Alonzo's got—" Beneath the overhang of a neighboring building, three gentlemen stood waiting to see if the serenade would call out the beloved or the duenna. The window opened, and there she stood, a pale shadow, her white nightgown and cap luminous before the faint and flickering light of candles deep in the room. Nicolas was transfixed. Even his friend made an admiring sound. One of the strange gentleman outside stepped before the serenaders and began to declaim a poem.

"Not another word, you preening parrot!" cried Nicolas, pulling his sword, and handing over his torch. "The lady is too intelligent to listen to your cheap hired verses." The musicians stopped, astounded.

"What do you know of this lady, you whoreson?" cried the strange gentleman, discarding his poem and drawing his sword in turn. "Speak her name, and I'll spit you like a roast." Nicolas's companion extinguished both torches and reached for his sword hilt.

"She despises you, you featherbrained dandy!" cried Nicolas. There was the slither and clatter of steel, but the two were clearly outnumbered.

Just then, from inside the room, they were distracted by a strange screeching sound, followed by a woman's voice shouting, "Señor Alonzo! No!" and something else unintelligible. Both men looked up, to see a stranger's hand close the shutters with a bang.

"Now look what you've done!" cried the strange gentleman, but looking around, he saw no one but his own musicians and cronies. Nicolas and his friend had taken advantage of the distraction to vanish into the dark.

"She screamed. I know I heard her scream. And then the shutters slammed. It was Alonzo inside, taking vengeance, perhaps beating her—"

"Nicolas, I swear I heard the duenna call out to him, 'No!', when swords were drawn. She was calling outside. That cry was the demoiselle, fainting. It was the man below the window the duenna was calling. That was Alonzo himself there, with his serenaders. You nearly had him." But Nicolas looked grim.

"Or there's two of them. The despicable Alonzo inside and that fop outside. I swear, I'll follow her until I find out the secret, and I'll be back. With you, with the others. Are you with me, Robert?"

"With you all the way. We'll soak them all in the river."

"And Alonzo must die," said Nicolas. "My honor requires it."

✣

"War," said the Queen of France. "War with the Empire. And for what? For vanity!" The heavy, gilded door had just closed behind the Old Constable, leaving Catherine de Medici alone with two of her most trusted *dames d'honneur*. The queen was breathing heavily, and placed a hand on her heart.

"For three nights now I have had dreams of death, dreams of falling, dreams of blood. And in them I saw my daughter Elisabeth's face. Ah, God, it was as white as a corpse! What can it mean? What if we are not the victors in this war? The king, my husband, must go to Biragues, to Gondi, to Montvert, to the Italian bankers. Without money, all will be lost. I must beg him to listen to my dream of blood."

"But, Madame, the Constable said the Guises would not have him go to our Italians. What do they think we women know of war and finance? Even though you have the gift of prophetic dreams, they have made their plans and will not listen."

"Not listen! Not listen! The king, my husband, mocks my powers, which he ignores to his own disaster! And who does he listen to instead? That dried-up, ambitious, money-grasping old woman who dogs my every footstep! I cannot even escape her in childbed, or when I am sick! There she is, running everything, telling him everything, as if she were me, and I were nothing! And where is he tonight? In her bed! Listening to her!"

"Surely—"

"Surely as snow falls in winter, she is telling him what a great warrior he is, and puffing him up so that he will have no doubts that the plans of her relatives, the Guises, will bring glory to France, a new empire, carved from Spanish possessions. I know her—she's already planning her triumphal entry into Madrid! She's already hired poets to praise the victory, and painters to make her new banners! She eats at my vitals, that woman, and even the hairs on my head despise her!"

"Majesty, you must be circumspect."

"I tell you, I sent word about my dream, and the king, my husband said he was occupied with affairs of state and could not be disturbed. But his affairs of state did not delay his visit to the Duchess of Valentinois this very evening. Oh, the shame of it! He risks the throne of my son because he is under an evil spell cast by that demon-woman. I tell you, I can deal with the devil, too." She turned to her closest lady of honor, Madame d'Elbène: "Lucrèce, I want you to call a page this instant and have him bring that Demoiselle de La Roque and her magic casket back from Paris. I want her here today, before nightfall." As Madame d'Elbène pattered off in search of a messenger, the queen addressed Madame Gondi, her other companion.

"Maddalena, get my black candles and my linen robe. Tonight I will not be content with prophecy; I will change things forever."

"Ah, Majesty—"

"Why aren't you hurrying? Haven't I given my command?"

"But—if you could consult Nostradamus—you'd know how it would come out."

"Do you doubt my dreams? Didn't I dream a black, hooded figure stood over a double cradle during my last pregnancy? And when I bore twins, I knew that my dream was true, and that they were born to die. My dream is a true warning! Besides, Nostradamus won't be back from Blois before the end of the week. By then, they will be well on their way to breaking the treaty. No, it must be tonight. Tonight, I will overcome the duchess's evil sorcery with The Master of All Desires."

✣

On our return from St.-Germain, Auntie had taken a lease on commodious rooms in a house on the rue de la Cerisée, convenient to the nicer district of the old Hôtel St.-Pol, where so many people of distinction now live. The location had brought out her long-buried passion for a life in society, and she hunted guests with the avidity of a tiger. But in one thing was she adamant: Philippe d'Estouville would receive no invitation.

"Let's see, on Tuesdays we might bring together a gathering of choice wits—"

"But, Auntie, why not M. d'Estouville?"

"I don't like him. He smells wrong to me. He will cause you nothing but grief—"

"But the poems, and the serenades—"

"Rank or no, he's much too conceited to be capable of true love—he's not good enough for you, Sibille. He'll just use you and discard you, as I'm sure he's done before. By God, if I knew that drunk who chased him off last week, I'd send him a bottle of his own choice—"

"But, Auntie—he seems so sincere—"

"Sincere, bah! So was my brother—now, let's see—for the Abbé, we must be sure to have a naturalist or two—let's see—yes, a free dinner always flushes out the poets—we need several, as a proper setting for you, as soon as—*oof*—this dreadful gout fades out a bit. Théophile, my dear cousin, I feel a spa trip coming on. Enghien, perhaps not as distinguished as Évian-les-Bains, but so very convenient. And the water—so agreeably sulphurous."

✣

All the plans had been made for the spa, and the horses had already been harnessed when an unkind wind blew in the first gray clouds. "Rain," said Auntie, surveying the sky as she put one hand out the window. "I felt a drop. I absolutely refuse to travel in the wet. It will make my gout so much worse that even the spa won't touch it."

"Surely, my dear cousin, you are premature," said the Abbé, but Auntie sent down word to put her litter back in the stable, and before we had even half unpacked, the gray wisps had turned to rolling black, with a hint of distant thunder. By the time we had taken out the *jeu de dames,* a waterfall was thundering down the gutters and battering the shutters.

"You see? I was right. My left knee always tells me when it will rain. Jump there, he's left a piece with a space behind, don't you see it?" said Auntie, peering over my shoulder.

"It's a trap, Auntie—see there? The Abbé is lying in wait for my piece like a wolf—then he can jump here—and here—"

"Cousin Sibille, how inconsiderate of you to spy out my plans—" There was a pounding on the door, and Arnaud showed in a boy and two soldiers of the king's guard in heavy cloaks, dripping wet, their boots and breeches mudstained with hard riding. The boy was a page we had seen in the queen's household.

"The queen commands that the Demoiselle de La Roque be brought into her presence today, and bring with her a certain coffer that she has in her keeping. She said you would know what coffer that is."

"As indeed we do," said Auntie. "But you must dry off and have a little something. This is not a fit day to travel without a bite to eat."

"Madame, we would be pleased to accept your offer, but we must ride more than two leagues before nightfall. Once Saint-Germain is sealed after the king's *coucher,* the Pope himself wouldn't be allowed in. It's been delay enough getting fresh horses from Les Tournelles—we must go—ah, I see the demoiselle is ready—" As I stuffed the silver-gilt box into its traveling case, the Abbé said:

"My dear cousin, what about the game?"

"Save the board as it is—I'm sure I'll be back in no time. And remember, I have an excellent memory—"

"Sibille, take care," said Auntie, as she pressed me to her effulgent front. "Promise me—"

"Madame, the Queen's own *dame d'honneur,* Madame Gondi, will have charge of her at the palace. And the Queen has commanded that we ourselves escort her back by tomorrow evening," said the page. But as I descended the steps, I could hear Gargantua, confined upstairs against his will, howling.

We took the empty streets at a fast trot, muddy water splashing everywhere, rain slashing at our faces, the only respite the brief pause beneath the city gates. Once past the walls and moat, we pushed the horses to a canter wherever the road looked reliable, cross-country away from the dark waters of the swirling river. Heavy mud clods flew from the horses' hooves, and as the rain let up, we were no drier, for we passed into forested lands where the trees spilled water from their leaves as we passed.

The light was almost gone when we at last spied, among the shifting dark clouds, the towers of the old castle glowering from above us on the bluff. Trees and outbuildings had become black shadows, and already the first trembling candlelight could be seen in the windows of King Henri's new château, built in the modern style beneath the black bulk of the old fortress.

"Thank God the gates are still open—the Queen would accept no ex-cuses." The boy shuddered, but I did not know if it was just because we were all soaked to the skin.

The Swiss guards were already in the courtyard when we entered, preparing to seal the gates, and lighting the four torches that were to burn all night in the corners of the court. The rain had stopped, but there was the distant rumble of thunder in the half-dark. The boy took my arm, so I wouldn't stumble on the slippery wet, uneven paving, for we were on foot. Only members of the royal family were allowed to enter the court on horseback or litter. Inside, the archers were already deploying on the staircases, and valets were lighting the torches to illu-minate the narrow stone passages, the long public halls, and the stair landings for the night. Palaces at night are like cities, with crimes and blood and secret whisperings in the dark corridors. Worse, perhaps, for in a palace one expects less evil than in a city alley. A palace must have its Swiss guards and its archers no less than a city its night watch.

The boy led me to an ornate, sealed door, where a lady-in-waiting an-swered his knock, dismissed him, and led me inside.

"Good," she said, "you arrived in time. Just hand me the coffer, and I'll send for a maid to dry you off."

"I can't give it to you, I'm afraid. The queen herself commanded that I never put it in anyone's hands but her own."

"I am pleased," came a voice from the depths of the room, and I saw there a short, plump figure in a white robe, standing beside a little table laid out like an altar, with black candles in silver candlesticks burning at each end of it. "I see you are loyal, discreet, and true to your word. I could wish for no more. Now give me the coffer." I took the coffer from its traveling case. The candlelight shown and flickered luridly across its surface. I hate this thing, I thought, as I gave it to the queen. I wish I were rid of it. You *could* wish for it, came the hidden voice of Menander in the depths of my mind. And the way you work, you'd give me my wish by killing me, I answered, just as silently, as I handed it to the queen. Of course, came the secret voice of the thing—that's how the others got rid of me.

But the queen had put the box on the altar between the two black candles, and though her back was turned to us, I could hear her chanting in some unknown language just like a necromancer in some drama. After that, she threw open the lid of the box. The lady beside me caught her breath and shuddered at her first sight of Menander. Somehow he looked more revolting than usual this night, his skin more like a viper's dead sheddings, the brown teeth of his ghastly, mummified mouth more like fangs, and his gangrenous eyes exuding pure evil. He knew that he had a victim, and that victim was a queen made reckless with desire and capable of anything, even selling her soul. I felt sick to my stomach, and the clammy cold of my wet clothes made me shiver.

But the queen spoke in a forthright voice, without a quaver. "At last," she said. "At last your magic is mine, O deathless one. And tonight I will do a great deed, one that I have long craved."

The lady-in-waiting beside me turned away, closing her eyes and covering her ears as the revolting object in the box moved as if to speak. At last the dead thing spoke in a rusty, thin voice, as if from another world:

"Great Queen, command me," said the undying head of Menander the Magus.

Carefully, firmly, Catherine de Medici repeated the words engraved over the catch of the open box:

"By Agaba, Ornthnet, Baal Agares, Marbas, I adjure thee. Almoazin, Membrots, Sulphae, Salamandrae, open the dark door and heed me," said the queen.

"Speak your desire," said the head, and the aroma of things long rotten rose from it.

"I, Catherine de Medici, wife of the great Henri the Second, son of the mighty King Francis the First, command and desire that the influence of the Duchess of Valentinois over my husband shall be taken from her and cease forever."

"It is done," said the Master of All Desires. "Time will show you the truth."

"At last," said the queen, taking a deep breath. "I will have my heart's desire, and the means to secure my son's throne. From the Spanish—and from the Guises. All with one simple wish." As she closed the box, she turned to me. "Seal this thing up again and take it away—oh, you are wet. Maddalena, take the demoiselle away and have her dry by the fire; get her nightclothes and a bed—it will not do to have her catch a mortal fever. I am pleased to find the demoiselle a loyal servant." As I was bundling up the box, she asked suddenly, "Demoiselle, why have you not confided any of your desires to this magical box?"

"Majesty," I spoke, shivering, "it is because I am afraid."

"Ah," she answered. "That is because you are not a queen."

✢

That night I lay awake in my borrowed nightgown and cap, listening to the breathing of the other two ladies-in-waiting in the bed, unable to sleep for the terrifying dark that lay clustered inside the bed hangings. I thought I could hear Menander's soft and sinister breathing from his box beneath the bed, and then his voice, a whisper like dead reeds rattling in the winter wind.

"You should kill yourself. It would be easy. Just rise and jump out of the window." My heart began to pound. What was this new trick of Menander's? Wasn't hounding me to make wishes enough to satisfy him anymore?

"It would be far better for me if I were to belong to a great queen, instead of to a nobody like you. How much grander my scope, how much greater my conquest of souls. Who are you, an ugly old maid, to possess such a treasure as myself? You make no wishes, you acquire no grandeur, and what is more, your poetry is despicable, a joke. No one likes it. Rise and go to the window. You would be better off dead." In the dark, tears squeezed out of my eyes. He was right. Why didn't I? But something solid in me stood apart, watching, and said to me: Menander can't get you to wish yourself out of the way, so he wants to drive you to suicide. He sees how much more evil he could do if he belonged to the queen instead of you. I won't listen to you, you dried up piece of bacon in a box, I said to him in my mind.

Oh, but you have to, said the secret voice of the Magus. You won't let me go, so I won't let you go.

Menander, you're nothing but a cheap social climber.

If I can't have your soul one way, I'll have it another. Rise and go to the window.

I won't, I answered, grubbing the tears from my eyes with my fist. Then I pulled the covers up tight around me and began to make a noise in my head to drown out Menander's voice, the hideous temptation. In my mind, I sang the psalms of Marot, noisier and noisier. At the sacred words, I could hear the diabolical little thing shriek, then go silent. Outside, in the real world, the breathing of my two bedmates was as steady as ever. How long was it we wrestled there, in the mind's dark, until I fell asleep, exhausted? Perhaps minutes, perhaps hours, but it seemed like eternity. And I knew that now my nights would be full of struggle and horror, until such a time as either I or Menander the Undying had perished. Each night, every night. Nostradamus, said the observer in me. You must see Nostradamus again. He has the answer.

✤

The next morning, at her levee, the queen dismissed her flute player, and while Madame de Saint-André handed her her chemise, she had Madame Gondi read her an unusual dialogue on virtue from a slender volume, professionally hand-copied on vellum, and bound in very handsomely tooled morocco leather.

"Clever, that remark the Demoiselle de La Roque has put in the mouth of Athena," said the queen, as her hairdresser fussed over her elaborate curls. "This work seems ever so much more brilliant than the

poems, which are rather ordinary. It's quite original, too. Read again
that section on the sacredness of marriage, where Hera speaks. I like the
sentiment." The queen was unusually calm and peaceful this morning,
but she noticed that Madame Gondi's hand shook as she turned the
pages back. *She is not fit to be a queen either*, thought Catherine de
Medici. *Her nerves are too weak. Kingdoms are lost by the weak-
nerved, and then the winning prince slaughters the heirs. That is what I
learned in Florence, when the enemies of my family tried to hang me
from the city walls for cannon practice. Machiavelli, who wrote for my
father, what does he know of these truths? He scratches with his quill,
and understands only with his mind, but I, I know these things in my
heart and my stomach as well.*

"'—and for that reason marriage is ordained as a holy sacrament—'"
The queen looked about her at the richly tapestried room, the ingratiating servitors with hidden hearts and veiled eyes. *Any one of them could
strike from behind. To be a queen is to be different from other people:
the stakes of the game are higher.*

"'—and as children born of affection are more beautiful, even so
those of married affection are superior even to them—'" read Madame
Gondi, her voice somewhat quavering. There were dark circles under
her eyes, and her skin was ghost white. Her sleep had been filled with
nightmares of the mummified head that spoke.

"Stop reading awhile, is that where Hera rebukes Aphrodite?"

"N-no, it is the part after, where the Archangel explains true Christian marriage—"

"These are elegant sentiments—I find it not an embarrassment that
this little work is dedicated to me. The first printing shall have my official patronage. I think, perhaps, I will drop hints that I have in mind a
reading at one of my afternoons, and perhaps a debate of ladies on some
of the major points. That ought to redouble the demoiselle's devotion
and loyalty to my person, don't you think? My, what's wrong—do you
have a fever like she does?"

"N-no, Majesty—it's just a little draft." *Good Saint Maria, Holy
Mother, I'll give up playing with enchantments and good-luck charms
forever*, Madame Gondi was saying in her mind as the horror of last

night overwhelmed her again. I swear to you, Saint James, I'll go on a pilgrimage and buy myself a hair shirt. Just keep that dreadful thing's curse from me—

"Good. Fernel assures me it's nothing, but I've sent one of my own little home remedies that is absolutely sovereign for fevers—the plaster of rose leaves and hens' eggs that worked so well for the Queen of Scots's last illness—" Three ladies were lacing up the queen's gown behind her and attaching her ruff with pins. When at last they pinned her headdress and luminous silk veil—the exact shade of yellow of her petticoat—on the hairdresser's work, the queen turned to Madame Gondi. "What do you think of the plan of extending to her the promise of a husband of rank? I believe it would seal her to me forever. It is perfect: as guardian of the coffer, she takes all the risks, but I have it at my service whenever I want it. Don't you think it's just right?"

"Oh, Majesty, what man of rank would take a woman so old without a great fortune? Why, when you were married at fourteen, not only were you an heiress, but you were at the height of your own great beauty, and the demoiselle is already looking a little dried out, in my opinion."

"Ah, my dear friend and matchmaker, that is where I count on you. Find me a man who is in disgrace, who would do anything to gain my favor, or a man with confiscated property but of sufficient family—or, you know, a man of of inadequate rank who wishes to rise and an expendable younger son who must make his fortune—" The queen swirled her hand in the air to indicate all the sorts of men who could be acquired cheaply. "Make me a little list, Maddalena."

"Any particular age?"

"Oh, anything will do. Just so he's compliant, bought with very little, and grateful to me alone. Perhaps I will set her a choice. It really doesn't matter; they can live apart if they don't like each other—ah, who is that in the outer chamber that I hear? What a dreadful commotion—tell him I cannot see him. I have letters to write this morning, and do not want to be interrupted."

But the man in the antechamber twisted free of the guards, and ran into the queen's bedchamber, where he flung himself at the feet of the queen, right where she stood in front of her own canopied bed. "My queen, my queen," cried the man in black leather as he wallowed on the carpet, "do not, I beg you, make a mistake that might cost you everything."

"Cosmo, you pest, get up. How did you find out that the demoiselle has come to me and brought me my *little box*?"

"I tell you, it is accursed, accursed," said the man in black leather. "It brings only ruin in its train."

"And exactly what is your point, Cosmo, since it was you who first proposed to get it for me?"

"It is a danger—a terrible danger—if it is not handled by a professional. Why, just the wrong word, a careless wish—"

"Oh, so that's what you're after, Cosmo. Well, I'll have you know I am not unskilled in these matters myself. I thought of how to do everything I want with one wish only, and that most carefully worded." The astrologer, now on his knees, gasped.

"Then it's done? What was it?"

"And why should I ever tell you? I know what you want. A monopoly over my little box, knowledge of my secret thoughts, and a hand in all my business—I have better arrangements in mind. And other wishes, too."

"Great queen, I beg you, do not sully yourself—let one skilled in the Art—"

"Say, Cosmo, are you still unmarried?" said the queen, looking at him with new, assessing eyes.

"Start your list with him," said the queen, gesturing to Madame Gondi, who put down the slim volume and took pen, paper, and a little box of sand from a drawer in the queen's own desk. Laying the sheet out on the desk, she dipped the pen into an ornate inkwell supported by a trio of cupids, and scratched across the top of the blank page: "Cosmo Ruggieri, 43, short and dark."

"What is this?" said Ruggieri, newly alarmed. In his service to the Medici, he had seen many a list, drawn up by the stars, drawn up with secret, suspicious glances. Enemy lists, death lists.

"Why, I was thinking you might like to ally yourself to a fine old

French family, with perhaps a bit of money and a title thrown in." Beads of sweat stood out on Ruggieri's forehead, and his eyes searched frantically for an exit. It was inherited, this trick of irony, he thought, this sporting with the doomed. And now it had come out in the Duchessina at last. Why him, why him? Now he had to have that coffer. He had to wish himself off the death list that the queen was drawing up so casually as her ladies selected her jewels.

"Ha! Just look at him run!" said the queen.

"Are you sure he should be—?"

"Oh, perhaps not. After all, why put the box into his hands through marriage? Think of someone else. Somebody useful to us, who needs to be tied to me more closely—an ambitious man, who knows how to be quiet—let's see—what about the banker, Montvert? Is he married still? No? What about a son or a nephew?"

"I think there's a son."

"Good, list him, too. And get me a few others—I'll let you know when I think of any more—"

✤

It was a decree of King Henri II that made fencing schools, those gathering places of riffraff and tradesmen's sons, illegal within the walls of Paris. But in a disreputable alley off the rue St.-Jehan on the Left Bank, at the Sign of the Black Boar, there is a long room behind the tavern from which the clatter of swordplay may be heard. If a grizzled old *escrimeur* from the time of King Francis just happens to be there, and if students and farriers' sons just happen to be practicing self-defense, and if money just happens to change hands—well, it is nobody's affair. The owner of the Black Boar, who seems to have a hearing problem, has no idea where all the noise comes from, although rent and customers for his dreadful wine and cheap beer seem to emerge regularly into his tavern through a low back door behind the casks.

Through this dank cavern of drinkers, a tall figure moved briskly, threading his way through crowded tables and drunks lying on the hard-packed dirt floor.

"Holà! It's Nicolas the Italian!"

"Nicolas, I thought you weren't coming in today!"

"Nicolas, how's the lady? Still cold?"

Something curious happened to Nicolas's posture as he walked through the room toward the *salle.* He no longer slouched, half lounging, as he did in his father's house, but walked as straight as a lance, his pace quick and collected, his glance fierce and bright, like an eagle's. This was his place, the place where neither mother nor sister would ever dare to pray and mumble over him and call him a lost soul. This was the place where the hours he'd wasted all over Europe were not wasted. This was the place where hardened ruffians saluted when he laced on his heavy leather plastron and took up the practice foil, tipped with a big ball of cork to prevent putting out the eyes. Nicolas Montvert was a do-nothing dreamer. But Nicolas the Italian had cheerfully abandoned stud-ies of law, philosophy, and theology at several distinguished Italian universities in the pursuit of the maestros of fencing in the new style, in lounging, practicing, and quarrel-picking among the best. As a result, he was an extraordinarily competent rapier fencer in the Italian style, still a novelty in Paris, and not at all bad with rapier and dagger, rapier and cloak, or even the old-fashioned sword and buckler. His father wouldn't have recognized him in Maestro Achille's fencing school. And if he had, he would have been horrified.

"Speak my lady's name, Jean-Claude, and you're a dead man," said Nicolas, but his voice was cheerful.

"Now, now, just joking. Will you be available for practice today? The *botte* you showed me, I'm still slow—"

"Not today, I've just come to see Achille."

"Does he still owe you that two crowns, Nicolas?"

"Just as sure as I have a bill at the Four Elements," said Nicolas.

"A drink, then—stay with us awhile—"

"I can't—business—" Nicolas vanished through the door behind the casks.

"You know what business that is?" said one of the drinkers to another as soon as he was out of earshot. "He follows some lady of the court all over town like a sick calf, trying to get the opportunity to speak to her."

"*Nicolas?* Surely, any woman should fall at his feet. He's good-looking, his father's rich, and he's a damned fine fencer. That ought to be enough for any woman—"

"Not this one. I've *seen* her, Jean-Claude—she's very refined—tall and snooty. Stuck-up family—writes poetry—and there's a man with a title after her. Some rich Spaniard, he says."

"A title? Poor Nicolas—he hasn't got a chance."

"Oh, I don't know about that. I've never seen him more determined."

"Determined? Knowing him, then, his father must have forbidden it."

"Haw! You're right there! Want to make a bet on the outcome?"

"Nicolas, five deniers, odds, two to one—"

✤

His gout temporarily mended, Nostradamus and his servant set out on a pair of bad-tempered royal post-horses for the Château of Blois, where the royal children were being raised in isolation from the latest infection at court. Despite the agreeable air of the fall days, and the beauty of the lazy green river whose banks he followed, he found the trip disagreeable. The innkeeper at the Three Kings in Orléans overcharged him, and a dish of boiled tripe that had tempted him at a local tavern had given him dyspepsia. Then Léon's horse threw a shoe near Beaugency, and even the display of the queen's orders did not hurry the stubborn local blacksmith. Standing at the door of the thatch-roofed smithy, surveying the boats passing languidly by in the river beyond, Nostradamus resolved to make no more trips, no matter who commanded him. Lauricus did his horoscopes by mail, after all, and nobody bothered *him* to ride bad horses and get dyspepsia and deal with dense-minded smiths just to get an entirely inadequate fee.

His resolve redoubled itself when he presented himself to the guards in the courtyard of the château and was told that as a servant, he must enter up an obscure back staircase. Only after a great fuss, and several messages sent back and forth to M. de Humières, the children's governor, did the word come that in this case, and this case only, was the celebrated Maistre Nostredame allowed to mount by the great octagonal stair. As Léon, laden with books and instruments, puffed up the steps behind him, Nostradamus appeared lost in deep philosophical speculation, his lips moving silently in some mysterious formula. If the awed servants and hangers-on could have heard the mystic words, they would have heard: "not worth it, distinctly not worth it, definitely not worth it. Waste of time. Blasted stairs. A man never gets any peace."

After a conference with M. de Humières and the inspection of the queen's order for horoscopes to be drawn for all of the children, including the Queen of Scots, Nostradamus found himself assigned to a room with an obscure view of part of the roof of the chapel nave and a half-dozen curious pigeons, where the bed was of a despicable lumpiness and the candle was not beeswax but cheap tallow, the kind that always gave off a smell that gave him a headache. Never again, he resolved. Even to save France. France can be saved by mail.

The following morning, much fortified by a really excellent breakfast that included rolls agreeably light, a delicate little dish of smoked fish, and butter fresh from the churn, he set about the task of inspecting the Children of France for their brooding, anxiety-laden mother. Servants, gentlemen, and women of the household, and Monsieur and Madame de Humières themselves crowded into the long, blue-painted *salle* to watch, along with several large hounds, three dwarves, one bearing a pet parrot, and a lady with a white ferret on a silver-mounted leash.

But when François, the heir to the throne, was brought before him, the shrewd old doctor's stomach suddenly felt like lead. The truth shrieked at him through the pulsating, confused aura of the crowd that surrounded the boy. In the gray, shivering air around the throne heir he could read madness, sickness, and then death, and not in the distant future. Inspecting the child's body closely, the signs were there, even for a man who was no mystic. The mother must read them, he thought, and the world tells her she is wrong. That is why she has sent for me. She has to know, and yet she cannot be told. The thirteen-year-old Dauphin was undersized, the head bloated, the eyes dull with stupidity, the face eaten with some pustular disorder. As he watched, the boy wiped his runny nose on his sleeve.

"Do the ears run, too?" asked the old doctor.

"A cold; it is nothing," answered the Dauphin's governor. But Nostradamus had caught a glimpse of the boy's front teeth as he snuffled. Notched. The family was doomed. What madness, what destruction would these tormented, damaged, children wreak before their inevitable end? The Italian disease had tainted the lineage of the Valois, and these undersized, sallow-faced children were the result. What philandering ancestor had blighted these innocents before their very conception?

How long, what form would the disease take before they died in agony? The mother knows, thought the old prophet. In her heart, she will fight against fate until the very end. She will plan, scheme, struggle to make them what they are not. They are all she has. And I, as I value my own cozy home, cannot be the one who tells her that what she sees secretly is truth. "This boy is destined to be a great king," he intoned, and the ladies all nodded, and there was a buzz of conversation in the room.

One by one he inspected the throne heirs, four boys, each worse than the next. After thirteen-year-old François, came six-year-old Charles, with a ratty, narrow little face and malicious eyes that reminded the old man of an infant Caligula. Ah, here was another—pretty, but something twisted within his soul. She thinks this one, Henri, is normal, the old man thought. Then there was the infant, Hercule, with the telltale big head and even uglier features. There was a girl, Elisabeth, with an elfin face and intelligent eyes, but marked all the same, and a younger daughter, Claude, already twisted and crippled. Then a baby girl in leading strings, merry and flirtatious. Barren from birth, said her aura. No man will ever get an heir from her.

Ah, but here is the exception, said the old man to himself, as he was introduced to a tall, titian-haired fourteen-year-old, with a rose-and-white complexion, and clear, sparkling eyes. The Queen of Scots, the intended bride of François, the Dauphin, is whole, and well formed. I see in her the Guise blood, brightened by the ruddy-gold strength of the Scottish line. No wonder the king favors her. He thinks her health will renew his line. "Too late," sighed the voice of Anael in his ear, but the old prophet dissembled, told them all a glorious future awaited, beamed and bowed at the crowd around him, then spent much time ostentatiously taking notes in a shorthand of his own invention that none could decipher. And all the while, a voice echoed in his inner ear, the king will have no other marriage for his son, no matter what anyone says, and from this marriage will flow the sorrow that will rend France to the bone. War and death, brother against brother, the Guises trampling their enemies to be trampled in their turn.

❖

"So tell me, Anael," said Nostradamus to the angel of history, "what if a cruel future hinges on the life of a pretty little innocent? What would happen if I spoke the truth?" It was night, but the shutters of the prophet's little room with the bad view were thrown open. Six stars, no, eight winked down at him from above the dark shadow of the roof opposite his window. Anael sat on the windowsill, his shadowy blue body with its twinkling lights only slightly lighter than the night sky. A single candle illuminated the complex diagram of a horoscope beneath Nostradamus's hand. He made a series of notations at one corner, near the sign of Mars, then set down his pen with a sigh.

"You mean, could you abort history?" Anael grinned, ruffling the feathers on his raven-black wings. "You? A mortal old man? You don't need your divining rod to know the first thing that would happen is that someone from one of the factions would murder you."

"Are you implying that my silence isn't purely moral?" Nostradamus had been up too late, finishing all those horoscopes, and when he'd sent to the kitchen for a little snack, there wasn't anything left and they sent word the fires were out. As a consequence, he sounded rather testy.

"Oh, don't get so huffy. It's just mixed, like all you people make." Anael lounged there, his legs crossed and swinging, looking so content with himself that it irritated the old prophet even more.

"Well, if you're so perfect, why don't you make history better?"

"Not my job. I just keep the cupboard. Besides, it doesn't matter what any of us do at this point. A big thing like a religious civil war—why, it's like water rolling downhill. You can't stop it; it's going to go by one path or another, so you might as well leave things alone and get out of its way."

"Was there a time it could have been stopped?" Nothing interested Nostradamus more than a serious philosophical argument. He cheered up at the prospect of debate.

"You mean, by assassinating someone like M. Calvin, who is not half as attractive as that pretty little Guise girl?"

"We—ll, I didn't say *that*—"

"Or perhaps you had in mind going back farther, M. Luther, for example? I assure you, sooner or later, that old, corrupt institution would have cast up its own ruin—"

"Well, what about the corruption then? Couldn't that have been stopped? What about the inventor of the plenary indulgence?" Anael laughed, and Nostradamus brought his fierce eyebrows together in a frown. He felt he was, after all, of an age to be taken more seriously. Sometimes he forgot that to an immortal like Anael, he was hardly newborn.

"You think only one person would have had a bright idea like that? The seeds were there. When something is ready to be corrupt, it's ready to be corrupt—"

"Yes, yes, like water running downhill, you've already said that," said Nostradamus, irritated at being condescended to.

"And besides, just think of the art and beauty all those indulgences purchased. Would the world be better off without them? The rose is most beautiful just before it decays, you know. And all by means of a transfer of funds from the artless and gullible to the artful and crafty— who's to say that isn't appropriate—"

"Anael, you are the most profoundly amoral creature I have ever encountered—"

"You expect History to be moral? Michel, I never expected your depths concealed such shallowness—" There was a timid knock on the door, and Anael concealed his tall, graceful form among the shadows in the corner opposite Nostradamus's candle.

"Come in," said the prophet, wishing it was his snack after all, but knowing better, all at the same time.

Two little girls in nightgowns and caps, all wrapped up in heavy, furry *robes de chambre,* stood in the doorway, while behind them stood their governess, Madame de Humières, with her gray hair in a night braid beneath her cap, the lady of the castle that he had met that day in the great *salle.* Behind them were four sturdy armed guards, two of them bearing torches. A conspiracy, thought Nostradamus. They shouldn't be up at all, let alone here, but he was touched all the same. He fussed and smoothed down his gown and tried to make his table look a little neater. After all, if one is the object of a child's secret night adventure, one must live up to the part.

The youngest of the little girls had the big brown eyes and receding chin of her mother. Tight, dark curls peeped from beneath the white ruffles of her nightcap. It was the little Valois princess, Elisabeth, daughter of Queen Catherine. With her was her taller, older friend, with whom she shared a room and a big, canopied bed. The unmistakable titian hair flowed in two heavy braids over her shoulders, her porcelain complexion had turned pink with excitement at their daring nocturnal excursion. Mary, the girl-queen of Scotland, who had not set foot in her homeland since infancy. They stared at the instruments and charts he had laid out on the table. Mystery and magic, that's what they'd come to see. Strange vessels, with imps sealed in them, perhaps. Nostradamus could tell he was a bit of a disappointment.

"Maistre Nostredame, we have come to know more about our futures," the little dark-eyed girl spoke up boldly. Nostradamus, with a gesture, had swept away the chart he was working on, just in case one of them might catch a glimpse of the figures on it, and be able to decode any of them. On it was written the future the stars had ordained for the auburn-haired girl who stood before him: widowhood, exile, betrayal, imprisonment, and execution. All of it unfolding in the shadow of her uncles' ambition, from blood heritage, just as surely as disease was the inheritance of the dark little pixie-faced girl who stood beside her.

"Yes, we want to know about our lives when we are queens; what palaces we shall have."

"And our jewels; will we have splendid ones?" Nostradamus sighed, and they took it for impatience.

"We will reward you when we are great," said the auburn-haired girl, her tone very grand and condescending, as if imitating someone else.

"We would not have come so late, but they said you were leaving soon, maybe tomorrow," added the dark-haired one.

"It's quite all right," said the old man. "Just don't give the others the idea, will you? I'll read your fortune in your palms. Stand here, by the candle, while I look first at yours."

"No, you must look at Mary's first. She is a born queen, and father says she must go first in everything, even through doors."

"Very well then. Hmm. Hum. Yes. You shall be a queen of two realms." Above her head he saw hovering the black-hooded shadow of the executioner.

"Two, not three? I am queen in Scotland, shall marry France, and in-herit England." Her assured little voice resonated in the silence.

"No, not three. The signs say two. But you shall beget a line of kings—and . . . and you shall excite the passions of men wherever you go."

"Oh," sighed the girl-queen. "That will be splendid." Not if you knew how selfish and how full of hatred some of those passions shall be, thought the old man to himself. Damn that Menander for making every prophecy an agony. How he laughed when I made my wish, and how cruel wisdom is.

"Now my turn," said the dark-haired eleven-year-old, extending her little palm.

"Ah, what interesting lines," said the old man, pretending to pore over them. "You shall be a very, very great queen, with closets full of splendid dresses, and more and greater jewels than you could wear in a lifetime—the riches of a great empire." Her chart lay rolled in a drawer of the desk before him. He intended to revise it sufficiently to please her mother in the finished version. In it, he saw the bleak, ornate palaces of the Spanish king, marriage to a loveless old man, the frigid stares of ri-vals, and, young, so young, poison.

"And will I be the mother of kings, too?"

"Of daughters, my dear, but you will not regret it. You will be so beloved by your people they will call you the queen of peace and bounty."

"Is there more?" said Elisabeth, who was very clever and her mother's favorite, for she had caught an unusual look in the old man's eye.

"Why no, nothing more," said the old prophet. "That's all the lines say, except that you are a very intelligent young lady, and good at your studies."

"But I knew that already."

"Exactly, which is why I don't have to tell you," said Nostradamus. When the girls had made their farewells, he saw Anael stretch himself in the corner, then fold his arms and snort.

"Change history, ha! You haven't the heart to blot out anyone. You haven't even the heart to tell those two little girls they will be murdered."

"What would it do for them? Nothing but steal whatever pleasure they can find in their days," said the old man, his voice sorrowful.

"And so you hide your predictions in code. Can't bear to tell, can't bear not to tell. Has anyone told you you're an odd bird, Michel?"

"A large number of people, Anael. Oh, God, how ignorant, how accursed I was when I craved to read the future."

"It's all your own fault, you know."

"Yes, and knowing it only makes it worse." He sighed. "I was young, I was foolish, I was crazed with a lust for the mysteries of the East. But at least that damned mummy in the box didn't belong to me. And I was fortunate indeed that somebody stole it from its keeper in Constantinople before I had a chance to make another wish."

"And so you were saved from yourself. But really, I should consider your regrets an insult. Is it that bad making my acquaintance?" said the Spirit of History.

"No, Anael, it's had its points. But tell me, how can we get rid of Menander the Deathless before he destroys France?"

"Really, Michel, you are transparent. Do you actually think repairing history is as easy as that?" The angel grinned, showing lovely, even, white teeth, and unfurled his raven wings, so that their glistening feathers shone iridescent in the candlelight. Nostradamus heaved a great sigh. "Don't be so downcast, old mortal. I'll give you a hint. It's in that girl's horoscope."

"Her? The little queen?"

"No, the girl whose godmother poured hex powder into Menander's box."

"Her? Her dog ate my slippers. I never want to see her again." The angel shrugged his shoulders, and the little twinkling things inside his dark, translucent body whirled and danced.

"Have it as you will. Slippers or France," he said.

"Well, if you put it that way. But, Lord above, what irritation! The social climbing, the chattering, the snooping, the *know-it-all-ness*. And that awful poetry—did you know she sent me a villanella of her own composition? The rhymes—ugh—they put my teeth on edge."

"The horoscope, Michel, don't forget," said the Angel of History, as he faded from view.

Fifteen

Monsieur:

   This Saturday, the 29th of November, 1561, I received your letters sent from Paris on the 12th of October of this year. And it seems to me that your letters are full of spleen, quarrel, and indignation that you have against me for I know not what reason. You complain that when I was in Paris paying reverence to Her Majesty the Queen you lent me two rose nobles and twelve crowns, which is right and true.... As for writing me that I left Paris ungrateful for your hospitality ... it is totally outside my nature. As for my fine reward I had from the court, when I got sick, His Majesty the King sent me a hundred crowns. The Queen sent me thirty, and that's the lovely sum I got for having come two hundred leagues and spent a hundred crowns—thirty crowns. But that's not the point: after I returned to Paris from Saint-Germain, an honorable great lady whom I did not know came to see me ... and told me that the Gentlemen of the Justice of Paris were coming to interrogate me about what methods I used to make my predictions. I said ... that they needn't bother, that I planned to return to Provence the next morning, and I did.... But you'll think that with all these words that I write that I intend to put you off without paying. Not so. I send you in this letter two little notes, which, if it pleases you to deliver them, I am sure that your money will be repaid promptly....

Excerpts from a Letter of Nostradamus to Jean Morel
Fonds latin No. 8589, French National Library

"Another cushion, Léon, before I perish of the Cardinal's luxury." Having returned to Paris from his trip to Blois, Nostradamus had settled himself into the overwhelmingly large, dark, carved wooden chair, entirely devoid of comfort, which was provided in his room in the Cardinal de Bourbon's palatial establishment. Nostradamus's days as a houseguest were beginning to pall; the food and company were excellent, but the open, high-ceilinged stone rooms, so chill and drafty, the constant annoyance of strange servants, the busy carved faces of grotesques and beasts that peered at him from every piece of malignant, hard-edged furniture made him long for his own cozy house, his sweet-tempered wife, and the joyful sound of his own children. Then there was the matter of his books, from which long parting annoyed him, and the nattering of the ignorant, who hadn't yet paid him enough to return his loan to the trusting Maître Morel. "Don't let a soul in; I want to finish the dauphin's horoscope."

"I thought you'd finished it already," said Léon, looking at the mass of annotated papers that lay on the lion-footed table before the large, ugly, hard-edged chair in which the old prophet sat.

"I did. This is the new, improved version. I need the queen's fee to get home, and I see no reason to put her gratitude in jeopardy."

"In short, you are taking out a fatal illness and substituting a period of great risk—"

"You presume upon your long service, Léon. The dauphin will be the greatest king in Europe once he has passed the period of great risk."

"Exactly," said Léon, settling another cushion behind his master's back, and rearranging the footstool for his gouty foot. "Will you be wanting your dinner brought up to you here?"

"Of course. But no more cream sauce. It unsettles my digestion." As Léon departed, Nostradamus dipped his pen back in the inkwell and wrote, "In his seventeenth year, the Lord Dauphin must give up hunting entirely if he wishes to pass by a period of great risk successfully." It's just as well Léon can't read, thought Nostradamus, or he'd throw me off with his snickering. We both know well enough the dauphin will never give up hunting. . . .

There was a rustle and a snort of amusement behind him. Without turning his head, Nostradamus said, "Anael? You should be ashamed, snooping like this. I didn't even call you."

"I told you, Michel, I go where I want."

"*Doctor* Nostradamus, please."

"You call me by my first name, I call you by yours."

"You have other names?"

"Of course. Dozens. And titles, too. I'm just not vain, like *some* people."

"Always, criticism. A man can't get anything done without someone offering irritating suggestions—"

"—or snickering at the sight of the great Prophet doctoring a horoscope for money to get out of town."

"Go away, you pest, and come back when I call you."

"Oh, I wouldn't think of it. You wished for the spirit of prophecy, and you *get* the spirit of prophecy, my own self, whether you like it or not." Here Anael nodded his head mockingly and made a flourish, as a gentleman would when introduced. But somehow it did not look the same when the gentleman had no hat and plumes, or even any clothes, and, in addition, filled the entire space from floor to fourteen-foot ceiling. "Besides, I was feeling a bit of that ennui of eternal existance, and something amusing is going to happen, so I dropped in." Nostradamus, who had studiously evaded the angel's gaze, in order to avoid giving him any additional satisfaction, now glanced up from his papers and realized that Léon had left the door open. In the door frame stood the gawky, tall, bony figure of the most annoying, pretentious poetess in the whole world, clutching a package tied with a fancy ribbon to her bosom. Oh, God, thought Nostradamus, an entire package of poems, and I'm probably expected to read every one of them. But she was standing stock still, not saying anything, for once. And suddenly the prophet realized, she is seeing Anael. He is not invisible to her.

"Um—I didn't realize you had a guest," she said, inspecting the towering, raven-winged, unclad figure. "I'm sorry, Monsieur—ah—Anael, I believe—I will return when you have finished your toilette."

"Oh, no, don't go just yet," said Anael. Addressing Nostradamus, he added, "You see? There's someone who knows about polite address."

"And just how did you know Anael?" said Nostradamus. "And how did you see him?"

"Oh—I often see—things" she said, still rather wide-eyed with shock. "And I do *read,* you know." She hesitated. "Monsieur Anael, dark blue, very good-looking—the Angel of Venus—" She blushed. "I didn't know about the little twinkling sparks. Like the night sky. And they move about—" While she was distracted by staring, the prophet suddenly came to himself, and covered up the draft horoscope with some blank paper, then weighed it down with a book and his inkwell.

"Have you brought that—hound of yours?"

"I know you don't like Gargantua, so I left him at home."

"And the interfering aunt?"

"She's having the furniture rearranged in a nice little apartment we've just rented. It's really not so far from here. I've brought you—"

"Just leave them here," said the defeated prophet. "I'll read them later. You haven't gone and dedicated them to me, have you? I simply can't have that—"

"It's—it's your slippers. We had them made up from the old ones—exactly alike—" Nostradamus suddenly felt very mean and small when he noticed her eyes had started to swim. "My father never liked them either—but I thought—the queen said they were very admirable, and M. Montmorency, too, especially the one I wrote about you—pardon—" She wiped away a tear and shook her head so that no more would come.

"Do sit down here, Demoiselle Sibille," said Anael, sitting his huge figure on the big, canopied bed that stood in one corner of the room and patting the place beside him. "Not everyone has every gift, you know. And your prose dialogues have many passages that are very sharp and witty. I know many consider them your best work."

"You think so?" she said, hesitating to sit down.

"Absolutely," said Anael. "The secret of being truly admired is to write where your strength is. You need to know who you are before you take up the pen—" Sibille looked at up at Anael's vast, shadowy bulk, and her face seemed troubled.

"—and you should try history. I've a knack for that, myself. I could help you out, there. Michel, you are a rude oaf. You never even offered the lady a seat."

"Oh, umph, so sorry. Don't know what I was thinking about. Don't mind sitting next to Anael. He may not be clad in the fashion, but he's very mannerly." When Sibille hesitatingly sat down next to the immense, bare figure, Nostradamus noticed that she carefully arranged her hem to conceal her generously sized feet, and he felt sorrier than ever for what he had let slip. There is nothing sadder than an old maid who knows it, he thought.

"I thought—perhaps—this was the time for my Art to be recognized— I mean, my readings have done so well, and even—you don't suppose it was all that horrible Menander's doing, do you?"

"Have you made your wish?" said the old doctor, horrified.

"No, but half the world would do it if they could get at him. The queen keeps me close by, and you wouldn't believe who courts me for a peek at him. I was thinking—maybe—some of it was sincere. But I guess he was right. It's all flattery."

"What do you mean, he told you? You mean Menander? And where is he, anyway? I thought he followed you about. He should be materializing about now."

"Menander told me that he was giving up on me until I realized that the only way I wouldn't turn out a lonely old maid was to wish for a rich, good-looking husband. And then he said he had better people to associate with—"

"Better people?" The old prophet could feel the hair standing up on the back of his neck.

"A man broke in and stole him two days ago, and I've heard the Duchess of Valentinois has him now. It's been such a relief, even if the queen *is* frantic. He—he talks to me at night, you know, and I can't sleep. He—he says if I won't wish, at least I should get out of his way, because he has much more important people to belong to than me. And just when I'm happiest, he'll come back and spoil everything—"

"Demoiselle Sibille, don't you realize he's just working on you?" said Anael.

"I know, but it hurts anyway."

"He always works on weak spots," said Nostradamus. "And, being

deathless, he has all the time in the world to do it. You shouldn't underestimate how sly and nasty he can be."

"That's what Auntie says, and she says I should be happy in order to
spite him, but he steals all my pleasure. He's worn me out 'til I hardly
feel like living."

"And he will keep it up until you've wished, and he's stolen your
soul into the bargain. It is clear that if he can't have that, he'll try to
wear you down until you perish. Your will must stay powerful! Sages
and seers have given in, but *you* must withstand him!" Nostradamus felt
himself aflame with indignation, with sympathy, with the desire to defeat Menander the Deathless at his own dirty game. He never noticed
Anael's quiet smile as he spoke.

"First he said my pretty new dresses were unbecoming, and then
they looked all plain and dowdy to me. Then he told me I was ugly anyway, and I didn't want to look in the mirror anymore, because every
time I did, all I could see was a flaw—my nose, this eyebrow, a pimple—
you know." Sibille's face was pale and sad. She smoothed the wrinkles
out of her skirt, looking down as she spoke.

"Then I thought, well, at least I'm healthy, and he reminded me that
health never lasts, and the most sinister diseases start with the tiniest
signs. Now every time I get a cold, he says he knew someone who died
from it, and then I feel worse than ever. When I became popular and
got invited to the queen's cultured afternoons to read, he said it was all
flattery because they wanted to get to *him* and they were laughing behind my back.

"Then, I swear, Maistre Nostredame, I could hear whispering behind
me wherever I went, and I could never hear anyone say anything good
or kind without listening for some hidden slight. But still I didn't wish,
you see. I didn't wish for beauty, I didn't wish for eternal youth and
health, I didn't wish for everybody to admire my writing—I was strong."

"I see, I see. You've held out longer than anyone I've ever heard of—"

"Then M. d'Estouville came to pay court to me, and hired men to
play viols and lutes beneath my window. Can you imagine? The most
handsome, dashing man I've ever met! Rank and fortune, and admired
by my brother and my father! I was ecstatic! Menander sat on the
cupboard and gloated that he was only after the money Auntie was

going to leave me and told me exactly how many debts he has, and how his rich uncle is too healthy to die just now—" All true enough, thought Nostradamus, who had drawn up the dashing M. d'Estouville's horoscope.

"You see? Auntie won't have Philippe in the house because of it, and even you know it's true," said Sibille. "Then when I decided that at least I had my Art, Menander told me it was awful, and I've lost all my inspiration. My muses have flown, and I'm going to die of starvation in an attic and they won't find my body until it's mummified, just like he said—"

"That's nonsense!" said the prophet.

"I said so, too. I have Auntie, I told him. And he said she only bought me from father to spite him, and my own family didn't even love me, so what did I expect—"

"Your father *sold* you?"

"Well, in a manner of speaking. He let Auntie adopt me when she offered to pay his debts. Don't you think a father who really loved me would have said, 'Never!' or perhaps maybe just loaned me for a while? It's all so awful, you see—and when I told that awful mummy that the great Nostradamus said I had an important future, he said you were a quack—"

"That does it!" said Nostradamus, leaping up in such a fury that he forgot to favor his bad foot. "I swear, I'll see that wretched piece of garbage in a box destroyed if it's the last thing I do!" He pounded with his fist on the table, and the lid rattled on his inkwell. "Take heart, Demoiselle! Do you think I can read so little of the human essence that I think you will end as he said? That evil, sneaking, creature takes speckles of truth and distorts them until they are huge stains. He works on your will, and he has had a thousand years to learn how to do it! Can't you see what he wants? If he drives you to despair, you'll take your own life and he'll have your soul without even having to do the work of carrying out a wish! It's nothing but a new game for him! After all these centuries, he's bored, and this is the way he amuses himself! But I, the infallible Nostradamus, will draw your horoscope entirely gratis, without charge, and show to you that all his evil prophecies are false! Quack, indeed! I'll grind that despicable Menander into dust!" The old prophet was so furious the arteries in his neck stood out and his hair stood on end, and he never even noticed Anael's broad, triumphant smile.

❧

That morning Nicolas Montvert had awakened from a dream that his father stood over his bed, lecturing him on the virtues of early rising, the expense of the waste of candles in late nights, the expense of the education and travel showered upon him, all of which was wasted, his advancing age and failure to show himself responsible, and he was, in the dream, just preparing to answer, "But I don't *want* to be a banker," when his eyes popped open, and he saw his father, his somber silk gown, gold chain, and flat hat, his long beard wigwagging over him even as the words,

"—shameless waste—your grandfather is turning in his grave—your mother weeps—even the angels weep—sloth is one of the seven deadly sins—"

"Uff, oof," said Nicolas, who was deeply entangled in the sheets.

"—and pretending to be asleep, it is insulting! How many burdens must an old man bear? Soon I'll be in my grave, and you will be the cause of it, yes, you, your ingratitude—"

"I'm up, I'm up," said Nicolas. His hair was sticking every which way, and the previous late night had left dark circles under his eyes.

"I want you to survey accounts with me, then this afternoon I take you to meet the keeper of the queen's household accounts, you have no idea the time I've waited for this appointment; you should be grateful for such an opportunity—"

"I am, Father, I am. I swear I'll be there—what time?"

"And *where* are you going, that you are dressing in such a hurry?"

"Ah, um, to mass, father. I—I've been feeling a need to worship in a more wholesome fashion, more profoundly, lately—"

"Weekday mass, and not Sunday mass? Oh, I am a foolish old man, to believe you once again—go, go—ah, God, God, how does it happen in a family that one child gets all the virtue, and the other collects sins like loose dog hairs?"

After all, it's a kind of worship, said Nicolas to himself, as he walked through the narrow streets of the Marais, emerging at the rue St.-Antoine, and found himself, almost without effort, at the doorstep of the house on the rue Cerisée. This doorstep, it's the altar of Venus. Every day, Sibille's beautiful foot touches this doorstep. And today— today's the day my watching will pay off. I'll discover the identity of the wicked Spaniard and then, why, I'll insult him, and cause him to chal- lenge me, and when he's dead on the field of honor, it will erase the stain—

At that very moment, the door opened, and his heart gave a leap when he saw it was her, her alone, her without the litter, the duenna, the huge, slavering dog, the lackeys. On foot, in a plain, dark cloak, clutching a mysterious package to her bosom. Carefully, she looked both ways, and assuming the street was empty, sped away with swift and determined steps. Taking care to stay on the shadowy side of the street, Nicolas followed as quickly and quietly as a cat—no, a tiger, or perhaps a lion—well, he followed swiftly, while deciding on a suitably becoming image for himself, finally settling on a gigantic, silent, slither- ing serpent. This time, the Spaniard will not escape me. But suppose it is the second lover she is meeting clandestinely? One or two? Well, what does it matter: I'll challenge them both, and fight them on succes- sive days, he thought. It will make me famous. He imagined her old, sun- ning herself in a convent garden, and someone saying, "*Her?* The famous double duel of Montvert was fought over her?" and then the answer, "But, my dear, that was long ago. You cannot imagine her beauty in those days. But all wasted. After the victory, the Chevalier Montvert refused ever to speak to her again on account of her dishonor, and here she has been since, simply numb with grief for fifty years."

But he had hardly got to the best part of his daydream when she passed the Swiss guards at the courtyard gates of the Hôtel de Sens and when he tried to follow, they most rudely demanded his standing, and his business there. Quickly it an through his mind: what could he say? Nicolas Montvert, Philosopher and Observer of Life? Nicolas Montvert, quarreler in student taverns through half of Italy and France, hanger-on with the rogues at cheap fencing studios, and author of an as- yet-to-be-published treatise on *The Secrets of the Italian Art of Fencing?* Nicolas Montvert, banker's son, but no banker? None of it was a worthy enough description of his special and higher relationship to the ordinary run of mankind, the glorious but unspecified future that he intended for himself. I need a title, he thought sulkily, as he lurked by the gate, waiting for her to come out again. I need something grand enough that I don't get turned away from courtyard gates by hired Swiss guards, like some peddler of trinkets.

✣

Then he noticed he had a fellow lurker, a dreadful figure of a demobilized soldier in filthy old rags, quite drunk even early in the day. He's the sort that gives a bad name to people who lurk for legitimate purposes, thought Nicolas. The sinister man was also eyeing the gate, watching the visitors, priests, merchants and petitioners go in and out, waiting for somebody. A hired bravo, decided Nicolas. I've run into enough of them here and there. How desperate—or how well paid—to attempt an assassination in broad daylight. A woman with a tray of meat pies came by and the lurker bought one, and as he munched, Nicolas remembered he hadn't had breakfast, and this led him to a contemplation of his father's extreme stinginess, which had left him entirely without funds for a similar purchase and this in turn led him to ponder how misers never end well, and just as he was imagining his father on his deathbed repenting, and begging forgiveness from his long-suffering son, who was reduced to a pitiable human skeleton, *she* came out of the gate, looking unhappy, and without the package.

"Demoiselle Sibille de La Roque?" asked the sinister fellow, blocking her way. Then she nodded, looking puzzled, and everything happened at once.

"*This* from the Sieur Villasse!" cried the man, raising his arm, at the very moment that Nicolas leapt upon him, sending the object in his hand flying. As the shower of vitriol spewed harmlessly between them, acid drops ate unnoticed into his sleeve, while Sibille screamed, "My hand! My hand! Oh, God, it burns!" and Nicolas hammered the assassin's head into the cobblestones shouting, "The Spaniard! Tell me where he lives or I'll kill you here! Who is Señor Alonzo?" and the Swiss tried in vain to claw them apart. "Insanity! No, a fit! No, a murder attempt!" cried the strangers who began to run to the struggling mass of bodies.

"Assassin!" he cried, as they separated him from the ragged man. Behind him, someone was saying, "Oil of vitriol—it's everywhere— look at it eat into the stone—" while behind him he heard his beloved screaming.

"She's fainting, the demoiselle is fainting!" he cried, turning and scooping her up. "Quickly, where is a doctor?"

"No—no—don't touch me—my arm, my hand—" she cried, shaking all over. "Water, for God's sake, water!" But then she looked up and saw Nicolas. "You! You've been following me again. But I saw you—you knocked his hand away—"

"You're burned—you've lost your mind—quickly—we must have a doctor—" They were inside the gates now, and swarms of people were running up.

"You are acquainted with the demoiselle?"

"Her cousin is my best friend—" A tiny exaggeration, justified by circumstances.

But Sibille was crying over and over, "It's burning—it's burning! Oh, bring water! Help!" Someone splashed water onto the hand she clutched to her, wetting them both, but not stopping the terrible burning as skin and flesh dissolved. "It still burns, Jesus, it's burning me away!" There were cries and the sound of footsteps as servants ran into the vast old building to find aid. Then there was a tap-tap-tapping of a malacca cane, but the sound was lost in the general commotion.

"We have to cut away the sleeve, Demoiselle, here, into the bucket, yes, the whole arm—" Nicolas found himself kneeling on the hard stones of the courtyard, supporting in his arms the body of his Divinity as an old man in a doctor's gown dipped her burned arm in a bucket of water mixed with wood ash to neutralize and wash away the searing acid. He could feel Sibille's pulse, he could feel her breath, which came in quick gasps, and he could feel her tremble.

"He was aiming at my face—my eyes—"

"You are lucky," the doctor was saying. "Léon, more water, and stir in plenty of wood ash—we have to dissolve every trace away or it will burn deeper. Lucky that he missed, lucky that I know that water alone will not stop oil of vitriol's evil work."

"We have the man, Demoiselle," said one of the Swiss. "This fellow here saved you."

"Ah, yes," said the old doctor, looking directly at Nicolas. He had a beard almost like Nicolas's father, but somehow it didn't quite look the same. The eyes above it, that was the difference, perhaps—they were shrewd with understanding.

"Sun in Leo," he said. "You'll do nicely."

"Wh-what do you mean? A fiend has tried to throw oil of vitriol on the demoiselle, and you are telling me my birth sign?"

"Young man, I am Michel de Nostredame."

"The *astrologer?*" Nicolas could only gape. Did that mean that Sibille had not been on an assignation, but consulting a *fortune-teller?*" How terribly weak-minded. A flush of relief and disappointment—for the famous double duel had blown away like smoke—washed right through him. But Maistre Nostredame was busy saying:

"—and you really should not walk home unescorted after a dreadful shock like this. Have this young man take you home, and greet your aunt for me. Remember, water and wood ash, should the burning recur, and then a poultice of honey and eggs, to make the scarring less—keep it very clean, the skin is gone—but even so you are fortunate—the hand and arm are saved—"

But now the archers had come to remove the attacker, and the crowd departed to follow the better spectacle, the howling prisoner who was proclaiming his innocence. "The effrontery of that criminal," Nicolas heard one of them say.

"Ha! What fool hired a drunk to throw vitriol? He missed," said another.

"Probably the idiot paid him first, and he got drunk before the job."

"*And* she can still see, so she can identify him—"

As Nostradamus's back receded from them, Nicolas made his heart-felt plea: "Ma Demoiselle, do you see where all this has gotten you? Leave this terrible life, leave that despicable Spaniard—"

"What Spaniard?" she said.

"Oh, don't play the innocent. I know all, but I forgive. But you understand, I cannot with honor pay my addresses to you until I have killed him."

"Killed who?"

"The one who has led you into this dreadful life, the one who debauched your innocent beauty, the odious Señor Alonzo—"

"Señor *Alonzo?*" she said. "When you come home with me, I'll introduce you to him—" How could I have so misjudged him? She was thinking. I thought he was a trailing pest—another fortune hunter. But no, his was real devotion, and he was sent by God to save me, a miracle— and, and—

All the way to the rue de Cerisée, one word he had spoken resonated in her mind, mingling with the pain, the confusion, the sorrow and shock. It grew bigger and bigger, and it threw an even bigger halo around the tall, dark-haired young man who escorted her, one arm protectively about her shoulder. It hyphenated the sorry "Montvert" with a dozen noble chivalric lines, and made his bony, intense face handsomer than that of Apollo.

The word was "beauty."

✤

It was almost midnight, and Nostradamus's candle was burned down nearly flat. Léon was snoring on the trundle bed that pulled out at the foot of the great, canopied bed that stood against the wall. Servants had quit stirring and hustling in and out through the doors of the room, which served also as a corridor in the curious old palace, and even the mice had at last gone to sleep. But the old prophet was still up, doggedly struggling with a horoscope that contained many crossings out and several ink blots representing pure frustration.

"Still it doesn't come out, Anael," he said, consulting a little volume of astronomical calculations. "It's driving me mad. Look, here is the hour and the birthdate she gave me, six o'clock in the morning on February eleventh, and here is the character and the future, and none of it fits that girl, or what I read in her aura, in the least."

"*Hmm,*" said Anael, folding his arms across his bare chest. "I see what you mean."

"You don't see at all. You're not even looking," said Nostradamus.

"You forget. I don't *have* to look in order to see things," said Anael, sounding superior. The old prophet grunted, and went back to work.

"Just look at this, just look. According to this, she is a frail, sensitive, poetic girl destined to die two years ago, before she reached her twentieth birthday, in childbirth. And here she's a great, healthy horse who isn't even married."

"She does, however, consider herself sensitive and poetic."

"Her poetry is awful, and as for her sensitiveness—well, she has the skin of a dragon when it comes to pushing herself into places she doesn't belong. And all the while she carries on about being a tragic, drooping lily, she conceals a sarcastic wit that could grace a comedy on the stage. It's all pretense, Anael."

"Maybe she lied about her birthday. She's a little sensitive about her age," observed Anael, in a tone of false helpfulness.

"No—I know from her aura she was telling the truth, at least this once. She said she checked it with her godmother, just to make sure," said the prophet, running a hand through his hair until it stood almost upright on one side. Anael chuckled. The prophet rolled back his sleeves so the ink wouldn't stain them and fussed again with the chart. "It's almost as if she's *trying* to be the person that this horoscope describes," he muttered to himself. "It just doesn't make sense."

"Perhaps you should sleep on it," suggested the Angel of History.

"You know I can't sleep in this awful bed. The pillow—it's stuffed with very cheap feathers, not good goose down like my own. It gives me bad dreams. All night, I see riots, death, and the war of brother against brother. I could hardly wish for worse nightmares. If I weren't waiting for the queen's payment, I'd have left yesterday—no, before yesterday. I didn't like the quails at the table yesterday. Tough, bony little things, and the sauce tasted tainted. I've been bilious ever since. And these northern cooks just don't understand the value of garlic."

"Just because they don't chew it raw, like the Béarnais—" But the great Nostradamus had fallen asleep over his papers. Anael leaned over his unconscious form and blew out the guttering candle.

❧

"—so you see," Auntie was saying, "although we possess several items from his treasure, the original Señor Alonzo, being an old enemy of my husband's, is at the bottom of the ocean, but Monsieur Tournet bestowed his name on my darling little creature, here, who was for many years a poor old widow's only consolation, especially since she had such an arrogant and ungrateful brother. Here, sweetie," she clucked, as she offered the monkey another piece of candied orange peel. "Just look at his dear little hands, such tiny fingers!" Señor Alonzo scrambled up the curtains to perch on the rod and make one of his horrible grimaces at my brave, heroic rescuer, who was blushing with becoming modesty and trying to excuse himself as he edged toward the door.

"A monkey," he was mumbling, "a monkey—and you're her godmother—I—I have to leave—business—"

"And just what business is that, Monsieur Montvert?"

"Ah, um, I have to join my father at four o'clock sharp at the Louvre—an appointment—very important—"

"Why, it's nowhere *near* four o'clock; it isn't even noon yet, and I'm sure you haven't eaten." It is a good thing Auntie had words enough for two, because after all the turmoil, I couldn't manage to say a thing. My words had just dried up in favor of my sight, blessed sight that he had saved, so that I could the better behold him. And I just couldn't see enough of *him.* Why had I never noticed before the charming way he left his shirt unfastened beneath his doublet, the lace trailing carelessly at his neck? Why hadn't I appreciated his simplicity in shunning a tight, formal ruff, and carefully oiled and combed hair? How could I have failed to notice his arm and delightful brown eyes, at this moment filled with some unspeakable emotion, or his long, aristocratic hands—surely from some elegant descent on the non-Montvert side? Yes, simplicity, insouciance of dress—how they become a truly handsome man, one of noble spirit, such as my rescuer.

"But—um—I have to change—my clothes, ah, yes—change clothes—" He looked uncomfortably about him. His eye seemed to fix on one of Auntie's more lurid tapestries, the *Judgment of Paris*, with three naked goddesses.

"Oh, your poor sleeve—just *look* at those terrible holes! Vitriol is wicked, wicked stuff—I'll have my tailor take your measure and send you an entirely new doublet and shirt, as a token of my gratitude— are you sure you can't stay to dinner?" Auntie didn't seem to notice anything amiss at all—with him, with me. How could she not hear the loud thump-thump of my heart in the embarrassed silences of our conversation?

"Do stay," I managed to choke out. How delightfully rakish his hat looked, perched over one eye like that. What a delicious angle his jaw made as it rose to meet the cheekbone—was that a beautiful blue vein I saw throbbing at his temple?

"You—you'd have me, even after—after—Señor Alonzo—I made—such a misjudgment about your reputation?"

"After what? After you saved me. Saved me from the terrible vengeance of Villasse—"

"Villasse," he said, losing his crimson color and straightening up. "I will find him and kill him for this. I will call him out, and destroy him on the field of honor." A beautiful lightning glance, like a bold eagle, lit up his face.

"I beg you, Monsieur Montvert, leave him to the king's justice. His creature will confess everything and you will not have to sully your blade," said Auntie.

"That's the coward's way," he mumbled.

"Monsieur Montvert—in how many affairs of honor have you participated?" asked Auntie.

"Well—um—none—well, not the formal sort—ah, as yet," he answered. "But—but I know a great deal—I've traveled—the new Italian *bottes*—"

"I have known Villasse for half a lifetime—he's old, but malicious. In his youth, he survived a number of duels, mostly by trickery. Do you know once he secretly oiled a spot on a dueling ground, and drove an opponent across it? No one ever placed the blame on him. He's as sly as a serpent, that one, and if you're the one who calls him out, he will demand the choice of weapons—"

"Still, I can't in all conscience—"

"But of course, we can discuss it over the meal. You must be terribly hungry, after all you have done for us, quite without a thought for yourself. Such gallantry! Surely you would not deprive us of your company—"

"If the demoiselle w—wishes—"

"Sibille," I managed to say. "You must call me Sibille—"

"If Sibille wishes—" Silently, I nodded.

"Well then, take my darling's arm, and escort her in, will you? I do believe the hour has come." All I remember is that I nearly fainted at his touch, and for the life of me, cannot recall a word of the conversation or any of the dishes.

✤

"Are you certain this is respectable?" asked the Duchess of Valentinois. She was standing before the fireplace in a handsome antechamber in her lovely, white towered palace at Chenonceaux, the gift of her doting lover, the king, the envy of all who saw it, especially the queen. The marble mantelpiece was ornamented with carved and painted HD's entwined, for Henry and Diane, the walls were hung with exquisite tapestry, and on a squat, ornate table, rested a silver box, engraved with strange antique symbols and a rooster-headed god in a flying chariot. Outside, the cool, green waters of the Cher rippled beneath the piers of the great gallery, the sky was that divine, chilly blue that can only occur on the most perfect days in autumn, and the leaves of the forest beyond were just beginning to lose their summer green. In the distance, the calling of hunting horns echoed through the woods as her party of guests rode ever farther from the château.

"I assure you," said Simeoni, a tall, gaunt magician in a shabby black robe, "this Menander was of noble descent, although of his own people. A kingly descent."

"Oh, then I'm certain it must be correct. So many of these relics are of nobodies—hanged criminals, dreadful little shopkeepers, beggars of some sort or another. I don't wish to be revealing my secret desires to some—ugh, *peasant,* you understand."

"Oh, lady, I would never even dream of suggesting such a thing to one of your illustrious ancestry and refinement of taste."

"Well then, Master Simeoni, let us proceed. Do I open it up, or does the repetition of the magic words cause it to open by itself?"

"I will open it, but you must promise not to be shocked." The duchess nodded her assent, then drew back when she saw the wrinkled, mummified head in the box.

"Oh, it's all dried up! How dreadful!" she cried.

"No more mummified than yourself," said Menander, opening one of his leathery lids and rolling a hideous, living eye at her.

"Really, Lord Menander, for decency, perhaps a bit of cucumber cream for those dreadful cheek creases," said the duchess, her tight little mouth prim. "I am shocked that a person of your standing would let himself go like this." With a white, manicured finger, she pressed a stray wrinkle from her lushly embroidered oversleeve.

"Get on with it, you silly woman," said Menander. "I suppose you want eternal youth."

"Certainly not from *you*," replied Diane de Poitiers. "Since you hardly have attained a desirable state of preservation of your own complexion. You really should try a bit of my rose oil on those crow's-feet. You've let them get *entirely* out of hand."

"Simeoni, I will revenge myself upon you for this," said Menander in a low growl.

"I beg you, Madame, make some allowance for Lord Menander—he is, after all, nearly two thousand years old."

"That really is no excuse for such—ugh—poor personal maintenance," said the king's mistress, "but still—I suppose—well, he is not French, after all, and therefore can't really understand refinement—yes, I can understand—"

"—and you must consider the company he has been in lately," said Simeoni, thinking desperately of ways to salvage his fee.

"Well, then, it is entirely understandable. That dreadful little queen from the foreign pawnbroking family—nouveaux riches like those awful Gondis, that dismal poetess—you are entirely forgiven, Lord Menander, since you have suffered."

"I should hope so," said the mummified head in the box, with an irritated sniff.

"Very well then. Simeoni, you tell him what I want."

"Madame, I cannot do that. You have to recite the magic words yourself, and then speak the wish directly to Prince Menander."

"If I must. Let me see—they're written here. 'By Agaba, Orthnet, Baal, Agares, Marbas, I adjure thee, Almoazin, Membrots, Sulphae, Salamandrae, open the dark door and heed me.'"

"Speak your desire," said the hideous head, in a voice that whispered like the dust in old tombs.

"I, Diane de Poitiers, Duchess of Valentinois, command and desire you, Lord Menander, to prevent the queen from ever gaining influence over King Henri II of France, no matter what kind of magic she uses."

"It is done," said the head of Menander the Deathless. "Time will show you the truth." His living eyes glittered evilly, and for effect, he caused a dark cloud to fill the room, and a smallish bolt of lightning to surge through it with a *crash*. Simeoni fell to the expensive carpet, groveling in fear, but the Duchess of Valentinois tapped her narrow, musk-anointed, silk-shod foot and said:

"Really, how common. My rose oil, Menander, and avoid vulgar effects. It will bring you a better clientele."

"Who do you think you are, talking to me like that? I'm not your *hairdresser!*" shouted Menander, as he snapped his box shut and faded from the table, leaving a singed place on the varnish just out of spite.

I had best leave the country for a while, thought Simeoni as he tucked the Duchess's fee into the old leather purse at his waist. He had heard about the queen's wishes on the magician's grapevine, and although he could hardly predict that Sunday would come next week, he had suddenly had a great surge of understanding come upon him, and in that awful moment, had figured out how Menander the Deathless could make both the duchess's and the queen's wishes come true at the same time with a single dreadful event. If I'm gone, he thought to himself, they'll blame someone else. No use ending up like Guaricus, now. Sea air, and maybe that post with the Duke of Urbino. They'll do old Simeoni good for the next year or two. These French just don't appreciate a first-class astrologer, anyway. The following week saw him already beyond Orléans, traveling the dusty road to Toulouse and points south, mounted on a heavy-laden old yellow nag and trailed by his servant boy on a donkey.

❧

"Let's see," said Auntie, examining the spread of the *tarocchi* that she had laid out. "The lovers, the sun, all excellent—except for this one here, crossed by the Queen of Swords—I just don't like her in this position. But there's really no question. Nicolas is the one for you, Sibille. It's perfect."

"The cards approve, and I approve, too," said the Abbé. "He plays an excellent game of checkers. Passion never lasts, but you can play checkers forever. Wily, that boy. Did you see what he did to my king last Thursday? Now hurry up and finish that game, Sibille, I want to regain my honor."

"Can't," I said. "Nicolas has me in a corner, here, and I must fight my way out. Besides, it's not nice to talk about people behind their backs." We were hunched over the checkerboard, and it was the end game, all kings on both sides, and neither of us was giving any quarter. Time had been going by in an enchanted haze, since Auntie had given him permission to call every day. We read poems, he played his mandura and we sang duets, and warred at checkers, where we were merciless with each other. When we were close, our hearts beat in the same rhythm, and when we were not together, we felt as if we were missing half of ourselves. "Aha! A jump! Too bad, Nicolas!"

"You've fallen into my trap! Jump, jump! Good-bye two kings!"

"But now—just look—" The Abbé wandered over to inspect the board.

"Well, well, both of you are stuck now. I call it a draw. Yes, it's a draw, definitely. That's the problem with you two. Too evenly matched."

"And well matched, too. Nicolas, I have a plan to arrange for a go-between to speak to your father. I'm sure I can make the terms attractive for him. All this nonsense about sending for some foreign bride—it just won't do. You must explain to him that my darling is a woman of virtue, that you are properly chaperoned, that there is a handsome dowry. Surely, he will relent when he realizes your happiness is at stake."

But Nicolas looked devastated. "Oh, Madame Tournet. Every time I even hint about a French bride, he says Frenchwomen are shameless flirts, that a French wife will only make a fool of me and give me a set of horns, and that he knows best. Then he shouts about the Bastille, or sending me off to my cousins in Genoa—what shall I do? You know there will never be any bride for me but Sibille. I'd rather die than live life without her."

"Hmm," said Auntie. "This is a problem. If you elope, your father will never forgive you. He has the right to lock you up, have the marriage annulled—all that and even more. And I want my Sibille to be honored in your family. We must win your father over somehow. I'll just have to think of something. Don't worry, I always have."

❖

"Cease that vulgar banging! Didn't they tell you I'm not seeing anyone today? I have a headache!" shouted Nostradamus at the sealed doors. All day long, servants had tiptoed around the long way rather than cut through Nostradamus's room, ever since he had thrown his inkwell at the Cardinal's own barber and gotten away with it. Nostradamus didn't consider it his own fault at all, not in the least. He was plagued by devils, not the least of them the elusive Anael, who hadn't showed him a single vision in days. Then there were the despicable Ruggiero brothers who had raised a phantom in phosphorescent armor to predict the greatness of that runny-nosed boy, the dauphin, when he had become lord of three realms, which had sent the queen fluttering after them like an adoring schoolgirl. And finally there was Menander's vulgar taunt and that spotty piece of paper on which was depicted the only horoscope he had ever drawn up that wouldn't come out. Then just when he had reattained equilibrium of mind through a really excellent ragoût and a pleasant old Bordeaux, a lackey in the king's livery had delivered two purses, and Nostradamus counted them out to find that the king had sent him a velvet purse with a hundred crowns for his services, and the queen had added thirty more. Barely enough to cover the cost of his travel.

"Beware the generosity of kings, Léon," the old doctor had growled as he tucked away the money in his own worn leather purse. After that, the day hadn't gone well at all, not at all, and now some lackey was banging on his door with a stick.

"Open, open," called a woman's voice. "I have important news for the great Master Nostredame."

"Go ahead, Léon, I am destined to be martyred," sighed Nostradamus. But when he saw the vast figure that filled his doorway, silver-headed walking stick still raised in mid-knock, he paled, then sighed deeply, and rose from his worktable. "Madame Tournet," he said, "what brings you here?"

"News of the utmost importance to you. And, of course, I've come for my goddaughter's horoscope. You promised to send it over three days ago. Surely, you haven't forgotten."

"It's not done," said the exasperated prophet.

"Not done, not *done*?" she said, advancing her formidable figure into the center of the carpet, from whence she could spy out the contents of the papers on the prophet's worktable. Quickly, he moved himself in front of the table, but it was too late. "What's that I see lying there? That one with all the ink blots? Sun in Aquarius; surely my god-daughter. We'll take the draft."

"You will *not*," said Nostradamus, drawing himself up to his full height and giving her his most commanding stare. But women who have been married to pirates are not so easily put off.

"Of course we will; you have to be leaving immediately and won't have time to make a fair copy—I'll just have that now—" But Nostra-damus grabbed the offending document from the table ahead of her questing hand, and he held it behind his back, where the rudeness re-quired to seize it was greater even than Madame Tournet could muster.

"What's this about leaving? I plan another three weeks at least," said the prophet.

"If you stay the three weeks, you'll be staying here forever."

"And they accuse me of being cryptic. Speak up, Madame, or I shall never give you the horoscope."

"I mean that you'll be leaving your bones here. I have it on the best authority that the theologians of the Sorbonne and their friends from the Justice of Paris intend to investigate the source of your powers. And we both know they don't use delicate means. Even if you are spared being burned alive, there won't be a whole joint left in your body."

"How do I know you aren't just lying for some ulterior purpose? You've been consulting with that Lorenzo Ruggieri—that's it—or Simeoni. How much did they pay you, what favors have they offered, to convince me to leave? You know it is only I who am great enough to devise the means of ridding your goddaughter of Menander the Deathless."

"I'm telling the truth; I heard it from a parlementary counselor's wife at a card party. They're jealous of the favor the queen has shown you, and want to make an example. You must flee at once."

"You've lied to me before," said Nostradamus.

"Never," said Madame Tournet. "I am the soul of truth." But here Nostradamus played his *coup de Jarnac,* his brilliant fencing trick. It was also a stab in the dark, but a wisely chosen one. These things, after all, are known to happen in the best of families.

"You are a liar. You have already lied to your niece, and through her, to me. You lied about your goddaughter's birthdate, and thereby sent me on a wild-goose chase that has wasted many candles. And now here you are, as bold as brass, demanding her horoscope and trying to get me to leave for some devious purpose of your own." The prophet braced himself for a storm of furious denials, but instead, to his surprise, the vast, pallid figure of Madame Tournet seemed to wobble and shrink inside her immense, padded-out skirts. Her face became even whiter than her white lace ruff, so that the little black mustache stood out in even bolder relief. Her dark eyes started to swim with liquid, and blindly she sought out the chair, plopping down into it with the sighing, hissing sound of an inflated pig's bladder that has been suddenly pierced by playing children.

"I swore before the altar of God that I would never tell. There are only three people on this earth that know the secret. You are the fourth. Swear to me, swear, you will never tell her. It would break her heart."

"The other two?"

"Will take the secret to the grave."

"Then one of them must be the priest who baptized her."

"You see too much, Master Prophet."

"And the other?"

"My best friend on earth—but no more, no more—I must not think of it or I will die of it."

"But, there is one more thing. I must have the true date—"

"I can't—"

"It is either that, or Menander the Deathless will at some point finally win his battle of nerves; then she is lost, and you, more than anyone, can understand that."

"I—I—well, then, I must—" The prophet waited for the war inside the old lady to subside.

"I can send word as soon as the work is complete," he said, his tone gently encouraging. "And if you need to hide it from her, I'll just send it direct to you when it's finished. I do most of my business by correspondence, anyway."

"Come close, and I'll whisper," said Madame Tournet, and wiping her eyes and a large swath of damp rice powder from her face, she looked about to see that no other human was nearby.

"Ah, I see," said Nostradamus very softly, still leaning over her immense figure to catch her low-voiced answer. "That changes everything."

Sixteen

In hope of catching the king alone, the Cardinal of Lorraine had remained in the council chamber until the last of the supporters of Montmorency had departed. It had been a hard winter, following on famine, and it promised to be a hard spring. Outside the narrow, diamond-paned windows of the Louvre, an unseasonable late spring sleet slashed at the towers, the streets, and the few hurrying passersby. The Old Constable was at the northern front, and the king felt nervous and unsure without his stabilizing presence. Lorraine's older brother, the Duc de Guise, was triumphing on the southern front, his Italian victories bringing glory, but his absence removing him from the center of power. It was time for Lorraine to act, in the interests of the House of Guise.

"Your Majesty," he said, just as the king was anticipating a rapid exit. "Your Majesty, I have news from Rome that will cause your rejoicing." Henri II turned a calm, grave face to his counselor, but an errant muscle in his right hand quivered. He had noticed a distinct thickening of his waist lately, and craved the indoor tennis court. He nodded silently, as if interested, then stroked his narrow black beard. It was his favorite gesture, and gave him an undeserved reputation for deep thinking. "Your Majesty," Lorraine continued, "our petitions have at least been answered. The Pope has ordered that the Holy Office begin the cleansing

of our realm of the new heresy." A chill, errant draft caught the tapestries of the council room and set them in motion. A mouse skittered
from beneath the arras and under the heavy wooden council table.

"Ah," said the king, nodding again as he moved toward the door,
"and who has been appointed Grand Inquisitor?"

"Myself," said Lorraine, following him into the corridor as he
edged ahead of the king's tennis companions. "But regretfully, the Pope
could not avoid the appointment of the two other cardinals, Chatillon
and Bourbon. A matter of precedent, you understand, no matter how
regrettable."

"What is regrettable about having three mighty lords to accomplish
a task so great?" asked the king.

"I have reason to suspect, Majesty, that Chatillon—Chatillon is one
of *them*." Chatillon. A Montmorency. How delicately the treacherous
Guise Cardinal cast suspicion on his rivals—suspicion of heresy, suspicion of treason. A knowing glance, a hint of evidence, and a whisper
too soft to echo in the stone staircase. The king paused in his rapid descent and looked back up over his shoulder at the Cardinal of Lorraine.

"Oh? Has he letters from Geneva, then?"

"Nothing so direct. He gives them sympathy. He tolerates them more
than he should. By these signs, I know what he conceals from you, and
from the Holy Father. In his heart, heresy has found a foothold." They
had entered a lower passage; a page carrying a huge ewer of water
paused to stare. From inside the court at the end of the passage came the
inviting sound of a man's shout, a patter of applause, and the thunk of a
struck ball.

"But even were he to doff his silk and address a *preche* at their Temple, which I do doubt exceedingly, you would have Bourbon to side
with you in this inquisition. Bourbon, I know, is a good Catholic." They
had reached the open door of the tennis court. The rope was up, curious faces were peeping from the upstairs galleries. The court smelled of
sweat, of urine, of old leather. Lorraine spoke faster, trying to keep the
king's fast-waning attention.

"That is true, Majesty, and your discernment of his sympathy is
perfect. But have you not noticed a certain laziness about him, a certain fondness for soft living and amusements that might sap his energy

in pursuit of these treacherous heretics? His good temper, his love of novelty—they lead him to tolerate much. Why, only last fall, he had as a houseguest that charlatan, Nostradamus. I hear he had him at his table almost every evening, and reveled greatly in the company of all the ladies of rank who came to have their fortunes told." At the mention of fortune-telling, the king turned toward Lorraine, his voice irritated, his attention fully caught, at last.

"Superstition, my dear Cardinal. I despise it, but it is everywhere. Fortunately, it is not the same as heresy. The queen my wife, you know, is utterly taken up with the most preposterous superstitions—and yet you will find no more faithful Catholic on this earth. Masses, prayers— she can't get enough of them. It's in the blood. No balance. Italian, and the niece of a Pope. No, superstition is not enough to suspect a man—" The king paused, the expression on his long, morose face unfathomable.

"Your reading of his character is brilliant, Majesty. But sometimes— sometimes I have concern that, good Catholic that he is, he might favor his family excessively. His brother—" A spark of irritation lit the king's eyes.

"The King of Navarre? He changes his mind with every passing wind. I never concern myself with the King of Navarre. He rants and raves and schemes uselessly to regain the Spanish half of his kingdom, and will never care for anything else. He is here, he is there, a useless fellow. He may be a Prince of the Blood, but I am glad that three throne heirs separate him from power in this realm. He would sell away France in a moment, out of pure forgetfulness, or because someone temporarily amusing told him it was a good idea. No, he has not the force of will to be a dangerous heretic."

"Yes, but his wife does, and is. Her court is a haven for them."

"A woman? Hardly worth considering. And remember, you are speak- ing of my own cousin, the daughter of my aunt Marguerite, the beloved sister of my father, King Francis." The king looked away impatiently; this time Lorraine had gone too far.

"Oh, consider it not said, Majesty. Doubtless, she has fallen under the spell of Navarre's younger brother, Condé—he is one of them, too, I am sure."

"Really? I have not heard of that. Very well, I suppose I must have him watched more closely. But as for the Queen of Navarre, I want her left alone. Royal blood—greater than yours, Lorraine—if she wishes to be eccentric, that is her own matter." The king had edged through the low, arched door of the tennis court, as Lorraine followed him close at his left elbow.

"And the orders for the required death penalty for all Protestants?" The king unfastened his gown and handed it to a waiting page. Stripped to his doublet, he acknowledged the joyful shouts of his tennis partners and gestured for a racket.

"Of course, of course—just follow the existing law—they are, after all, the worst of heretics—but leave the German mercenaries alone—their Princes, you know, so fussy—some things, you understand, must be overlooked temporarily." The king waved his hand as if it would all be taken care of by some invisible force located slightly above his left elbow and abandoned the Cardinal, there on the edge of the court, as he took his place to the sound of scattered cheers from the gallery above.

The seeds are planted, thought Lorraine, as he paced alone through the damp, stinking stone corridors to leave by the courtyard entrance. I have made the Bourbons suspect, as well as the Montmorencys. If only a kind God would allow the Old Constable to be slain in battle—why then, a snake without a head is a dead thing, and so will be the influence of the whole Montmorency tribe. That clan is riddled with too much independence of thought. Heresy is the next step. They may be heroes now, but with little effort, I can reveal them as traitors to the faith tomorrow. The Inquisition will gain strength, and with it the Guises, the only true, unquestionable Catholics. And I, I shall control the Inquisition. Time, time—it is only a little time, and the Guises will reign over three kingdoms.

❖

It was a beautiful spring day, two months after Lorraine's sinister conversation with the king. Birds sang in the trees, playing children called from the alleys, and housewives leaned out of their upstairs windows to shout gossip over the laundry. But above all these sounds of spring, the comfortable house on the rue de Bailleul was resonating from cellar to roof beam with the loud, aggrieved cries of Scipion Montvert, banker, substantial citizen, and paterfamilias. All the servants, even the little boy who sharpened the knives in the kitchen, were tiptoeing and shushing one another, pretending that they didn't hear the bellowing outside the closed door of the son and heir of the House of Montvert.

"How DARE you bar your door to ME, your own FATHER? Open, I say, or I'll sign the papers to have you consigned to the Bastille as a wayward son! THAT'S better! When I say open, you open—" The listeners heard a sort of indistinguishable grunt as a response. The lady of the House of Montvert placed her hand over her heart, leaning for support on the pallid, dark-haired daughter of the house, whose eyes were rolled upward in prayer.

"Have you not a thought, young man, for your life which is flowing away? When I was your age, I was up at DAWN, working at mastering my TRADE! Languages, law, finance! And here I've sent you to the finest universities: Bologne, Montpellier, Toulouse, and you've been thrown out of every one of them! And now you go out all night and sleep all day!"

Mumble, mumble, mumble.

"Don't make excuses! You've sampled every den of sin in six nations! And with whom do you associate? People of substance, who can help you? Or lowlife tavern-keeper's sons, fencing school rowdies, impoverished scandal-mongering writers and gallows-bait fiddlers, no, THOSE are the people to whom my son is drawn, like some perverse lodestone!"

Mumble, mumble, grump, mumble.

"Mother," whispered Clarette, sensing a break in the invective, "may I take Bernardo to accompany me to mass?" Nicolas's virtuous younger sister had a prayer book in her lily-like hands, and was wearing a large cross upon her bosom.

"WASTREL!" came the shout from upstairs. Nicolas's mother shuddered at the sound.

"You know your father has asked Bernardo to follow your brother everywhere, to keep him out of taverns, quarrels, and public stews. And don't you hear? He's almost up."

"Oh, Mother, you know it is Nicolas who should accompany me, and not a servant. If only once he would set foot in church—It is my dream that someday I will be the means by which he can enter into the presence of God's love."

"Oh, my darling, virtuous girl. Why did God give so much goodness to you, and no portion at all to your brother? I swear, he will be the death of me yet."

"If only—" And here she sighed, rolling her eyes upward. "If only you could convince Father to let me enter the convent."

"You know it is not your father's wish. Who, who would remain of the Montverts if your brother—ah, God, how I suffer over him—"

"At your age I was a sober young man of BUSINESS! I was married to your mother! I had a FUTURE! What is there for you but a career as a mercenary or hired bravo or professional gambler? Eh? Answer me that!"

"Very well, Father, I'll turn over a new leaf—" At this, all motion in the house below stopped. The two women, mother and daughter, strained to hear—but discreetly, as if they were in deep contemplation. "Yes—this very day. Give me permission to marry, and I'll establish myself in some worthy profession—law—just as you've always wanted." Clarette and her mother gasped.

"Not so fast, you weasel. You've failed to finish your legal studies in three universities, at my last count. Who's to say you won't enter school and do it all over again? No more, I say. An honest apprenticeship—say, in your mother's cousin's banking house in Genoa, and I'll arrange a marriage with a sober, pure young woman of substantial family—"

"Actually, Father, there's already a demoiselle—"

"A WHAT? You DARE to practice this sort of trickery on me?" Clarette and her mother crept quietly up the stairs, their eyes large.

"She's beautiful, of high birth, she worships me, and I—I am so in love with her that I'd do anything—even be a banker—for your blessing, Father."

"You have been PAYING COURT to a WOMAN without my PERMISSION? I WARNED you not to do that EVER again!"

"You *said* I should make the acquaintance of people of good blood and high connections—"

"MEN, not WOMEN, you ninny!"

"She's from an excellent family—nobility of the sword—very old—the Artauds of La Roque-aux-Bois, and has the most important connections at court—with the queen, herself—"

"You, you, you—WHAT? A COURTESAN? I know all about that woman! Knowing what you are—a fool—I made inquiries when you first laid eyes on that hussy, and I learned more than I ever wanted to know about that dreadful woman! Sibille Artaud de La Roque, whose cousin Matheline is a wanton from birth, and has caused her good husband infinite suffering! The only one worse is her *cousin,* who abandoned her decent family, took up with her wicked aunt to gain an inheritance that belonged by right to her father, and now has mysterious connections at court! Sinful connections, without a doubt!"

Nicolas's mother and sister were almost at the head of the stairs now, just out of sight of the quarrelers in the doorway. They paused, more silent than silence itself, and in that silence, you could almost hear their ears growing longer.

"My son, my son, have you lost the last of what little sense you ever had? Don't you know why a woman of that sort would be interested in you? A woman who waits on the queen? Who shows herself in public, reads at literary gatherings, and, what's worse, has books printed *in her own name*? She wants a husband of a rank that she can command—a cover for her sins, for her affairs, which I have no doubt are already as numerous as the stars in the sky. That's how those women live, those women with high court connections. Don't you understand? They're not like us—"

"Father, it's you who doesn't understand. Her conversation is elevated, her associations virtuous—" A look of sudden, furious realization crossed his father's face.

"You've been *calling* on her—don't deny it, I can tell by your face—calling in secret, without my permission! How long, for God's sake? Have you promised her anything? Is she pregnant?"

"Father, she is pure, she is constant—no woman you found could be finer, more devoted—we could be happy together—"

"My God, haven't you learned anything? The lawyers, the expense—how much to buy this despicable harpy off?"

"Father, she's not after anything. Look at me, can't you see? This is true love. Our minds and hearts are one. I'll die if I can't have her."

"You'll die if you *do* have her. The thousand deaths of cuckold! Enough is enough. I, your father and your master, am locking you in this room until you understand that you either agree to go to your cousin's in Genoa to learn new and sober ways, and a business that is appropriate to your station in life, or I'll sign the papers that commit you to the Bastille for your wayward manner of living—" The sound of the slamming door reverberated through the entire house, and the two women on the stair slipped quietly away.

✣

"An English herald is here?" said King Henri, his foot already in the stirrup held by a valet. Spring was busy passing into summer. The horses were gathered in the stable courtyard at Fontainebleau, the excited staghounds were barking, and half the court was already mounted for the hunt. Even Queen Catherine, who, despite her dumpy figure, rode sidesaddle with the courage of a man astride, was on her rangy gray hunter, reins gathered in her podgy fingers, breathing deep the promise of the bright morning, and anxious to ride out. "Let him wait," said the king, swinging up into the saddle. "A man of honor does not waste his time on declarations of war made by a woman." The French nobility who overheard laughed, and repeated the comment until everyone of gallantry and spirit had enjoyed the joke. And so it was in high good humor that the king and his court rode out to kill stags, and the English herald was left to cool his heels for the next few days, until it was convenient for the king to hear that England had declared war, and joined the troops of the Empire massing on the northern front.

✣

"Have you the honey, Madame?" said the queen. Lucrèce Cavalcanti extended the little glass jar in its silver stand.

"It is right here, Your Majesty," she said, placing it on the wide oak table within the queen's reach. The queen did not even look up. Next to her right elbow lay an open book with handwritten notes in it.

Catherine de Medici, clad informally for the morning in a sacque of primrose-colored taffeta and a plain lace cap, was busy grinding up a grayish powder in a mortar. Entirely globular in form without her stays, her pudgy face was bright with focused intelligence, her eyes intent on the process. At last the mass in the mortar seemed to satisfy her, and she turned, with a sharp rustle of taffeta, to the waiting lady.

"There," she said. "Powder of geranium, and a pinch—just a pinch— of powder of nutmeg. It is sovereign for these summer fevers. It quells the aching and shortens the catarrhal discharge. And now—the honey— my little girl will never taste the medicine." Busily, she mixed up the fever potion and decanted it into a covered china dish, painted with mythical figures.

"Majesty, you are not only a great queen, but the kindest and most thoughtful of mothers," said her *dame d'honneur,* gesturing to a serving maid to come and clean up after them. The queen sighed.

"I try, Lucrèce, I try. But despite all my wisdom, I lost my little twins."

"Sorrow is the lot of every woman."

"But now, I pray, for my daughter." Accompanied by a page to announce her, the queen and her companion made their way through the corridors of St.-Germain to Elisabeth Valois's sickroom. Not even trusting her close companion, the queen herself carried the remedy in her own hands, as if somehow the maternal virtue might be imparted through the china itself. But on the threshold, they paused. They were already too late. The Duchess of Valentinois stood beside the huge, draped bed where the queen's daughter lay. Behind her, a physician held a vial of urine up to the window to inspect the color. Another physician, in a long robe, was giving orders to a surgeon, who had already opened a vein in the wrist, and set a copper bowl beneath the arm to catch the dark blood that was draining out. Beside the bed, at the duchess's elbow, stood the tall, titian-haired girl who was Elisabeth's closest companion. The Queen of Scots, the Guise protégée of the duchess.

At the sight of the queen, they all looked up, suddenly silent.

"I've brought a remedy for my daughter," said Catherine de Medici, advancing into the silence.

"A remedy?" said Diane, one eyebrow raised, a condescending smile barely visible on her face.

"Powder of geraniums," said the queen.

"Fernel has already advised us," said Diane, and the bearded doctor with the vial of urine turned toward the queen and bowed deeply.

"Gracious Majesty, I have prescribed a course of purges that are infallible in these cases."

"I see," said the queen, looking at her pale daughter, her lifeblood flowing into the basin.

"Mother, I would like your remedy," said Elisabeth.

"Nonsense," said the duchess. "You'll just disturb the treatment. Trust your physicians, my dear. I have summoned the best in the kingdom. Your mother did not need to trouble herself to come."

"I see," said Catherine, her voice as cold as ice. But as she turned to go, she heard the duchess, in a sharp, audible whisper, say to the Queen of Scots:

"The three Medici balls—they seem to be apothecaries' pills." The teenage girl snickered. Outside the door, the queen paused and took a deep breath. Her eyes were blazing, but her voice was icy.

"Lucrèce," said the queen, her face set like iron. "Send for the Demoiselle de La Roque."

"Majesty—" Lucrèce Cavalcanti turned pale.

"I desire that my daughter be raised higher than the Queen of Scots, that my children shall see the Duchess of Valentinois in the dust beneath their feet."

"But that thing—it is accursed—" whispered her *dame d'honneur*.

"That is no concern of mine. Tonight I shall charge Menander the Deathless to grant all of my children thrones, and to raise my daughter Elisabeth to such a rank that Diane de Poitiers—that barren old hag—will not be fit to tie her shoe."

❧

"My! Just breathe that in! The most sulphurous water in all of France! All the way from here, you can just smell all that health! Soon, Sibille, you'll shake off that bad mood, and feel quite like your old self again." We had left our baggage with the Abbé's, in our rooms at the spa, and the two of us had gone to inspect the baths. Beyond them, the lake, spotted with swans and the occasional pleasure boat, sparkled serenely in the sun. On a path by the shore, old ladies, leaning on the arms of their attendants, strolled, awaiting the inevitable call of nature that attends the drinking of spa waters. Before us lay the stone bulk of the bathhouse with its changing rooms, tubs, masseurs, and shady arcade all hidden behind the high wall of the enclosure of the main bath. Here one could get a cupping, a bleeding by the resident surgeon, or the inspection of one's urine by a physician of sound medical training. Beyond the wall we could hear the inviting sounds of bathers splashing in the great outdoor pool, calling for assistance, babbling in conversation. Over all lay the stink, a cloud straight out of hell.

"Pardon, *ma tante,* but it smells as if ten thousand rotten eggs have been broken open all at once. Surely, one feels better only by contrast, on finally being able to remove oneself from this place."

"You see? You're feeling better—your old wit is coming back. Soon you'll be inspired to finish your lovely epic on the life of Queen Clotilde. You've drooped too long; it's obviously your liver, as Doctor Lenoir said. You need to regulate your bowels better—"

"But you know it's not that, Auntie. My Nicolas went to ask permission to marry, and now he's gone. I'm sure he's been locked up like a thief. His horrible old father is capable of anything, just to keep him from me forever. And my heart is all cracked in pieces, I haven't any appetite, and all the sulphur baths in the world won't fix it." And every night, though I did not tell her, Menander sat on my chest of drawers, whispering, "Don't you know he's given in to his father? Why not? Out of sight, out of mind. He doesn't love you anymore. They've found him a beautiful bride, just sixteen and fresh as a rose, with dainty feet and hands, and now he's realized *you* are a big, ugly, scarred monster. It was just infatuation, and now he's gone. Why don't you wish for him back? It would be easy, if you weren't as stubborn as you are stupid. No man will ever love you without my help. Wish! Wish! Why don't you? It's so simple." But even though I tried to keep my sorrows to myself, as I began to droop and grow dark circles under my eyes, Auntie noticed anyway, and decided to apply her cure-all: the sulphurous waters of the nearest spa.

"You need to cheer up, Sibille, and you will when I tell you that his father has written to me—"

"Has he relented?" My heart gave a leap.

"Well, not quite—but reading between the lines, I think you needn't worry that Nicolas has given in to him: his father has offered you money if you'll relinquish your claims, and write a letter to Nicolas telling him that you do not love him anymore."

"Auntie, how despicable! I'm mortified! What an evil, unnatural old man! I hope you told him off!"

"Hardly, my dear. You see, he has opened a dialogue. He writes, I am required to respond. With the help of my dear cousin, here, I have written a wily letter to entangle him deeper—give me credit, my dear. You may yet be seeing your Nicolas again."

"My, my, what a lot of new rules the governor of the baths has posted here," observed the Abbé, as if to change the subject. He squinted a little to read the tablet posted at the gate. " 'It is forbidden to all people, of whatever quality, condition, region, or province they may be, to use provocation in insulting language tending to lead to quarrels; to carry arms while at the baths aforesaid; to give the lie; to put hand to arms under pain of severe punishment as breakers of the peace, rebels, and disobedient to His Highness.

" 'Also it is forbidden to all prostitutes and immodest women to enter the baths, or to be found within five hundred paces of the same under penalty of whipping at the four corners of the town. . . .

" 'The same penalty will fall on those who shall use any lascivious or immodest discourse to any ladies, or damsels, or other women and girls who may be visiting the baths, or touch them in a manner unbecoming, or enter or quit the baths in ribald fashion, contrary to public decency—' "

"Oh," I gasped. "Do men and women bathe together?" I hadn't expected that. Here I was, sick with grief, and they expected—I couldn't, I just couldn't—perhaps if I pretended to be sick in my room—

The attendants at the gate opened it for an elderly gentleman twisted with rheumatism, who was being carried in on a litter. I could see them bow in greeting.

"It is really very decent, cousin," said the Abbé. "Every man wears a linen jacket, and every woman a shift. You will find the most genteel persons here."

"In my *shift?* Auntie, you didn't say—"

"Don't think to pretend you are sick in the rooms, Sibille; we'll just have you brought down in a litter the way *he* was. You require repairs, and this will do you infinite good."

"All of you?" asked the attendant at the gate, eyeing our procession, for we were an odder sight than any old gentleman in a litter. First came the Abbé, all shrunken up, in his broad hat and black gown, his eyes as bright and observant as a squirrel's. On his arm was his old mother, of a truly astonishing antiquity, barely able to walk on her frail bones. Then Aunt Pauline, vast and resplendent in yellow silk, leaning on her silver-headed walking stick, and followed by a lackey holding a little sunshade of ornamented muslin over her head, then myself, as tall and mournful as a stork, followed by two lackeys bearing towels and robes, and two boys in Auntie's green livery bearing Señor Alonzo in his big gilt cage, which was fitted out with a pair of handles at each end for easier carrying.

"All," said the Abbé, pressing a handsome tip into his hand.

"The monkey is extra—"

"Tell him, dear cousin, that the monkey does not bathe."

"The monkey is extra anyway—"

"We should charge for the exhibit of the monkey, since he will be a source of amusement," observed the Abbé, as he produced another few sous.

"Animals not allowed. I'm only letting you in because he's in a cage."

"I simply cannot live without the sight of my dear monkey," announced Aunt Pauline. "And he droops, positively droops without me."

"Hmm. Yes," said the attendant, still holding out his hand. Señor Alonzo stretched out his mouth with his fingers to make an ugly face at the attendant. The Abbé increased his offering, and we passed through into the bathhouse. Actually, we had to have Señor Alonzo, not for himself, but for his cage. In the bottom, beneath a board, lay the Deathless Menander's box, and by keeping him in close proximity to us, he was unable to flit about and embarrass us by materializing at the water-

side, after having been left up in our rooms. Of course, he had been furious at the notion.

"My beautiful box, in the bottom of a monkey's cage! I tell you, I'll
have a terrible revenge!"

"Nonsense," Auntie had told him. "I'm tired of your limiting our little
pleasure excursions. It's time we went to the spa, and you're just going to
have to settle for the monkey's cage. No supernatural phenomenon has a
right to be a social embarrassment."

"I tell you, I'll squeak, I'll howl!"

"And everyone will assume it's Señor Alonzo, and ignore you
completely."

"Never, never in eighteen centuries—"

"You're *spoiled*, Menander, that's your problem. You've had your own
way far too much. It's high time you were taken in hand."

So there we were, monkey, lackeys, Menander and all. Only Gargantua had been left behind in the rooms, to his great grief, since he considered himself a far more worthy companion than Señor Alonzo, his
mortal enemy.

Now I had never taken the waters before, since not only did I always enjoy perfect health, but father was a great hater of spas, saying
they were nothing but dens of sin, where men and women went to devote themselves to orgiastic pleasures, and only a wicked woman like
his sister would ever persist in such flagrant behavior. But the great
bath inside the arcade looked to me more like the aftermath of sin than
sin itself, resembling those paintings in church where the souls of the
wicked are stewed in steaming sulphur pools. The pool had shallow
steps descending into the water, and men on crutches, women twisted
into the shape of gnomes, and even pallid children with withered and
useless limbs were being assisted down into the water by various attendants. At one end, a canvas awning was stretched, and there Auntie
was assisted to a seat on the sunken steps, her immense shift billowing
about her in the water. There, she was immediately surrounded by a
number of other old ladies, all trading notes on their ailments at a rate of
speech almost too fast to follow. Over all, the hideous smell rolled like a
curse. And for myself—well, I was just praying that no one would

notice me there, so gawky, so undressed, my wet shift clinging to me. Where to hide? Only deeper in the water, crouching so it came up to my chin, in the center of the pool, my eyes tightly closed, away from the cripples splashing in the shallow water on the steps.

"Sibille, Sibille!" I could hear my godmother calling. "Over here—there are some ladies I'd like you to meet!" I opened one eye. All around me, the pool of the damned, except the attendants didn't have pitch-forks. "Don't stay in the sun, Sibille, you'll spoil your complexion!" I opened the other eye. In front of me, a woman with the biggest nose in the world. Another, with a china eye and a huge wen. You may be plain, but you're not as awful looking as *that,* said my Lower Self to my secret mind. I turned my head to the source of the sound, and saw the old ladies all bobbing in the water beneath the canopy. And at least you're not as old as *that,* whispered that regrettable, low element of my charac-ter. Sorrowfully, I thought of the new, vicious scars that spoiled my left hand and arm. But even though I'm young, my pretty hand has been spoiled, I thought. I wiggled the fingers. The scar still felt tight, and it looked horrid, all red and lumpy.

A frail boy with paralyzed limbs was being lowered into the water by the attendants. I knew I should feel sorry for him. But my mean-spirited little Lower Self said, well, at least your arm is better than *that.* Then I thought, what a low person you are, Sibille, and not sensitive and sympathetic at all the way you thought you were—instead of feeling compassion for the unfortunate who are all around you, you are begin-ning to feel better because you see other people worse off than yourself. Now I felt guilty about feeling better, so I felt just as bad as ever. Slowly, my conscience eating at me, I made my way through the stinking water to the shaded spot beneath the canopy.

"Ah, here you are at last," exclaimed Auntie. "Sibille, I swear I see a freckle! You must be more careful!" And the ladies left off discussing a woman whose womb had fallen after the birth of her fourth child in or-der to consider my own case, which they found quite scandalous.

"Imagine! A hired attacker with vitriol! My dear, how fortunate you were to be spared from marrying him!" Well, they were certainly right there. Just think, no matter what, I'd been spared marrying Villasse. And while I did feel guilty, it was not as guilty as if I'd been a murderess, and besides, now everybody who wanted me to marry Villasse was shown to be wrong. As they chattered, I began to feel my bad mood shrink. Perhaps Nicolas hadn't been convinced, perhaps Auntie could manage something after all.

"Why, the scarring is not bad at all—a glove, or you could hold a fan just *so*—"

"My poor niece is devastated because her admirer, her brave rescuer, has been forbidden to marry her by his father, and now he doesn't call anymore. I'm sure she's secretly afraid it's because she's scarred."

"Why, that's ridiculous! A beautiful, virtuous girl like your niece? The old man ought to praise God for his luck!" The old lady turned and inspected me closely. "Besides, look, not a drop hit your face, dear—why, if I had your complexion—Trust me, his love will only grow stronger once it's forbidden. And when a boy's in love, he'll find a way. He'll get a message to you—who knows, maybe one has been intercepted already—and then—ah, love!"

I began to notice that the sky above the pool was very blue. The company was amusing and lighthearted. The shady arcade seemed graceful and inviting. I could hear birds in the trees beyond the bathhouse wall. The sulphur stink had quite faded out, I hardly smelled it at all. My goodness, Auntie was right after all—these waters were very restorative.

"—your hair, it is so thick and handsome, and with the curl, it will hold the new style. Just a glimpse, and he'll fall in love with you more than ever. I'll send my hairdresser, he's a genius—"

"Now you see, Sibille? I told you you needed to take the waters. Your face is looking brighter already," said Auntie.

✤

"A tall girl and a very large lady with a cane? Yes, they're inside," said the attendant.

"Then let me pass," said the captain, trying to push by.

"Oh, no. Not without the fee. And you have to leave your sword with your man, here. See the rules?" The attendant pointed to the placard posted at the entry.

"Those rules are not for people of birth." The captain was splendidly dressed, his high white ruff trimmed with lace, his brown velvet doublet slashed with cream-colored satin, his wide, sleeveless gown fur trimmed and embroidered with crimson. At his side hung a rapier and dagger, and though he was on foot, he had not taken the spurs from his boots. With all his elegance of dress, few present would have suspected he was a chaser-after-dowries, a debtor living beyond his means, and a man who was capable of stooping so low as to purchase a love potion from Lorenzo Ruggieri to seduce the wealthy sister of his best friend and comrade-in-arms, Annibal de La Roque.

"Oh, no, they're the king's rules, and they're for everybody. No weapons, no quarrels."

"I have no intention to quarrel. I simply want to see Sibille de La Roque."

"No indecent proposals. Them's the king's rules, too."

"Fellow, I could strike you down for your insolence."

"Don't complain to me, complain to the governor of the baths. You can go in if you want to bathe. That's all."

"Well, then, I want to bathe," said Philippe d'Estouville, fishing in his wallet.

"No swords," said the attendant.

It was without a sword that Captain d'Estouville surveyed the great bathing pool from the shade of the arcade. Nowhere did he see the dark, curling head of his rival. His spies had told him right. The wretched interloper was no longer calling on her. Doubtless sent away. Now her heart was free. Good. The ladies, where were they? Aha, over there under the canopy. Yes, there she was, right by that vulgar old aunt who refused to allow him in the house. But sooner or later, Sibille would get out of the water, dry off, perhaps want a refreshing drink under the arcade. Perhaps the old dragon would vanish in to the bathhouse for a massage, or a cupping. Then he could offer the niece some light refreshment. It was astonishing to him how simple the concept of a love potion was, and how difficult to carry off its administration. Particularly when one must attend to a demanding superior, who traveled between his estates, the court, and now the battlefront, and when a suspicious old duenna manages to intervene on every social occasion. This time, this time he would manage, and Sibille would fall hopelessly in love with him, and his money worries would be solved forever.

❧

Outside the bathhouse gate, a beetle-like figure in black leather had been barred from entrance by the attendant.

"But I have no intention of bathing. I simply want to visit," Cosmo Ruggieri was saying.

"It doesn't matter. If you want to go in, you must pay. And no swords. No daggers, either. Read the rules there. Those are the governor's rules, on orders of the king. And no going in just to pay addresses to some lady. That's forbidden, too."

"I am not going in to pay addresses to a lady," said Ruggieri.

"Well, then, what do you want?"

"I—I have a very bad back. I—I need a massage, and a bleeding," said Ruggieri, rather unconvincingly, as he fished in his wallet for the admission price. Within minutes, he, too, was standing in the arcade, also clad only in his long undershirt, looking about for d'Estouville, whom he had followed in. God, there he was in the water, floundering about like a fish, making his way toward a group of ladies seated on the steps in the water beneath a shady canopy. What a bumbler. A Florentine, given any potion whatsoever, would not fail in a clever ruse to administer it speedily. But this wretched, arrogant, useless Frenchman, what a hopeless case! He moped; he traveled; he sent serenaders in an attempt to get into her house; he followed the sorceress about the court instead of joining her at supper in one of the great houses where she was invited to read her poetry. All he had to do was get her to sit down and drink with him just once. A failure, an utter failure, this ridiculous French captain. And a terrible annoyance to him, Cosmo, who had to trail this bumbler everywhere to grab The Master of All Desires the minute it was ownerless! If I hadn't found out she was going to the spa, and suggested this scheme, he'd still be pouting outside her door, thought Ruggieri. The French, how incompetent!

Where could they have The Master of All Desires? They couldn't risk traveling this far without bringing it. The wily Florentine hunted about among the loungers, the strollers, the bored valets, the attendants laden with towels. No box in sight. And yet it could not be far. Otherwise, it would follow them and materialize at the poolside. It must be in the dressing room. How like them—to hide it in the ladies' dressing rooms. Where were they? Ah, yes, there where the two arthritic old ladies were being assisted by a powerful matron to move, crab-like, toward the healing pool. As quietly as a lengthening shadow in the evening, Cosmo Ruggieri moved toward the unguarded door and slipped in. Suddenly, there was a powerful shriek, and several attendants rushed toward the sound, emerging with the unlucky Cosmo firmly in their grasp. Sputtering protests, he was dragged unceremoniously toward the bathhouse gate and pitched out.

"If you even think of trying to get back in, we'll have you in prison so fast your head will spin," shouted one of them, as the gate slammed shut. A ripple of laughter and the buzz of conversation spread through the sulphurous fumes. There is nothing like a scandal to excite conversation among strangers, and Cosmo had created a worthy one.

"Just what did he think he was doing?"

"A thief, obviously."

Sibille and Aunt Pauline looked at each other meaningfully, and their eyes lit up with amusement as Señor Alonzo began to dance and chatter in his cage. Sensing his opportunity, d'Estouville sloshed his way to the ladies under the canopy, and entered the conversation. "A scandal, what a dreadful fellow. It is such a relief to know that these baths are so well governed—"

❧

A delightful June breeze ruffled the waters of the lake, and carried the sound of a young man playing the lute for his lady-love from a boat drifting far out on the placid surface. But the melancholy fellow feeding the swans took no notice of the pretty sight. He had managed to escape from his father's house, followed only by a single minder, for this brief moment only, on the grounds that he had lost so much weight that he should take the waters to restore himself before the long and risky trip over the Alps into exile. Over and over, he rehearsed what he was doing to say. His Sibille was there, the greatest love of his life, and he would have only a brief moment to say farewell. Suppose she thought he had abandoned her? Suppose another man had taken advantage of his absence to lie about him, to sow doubts, to win her over? Suppose she refused to speak to him? Then he'd just leave silently, and languish and die—would it upset his father more if he languished and died on the road, or once he was at his uncle's house in Genoa? Never mind, a cruel fate would arrange it in the most tragic fashion.

"Master Nicolas, it does no good to droop and dawdle here; you need to take the treatment so you will be well enough to travel." Hmm, thought Nicholas, how am I to get rid of Bernardo? It was a fortunate thing that I discovered *she* would be here. But what will be the good, if I can't break free of father's lackey? He'll report everything. Languidly, he drifted toward the bathhouse gate, the old servant following close behind.

"Goodness, just look at that placard," said Nicolas, still at a distance from the gate. "I can't take my sword or my knife inside. Bernardo, could you take them back to the room?"

"Not until I see you're safely inside, Master Nicolas. As long as you've clothes on, you might escape."

"Not without my sword. You know it's too valuable to leave behind." Grudgingly, the older man watched as Nicolas leaned against a tree and fumbled in the purse at his waist for the price of admission. He looked even skinnier and more hollow-eyed than he had ever been since he had fallen in love with that canon's niece at Bologna, who had promptly been sent off to stay with relatives in the country. Poor old man, thought the servant; this ungrateful, useless fellow is the only son he's got.

But hardly had Bernardo departed when the strangest old woman hurried past the languid, heavily sighing Nicolas. The hoops in her far-thingale joggled this way and that; she trod on her hem, and a distinctly masculine curse emerged from beneath the heavy veil she wore. Nicolas's eyes brightened.

"Your beard is showing," he said to the strange old woman.

"Young man, I have a terrible disease," whispered Cosmo Ruggieri in a hoarse voice.

"Terrible indeed—you are so badly crippled you walk like a man," observed Nicolas, his left eyebrow raised sarcastically.

"Listen, you have to help me. If I lean on your arm, and you pay for both of us, the gatekeeper will never see through my disguise."

"Why should I help you?"

"Because I am planning a rare prank. A clever young fellow like you will be able to dine out for years simply retelling the story."

"A prank? On whom?"

"On a snobbish gentleman who thoroughly deserves it. Monsieur d'Estouville, if you've ever heard of him."

"Heard of him? Why, he hired serenaders to steal a lady's affections from me. I was forced to drive them off at sword's point, the wretches."

"A lady? Could that lady be—Sibille de La Roque?"

"Why—yes—was I that notorious?" asked Nicolas. Cosmo's eyes narrowed slyly beneath his heavy veil.

"Well, at this very moment, *Monsieur* d'Estouville is paying his addresses to her inside." Nicolas first turned pale, then crimson with concealed rage.

"Take my arm, old lady, you're too weak to walk without a cane," announced Nicolas in a loud voice, and together they passed through the bathhouse gate.

As Nicolas emerged from the bathhouse into the arcade, he noticed the strange old woman was nowhere to be seen. What a fool I feel like, with my shirt flapping about me. How can I say good-bye like this? But then he caught sight of d'Estouville's fashionable little beard, and his flashing smile, and heard his light laughter as he escorted Sibille to the edge of the water. *His* Sibille, looking more beautiful than a nymph, her head and neck emerging from the water. And beneath that, her wet shift, clinging and floating—he could feel himself tremble all over. Sacrilege! That odious womanizer, so close, so foul!

At that very moment, Ruggieri, divested of his feminine attire, was slinking behind the pole that supported one side of the canopy, not far from the backs of the jabbering old ladies and the monkey's cage, which had attracted several curiosity-seekers. Señor Alonzo, pleased with his audience, was entertaining them with several of the extraordinarily vulgar acts of which only monkeys are capable.

"Again! Oh, look at that!" There was a patter of applause. A groan came from the bottom of the cage. Cosmo edged closer. Yes, definitely, that was not a monkey sound. In the midst of the laughter, he could distinctly make out words:

"Never, never have I been treated so rudely—"

Yes, that was it! It could only be The Master of All Desires, set be-neath a board in the bottom of the monkey's cage! Quickly, Cosmo looked at the pool. Sibille was emerging behind a large sheet being held by an attendant, and d'Estouville was following, all dripping wet. Soon enough he'd be dressing, then offering her a drink—

In a single bold movement, so swift that the onlookers only gaped, Cosmo Ruggieri unlatched the monkey's cage and dug beneath the floorboard.

"Stop him! My dear Señor Alonzo!" cried the billowing figure from beneath the canopy.

"The monkey! He's letting out the monkey!"

"Aiee!" screamed Ruggieri, as blood streamed from his hand where the monkey had bitten him to the bone. Instinctively, he pulled it out, and just as instinctively, Señor Alonzo burst from his cage, screeching joyfully, and swung up to the canopy.

"Catch him, catch him!" cried the onlookers, as the bath attendants scrambled to the canopy. With a splendid leap, the monkey sprang to the gutter that ran along the rooftop, then scampered to the peak of the bathhouse roof. Cheers and laughter accompanied him.

"Oh," cried Sibille, peeping, half-dressed, from the exit to the ladies' dressing room, "someone has let out Auntie's monkey. She'll be devas-tated if she loses him."

"You again!" the bathhouse attendants, who, unable to catch the monkey, had caught Cosmo Ruggieri instead. "You'll answer to the governor—this time it's prison for you."

"I'm the queen's servant! I'm on a secret mission!" screeched Rug-gieri, as they hustled him to the exit. "Call the queen! Call her maître d'hôtel! Call her captain of the guard!"

In the shadows of the arcade, Nicolas, astonished and delighted with the hullabaloo, found his joy expanding infinitely as the odious Philippe d'Estouville, wrapped in a towel and still carrying his clothing, emerged from the changing room crying, "Never fear, *ma Demoiselle,* I'll catch him!"

And while Sibille wrung her hands, the gallant captain dropped his clothes on a nearby bench and shouted, "Come down at once! Come down!" while he shook his fist at the monkey. As if to tease him, the monkey, as lightly as a feather, skittered along the peak of the roof until he was almost over the captain. Little black eyes beady with anticipation, the monkey watched as d'Estouville clambered up a large ornamental statue of a nymph with a vase, then descended to the gutter just above the captain's reach. Then as d'Estouville grabbed for him, the creature, in a single brilliantly swift motion, swung down from the gutter, leapt to the bench beneath, and snatched up the captain's doublet, to the accompaniment of joyful applause from the watchers in the bath. The captain, marooned on the statue, could only shout.

Screeching and chattering, the monkey dragged the garment to the rooftop and poked at it, shook it, and then tried to put it on. "Bring it back, bring it back this instant, or I swear I will kill you!" cried d'Estouville.

"Don't you dare kill Auntie's monkey!" shouted Sibille. At the other end of the roof, two attendants had placed a ladder, and one of Auntie's footmen was climbing up, clutching a rope with which he hoped to catch the wayward monkey.

"Señor Alonzo is like my child; if you touch him, I'll drag you through the courts until nothing is left of you," shouted Aunt Pauline, who was being dragged out of the shady end of the bath by several attendants.

Unable to put on the doublet, the monkey shook it, then flung it away. Something hard and bright caught the sun as it flew from some secret recess of the garment, something like glass. It skittered down to the edge of the roof, where it caught in the gutter, then slid down the rainspout. The flash caught Nicolas's eye, and he put out his hand beneath the downspout to see what could be rattling down it. The heavy little green-glass bottle had not broken, nor had the tightly wedged cork come out of the neck.

"Why, look at this," he said loudly, as he inspected the offering that had dropped upon him from heaven, as it were. "It's a bottle of *love potion!*"

"Give me that, you lowborn little bastard!" cried the captain, clutching his towel and turning his attention from the monkey on the roof to his newly perceived rival in the shadows.

"Love potion! *Love* potion!" shouted Nicolas as he evaded the captain's grasp. "You couldn't win her with your dreadful serenaders, so

you were going to poison her heart with *love* potion! What a lover! Pan-
taloon on the stage!"

"Nicolas! Oh, Nicolas, you're back! I've missed you so! Where have
you been all this time?" cried Sibille.

"How dare you insult a d'Estouville! I challenge you to meet me on
the field of honor!"

"*You* challenge *me*? No, I challenge you, you bag of wind!"

"No challenges within the bath! Throw them both out! You'll answer
to the governor for this! You're banished for life!"

"Banished from this despicable establishment? You'll be hearing from
my uncle, the *Seigneur* de Vieilleville—"

"Come to mama, come to mama, my little sweetie. Did all those bad
people frighten you?" Aunt Pauline, her dripping shift revealing propor-
tions of astonishing magnificence, was coaxing Señor Alonzo down
from the roof with one of the copious supply of sweetmeats she always
traveled with.

"Nicolas, don't go! Take me with you!" Sibille, unlaced, unbuttoned,
and unshod, her wet braid unraveled down her back, rushed from the
dressing room door to his side.

"I can't, Sibille, I have to leave before they arrest me," cried Nicolas,
as he snatched up his boots.

"Nicolas, I love you always!" cried Sibille, and, still damp and rosy as
a water nymph, she embraced him suddenly. Nicolas looked, all in a moment, shocked and then overjoyed, an right then and there, his boots
still in his hands, embraced her back. There was the sound of applause
from the old ladies in the pool.

"No indecencies! You're fined! The governor will deal with you!"
Two burly attendants grabbed him by the neck.

"Sibille, my father's exiling me—I love you always—I'll write!" Nicolas cried over his shoulder as he was frog-marched from the enclosure
behind his rival.

"Exiling you?" said one of the men who was hauling him to the exit.
"Hmph. I'm not surprised. Troublemaker."

"I tell you, I am from the noblest family in France. My uncle is
the king's most trusted companion—you'll regret this—" D'Estouville's
shouts floated back from the outer gate.

"Wonderful," said a crippled old lady, who had entered the bath with a crutch, but was leaving without its assistance. "Better than a play in the theater. My pains have entirely vanished." Then she turned to Sibille, who was staring after them and wringing her hands. "Young lady," she said, "you needn't worry. That one will be back for you if he has to walk all the way from Tartary."

✤

"What says the Pope's messenger?" said King Henri, looking toward the Cardinal of Lorraine. Around the council table, faces were grim. With war possible on two fronts, Guise's army had been called home from Italy, but the debt they had incurred in the past three months was tremendous. Four hundred and thirty-four thousand écus, and nothing remaining in the treasury.

"His Holiness has approved the collection of a new tax of eight décimes from the clergy."

"I want you to carry out an inventory of all the church's objects of precious metal," said the king. There was a long and deadly silence around the table. The last source of money in the realm, to be collected and melted down if the war continued much longer. France had entered the end game.

"You must go to the bankers of Lyons, the Italian bankers, the Germans. We must have a loan of at least five hundred thousand écus," said the Old Constable.

"Tell them," said King Henri, "tell them that I am a prince of honor, and will not fail to pay them their interest, unlike King Philip of Spain."

As the meeting wore on, plans were laid, and from these plans, the orders went out: the Old Constable would leave by the end of the month to take command of the war on the northern front, and every man at court able to bear arms was ordered to go with him. King Henri himself would go to Compiègne to be nearer the front, and join the army of the north in person early the following month. August, the season of heat, would be the month of victory over the Empire.

Seventeen

hat silver! What lovely linen! Oh, my dear Pauline, you have exceeded us all." As Auntie's guests entered our salon, there were little gasps of pleasure at the ornate dishes of dainties on the tables, the pretty little party favors laid out at each place, the two good-looking young men playing the flute and *épinette* in the corner. War, tragedy, and suffering—nothing interrupted these old ladies' social gatherings. They came in the flush of joy, in the black of mourning, in health, and with one foot in the grave. It was as if they'd lost all sense of decency about others' grief, especially mine. I had found and lost true love in an instant; I had heard not a word about Nicolas's fate—was he in the Bastille or on the stony road to exile at this very moment? What of the duel with Captain d'Estouville, who had vowed to kill him? Was Nicolas alive or dead? And here I was, living a shallow mockery in the center of false pleasures.

"Why, it is the very least I could do to honor you ladies, and, oh, my, *dear* Erminette, it's all because I could never hope to equal your splendid *salle.*" There they all were, just dancing on the tomb of my sorrows, the whole lot of them. Auntie was ebullient, generous. No one loved card afternoons more than she, and she had managed to collect around her a circle of raucous old ladies almost exactly like herself—widows and wives of minor gentry of the robe, of freshly minted and somewhat dubious titles, all thrilled that she had a court connection and all devoted to the art of gossip.

"And you never will equal them, dearie! Those cherries are my secret, and I won't even tell it to my daughter when I'm on my deathbed," the old lady cackled. The two strong lackeys the old lady had brought with her helped her into a cushioned chair, covered her vastly swollen legs with a lap robe, and vanished downstairs to pursue the kitchen maids.

"They say the fever kept ever so many away from the funeral of Madame Cardin. Only her grandson came, and him not even in full mourning."

"I hear the others were all disappointed in their inheritance—Thank your stars, dear Pauline, for such a levelheaded, dutiful daughter as your darling Sibille."

"And so talented, too!" cried another woman, immense in black satin and lace.

The flute player had put down his instrument and burst into song. "Sweet shepherdess, recall, how soon the season of love is over—" One of my most delicate verses, very admired by the ladies at court. How could I bear hearing it now, when all hope of love had fled!

"I've had them set a half dozen of her finest works to music," said Auntie, looking smug. For her sake, and her sake only, I had forced my suffering self downstairs to assist with her card-party. After all, the horrible scandal of the challenges at the spa was on every tongue these days, and the fascination of my presence alone would make her card-party the envy of her set. And besides, when I had died of grief, there would be more people to speak of me, which gave me a certain perverse pleasure.

"And all about the season of love. Too brief, too brief! And all her charming little verses even more in fashion than ever, now that the dear girl is the object of the most celebrated challenge of the season! Just think! D'Estouville, who has killed twelve men in affairs of honor. My, what a hero!"

"But *I* say, the duel won't be held. The king's edict against dueling, you know—they'll both end up arrested for violating the king's command. *I've* heard that the king is furious at the notion of losing officers to private quarrels. They will be forced to reconcile."

"I'd bet good money that duel will be held. You know these young men and their affairs of honor. When has any royal edict every stopped dueling?"

"Not when every available man must be at the front—the king has sworn to order the execution of anyone who appears on the field of honor, as an example—"

"Arrest d'Estouville? Never! His uncle Vieilleville stands too high at court for that—"

"Well, the other young man then—his family, well, it isn't—*old* blood, you know. Besides, I hear his father intends to have him imprisoned, or send him into exile, so that he can't meet d'Estouville."

"How lacking in any concept of honor. It would be far better to see him dead than run away from a challenge. But then, I hear his father's a banker—"

"*Oof*, money. Nobody nice ever talks about money—"

"Still, you know how it is these days. Don't annoy the bankers, for the sake of their loans, don't annoy the Lutherans, for the sake of our German mercenaries. Who is left? We are overrun with riffraff these days—"

"Don't take it personally, dear Sibille. D'Estouville gives the whole affair *style,* so the challenge won't lower your standing. He'll just trounce the fellow, if he turns up. And just think! After a fashionable duel like that, you can have any lover you want—"

"Lovers, bah! Don't mislead the child," cried one old lady, who had taken out her false teeth in order to speak better. "The best time is when the season of love is past. Then after the season of love, comes the season of cards! A vast improvement! Cut the deck, Pauline! I feel lucky this afternoon!"

"Never give in to love, Sibille, my dear! Men aren't worth it!" proclaimed Erminette from her throne-like chair at the far end of the table, puffing with the effort of laying out her cards and speaking all at once. "Why, just last week I saw Madame de Bonneville's chambermaid hanged for drowning her baby so she could keep her position. That's where love leads! The grave! We're lucky to have survived the season of love, I say! Aha! I have the queen!"

"They *say* a priest was the father—"

"Well, of course. Who else? Give way to my king, dear Erminette." Money rattled on the table. The crass heartlessness of these joyful old harpies, so entirely uninterested in my sorrows, which, after all, interested *me* greatly, seemed entirely too much to bear.

"Darling Sibille, you aren't playing today?"

"I'm not feeling very well—I'm sure I wouldn't have the least luck. I—I need to lie down."

"Take a nice glass of cordial, dearie, and you'll feel better in no time."

"Yes, we'll save you a place at the table," I heard them call, as I fled upstairs.

❦

Far from the callous observations of the cardplayers, I rushed forward, utterly dissolved in sorrow, to fling myself upon my bed for a good and proper weeping fit. Imagine, then, what additional shock was laden upon my already tormented breast when, rather than my cozy and well-made bed, a ready receptacle of sorrows, a scene of mortal horror met my eyes!

There, stretched out and dead on the carpet, lay my own truest and most devoted companion, my last friend on earth, Gargantua, his stomach bloated beyond recognition! At the top of the wardrobe, Señor Alonzo was contentedly picking fleas, so I knew at once that it was he who had done the terrible deed. Beside Gargantua's head lay a few well-chewed scraps of human skullbone, a fragment of lower jaw, a number of brown, ancient teeth—and the open box of Menander the Deathless. Hate rose in my soul, and I grabbed the nearest available weapon, a large brass paperweight in the shape of a lion's head, and flung it at the vile, furry little creature. "You horrible, horrible, monkey—you've killed my own dear Gargantua!" Lightly, the monkey dodged my missile, and leapt to the bed canopy. "I'll kill you, I swear I'll kill you," I cried, snatching up a large embroidery hoop, the nearest thing at hand, and climbing onto the foot of the bed, clutching at one of the bedposts, while I tried to dislodge the monkey with the other hand. At the sound, Baptiste came running, just as I slipped and fell to the floor, damaging my back too badly to rise for the moment.

"Why, that little devil spilled the box off the top of the armoire, and now that big hound of yours has eaten up your magic head. What a disaster!" He tried to help me rise, but I just moaned.

"Don't touch me. Just kill that evil little monster for me. Look what he's done to my dog."

"Come here, come here, you! Mademoiselle, he must have unlatched his cage."

"Oh, Gargantua, you were the only creature in the world that ever loved me truly." I wept, still lying flat on the floor and incapable of movement due to the dreadful shock I had undergone.

"*Mon Dieu,* what a disaster! He has entirely eaten up the magic head!" exclaimed Baptiste. "Now the queen will never call you again. All our good fortune—oh, dreadful, what terrible luck—how will I ever tell Madame?" What? The queen would never call again? The head was gone, and I was free? Oh, alas, poor faithful hound, who freed me at the cost of his own dear life. Maybe it wasn't too late. Maybe Nicolas hadn't left yet. I'd write—yes, as soon as I could get up, I'd steal away to his house, perhaps in disguise, and get word to him that I was waiting, and free at last of the accursed head. We could marry secretly; we'd escape beyond the reach of his heartless father; I'd share his bitter exile. Penniless, living only on love, we'd wander into sunnier climes. . . .

"Oh, poor creature, poor creature, he died to save me from that awful—thing." I put out my hand to embrace my faithful hound, but since I was temporarily unable to move, I could only reach a portion of his noble, self-sacrificial stomach, and not his faithful head.

"Madame will have my hide—oh, God, preserve me—"

"Oh, if only his generous heart were still beating—"

"You devil—you brown, furry devil—" cried Baptiste. "If I have to lose my place here over this, I'll see you flung out into the street first—" Baptiste threw open the window in a paroxysm of vengeance, and leapt upon a chair to seize the monkey and fling him out. Señor Alonzo leapt again to the top of the armoire, screeching with enjoyment at the chase, while the brisk, fresh breeze entered the room. But with the fresh air, did I feel something, something stirring, something not entirely dead in Gargantua's swollen belly? I heard a muffled gasping sound. Was my dog returning to life, or was the hideous Menander still alive within his dead carcass? There was another gasp, a breath, and a ripple down the dead hound's belly and then—

With a start, Gargantua's eyes flew open with an expression of pure horror. There was a choking, gurgling sound, and without even lifting his head, he began to vomit yellow liquid, with shreds of brown, revolting, disgusting, stinky stuff. But even as I jumped up, horrified by the hideous retching sound, and, I must admit, a certain low desire to save my silk gown, I could see the tiny shreds assembling themselves into bigger pieces, the bigger pieces joining together . . .

"Aaah!" cried Baptiste in horror. "It's still alive!" Even the monkey stopped chattering and leaping, and sat on the curtain rod, staring curiously at the sight.

"My dog—Gargantua—oh, live, live!" I cried, my mind torn between joy at seeing my dog alive, disgust at seeing that dreadful Menander reassembling himself, and fear that Menander had reanimated Gargantua in some dreadful fashion and would send him again into death when he was done vomiting up Menander's well-chewed and partially digested fragments. Now the brown teeth, with their long, dessicated roots, were crawling across the carpet like revolting insects, blindly seeking the jawbone from which they had been scattered. The skull fragments rocked and skittered as they drew together, then locked into place. Bits of flesh adhered, a pulpy mass reassembled itself as an eyeball—never in my life do I ever wish to see such a stomach-turning sight again.

"Never, never in eighteen centuries, have I suffered such indignity," said Menander the Deathless, shaking his head slightly as he nested into his box, the way a person might settle into bed at the end of a hard day. "The greatest magus of all time, reassembling himself out of a dog's stomach." The monkey on the curtain rod bared his teeth at Menander. There had to be something good in that monkey after all, I thought suddenly, if he hated that old mummy enough to dump him out on the floor. Not, mind you, that that made Señor Alonzo any more likable.

"My poor, sweet, brave Gargantua, are you feeling better?" I said, stroking my dog's back and stomach as I bathed his head with my tears. As I was rewarded with first a feeble, then a joyful wag of the tail, that spiteful old mummified head said:

"All that for a dog? You are the most birdbrained, sentimental woman that ever laid hold of a pen."

"What do I care for your opinion? My brave Gargantua risked himself to save me from you."

"He risked himself for a snack, you dumb female. He'd have done the same for a rotten ham rind in the garbage."

"Nonsense. You are so without honor you can't recognize it in any other creature."

"Honor, ha! After all I've done for you, you should be weeping over me and stroking me! Where would your awful writings be without the queen's favor, which I may point out, *I* secured for you, gratis? I've half a mind to bring about your bad fortune."

"Mademoiselle—" said Baptiste, his teeth chattering.

"Nonsense. Menander can't do a thing unless somebody wishes it, and the people who see him are too busy wishing for themselves to wish anything about me. And I'm the one person who doesn't want him and here I am trapped with him after all."

"You could always wish that I'd go away—" said Menander suggestively.

'Baptiste," I said, stroking down my dress, "I am in shock, terrible shock. Bring me a glass of that cordial Auntie saves beneath her bed, or I shall faint away and become permanently ill. And send up Marie—I want this mess on the carpet cleaned up." I sighed a great sigh. I couldn't disguise myself and run off with Nicolas after all. The head would follow, and where it followed, so would the queen, the duchess, their astrologers, their relatives—a regular parade, an army, all clamoring to tell their horrid secret desires to that awful box. And, then, oh, God, the thought suddenly came over me, the worst thought of all: suppose Nicolas and I *did* manage to get married? Menander would be there every night in the bedchamber, making loathsome little comments about our most intimate moments. How could we ever hope for happiness? If only Gargantua had a stronger stomach— Damn, damn, and a thousand damns. "Well, Gargantua, at least you tried," I said, sitting down on the bed, but carefully, so as not to annoy my injured tailbone. He looked up at me with his big pink tongue hanging out of his mouth and thumped his tail cheerfully on the rug, just as if he had not ever attempted to consume the most filthy dinner in the world. As Baptiste left the room, Menander called after him,

"You could wish for a better place—" and Baptiste answered with a growl,

"You don't catch me wishing on no heathen, talking head—"

❧

The smell of dirty diapers and cabbage penetrated from the back rooms into the magician's little reception chamber. The large man settled his body down gingerly, wrinkling his nose as if he feared contamination by the dark, low wooden chair on which he had seated himself. He had worn old clothes for this visit to the wrong part of town, anonymous dark wool trunk hose and doublet, covered by an undecorated black wool cloak, but still, he felt they would have to be laundered or given away when he returned home. He was an immense, sinister man, his plain black beaver hat pulled low over greasy, graying hair and barely skimming an eyepatch that covered his left eye. He tapped a finger impatiently on the table that separated him from the magician as he spoke.

"The oil of vitriol, Maestro Lorenzo, it did not work."

"Surely it did not fail to burn, Monsieur. It was of the finest quality," answered Lorenzo Ruggieri.

"It burned most powerfully, but some unlucky star made her dodge so as to save her face."

"Ah, as I warned you. Opportunity is everything with vitriol—you must get close enough not to miss the target. It is entirely different with the death-spell. It is impossible to dodge a well-cast death-spell, Monsieur Villasse, or hide from it, even at the farthest ends of the earth."

"A spell? I mistrust spells. How do I know that I've got what I paid for? No, I want something stronger, more certain. Something that will cause terrible suffering—"

"That can always be managed. I am, after all, a master of my craft. Now tell me again all the things you wish accomplished. As I recall, it is rather complicated."

"She is a great heiress now, a favorite of the queen—God alone knows why—and is being courted by an officer of high rank. Once he marries her, the property I wish to possess will be beyond my grasp. The vitriol, it might have stopped that, but now—no, it is better that she die. Besides, there are—ah—others with an interest—"

"Ah, another heir to the land."

"Yes. More beautiful, more agreeable to me, and anxious for marriage."

"Marriage? I thought you had said that a brother was next in line."

"One way or another, it doesn't matter. He is in the military. Things happen." Villasse shrugged.

"Ah, I think I am beginning to see," said Lorenzo Ruggieri, tapping on his forehead. "First the woman, something painful, then the man, something quiet. Am I right?"

"Absolutely. You read my mind, Italian."

"I can't help admiring a wily fellow who thinks so many steps ahead. It's an advanced skill. So few possess it but us. But continue—would you also like a love potion?"

"Ha, I don't need one. Those who hate the same person must needs love one another. The woman stole her younger sister's admirer, and when the sister heard the two would marry, we became one in our vengeance. Why, she even thought of the vitriol—"

"I thought that sounded like a woman's idea . . ." murmured the magician to himself. But Villasse went on, unhearing:

"She needs position; a proud family, but poor. My speculations and monopolies make me more wealthy by the moment; a wife of old family would suit me well. And she is beautiful, respectful, feminine—as unlike her murderous, lunatic elder sister as it is possible to imagine—"

"I should warn you, Monsieur, these urges to kill tend to run in families—you should be wary. Now, a proper love potion—"

"You'd do anything to enlarge your fee, wouldn't you? First the expense of the vitriol, and now you're trying to sell me three jobs rather than two."

"That's because I always think only for my client's benefit. You said you wanted suffering for the first job?"

"Yes. Slow, terrible suffering. For the second, I need only speed and undetectability."

"The second is easy. White arsenic—it will be mistaken for camp fever. The bowels come undone. Send it in a package of food from home. Sausage always does well. People always blame sausage . . ."

Lorenzo looked dreamily into the air, remembering former triumphs. Villasse drummed his fingers impatiently on the table, bringing Lorenzo back to the present. "For the first, hmm, let's see—" Lorenzo Ruggieri smiled sweetly and placed one hand on his heart. "Ah, yes, terrible suffering. You might consider poison of toad—not too quick acting, terrible suffering, and an inevitable end. I happen to have some on hand, so I can offer it to you for the same price as white arsenic and less than viper, which I would have to send out for."

"What is the—ah—type of suffering?" said the lord of La Tourette, his one eye glittering, his mouth half open in voluptuous expectation.

"Quite superior suffering. First light becomes irritating, then blisters grow on the surface of the eyes, gradually blinding the victim. In the meantime, the intellectual ability is reduced to the level of an animal, and sharp pains rend the body, especially, um, the generative parts—"

"Blindness and pain? Oh, splendid. Are you sure?" The stranger was rubbing his gloved hands together in greedy anticipation.

"As if you yourself had taken your will of her with a red-hot iron."

"Ha, and a bargain, too. I'll have it, if you can tell me how I can be sure that it gets to its mark."

"I must say, you really don't seem to like this woman."

"Don't seem to? Do you see this eye? See here?" Villasse rose to his full height, fury making the arteries stand out in his neck as his face crimsoned. "Look, look at that!" he cried, lifting up the eyepatch to show a hideously defaced mass of scar tissue, marked and seared with the permanent dark stain of gunpowder fired at close range. "It is she that struck it out."

"A powerful blow, that. How did she manage? It will be harder to taint her with the poison if she is violent, and cannot be lured close to you."

"She shot me in the face at close quarters with her father's blunderbuss. But being a fool, she had not loaded it properly. She forgot the shot, and only fired the wadding."

"Hmm. Quite a shrew, I'd say. She won't be inviting you in for a cup of wine, then."

"I should think not."

"Well, then, I can't offer you this ring," said the younger Ruggieri, pulling aside a curtain that concealed a number of shelves with boxes and bottles, and taking down an interesting, ironbound coffer. He set it on the tale and opened it to reveal a number of cloth-wrapped objects of various sizes. "See this?" he said, unwrapping a little one. "A beautiful thing. It has belonged to three Dukes, an Emperor, and even a Pope. Look at this—a tiny spring, and it opens to drop the poison into a cup when you merely pass your hand across it."

"Charming. But not for me."

"Obviously. Now here are several little mechanisms that send darts across a short distance—"

"No darts. I've wasted too much time hiring that rogue to trail after her and throw the vitriol. I want something that works by itself."

"Well, you might send her a gift—"

"Not from myself."

"Why not from that generous, aristocratic fiancé of hers? Have it delivered to her door in his name." Lorenzo Ruggieri donned a pair of gloves and unwrapped another little packet containing a crimson velvet case. He opened it and gingerly picked out of its satin-lined center an exquisite jeweled brooch with a sharp little pin at the back. Shaped with two ornate branches, almost like the upper wings of a moth, its center was formed by a great pearl, surmounted by an emerald, and then a smaller pearl. A short pendant chain formed of small pearls interspersed with carved gold beads hung from beneath the large central pearl. The golden side branches, cunningly ornamented with carved flowers, shone with brilliants and tiny seed pearls. Even Villasse gasped at the loveliness of the thing. Then he grunted.

"Hmph. All those pearls. Beyond my price, I should think."

"The pearls are false, but no one who has received it has had time to discover the fact. And if you can retrieve it when it has done its work, I'll buy it back at half price."

"She'd be dazzled. Any woman would. How does it do its work?"

"See these little flowers? All sharper than knives. The pin at the back has a clasp that is hard to undo—and it is made of spring metal. So easy to prick oneself. And then, even if one is not pricked by the pin, just settling the thing on one's gown, or into one's hat, one is bound to be scratched by the flowers. Such a little scratch. One might put it in one's mouth, or perhaps not. The wings, they are hollow, the holes that feed the surface too small to be seen by the eye. And then, of course, if the poison is colorless, as it was last time, even the surface of the jewel can be painted—"

"Last time?"

"I can assure you, it has never yet failed to do its work."

"Excellent. I'll hire an old soldier to deliver it. She'll never suspect a thing."

"I admire a man of decision. Now, how about the boy at the front? Will you be sending the package yourself?"

"The problem is the letter that accompanies the gift. He'll know the writing. Better it should be a gift from his sister."

"The one who shoots guns?" said Lorenzo, opening the back of the brooch with heavy gloves, and transferring several drops of a vitreous liquid from a bottle into a tiny opening, almost invisible, behind the catch.

"No, the one who adores me."

"Monsieur, I must speak to you as one whose profession is deceit. You are a master of the first rank." He sealed the opening behind the catch and replaced the brooch in its velvet case.

"Why, of course," said Villasse, counting out gold pieces from his purse, tucking a little glass vial into his wallet and then wrapping the velvet box in a linen handkerchief for safe transit. "An unfair life has taught me all her tricks. They have cheated me for the last time, these coldhearted people of old blood. That property was meant to be mine. This time, the goddess of revenge has made me brilliant." As the door shut behind the black-cloaked man, Lorenzo's wife called him to supper. Carefully, he removed his gloves and replaced the box on the shelf behind the curtain.

"Oh, Beatrice, what work!" he said, settling down before a bowl of steaming potage. "But today alone, I've earned little Fortunato's school fees for the year. But you—and Roger, too—I must warn you again: don't open any packages that are delivered here. A man of that type, when he's done his work, will doubtless have his miserable little lizard-brain turn to thoughts of getting rid of any witnesses. Praise Asmodeus, I am shrewder than he."

"Some people just have no gratitude," said his wife, ladling out a second helping all around.

Eighteen

Geometrical reasoning proves that the cut is therefore in fact inferior to the thrust, for a circle has a longer path than does a straight line. The cut is preferred only by those accustomed to weapons of the old school, French and English gentlemen who do not easily come to the new Italian rapier, but whose vain words and posturings are like the blowing of wind. Meet such, then, by awaiting the attack, for they will reveal themselves and leave the defender in the superior position. Should such a one attack by a cut, you may thrust beneath his blade. Should he attack by thrust, which is alien to his nature, you may parry with the blade or with your left hand, which you must furnish with a stout leather or mail glove. . . .

To meet an imbroccata *in low ward, beat aside the thrust with the left hand at mid-blade, then as you oppose his blade with your own, seize his rapier guard with your left hand and in this way disarm him. This* botte secrete *was imparted by Maestro Francesco Altoni to very few, since if ill-practiced, it can lead to death. . . .*

From Secrets of the Italian Art of Fencing
Montvert, N., Sieur de Beauvoir et
Châteauneuf-sur-Charentonne, Lyons, 1571

In the rue de Bailleul, the rattle of drums and the crunch of marching feet rose to the windows above. A company of city pikemen, banners flying, officers on horseback, was marching to join the troops massing at the northern front. Women shouted and threw flowers down from the upper stories of houses that lined the street, and ragtag little boys ran beside and behind the booted, motley-clad soldiers, cheering and waving. But one window, a window in a square tower with pointed roof, was closed. From behind its warped, greenish little panes, a heavy-set man with a square-cut beard, gowned in silk, with a heavy gold chain, pondered the glinting steel pouring through the narrow street like a river. *My* boots, *my* pikes, *my* horses, and *my* advance on salaries, thought the banker Montvert. I wonder if the king will pay the interest. Of course, if we lose, the entire investment is moot. How much more practical to finance both sides, then one would ensure collecting from at least one of the kings. He sighed. Kings were so touchy about this sort of thing; they always seemed to think a man has to be on just one side. And, after all, one did have to choose a place of residence. He sighed again. The kings take your money, he thought, and their servants pick quarrels with your idiot son, who is blinded by their flash and dazzle and lies of chivalry. Who, who is on *my* side?

But there, drifting to his side like a frail leaf of autumn, was his pallid, saintly daughter, Clarette. Her cool hand brushed his brow, and she said, "*Padre mio,* you have such terrible cares, confide in me and I will pray for you."

"Is your brother still pounding on the door upstairs?" he asked.

"As loudly as ever, since the day you locked him in. He says you have destroyed his good name since you have prevented him from meeting d'Estouville on the field of honor."

"What else?"

"A thousand other things, Father, many of them in appropriate for female ears."

"Then you've been listening again," said the old man.

"Oh, no, Father, I just can't help hearing, since I kneel in prayer for the salvation of his soul right outside the door."

"Ah, I see, I see. Well then, my lily, my diamond, pray also for the salvation of his body, and that he learn a proper calling in life and marry. Otherwise, you will have to provide the grandchildren." The saintly, pale child shuddered, and touched the crucifix—one of a large wardrobe of them that she possessed—that hung around her neck.

"Father, the Carmelites—"

"I have told you, and told you again, Claretta *mia,* my beloved white rose, that I cannot sacrifice you to the altar of Christ. As soon as d'Estouville departs for the front, I plan to pack your brother off to his mother's cousins in Genoa—in chains, if necessary—and I will then send to Florence to enter negotiations with the Pazzi family for a suitable bridegroom. Would you rather have Giacomo, who is two years older than you, or Guiseppe, who is six months younger, but, they say, the handsomer of the two?" With the cry of a wounded fawn, the pallid girl blew, wraith-like without even the sound of a single footstep, from the room.

"Idiot," said her father, as he watched her retreat. "The sooner she's married, the better—before she evaporates entirely."

Upstairs, Clarette took up her accustomed spot in front of her Satan-possessed brother's nailed-shut doorway to begin again her prayers for his salvation. The servants, her mother, tiptoed around her, speaking in reverend whispers as they saw her rededicate herself to her holy mission.

"A saint—a saint—" they whispered, and so self-denying was she that she pretended she didn't even hear them.

"Oh, Madame, your daughter is a blessed virgin," whispered her mother's old nurse, who had also been hers and Nicolas's.

"God has made me suffer," she heard her mother reply. "He took my little twins, my father, and my brother—but then He repaid me a thousandfold by sending me that blessed child for consolation..." The voices faded off down the hall, and Clarette's heart grew warm—but then, again, it may have been the effect of the praying.

She raised her voice, slightly, expecting the divinely fulfilling dialogue with the devils inside of Nicolas to resume. She would recite, and he, the madman, the lost soul, the extraordinarily bored prisoner of the bourgeoisie, would shout all kinds of extremely interesting things back through the door. Sometimes, she would pass him some holy work or pamphlet of sermons for his improvement, and it was then that Satan himself seemed to spring forth from her brother's tongue, steeling her in her divine mission. After all, if she could not enter the convent just now, what higher jewel in her crown could exist than the salvation of her poor, lost, older brother?

But instead of the expected imprecations, an eerie silence ensued. In the door, a slot had been cut, for the passage in of food and drink, and the passage out of the chamber pot. It, too, had been fitted with a bar to prevent the prisoner's escape by some ruse. The silence boded well, thought the white lily of the Montvert family, perhaps he is ready to contemplate his errors. She took down the bar so that she could slip though the slot a particularly potent prayer, copied in longhand by herself. But no grumbling and growling met her ears. And when she peeked into the room, she saw no caged tiger, but an unmade bed, a broken window, and the end of a sheet tied to the bedpost.

Her screams brought the family, and in the milling around and general hand-wringing, she heard, as in a dream, her father's voice giving orders to unseal the room, and the pounding and prying of crowbars. All of them, father, servants, mother, old nurse, and sister rushed into the room.

"My boy is gone! Gone to his doom!" cried her mother, half fainting.

"Out the window," said Bernardo, peering out at the rope of sheets and old clothes, "and his sword and poniard are missing."

"Damn!" shouted Nicolas's father. "I didn't know they were locked up with him—I should have stripped the room first before I nailed the door shut—"

"I have failed," cried Clarette, rolling her eyes up into her head, and turning paler than ever, but nobody even noticed her in the hullabaloo. How irritating it all was. As usual, everything was about Nicolas. What a curse to be born younger, and a girl. "I shall pray to the Holy Virgin," she said, a bit louder, but nobody heard her. Her mother was weeping. "My boy, my boy, dead!" Her father was calling down really extraordinary curses, and even the servants were too busy attending them to notice the poor, pallid, self-sacrificial soul in the corner. While they all were inspecting the sheet tied at the foot of the bed, she sat down at its head, mortified, bitter.

It was then that she noticed something unusual winking and blinking in a stray shaft of sunlight. A bottle, a green-glass bottle that her brother had got somewhere, set up like a trophy on the nightstand. Curiosity grew in her. Was it perfume? Was it medicine? She picked it up, and saw that it was tightly sealed with wax all around the cork. She turned it over, and saw a legend engraved in the glass: LOVE POTION. What an amazing thing, she thought. Was this how Nicolas made himself the best loved? How had he found it? Did he drink it every day? Or did he pour it in the glass of wine he shared with that wicked courtesan he'd been forbidden to marry, so that she would prefer him to all her other lovers? Did it make people love you, or you love other people? Did it require a drop, or the whole bottleful? Questions began to eat at her, and she tried to think of holy things, but the diabolical little bottle kept interrupting the most edifying thoughts. Where had he got it? Was it expensive? Was there more? Quietly, she slipped it into the bosom of her gown, where the cold glass seemed to make her skin prick and her heart tremble. If anyone had noticed her drift soundlessly from the room, they would have seen two distinct pink patches beginning to form up on her sheet-white cheeks.

✤

"Go and have Arnaud see who's banging on the front door, Sibille, I am entirely too wretched to rise. If it's Doctor Lenoir, tell him his last purge brought forth nothing but green bile, and my gout is worse than ever." Aunt Pauline lay, moaning, her body like mound of cushions beneath the bedclothes, the sheets turned back from her bad foot, for she could bear nothing touching it when the attacks were on her like this. On these occasions, her massive, carved canopied bed became, to use her phrase, a "temple of suffering," and she would call for the doctor, the last rites, and announce that "soon it would be all over—don't forget the little ivory box on the mantel, I especially want it to be yours." Then, of course, company, fuss, and purgation would make her better, and she would rise grandly, order her long-suffering maid to dress her in her finest, and say, "All the while I lay in my bed of pain, I kept remembering that splendid little Italian velvet I saw in that little shop in the Palais. Don't you think it would make a lovely hood? Let's go and see if it's still there. My recovery is a miracle, a miracle, I say—I need to go to the cathedral and give thanks to God—a new hood would be the very thing—out of respect, you know. Perhaps a silk lining in sky blue—" and the crisis was over.

But this time it wasn't the doctor. On the threshold stood someone entirely unexpected, his hard, lined face in sagging folds, his beard and hair in disarray, his gown splashed at the hem with stinking Paris mud, testifying to his rapid trip across town.

"Tell Doctor Lenoir that I need another eternal pill; my maid has failed to recover the last from the chamber pot, and I am devastated. The lead in pills these days is such poor quality I'm sure a new one won't work as well. My mother left it to me in her will." Auntie's voice came floating out of the bedroom.

"It's not the doctor, *ma tante*," I called, "—it's Nicolas's father."

"Tell him he's not welcome in my house," came the response. "He has failed me utterly, and I no longer wish to speak to him."

"Demoiselle, I beg you, has my son been here?"

"Not since you locked him up. The last I saw of him was when he went to ask your permission to marry me—and never returned. Then when he came to the baths to say farewell before going into exile, you locked him up again, and gave out to the world that you were sending him away to keep him out of my clutches. Monsieur Montvert, you are a bad man who has trumpeted to the four corners of the earth that I am a courtesan who seduced your son to entrap him into marriage. You have spoiled my reputation, and I must bid you farewell, as my aunt desires."

"Your rep—" He began to turn quite red in the face, then checked himself. "Demoiselle, you are the only one to whom I can turn. Nicolas has escaped, and it is the day appointed for the duello you caused at the bath. I am sure he plans to meet d'Estouville this forenoon outside the walls, where he will either be slaughtered like a calf or arrested and exe-cuted. The very least you can do, since it is all your fault, is to plead with him to stop this deadly so-called affair of honor. Malicious as you are, surely you do not want him to die."

He's out, and didn't even send me notice? I thought. He doesn't love me anymore. Auntie was wrong. The old ladies were wrong. He's for-gotten me. And it's all his father's doing. I felt my heart crack at the

thought of it. He'd won, that cruel, selfish old man. But I was determined not to show a thing in front of him.

"If he's gone, how do you know he's meeting d'Estouville?"

"Because he took nothing with him but his sword, cloak, and
poniard. His money, everything else—remained in his room. Demoiselle,
he will not listen to me, but perhaps if you beg him, you will have
influence—"

"Why should I, an Artaud of La Roque, ask a man to play the coward? Honor is everything, and without it, life is valueless. Sir, you shame
yourself in asking such a thing."

"You needn't be so snobbish about it. I'd think you, of all people,
would know the value of a little accommodation to these so-called rules
of honor. My boy's only a student, he has no experience, and he can be
executed if the authorities find out about this duel. D'Estouville is not
only high enough in rank to escape the law, he's celebrated for having
killed a dozen men in duels. What is my son's life to a man like that except to boast that he has killed number thirteen? He'll spit him like a
roast, and I have only one son left. One, do you understand? And he's
my dearest treasure. If he ever learned anything useful, he'd really make
something of himself—something better than worm food."

"The *value*—? I? What do you take me for? My reputation was as
white as a lily until you besmirched it with your nasty behavior—and
now you've succeeded at last in poisoning my Nicolas's heart."

"Besmirch? You lure my boy into a public stew, where is he set upon
by your lover, who challenges him to a duel that will kill him? And for
what? So you may be known as a woman for whom men have died? Are
you going to make a poem about it, so that your lovers can sing it at
court?"

"My lovers? You horrible old man, leave at once! Nicolas was right
about you—you're just dirty-minded, and wouldn't know a pure heart or
an honorable intention if you stumbled over it in the dark. You don't deserve a son like him!"

"Sibille, what is that I hear, voices? I thought I told you that man was
not welcome in my house. Surely, he has already done enough harm to
you—" Auntie's voice came floating in from the bedroom.

"I did *not* lure him—he hates d'Estouville for what he is—a titled parasite and a fortune hunter who's after my inheritance, and I've never even let him in the house—"

"Inheritance?" said Nicolas's father, his eyes wandering suddenly to the furniture and tapestries in the room.

"And what's more, the spa is very respectable and ladies of the highest standing patronize it, and—"

"But you are seen in court, and unmarried—"

"I was invited by the queen herself—"

"But your cousin Matheline said—"

"Matheline? What has she to do with it?"

"She said—she said, your poetry had brought you lovers of the highest rank, and she was going to take up writing herself, it was all the rage with the court ladies now—"

"Lovers? Lovers? I don't dare have lovers! They'd just be after the queen's box that I can't get rid of! My life has been ruined by Menander the Undying, and the only person in the world who understood and cared for me was Nicolas, and you've stolen him from me. I hope you're happy about what you've done. It's all your fault, you did every bit of it, and he only came to the spa to say good-bye, and if you'd let us marry, it never, never would have happened—"

"Menander the Undying? Who is that?"

"Sibille, I've heard you both. I told you to send him away. But now that your tongue has wagged a little too freely, bring him in here. I need to look him in the face." Auntie's voice, quite strong for one in mortal illness, called through the open bedroom door.

"Who is that? I'm sorry, I must go—Nicolas—"

"Tell him to come in here or I will put a curse on him that will make his hair stand on end," Auntie said. "Family, fortune, all will fail if he crosses me now. Tell him that Menander the Undying wants his presence." I saw Monsieur Montvert go quite pale. Poised for flight on the threshold, he suddenly took a long look about the room, breathed hard, stepped back in.

"Sorcery," he whispered. "Not sin, but sorcery. What is it that you are entangled in?" I sighed deeply.

"Come and see," I said.

"Will it save my boy?" he asked.

"Only at a price you'd be unwilling to pay," I answered.

"I'd pay with my soul," he said, and at that moment my hate slipped away, and I felt sorry, so sorry for him that I could hardly bear the weight of it. I think I knew even more than he did exactly what he was saying.

"Don't ask Menander for anything," I said. "He's as evil as they come—he'll twist your wish and spoil it. He destroys everyone who gets involved with him. The great Nostradamus told me once he was the open gate into Hell. I'll—I'll go with you to wherever they intend to meet each other for the duello, even if it puts my reputation in rags. I'll beg Nicolas to betray his own honor for your sake. Just don't make me guilty of showing another man to his ruin."

The old man turned and looked me full in the face, staring, silent, haggard. His eyes were full of fear and sorrow. Then, with resolute step, like a man marching to the gallows, he went into Auntie's bedroom, where the open box of Menander the Undying lay upon an ornately carved, dark table by the window.

"Well, well," said Menander, his voice like the whisper of dry leaves, "another man anxious to shed himself of his soul. It's dead weight, Monsieur Banker, and you're bound to lose it anyway. Why not in good cause?" Monsieur Montvert walked back and forth before the table that held the open box, as if inspecting Menander from every angle, thinking, calculating.

"Because now that I see your nasty little eye, I have no doubt that you're a bigger cheat than the monarchs I lend money to. They never pay their interest, and rarely the principal. Have you ever paid off on your promises, Monsieur Evil Head?"

"I always pay—exactly what my devotees wish, no more, no less. I am exact. Confide in me your desire, and you shall have it—come now, it's so simple, and who sees a soul anyway? It is doubtless imaginary, and you'll be missing nothing—" But instead of temptation and desire, the old banker's face grew as hard as iron, and his lip curled with snobbery and disgust.

"I've known people like you," he said. "Hard dealers, sellers of repossessed goods and dead women's hair. All's fair, isn't it?" The old banker turned to me, his eyes assessing every shade and corner of my face.

"Tell me, Demoiselle, when did you take up sorcery as a hobby? Did you call this thing to you with some evil spell? Or did you animate this leaving from the gibbet yourself?"

"I didn't. This thing was in the hands of a stranger, and attached it-self to me by accident, and now I can't get rid of it, though I've tried dozens of times. But the queen wants it for herself—so I keep it for her, and bring it to her when she wants to wish for something. I'm not al-lowed to travel far from her presence, just in case something comes up suddenly that she wants to wish on."

"So that is the secret. How far it is from what I imagined. And you, Madame Tournet, I apologize for my intrusion. I seem to have got everything backward. I know the Sieur de La Roque-aux-Bois, your brother, Madame—"

"And you imagined his daughter to be as shameless as her father—a penniless adventuress who wormed her way into my good graces and then used me to go to court to make her fortune, and who now wanted a simpleminded husband as a cover for her affairs."

"Such things are not unheard of," answered Montvert the banker. "Ambitious women are more numerous than honest ones in these wicked days." He shrugged, as if to rid himself of old memories. "But now, since my son's life is in danger, I must ask you a few questions. This unpleas-ant, living, mummified head grants wishes, I take it?"

"If you recite the words on the box."

"And in bad spirit? That is, it takes your wish literally, and gives you precisely that?"

"Yes, indeed. I recommend you be very careful with the wording. If you wish for your son's life, he may be blinded. If you wish for his health, he may lose his mind. Menander's game is to get you to make an-other wish to mend the first one, and so on, until you sink into your grave from horror and regret."

"So he not only takes your soul in trade, but is so greedy to collect that he hurries you to give it up to him ahead of time?"

"That's more or less the idea. We've watched several foolish people do exactly that since he first came to us."

"And the queen?"

"She's iron-willed—she apportions her wishes very carefully."

"And you?"

"We don't wish. He hasn't got a body to force us to, after all, and he can only act when people wish for something, so he can't do anything to us on his own."

"He does whisper in the night, though. He says horrible things," I added.

"Whispers all night, tempts people to lose their souls, causes strangers to traipse through the house. I'm afraid, Demoiselle Sibille, though I have now formed the highest opinion of your character, that this is not the sort of encumbrance I wish my son to have in his life. He could not make much progress in a career with all the nocturnal interruptions, and, I'm afraid, he's very weak-willed."

"I understand entirely," said Auntie. "It's the sort of thing that even the immense fortune that she will inherit from me would hardly offset." When she saw that her dart had hit home, she smiled a very tiny smile under her black mustache, so small that her powder didn't even crinkle beside her eyes.

"Well, then, my mind's made up," said Monsieur Montvert.

"And your wish?" said Menander, one eye glittering evilly beneath a tattered, scaling eyelid.

"My wish is that Sibille make good on her offer to come and convince my boy not to fight," he said. "You're worse to deal with than the King of Portugal."

"What?" shrieked Menander. "You're not wishing?"

"Of course not," said Scipion Montvert, his voice brusque. "I am a banker, and I make decisions based on costs and benefits. Your cost is high, your benefit dubious, and you haven't got a means of force. The King of Portugal does. Let some other fool drown in your magic." Auntie laughed out loud.

"Banker, I like your brain," she said.

"And I, Madame, respect yours," he said, bowing to her where she lay in her huge canopied bed. "And now, if I may ask your permission, I have below a fast horse with packed saddlebags and a letter of credit. If Sibille will tell me where they are to meet and you will let her come with me, he will be on that horse and out of the country before d'Estouville and his seconds arrive."

Auntie nodded her head in assent. "Bring her back safe," she said. "She is the greatest treasure I possess."

"That I promise, Madame," he said.

"But—an extra horse? You knew all along I'd come?"

"Demoiselle. I am foolish sometimes, but never stupid. And I know love when I see it. I never doubted that when you saw the case rightly, you would aid me." But I knew that in his mind he had added, *even if it costs you Nicolas forever.*

❖

"Well, my friends, it looks as if the coward has fled," said Philippe d'Estouville, surveying the dueling field. The flattened, half-dried weeds of late summer testified to the spot's popularity as a place for illicit encounters. The narrow tracks that counted for roads bypassed the place, and only a few isolated windmills overlooked the abandoned spot. At a distance, a handful of early travelers could be spied on the trunk road to the Porte St.-Antoine, the route by which the dueling party had left the city. Inside the walls, on the dark towers of the Bastille, bright pennants fluttered in the morning breeze. Already, the day promised to be scorching. D'Estouville had dismounted, and with his seconds, paced up and down, surveying the distance for signs of his rival's party, and the immediate ground for whatever advantage it could hold.

"Wait a little—there's someone passing through the city gate, no, two—three."

"On foot. Surely, it's not them. Even bankers' boys have mules." The group of officers laughed.

"The sooner you kill him, the better," said d'Estouville's second. "My sister has disgraced the whole family by allowing such a fellow into her company." Annibal de La Roque flicked a green bottle fly off his sleeve. The buzzing of many flies rose from the dark stains on the earth. The blood of the last man to lose an encounter in this neglected place still lay beneath the weeds.

"They're coming closer. Well, well, it looks as if I will have my thirteenth man after all."

"Who are those seconds? Gentlemen? One looks like a student."

"I know the other—the innkeeper's son from the White Horse. His father tried to buy him a place in the company of Monsieur St.-André."

"And even that corrupt Lieutenant Peyrat wouldn't have him?" Again, the officers laughed.

"Well, look at that, I do believe he's brought a rapier. I didn't know people like that had them. What a pity he wasn't the challenger. Then he could have named the weapon—dinner knives, I imagine."

"They say the English allow the one challenged to name the weapons—"

"That's the English—they get everything backward." As Nicolas and his seconds approached, d'Estouville called out, "So, Montvert, why have you come?"

"I have come to defend my honor," said Nicolas, making the formal statement required by the code of the duel, and then added, "Not that yours isn't long gone, you and your *love potion*. I've got it at home as a souvenir of our last encounter, and I'll add your arms to it, when I have defeated you."

"Love potion? You used *love potion* on my *sister*?" said Annibal, while his friend turned deep crimson with rage. Noting his state with alarm, his other second said, "Philippe, don't let him unbalance you with crazy talk. It's a trick." Then, while d'Estouville fumed, the seconds checked the lengths of the blades, forgetting entirely their primary duty, which was to try to resolve the quarrel.

Quite unseen to the group of dark-clad men conferring in the field, a half-dozen mounted archers had left the city gate, and turned from the main road to the track that passed the windmills. Their captain had with him written orders to enforce the royal edict against dueling. D'Estouville, in deference to his family connections, was to be stripped of rank and packed off to the northern front posthaste. The Montvert boy was to be executed as a lesson to others. "Over there," he said, as he spied the knot of figures and watched them suddenly separate. At his signal, the horsemen, harness jingling, pushed to a trot. Then, suddenly, the captain put up his hand to halt. "The salute—they've begun," he said. "It looks like a good fight. Let's wait until d'Estouville has preserved his honor."

"Ha, number thirteen lucky! I put six crowns on d'Estouville."

"That's no bet. Bet on how long the student lasts before he's skewered."

"But if he's killed, how can he be executed?"

"They'll just expose the body. That ought to be enough to put trades-men's sons off trying to ape their betters."

The archers pulled up at a short distance from the quarrel. Mounted, they had an excellent view—and an illegal duel to the death? It was bet-ter than a bull-baiting; it was the highest of the blood sports.

At this distance, they could hear the clang and slither of steel blades. In front of them were two men, left arms enveloped in cloaks, right arms wielding heavy Italian rapiers of the new style.

"Look—a mistake—he's in high ward—ha, now the other comes in low!"

"A hit—no, look, d'Estouville has a cuirass beneath his doublet—"

"A thrust—there's a neat parry!"

The swordsmen were close and vicious, glaring and sweating. Then, suddenly they sprang apart, and there was a quick scramble, so fast the eye could hardly follow it.

"His feet, I haven't seen anything like that—"

"D'Estouville—the cut—no, he's missed—"

"Don't move in on them now, you'll spoil the attack," the captain of the archers said.

Opposite the soldiers, a small group had gathered to watch the progress of the duel. Some were curiosity-seekers who had followed the soldiers to watch the arrest, and been rewarded with an excellent spec-tacle. These were shouting encouragement and laying bets. Beside them stood another knot of spectators and a valet who held two horses, one with a pair of bulging saddlebags behind the saddle. An old man held a restraining hand on the sleeve of a tall, angular girl.

"It's too late. No, Demoiselle, don't walk between the blades. My boy—no, he parries, now—yes, what is that, that lunge, that strange *botte*? Perhaps—my God, that bastard has a cuirass under his doublet. Nicolas is doomed—"

At the fork of the road by the windmills, a lady's mule litter, slung between two mounted riders, and followed by a man and a boy on

horseback, had turned toward the gathering in the field. Unnoticed by
the milling men and horses, as it drew closer, a girl's voice was raised in
prayer.

"Most High and Holy Virgin, graciously spare my brother's life that
he may redeem his soul through repentance and a future life of good
works—"

"Hurry, oh, hurry," called Nicolas's mother to the rider on the mule
in front of the litter. "Go on ahead, Maître, you may yet save him!" The
surgeon, his boy and his instruments laden behind his saddle, pushed his
bony roan to a trot ahead of the litter. Ahead of them, the clatter and
clang of weapons sounded exactly like business. One customer, maybe
two, and even more if the seconds got embroiled, as they so often did.

Clarette had clad herself in floating white muslin that morning, exactly like a virgin sacrifice, and combed her dark hair into braids set in
loops beneath her ears so loosely, so carelessly, that they might come
undone at the moment of tribulation, creating an image of divine and
pleading womanhood that could not fail to go unnoticed by the hardest-
hearted witness. As the litter approached the bloodstained field of
honor, she dismounted, placing herself directly between the mounted
archers and the struggling duelists, where the view was excellent. There
she knelt, saying her rosary and rolling her eyes toward heaven.

But there was something wicked in the grunting, the smell of sweat,
the sound of steel. Something that distracted her prayer, and caused her
eyes to swivel back toward the earth, and notice the most beautiful pair
of mustachios upon which she had ever laid eyes, a profile like an eagle,
a romantically bloodstained sleeve and a sweaty, slightly torn sleeveless
doublet. None of these things belonged to her ever-wicked and much
preferred brother. They belonged to the innocent, gallant fellow her sin-
laden brother was so evilly trying to kill. Suddenly, she noticed something tingling beneath the tight-laced bodice of her gown. It might have
been her heart, but it was in fact an alien object, a green-glass bottle,
that reminded her of its presence with its hardness. It reminded her of
love, and the thought itself, in the presence of the sweating stranger,
made a sort of twitching, burning sensation course through her body to
the oddest places. . . .

D'Estouville was soaking now, and breathing hard. His man was putting up an unusual fight for a person of little blood. Number thirteen would not come as simply as he'd expected. The Italian rapier was a new weapon in France, and a hard taskmistress, betraying the old-style cuts in which all good swordsmen were trained, and rewarding lightning thrusts, tricky parries, and secret Italian *bottes,* the hidden possessions of wily foreign fencing masters. D'Estouville opened too wide on the attack several times, his cuts left an opening, minute, momentary, beneath the right arm. But the defects of his defense were remedied by the cuirass, which had already parried two fair thrusts and a clever riposte, which had slid off the cuirass, caught in his sleeve, and torn a bloody, but shallow cut on his right arm. And he had parried a low cut clumsily, taking a wound over the left knee. The knee was beginning to give way, but he could see that number thirteen was tiring visibly, breathing hard, his point dropping. He had not the hardness of a soldier who trained daily. It was almost over. A rapid attack of the point, battering it down, spearing the target almost at the center, through the heart. . . . Love potion, indeed. His humiliation would soon be drowned in blood, and Sibille would be at his feet, worshiping him, as women always worship the victor.

But what was this sudden last, desperate attack? Rapid, hard, and not against his torso—no, where? Against his sword. Unheard of. The fellow had closed in somehow, and grabbed the guard of d'Estouville's rapier with his left hand, placing his right foot beside his opponent's left. Their two sweating faces were within inches of each other. D'Estouville held on tight and retained his rapier, but as he was pulled off balance over his opponent's foot and across the fellow's body by the strong yank on his rapier guard, a knee hit him squarely in the codpiece, and he dropped to the ground. The secret *botte* of Maestro Altoni. Not pretty, but very effective.

A woman's scream was the next thing he heard, as a heavy weight fell across his chest, adding to his agony and confusion. A sword thrust through the heart? No, it was a plain, doughy-faced girl in white, her hair coming undone, flinging herself between him and the victor's blade.

"Clarette, you pest!" he heard his opponent say, though he could not see him through the large amount of brunette hair that had been flung in his face. "Get off! I've won and his life and arms are forfeit."

"Nicolas, you beast! How could you!" The ridiculous woman had pinned him down; her hair made him want to sneeze, and he still could see almost nothing—then someone—a woman?—seemed to pull at number thirteen. "Don't waste another moment here—they've come for you—your horse—" he could hear the her say, and the sword point that had been hovering over his left eye vanished. After that, through a haze of dark hair scented with rose water, he could see a confusion of soldiers and hear shouts, footsteps, and the sound of a horse at full gallop receding into the distance. There was the clatter of armed men and contradictory shouting and the heavy weight on his chest crying, "Cowards! Don't you dare touch him! Don't you see he's wounded?"

"Captain, the other one's fled—"

"Well, we've got this one—"

"—I am a surgeon—his wounds must be attended to—"

"I have it—" said a woman's voice—the woman on top of him?—and he could feel movement, and another large flounce of muslin obscured his view. "It's—a—reviving tonic—"

"Get off me, woman," said d'Estouville. "You're disgracing me, whoever you are."

"Not—until—you drink this." Something searing was forced between his lips, and before he could even cough, the world went dark.

❧

The guards, who had hesitated to grab a maiden in muslin off the body of the duel's loser, stared in paralyzed astonishment as she pried the cork out of a little bottle in her bosom, forced a few drops into his mouth, and then drank the rest herself. Before she had even swallowed, she had fallen across the bleeding victim, exactly as if dead. The surgeon pulled them apart, and put his head to each of their chests. There was no heartbeat.

"Dead," he announced. "Both of them." The regret in his tone was genuine. The whole trip, a waste. Two expensive jobs gone, and probably a lot of time eaten up in some wretched official inquiry. Oh, Fortune, you bad tempered old harpy, he thought.

"My girl, my blessed girl!" cried a distraught, wealthy woman, who had dismounted from the litter.

"Who is this?" said the captain.

"My daughter, his sister—who would have thought she had such vengeance in her heart?" cried old Monsieur Montvert. "She has poisoned the challenger and then herself, to escape punishment."

"She was such a good girl, a quiet girl. She prayed all the time. Went to mass every day—" sobbed Madame Montvert. The soldiers, the watchers, the crowd all milled about the two bodies, their eyes wide with shock and horror.

There they lay, the handsome, bleeding officer, his mouth open like a dead fish, his booted toes turned up, and across his body, the romantic, muslin-clad maiden, her dark hair all undone, flowing like a river across the two bodies. Dead just like that, without warning, without the priest, without a prayer. It was simply too much. Many were overcome, and began to weep.

"Take them up," began the captain. "Wha—?"

There was a faint stirring of the dead man's hand.

"Look, she's moving—I hear her sigh," said someone.

"Surgeon, you're an idiot—they're alive—"

"I swear, there was no heartbeat—"

Slowly, with the deepest of sighs, the white-clad maiden raised her head, and looked into he face of the wounded man with passionate admiration. His eyes fluttered, and opened, and no one there could mistake the look he gave the girl; it was a look of deepest adoration. Their eyes locked, their cheeks grew pink. Their hearts, in such close proximity, began to beat in exactly the same rhythm. Love, love the absolute, love the infinite, had conquered.

"That nasty shoulder wound, that will want bandaging, Monsieur—" said the surgeon.

And Sibille, whose sharp eyes had not missed a moment of the drama, thought to herself: Thank God for all this crazy distraction—Nicolas is so far away they'll never catch up with him now.

"I—I don't understand," said Nicolas's father, looking puzzled.

"Didn't you know he was writing a book on the art of fencing with the Italian rapier?" said Sibille.

"No, I mean that stuff my daughter fed that fellow—what has she done?"

"I'm afraid they're in love forever," answered Sibille, picking up the discarded bottle and squinting at it as it glittered in the sun.

"In love—with a wastrel officer? A dandy? A parasite who'll live forever with his hand in my purse?"

"Well, at least he has good connections—and he's coming into a title someday, too, you know."

"The nunnery—why didn't I listen when she asked?" groaned the old banker.

❧

In the shabby apartment that smelled of boiling cabbage, Lorenzo Ruggieri was shouting at his wife. "Beatrice! Have you been using my white arsenic to poison rats again? The bottle's low!"

"Oh, my dear, not low at all. See the mark you made on it? I haven't touched it."

"I've told you a hundred times not to meddle with the tools of my trade. Suppose someone offers good money for a high-class poisoning, and I haven't got enough, and they take their business to someone else?"

Lorenzo's wife was balancing her latest baby on her hip and stirring a really splendid soup made with pigs' knuckles and garlic, which was her husband's favorite.

"Oh, baby mine," she sang quietly to herself. "When he tastes this soup, the storm will be over. He'll never notice I filled up his ugly old bottle with leftovers from the others. Oh, such a job I have, switching things around just to get enough rat poison to keep you safe and cozy! Sin, such sin in this wicked world! It's rats that need to be killed, not people. So what if that bottle's full of love potion and stomach remedies? What's so wrong with love? The world needs more of it, I say. More love and less rats, and we'd all be at peace, little sweetie."

The baby didn't say anything, but it beamed at the sound of its mother's voice, its face full of adoration.

Nineteen

he hot southern afternoon had driven Nostradamus to a shady spot in his garden, a cool bench beneath a tree, where he sat on his favorite cushion, reading a letter. Above him was the soft rustling of broad green leaves, and the sound of little creatures, hurrying, fluttering, chirping. Nearby, the sound of water trickling from a little fountain delighted his ear, and above that, was the sharp, joyful noise of playing children. Roses in full bloom sent their lovely odor in slow-moving clouds into the warm air, and only the sternest sense of duty caused the old doctor to avoid taking the delicious little nap that the afternoon invited.

The letter was from his old teacher, the brilliant and ancient Guaricus, who had combed the archives at Rome at his behest, and found, in a book of long-lost secrets, the original contract between Menander the Undying and his master, Lucifer, Lord of Hell.

"Hmm," said Nostradamus, re-reading the letter for the tenth time. "There must be something here—let's see, Eternal Life, and power over earthly Fortune, on the following conditions—"

"What are you doing with that paper, Papa? Reading a story?" Little César, curly headed, precocious, round eyed, was staring up at him. A baby still in clumsy long skirts, he was riding a stick horse with a painted head.

"Doing? Why, I'm saving France, my little César," said the old man.

"With just paper?"

"Paper and wisdom, my boy," said Nostradamus. "Someday you'll understand how much grief can be saved with the proper application of these two ingredients."

"I will have a sword—gallop, gallop!" shouted the little boy, as he trundled off on his make-believe horse to join his older cousins.

"And a better world it will be for you, with Menander out of the way," said Nostradamus, following the little boy with his eyes.

As the old prophet returned to his reading, he thought, no wonder Menander is the way he is. He went and signed this weasel-worded contract, and here his whole fate was written as clear as could be. Menander was deceived; his eyes were clouded and he imagined he would have more than is literally written. It's not suprising that now he wants to do the same to everyone else. Let's see—with the death of the body—*body,* ha!—the ability to make his own wishes ends—dirty trick, that. Hmm—and under paragraph 3B, he *has* to grant whatever is wished, unless it's logically impossible. How interesting, even Hell has its limits—now, that horoscope again. Let me see. . . .

Nostradamus unfolded the rough draft of Sibille's horoscope, with all the scratchings-out he had made to realign her fortune with the true birthdate that Pauline Tournet had given him. And what a birthday it was! The most fortunate possible, under the circumstances. And it made for a very different character from the frail, changeable lily of the later date. This creature, a Capricorn on the cusp of Sagittarius, was dauntless, ingenious, and passionate. Definitely an improvement in character over that person she's trying to be, he thought—but it's not just the date, there's something else. Let's count the months—hm, seven, eight, nine—now, let's assume, being the eldest child, they dated the false birthday nine months after the parents' marriage, so to get the date, we count again—yes, that's it. The girl was conceived three months earlier. Who was the real father? If he's not the man who raised her, we may have the makings of something here. . . .

That night, despite the heat in the little attic room, Nostradamus sat, all robed, in his secret study before the divining bowl, and called Anael.

"Haven't you any sense, Michel? You should be in bed. This little room is hotter than the hinges of hell."

"Anael, in your cupboard, do you keep the past as well as the future?"

"Of course. The past is just the leftover future. I've got it all in here somewhere—"

"Can you show me a scene from the past?"

"I wondered when you'd get around to that. Future, future, future, that's all they ever ask for. *Real* connoisseurs prefer the past. It's a far more elegant and refined taste. Would you like to see the coronation of Charlemagne? I've got it right up top."

"I was thinking of something else. You know what I want."

"Michel, you're a dirty-minded old man."

"Please, it's research."

"All for the sake of the higher good of getting rid of Menander, eh? Michel, you astonish me. Still, I think I've got something—" The upper half of Anael's torso vanished, and there was a rattling and crinkling and clattering as all sorts of things were shifted around in the cupboard. What they were, Nostradamus could hardly tell. They always made such odd sounds as the angel burrowed among them that the doctor was filled with curiosity as to what forms history past and future were stored in. They certainly didn't seem to be books.

"Stir up your dish, Michel. I can't find the actual act, but here's something that will do."

Nostradamus stirred the water with his magic wand, and as the ripples stilled, he saw a strange scene. It was dark, and men with torches were leaning over a dead man in the street. He was stretched at the foot of a ladder, and the spreading puddle of blood that seeped around him and onto the cobblestones beneath his body looked black in the torchlight. Beyond the torches, a boy was sobbing uncontrollably—no, not a boy—the long hair had come undone and fallen from beneath a low-pulled cap. A girl in boy's clothing. An elopement gone wrong. A gray-haired man that stood beside the corpse sheathed his sword, and, stepping swiftly, grabbed the girl by her long hair and held her face over the dead man's. The old man's face was swollen with rage, and his mouth was distorted, moving—but the vision was too old to hear what he said.

"How young that dead boy is," said Nostradamus.

"Just eighteen," said Anael.

"There's something familiar about him—the nose, yes—that's it. But she'd older. I swear, he's the image of Sibille the Dismal Poetess."

"I wish you wouldn't be so hard on her, Michel. I rather like her. And I told you, I'm going to get her into history just to spite you. She's got talent, you know. It just isn't used right. And she *cares* so much. You're just a jealous old man."

"That's her father, isn't it? Is the girl down there by the ladder pregnant?"

"Two months along, you narrow-minded old thing."

"Please, I'm a doctor."

"You're still a narrow-minded old thing. Now what do you intend to do?"

"I've figured out how to finish off Menander's wicked deeds for once and for all," said Nostradamus.

"And how is that?" said the Angel of History.

"I've looked at the original contract, and there's no way to kill him. However, there's another way—"

"So you think you can outsmart the Devil himself?"

"But of course—he is not French, and he is not Nostradamus," said the old man, tapping on his forehead and smiling an ironic little smile. "According to his contract, he has to grant whatever he is commanded to do. And I have noticed something about Menander. When two people are working at cross-purposes, it can take him a long time to figure his way out of the tangle. So the trick, you see, is to keep him so busy that he'll never do anything again. So if I can ask him for an internally contradictory wish, something impossible, he'll just have to keep working and working on it and never get to the end."

"Well, well," said Anael, folding his arms. "It took you a while, but you got there at last, old mortal. And no one can say that I told you, either."

"And with the information from this horoscope, it's simple now. All

I need to do is write to Sibille's aunt that Sibille must ask for some favor to be granted to her father, the Sieur de La Roque, and Menander's brain will be all knotted up forever, because her father isn't her father. And as for losing her soul on the wish, I'll tell her aunt she hasn't got a worry in the world, even if she wished for the moon. See the real birth-day? The aunt was so busy concealing it, she never thought of the sig-nificance. Midnight on Christmas Eve. The exact hour between the twenty-fourth and the twenty-fifth of December. Even Satan can't make a bargain with anyone born at the blessed time. Menander should have been so lucky."

"I can't say it's the cleverest wish, but it will certainly do," said Anael, looking a bit condescending.

"You knew it all along, didn't you?" said Nostradamus. "I must say, it's certainly not fair, the trouble you've given me."

"I'm just supposed to *keep* history, not change it," sniffed Anael. "I can't break the rules just for you." Nostradamus looked very hard at Anael.

"Anael, I swear—all those hints—you're a cheat, Anael. There's something almost human about you after all."

"Human? Disgusting. Of course not," said Anael.

❖

As the crossbow hit the outer edge of the distant target, there was a patter of applause from the gloved hands of the ladies-in-waiting, who clustered behind the shooter. As one footman in velvet livery removed the spent crossbow from the Queen of Scotland's hand, another wound a second bow, loaded it and placed it on the long, narrow table in front of her.

"It's the distance," said Queen Catherine, "and there's a cross-breeze blowing. Aim into it, my dear." For a moment, one of the drifting white clouds covered the sun, and the outdoor archery range at the Louvre, set up in the lists that had once been old King Charles's gardens by the Seine, was cast into brief shadow. Women and a few servants were watching out of balconies and windows, only a few gentlemen of rank were in attendance, and those only because they were too old or too ill for war. The Duchess of Valentinois, who sat apart beneath a canopy, shuddered and pulled her silk partlet closer about her white décolletage. She never partook in field sports, but would not consider absenting herself from any fashionable occasion. It was a matter of keeping her creatures, among whom she counted the two queens before her, in their place.

As the sun re-emerged, the willowy, redheaded girl took up the crossbow and said, with a haughty glance at the dumpy little Queen of France, "I will do much better this time." A feathered cap tilted neatly over one eye, her quilted, embroidered satin sleeves glinting in the sunlight, her pretty face wrinkled in concentration, she had never looked more like a fairy-tale creature as she took aim at the faraway mark. Beyond the target, and the high walls, the green river rushed by, leaving a dank, lingering scent in the air. The Duchess of Valentinois nodded and spoke to the Queen of Scotland's governess, one of the ladies who sat gathered around her, beneath the canopy. She had chosen the governess herself, as she had chosen all of the queen's children's attendants. Such were her public cares for the Infants of France that even the king himself had come to consider her, in his vague way, a sort of official mother to them. "Our little queen does well for one so young," said the duchess, her voice cozy and complicitous, just as if *she* were the mother and the queen, not the Florentine.

"Indeed, she does," said King Henri's homely queen, who had not failed to overhear the pointed comment. Catherine de Medici's tone was so calculatedly saccharine and outwardly agreeable, and so clearly contained a hidden barb, that certain of the older onlookers suddenly remembered how, as a fourteen-year-old bride newly come to France on the Pope's own galley, she had outshot the great King Francis the First in a similar contest. King Francis had laughed uproariously, and asked what other tricks she knew. But that had been the old days, the old court, before the country had begun its strange and eerie sinking into an unknown disaster, and back when laughter had somehow rung clearer, and with less malice. . . .

There was the crack of the mechanism and a whizzing sound as the bolt flew from the fifteen-year-old girl's bow and buried itself in the middle ring of the target.

"So much better, dear," said Catherine. "Let me try." She joined the girl behind the table as the footmen scrambled to load another set of crossbows. An elaborately slashed, embroidered, and massively petti-coated gown, a tightly crimped ruff, and ranks of artificial curls topped by an overly jeweled and plume-laden little silk hat had only compli-cated the dowdy queen's looks, not improved them. As the podgy little woman picked up the bow with a practiced hand, one of the youngest of the duchess's attendants suppressed a smile. How could the Italian woman hear a silent fragment of a mocking smile behind her? And yet she did, just as clearly as she felt the direction of the wind on her sag-ging cheek, and assessed the strength and tension of the bow while ap-pearing to be doing nothing at all. Her shrewd dark eye squinted along the sight, there was a *crack!* and the bolt landed square at the center of the target. Laughter and applause from the handpicked and loyal ladies of her "flying squadron" surrounded her, while beneath the canopy, there was silence.

As the footmen set up tables for the refreshments, the duchess was overheard remarking to one of her ladies, "Why, of course the king con-sulted me first—one cannot be too careful of appointments in wartime—and, of course, he has requested that I join him at his headquarters at Compiègne—"

The queen's mouth set small and tight. Was that a trick of the sun across her face, or were her eyes blazing with hidden rage at the indis-creet way the *dear* duchess's voice carried to her? Calmly, Catherine turned to Madame Gondi, dark and discreet in her dress of deep green silk. "My, my, so many choice new appointments, and so many to the duchess's relatives. I think it is time for a little—artistic interlude. Send for the Demoiselle de La Roque, and tell her to bring her *friend* with her—I want to discuss . . . poetry . . ."

❧

It was mid-August, the height of the heat, when open windows bring no breeze, but only the stink from the street, that I received another summons from the queen. There was a great sir and commotion in the narrow street outside when six armed riders, all in the queen's livery, clattered over the cobblestones and halted before our door.

"Aha," said Auntie, hearing the stir outside through the open window. "I do believe you'll manage to escape the heat after all. I *told* you this would happen. *La Reine des Epees,* she crossed my spread last night." We could hear the sound of strange men being admitted through the door on the ground floor, and voices saying, "—the queen's command—"

"I do hope," said old Monsieur Montvert, who had come to give Auntie a little financial advice, "That this is not a sinister sign." Since the duel had upended his family's universe, Montvert had more and more sought Auntie's advice on his entangled family life, and in return, given her some very clever hints about investments that had nearly doubled her fortune. "It's the sighing, the sobbing at the window, the letter writing that drives me mad," he would say. "Clarette's never been the same since she drank that stuff. My wife forced me to get in touch with d'Estouville's father, a dreadful old titled bloodsucker who's demanded double the dowry. The hypocrisy of it! If new blood carries such a taint, then how can mere money wash it away? Why didn't I listen to her when she wanted to be a nun? I could have endowed a whole convent at this price! Every greasy letter that preposterous popinjay sends from the front, she hides in her bosom, then she mopes and droops as if she had a quartan fever! All day at her writing desk! The cost of couriers! Ah, it's good to be someplace sane. Now if the learned doctor Nostradamus would only hurry and tell you how to get rid of that mummified head, your household would be in perfect order—" The old banker helped himself to several more of Auntie's little cakes and then settled back dismally into the cushioned arm hair usually frequented by the Abbé, who had gone off to hear a new flute player, of whom gossip said much.

"I doubt the Queen of Swords is a bad sign," said Auntie, leaning her large self toward him, her voice taking on a meaningful tone, "since the King of Deniers lay above her."

"I'm afraid I lack acquaintance with the Tarot. Just what does that mean?"

"My dear Scipion, *you* are the King of Deniers. Did you not suspect? Now, about this little annuity—"

"I can't recommend it, knowing the organizers, instead I'd recommend—" But he broke off at the sound of boots on the stairs.

"I'll get my things," I said, as the officer was shown into our little upstairs salon. I always get an impressive escort when I am sent for. The queen takes no chances with Menander.

As I rode off with the royal escort, with Gargantua running beside me and Menander's box in a canvas bag tied behind my saddle, I could not help thinking how much I hate going places with that old mummy. For one thing, he always smells dreadful in the heat, and for another, you can never tell what lewd comments he'll make in public, just to embarrass me. As we passed down the narrow streets on the way to the palace, I could hear him humming a filthy song, just so that people would think it was me. Luckily there was too much clatter and noise and vendors' singsong in the streets for anyone to hear. At last we reached the courtyard gates of the château, but had to walk the rest of the way because we were not royal, and the courtyard was wide and the cobblestones were uneven and hot, and Menander was stinking and saying horrid things under his breath, and I was wishing I could just *give* him to the queen, and go on vacation in the country.

We were hurried up the outer staircase past the honor guards, through the huge, ornate doors, and into the urine-soaked corridors, thronged with serving-men and -women and those few courtiers who were sick or wounded and unable to accompany the king to his headquarters on the northern front. We ascended two more interior staircases and at last were shown into a stuffy, windowless antechamber. Here the guards departed, leaving me in the care of Madame Gondi, the Italian lady who is one of the queen's closest confidential companions.

"That dog—he is huge. Must he be here?" she asked.

"Oh, Madame, a thousand apologies, but the only time I left him behind, someone tried to throw oil of vitriol on me. He's large, but very gentle." As if he understood me, Gargantua lay down at my feet and sighed with a gusty sound louder than a blacksmith's bellows.

"Oil of vitriol—" said Madame Gondi, almost to herself, "that sounds like, no, it couldn't be. What could she have against a woman who is no rival?" Then aloud, in a voice made dim with fear, she said, "Does someone know—has someone guessed—the secret of the deathless one?"

"Madame, no one knows but myself and my godmother, and neither of us have breathed a word. It is a horrible thing to own," I said, taking

Menander's box out of the canvas bag, "and it embarrasses me dreadfully to be in possession of it."

"Embarrasses?" said Madame Gondi, looking puzzled. "That's not
exactly the word I'd use." She turned and scratched on the inner door
of the antechamber, and one of the queen's ladies-in-waiting opened it,
and then excused herself. The queen had been writing letters; several of
them stood open on her writing desk. Letters to the governess about the
care of her children, letters requesting offices for Italian friends of hers,
other letters already folded and sealed. Beyond the desk, in a corner,
stood a little table with two black candles burning on it, even in the
heat of the bright summer day. She'd been expecting Menander; he'd
probably even been given his own appointment on her calendar: "Tuesday afternoon, consult deathless head." I could just imagine it. I saw she
had put on, over her court gown, a white linen adept's robe, especially
tailored with dozens of extra pleats at the shoulder and her own royal
crest embroidered in silver on the left bosom. Clearly, she was taking
her magic powers ever more seriously since getting involved with
Menander. What a deceitful user of human vanity that old mummy is, I
thought. He puffs people up in exactly the way they dream of, the better
to ruin them. But then a little voice in the back of my head said, "What
if he doesn't ruin them? Why don't you wish, and get what you desire,
too?" Shut up, I said to the voice, you're the Devil talking. I gave the
queen the box and bowed backward out of the room, plopping down
with a sigh on the bench in the antechamber, right opposite where
Madame Gondi was on her knees saying her rosary with a speed that
defied lightning.

But the door had not been latched, and the queen was too busy to
notice when it swung open a crack. Through that narrow opening, I
could hear her soft voice, muttering incomprehensible incantations, but
out of decency, I tried to avoid listening. Then Menander's cackling, sinister laugh cut through even Madame Gondi's prayers, and she opened
her eyes wide with a start. Both of us heard the Queen's voice, saying
firmly, "I wish to be respected in the counsel of my husband, in matters
of state,"

"It shall be even as you wish, Great Queen," we could hear Menander reply.

"And soon," she said. "Madame de Valentinois, that old, arrogant woman, still reigns supreme in my husband's heart, in spite of every-thing you promised, and you have done absolutely nothing about my last wish."

"Time will show you the truth, Great Queen," said Menander, but I thought I detected a hint of sulkiness in his voice. "Great things require great actions. I put thought into my work. Rome wasn't built in a day, nor a mighty king's heart changed overnight."

"Bend yourself to my magic, o disobedient servant," said the queen, and recited another spell. Goodness, she learns new things all the time, I thought, as I heard her slam Menander's box shut. Tonight I'm going to be kept up hearing his complaints. I wish Nostradamus would hurry up and send the secret of getting rid of him.

From the outer corridor, there came a shriek accompanied by the pat-ter of women's slippered feet. Then came a pounding on the outer an-techamber door. The queen emerged from the inner room.

"What is this?" asked the queen, signaling that the outer door be opened. There stood several ladies of the court, winging their hands, one of them in tears. With them was a messenger newly arrived from the king's headquarters at Compiègne, who knelt with a flourish, and presented his news.

"The king your husband sends word that the northern army, going to reinforce the garrison at St.-Quentin, has been defeated by the forces of the Empire—"

"The northern army is lost?" said the queen, with deadly calm, and the messenger nodded silently.

"Constable Montmorency has been wounded and taken prisoner, and Marshall St.-André is also captured—"

"What of my son, who is with the king at Compiègne?" she asked.

"The dauphin has been sent for his own safety south to Blois, and the king requests that you send the royal children and the Queen of Scots to join him there." The gathering crowd around us seemed stiff with shock. Several of the ladies began to weep.

"What else does the king, my husband, command of me?" The short, matronly woman stood firm and unmoved. Her eyes were shrewd and tearless. It was then I saw that within this despised, sugary-tongued, dumpy mother there was another creature hiding: a creature of steel and brilliance, yet with the quiet guile of an asp. She has hidden this brilliant and dangerous side from everyone, even herself, the thought flashed through my mind. Woe to anyone who ever liberates the true creature from her shell of jewels and feminine self-delusion.

"He wishes you to strip the jewels from the cathedral and royal tombs at St.-Denis, and send them into safekeeping in the south," said the messenger.

"The Constable, my old gossip, a prisoner, and wounded," said the queen, shaking her head in wonderment. That old, canny warrior, we all thought with her. How could this ever have come about? "Did they say Constable Montmorency lives?"

"No one knows. Four thousand are dead on the field of battle, and the heralds have not yet stopped counting." At this my heart stopped. My bold brother Annibal. Was he alive or dead? What of Clarette's single-minded passion, Philippe d'Estouville? What of the dozens of other young men of the court, lovers, sons, brothers. But Catherine de Medici was as calm as if she sat at her embroidery.

"Is St.-Quentin taken yet?" she asked.

"The constable's nephew, Coligny, holds the city still, but they are badly outnumbered."

"When Saint-Quentin falls, the way to Paris will be open. Paris has no funds, no troops. Guise is still in Italy. Who is left to defend our capital from the Imperial army? What of my husband, the king?"

"He is devastated by the loss of the Constable—he has sent for Madame de Valentinois to arrange for prayers for Montmorency's recovery, and has ordered Maître Paré to try to cross enemy lines to attend to his wounds. The council is being called, but has not yet gathered. He has also given orders for a solemn procession at Notre Dame."

"So," said the queen, quietly to herself. "That is how it is. He sends for her and not for me. The duchess still holds him tight and weakens his mind with her bad advice. And we must all beg Guise to return to save us, and when he does, he shall reign, no matter who sits on the throne." Then aloud, to the messenger, she said, "Return to his majesty the king, my husband, and tell him all will be done as he commands." And when the messenger had departed, the queen turned to Madame Gondi. "Send a message to your husband, that he and the other bankers who remain in Paris are summoned to an audience with me tomorrow. And then send my maids to prepare my mourning clothes. I will go with my ladies to appear in person before the Parlement."

"But Majesty, the king has given you no orders—"

"No orders? I am queen. He is gone, and I tell you, I will not lose Paris because he is under a witch's spell. These are *my* orders. I tell you, God has made *me* queen, and has set me here to act in the king's place. I, the queen, will beg the Parlement to raise funds for the defense of the city. You are all to dress in black, as I will, so they shall understand that the throne itself is in danger. Processions at the cathedral are all very well, but despite what all these *old families* say, armies run on money, not plumes and chivalry. And you, Demoiselle"—here she turned, as if she had just noticed me standing there with my mouth open—"you shall remain here until tomorrow morning. I intend to put *your friend* to the test. I want him to freeze the Imperial army in its tracks." How like a Medici, I thought, to hedge her bets, dealing with both God and Mammon at the same time, and adding the Devil for good measure.

⁂

The news spread quickly, and even as the defense of Saint-Quentin raged on, wealthy families dispatched their own surgeons to make the seventy-mile journey to find and return their wounded sons. Hideous reports from the road, of town halls and city arcades jammed with dying bodies, were brought back by the wounded who managed to drag themselves back to Paris for treatment. Poor Clarette was beside herself with anguish, waiting for the servants her father had sent north to find news of Philippe and Annibal. But they, too, vanished into the maelstrom, doubtless pressed into military service, and when no word returned, the worst was feared. "It's just as well Nicolas is out of the country, safe with his cousins in Genoa, or they'd snatch him up, too. They're taking every able-bodied man," said M. Montvert. And with that he began to lay plans with Auntie to remove his wife and daughter and the more significant of his household goods from the city with us.

"My dear Scipion, be assured, all of you will be welcome at my house at Orléans for the duration of this dreadful war."

"My dear lady, this removal will not be more than temporary. The war cannot last much longer. Both sides are bankrupt. The only question is, which will hold out longest. And if it is not ours, Paris will fall before the peace is declared."

"Scipion, sometimes I believe it is you who is the prophet, not Maistre Nostredame."

"No, I fear not. It is all common sense, applied in the face of hyperbole."

"Whatever would the world be like, if everyone applied common sense? Now, about the removal of your wife's jewels—my house has a buried strongbox, but I would suggest she sew them into her corset for the trip—"

It was during these strange weeks, when the whole city was waiting for the victory of the defenders of Saint-Quentin, that a messenger delivered to our house in the rue Cerisée, a little box that he said was for me from Philippe d'Estouville. But before we could question him further, he slipped away.

"Auntie, there's some mistake. Here Clarette hasn't had a letter for weeks, and he sends me this fabulous jewel? I simply can't touch it—it belongs to her, I'm sure." But then I thought, suppose it means he wants me for a mistress? Then if I give it to Clarette, it will break her heart. But it's too valuable to get rid of. So I put the little box in my dressing table, while I thought the whole thing over, and then, in the press of events, forgot about it.

❈

Rumors and news mingled in equal portion during this terrible time. Nevers would reinforce St. Quentin, Nevers had failed. King Philip of Spain had arrived to supervise the attack. King Philip's troops had been beaten back by a heroic attack. But at last, just before the turning of the month, word came that the city of Saint-Quentin itself had fallen, in an orgy of blood and looting. Now the hysteria set in, and the streets of Paris were jammed with carts of furniture with panicky women clutching babies perched atop their possessions, men of wealth trying to buy more horses, crowds of people on mules, on donkeys, on foot, pushing handcarts, all trying to pass through the city gates to the south. But Auntie and the shrewd old banker had already sent the better pieces of furniture and more valuable items south to her house in Orléans, and there remained only ourselves and his wife and daughter to be removed, according to a plan they had made weeks before.

"Good-bye, my dears," said Monsieur Montvert. "I will send news to you if the city is saved—if not, wish me a fortunate escape." He embraced us all around as he entrusted us to the care of the Abbé for the trip south, then turned away so we could not see his face. And with that our unlikely caravan swept from our courtyard into the hysterical crowds of refugees that swept down the rue St.-Antoine like a river. Auntie's litter, the cushions made lumpy with last-minute valuables sewed into them, swayed and jostled, causing Madame Montvert, who rode inside with Aunt Pauline, to cry out. And mounted double as we all were, we worried that our horses might panic and buck with the crowding, the sounds of shouting whips cracking over wedged-in carts and baggage mules. But it was not the fear in the streets that weighed heaviest in my heart. Rather, it was the certain knowledge that our pace must have us break our journey midway, at La Roque-aux-Bois. The thought of going home again made me feel plain and shabby; over and over again, I heard that last savage exchange between Auntie and Father in my mind. Even the thought of once more embracing my mother could not make it vanish.

Just beyond the city walls, as the crowd of refugees thinned out along the road, stretching itself into the endless dusty distance, Auntie lifted the curtain of her litter and spoke to me. "I can *feel* you moping out there," she said, just as if she could read my mind. "Quit worrying. There are laws of hospitality, you know, and I *am* his sister. He'll be thinking of my money the whole time. Besides, we have distinguished guests with us. He'll be on his best behavior, I assure you."

Home. Once it is shattered, can on ever go back? Of course, of course, I told myself over and over. It will be nice. We'll talk, my sisters and I, and read cards and gossip, just like the old days. I'll show them my pretty new things. I'll tell mother the news I couldn't write in letters.

We'll all be happy again. It will be good. It has to be good. Over and over I said it to myself, with the rhythm of the horses' slow hooves, as the landscape gradually grew more and more familiar.

✤

Two days later, a tall, heavy figure, enveloped in a gray cloak, appeared at the elegant glovemaker's establishment that stood across from the house in the rue Cerisée. He had a gray beard and shoulder-length greasy gray hair. One eye was concealed by a black silk patch.

"Well, what news have you for me now? Any illness in the house? Have they sent for a physician yet?"

"Not a one, and I've had my boy on the lookout every day since you were last here."

"Are you sure?" said Thibault Villasse, slipping a few coins into the woman's outstretched hand.

"Absolutely sure. I am the soul of honesty. But you needn't come anymore—the entire family left two days ago, and given this terrible war, I don't know when they'll be back."

"A pity, a pity—but you didn't see any signs of ill health?"

"Not a one. She was mounted on a big roan mule with her maid behind, and rode off as gaily as if to a ball."

"Damn! Maybe the messenger never delivered it—" said Thibault Villasse, as he departed to inspect the locked gates across the street.

Someone else was already at the gate, a dusty fellow in rusty homespun, a common carrier, banging on the wicket door, and not getting any answer.

"No luck, fellow?" he asked, and the courier turned to him, so obviously a gentleman, with some relief.

"I've tried for two days to make this delivery to Madame Tournet, and they're never home."

"I am a friend of the family," said Villasse, his voice silky smooth. "I'm afraid they've fled south. I plan to join them in the next few days. Would you like me to carry any letters?"

"Just this one is all there is—"

"Of course, it's not fair that you shouldn't receive your fee—tell whoever sent it that the Sieur de La Tourette will deliver it to Madame Tournet's residence in Orléans—" Villasse jingled a little purse before the carrier's dazzled eyes.

"Why, thank you, Monsieur de La Tourette, you are most generous—" said the carrier as he tucked Villasse's silver into his bosom. And as he departed, Villasse flicked a thumb under the seal, which he didn't recognize, and as he read the first sheet, a ghoulish smile gradually spread over his face.

"Why, just look at this!" A letter—and—ha! They've lied all these years! Her birthday is December twenty-fourth, not the eleventh of February at all, he said to himself. He counted the months backward on his fingers. That means—she was conceived out of wedlock—why, she might even be a bastard! Who'd have thought it of that righteous, mealy-mouthed mother of hers. What a secret! Too good for me, was she? Surely, a clever lawyer could do something with this to speed my case—

But as he read further, his jaw dropped in astonishment. Sorcery? The Master of All Desires? Who would want to stop up the abilities of a magical, undying head? Luckily, she does not know the secret of silencing it—I have it here—I must have possession of that thing—you won't find *me* trying to spoil something so splendid! Desires! Ha! I could keep it busy for the next hundred years! But I'll have to be devious; the queen owns it, it seems to imply here. But if I steal it, what can the queen do? I'll be able to wish that she can't get it back. Women—they're so foolish, they never think things through.

But suppose someone else gets it? Damn! She's bound to stop at La Roque on the way! Hercule de La Roque, you bastard, you'll never get your hands on *my* magic head—I must intercept her— And so busy was Villasse with planning his first wish, that he never even paused to read the second page, on which was written Sibille's horoscope.

✤

Villasse returned to the stable where he had left his horse to find the stablemaster in the very act of selling it illicitly to a stranger who wished to flee the city. Without the slightest thought, Villasse ran the stablemaster through and sent the other fleeing, then mounted, and joined the throngs crushing into the routes to the city gates. Single-minded, without looking to the left or right, he hacked his way across the Pont aux Meuniers with his riding crop, pushing foot travelers aside and leaving behind him a trail of curses. Beneath the bridge the mills of Paris still rumbled and groaned; the green waters of the Seine were jammed with heavy-laden boats, crowded with people and furniture, leaving the quays. At the gates of the city, he found himself waiting, cursing and fuming, as a detachment of Swiss mercenaries, newly arrived, entered with their banners flying.

Once in the open country, he rode fast, bypassing slow-moving carts and frightening other horsemen into giving way by the blazing gaze of his single eye. No one who saw him had the least doubt that this was a madman, bent on a mission of death.

It was only half a day before he saw in front of him, around the familiar bend in the road, the outbuildings of La Roque-aux-Bois, the familiar dovecote tower over the open main gate, the dusty courtyard lying within. Chickens fled from the heavy hooves of his sweating, hard-trotting hackney, and it was little time until he had crossed the bridge and flung his reins to the lackey at the foot of the stairs of the main house. Here he found that Laurette, who had spied him from an upper window, had hastened down to greet him at the front door. My, he thought, she's a pretty little thing, with her blond curls all damp against her pink cheeks in the summer heat. And no wonder she's so different from her sister, so feminine, so accomodating—she's only a half sister. God knows what lackey or priest crawled under her mother's skirts to get that first one.

But I really can't marry Laurette, pretty as she is, now that I know the secret. The family is just not respectable enough for me, now that I have plans to rise higher. First, I'll wish for rank, a place at court, then, several handsome estates with titles—oh, yes, and a nice little château well located for hunting—But I need Laurette for now—I need her to go through her sister's things and find me that head. It must be in a package of some sort. And once I get the Master of All Desires, I'll wish for a wife of rank and wealth, with a beauty more elegant. . . .

Villasse's face crinkled up in a benign smile, one that reassured Laurette that his infatuation was still intact, even after being in the city, with all those accomplished beauties in the latest fashions. Still mine, she thought, and it compensated her for the extraordinary irritation of having her elder sister turn up, beautifully dressed and apparently entirely unscarred, in the company of a wealthy big-city girl and her mother. Worse, the pallid, dark-haired creature with the silk underwear and diamond-drop earrings had paraded a potential engagement with *Philippe d'Estouville* in front of her, and confided that she had a dozen love letters from him tucked into her horrid, ugly, flat bosom! It was enough to send a girl instantly to church to pray that he be killed in the next Spanish attack.

"Darling Monsieur Villasse, have you brought your little friend anything from Paris?" said Laurette, batting her eyelashes.

"Why, I have quite a treasure for you," said Villasse.

"Is it here? In your purse? Is it big or small?"

"Why, big as big, you pretty little dolly, but it's for afterwards, not now."

"Not now?" Laurette pretended to pout. But what was it she saw in his face, peeping from beneath her darling curly eyelashes as she did? Something a little hard, a little distant, a little *preoccupied?* Had he seen someone prettier than her, more accomplished, better dressed, in the big city? Not prettier, surely—but possibly more soignée. Men's heads are turned by things like that.

"Has you sister arrived home yet?" said Villasse. A fist caught Laurette's heart in a tight grasp. Had he seen her sister's new wealth, new connections, and made up with her?

"Why yes, how did you know?"

"Half of Paris has fled, and when I found her house abandoned, I thought she might be here." That was it, that was it—he had decided to pursue her sister again, he was wooing Sibille again. What right had Sibille to steal her younger sister's one chance at marriage and estate? Oh, why hadn't her face been spoiled? It would have worked out so much better.

"She's here, with half the world. They arrived yesterday, like beggars on the road, with a wrinkled up old Abbé who has dyspepsia and can't eat anything, and Aunt Pauline who broke the chair she sat on, and a boring old Madame de Montvert and her stuck-up daughter. Father wanted to turn them away, but the disgrace of refusing hospitality to a relative was too great, so he gave in. They'll be gone in a day or two, as soon as they've eaten us out of house and home."

"Ah, how perfect," said Villasse, and Laurette grew truly apprehensive. "Will Thibault's dear little dolly do one favor for him?" I will *not* carry a letter, thought Laurette, her soul filled with spite.

"Your precious loves to make you happy," she said.

"Then, my darling, there's something I'd like you to take from your sister's things for me—a box—it's really mine, and I want it back. It's an unusual box—it has something, well, something nasty inside—you'll know it when you see it."

"But what *is* it?" asked Laurette.

"Well, um, it's—ah, an anatomical specimen. You know how your sister is always drawing bones—this one's a head."

"A *head*? A *person's* head?"

"Well, ah, yes. Just a head. An old one. Don't worry, it's all boxed up very neatly. But I need it back again. And when you bring it, your dear Thibault will have a lovely surprise for you—a diamond ring bigger than anything on the queen's finger—" As he saw her eyes light up, he smiled, that special smile that a man smiles when he has perfectly judged another's weakness. What's a diamond to a magic head? Just a trinket, he thought. I have her—she's my servant, I can do anything I like. "Let's go inside so I can offer my greetings to your parents. And as for the other—meet me by the old wall behind the orchard tomorrow just after the noon dinner. You know the spot—where the brook widens and the cattle drink."

"And will you have my darling little present?" I have him, thought Laurette. If there's something secret about this head, and he sent it, and he needs it back, then when I know about it, he'll *have* to marry me. If only I had a silk dress. . . .

"That and ever so much more, dear little treasure." Together they went in, and when Villasse had offered his greetings to her father, he departed.

"What was *that* about?" grumbled Hercule de La Roque when

he had left. "I paid him his interest on the new loan last month, and here he is, grinning like a wolf, offering neighborly greetings. I thought he was in Paris."

"*That* is doubtless about Sibille," said his wife, continuing to stitch on a new set of pillowcases.

"She should have had better aim," said Sibille's father.

❧

Since all the girls were sharing a room, it was a simple matter for Laurette to wait until after dinner, when everyone had gone downstairs or outdoors and then return upstairs to search for the mysterious box. The room was full of jumbled boxes and bags, both packed and unpacked, along with the litter cushions, which had been stitched lumpy with mysterious objects. A dozen beautiful silk and velvet dresses hung in the armoire, and boxes of jewelry and expensive vials of perfume had been heaped on top of the dresser with careless abandon. Clarette had hung a beautiful ivory rosary on the corner of the dim little mirror, and in an open box, in a clutter of elegant and dainty things, Laurette saw a bracelet of chased gold, set with brilliants, that made her heart ache. Sibille's or Clarette's? What did it matter? It was *Laurette* they would have looked prettiest on. I'll just try the bracelet, she thought, and this pretty ring here. Would the cross with the ruby at the center look pretty on me? Yes, it looked really elegant. What a pity my ears aren't pierced, she thought, as she opened a drawer, and then a box, and saw the coveted diamond eardrops.

Oh, my, what a wonderful silk scarf. Not a good color for a brunette—so much prettier on a blonde. She wrapped it about her shoulders this way, and then that, and then tucked it fichu style into the top of her dress, where it shone and glistened. I'll have things like this when I've married Thibault, she thought. Why, just look in the mirror—I could be received at court if I looked like this. If Thibault saw me looking so fine, he'd see that no one would be my equal, if he were to dress me right. Ah! What was this beautiful little crimson velvet box, all tucked away, and hidden as deep beneath these stockings as if it were some sort of secret? A brooch, and what a brooch! Such valuable pearls, such a delicate, feminine design—like a flower, like a butterfly. I'll pin it right here, to hold the scarf in flattering folds just beneath my face. . . . ow! What a sharp little pin it has! Yes, there it is. How beautiful I look now. *Madame de La Tourette*. Why, because I wasn't the oldest girl, I never even got to be the Demoiselle de La Roque. Just Laurette Artaud. Nothing's fair. Especially when the people who deserve nice things don't get them.

When Laurette was done sucking on the pinprick on her finger, she began to rummage about looking for a strange box, and it was not long before she thought to push aside the dresses in the armoire. There, glittering dully on the floor of the armoire, in the corner behind the flouncy hems and hanging hoops, was an antique silver-gilt box. She knelt and reached in for it, and as she did, she heard the oddest noise. It was exactly like a dog snoring, except there was no dog sleeping in the room, and nothing could fit beneath the low legs of the armoire. She pulled the box out, and noted the curious designs and strange words on it, then opened it up. Inside was a gruesome souvenir of some execution—a dried-up old head with shredded skin that let the white of bone show through here and there. Stringy old brown teeth showed behind its rotted lips, and the eyes were closed. But here was the curious thing: the snoring seemed to be coming from the ugly old thing in the box. Now there's an odd thing, she thought. How could a thing like that snore? It hasn't got any chest to breathe with. It must be a trick of the wind outside. But as for the head itself, she'd seen far worse human remains posted in quarters by the side of the road, and, after all, dead is dead and a diamond ring is a diamond ring. She didn't even wonder who it was, because she was not the wondering sort.

She wrapped the box in a pillowcase, then took a last look at herself in the mirror. It wouldn't really hurt to *borrow* these nice things for a bit, just to look good for Thibault, and remind him that she looked even better when set off by expensive things. It was only a matter of minutes to steal out of the gate and hurry through the orchard to the crumbling old wall by the brook. There, his horse tied to a low-hanging branch, in an old leather hunting jerkin and tall boots, sat Villasse, peeling his fingernails with his heavy knife. When he heard the rustle of her feet in the dry grass, he looked up eagerly. It's the jewelry, she thought. I look like a lady at court. He's surprised that I look so good.

"Do you have my box?" he said, without so much as a greeting.

"I do, right here, and where's my ring?"

"First, the box—I have to see what's in it." Hurriedly, frantically, he tore open the pillowcase and grabbed the box, hardly pausing to inspect the curious rooster-headed god before he opened the catch. At the sight within, even he paused and drew in his breath. The dead, mummified thing inside was moving and—horror of horrors, its shriveled eyelids opened to reveal two evil, staring eyes!

"What pests have stolen me now?" said Menander. "Work, work, work! I take a little nap and —oh, what a wonderfully evil face! I sense a soul mate. And the other one, too—what hard little eyes you have in that pretty face, my dear. Tell me what you wish, but be quick about it— I can't stay, even to collect another soul. Regretfully, I'm bound to return from whence I came."

"First, I wish for a very large diamond ring of a size to fit this girl, here—"

"No, no—what kind of sorcerer are you? First you recite the words written on the box—" Menander sounded testy.

"Thibault, what is this thing? Is it sorcery?"

"It is an ancient secret known as The Master of All Desires."

"Well then, when you are done, wish for a silk dress and a white mare with a silver harness, and when we are married, you can wish for a castle for me—"

"Married? You think I'll marry *you*? Why should I have you when the most beautiful women of breeding and wealth in the kingdom can be mine now that I have this magic? I don't need a country bumpkin for a bride."

With a scream, Laurette launched herself at Villasse so fiercely that Menander tumbled into the dirt at his feet.

"What are you doing you harpy—you've made me drop it. Quit this! Ugh, you little beast, your brooch has scratched me." With a powerful backhand blow across her face, he knocked her to the ground. Only then, as he was sucking the scratch, did he notice the brooch on her bosom. Horrified, he drew back. "Where did you get that brooch? Your sister's brooch?"

"If you can imagine, you ugly old man, I wore it to make myself more beautiful for you. Beautiful for you! That's a joke! You're as ugly as an

ogre yourself, you one-eyed freak! You deserve a toad for a bride!"
Blood was trickling from her nose as she spoke, and she wiped it away
with the back of her hand.

"If you weren't as stupid as a frog and as greedy as a bitch-hound
yourself, you'd have never touched your sister's things. I sent her that
pin, you ninny, and it's poisoned."

"Poisoned?"

"With a very slow, but mortal venom. Distillation of toad, as I recall.
But there's plenty of time for *me*. I'll just wish myself safe with the Master of All Desires here, and go to your funeral and weep. Think of me,
when you remove yourself from the earth for my convenience." Rapidly,
he scooped up the mummified head, threw it in the box, and mounted
his horse. Screaming, the girl ran after him, through the brook, but the
fast-moving horse only splashed her and her finery from head to foot
before Villasse flashed away toward the main road. Sobbing, wet, and
bloody, Laurette staggered back to the house, where she met her father
coming from the stables.

"V—Villasse—" she managed to say.

"Has he stolen your virtue?" said her father, his face flaming with
rage.

"N—no, he stole my magical head that grants wishes—"

Hercule de La Roque looked at his hardheaded, pretty little daughter.
Just like him, she was, and he loved her for it. Blood was trickling from
her nose, a black eye was starting to show, and her clothes were
splashed with water and mud.

"Where did you get all that jewelry? From the magic?" he asked. His
eyes were shrewd and assessing. That brooch, there, worth a king's ransom, with that big pearl in the center.

"N-no, from Sibille's things. The brooch—the brooch, he says it's
poisoned with slow poison, and I scratched him with it. I have to have
the head back, Father, so I can wish myself well. He's taken it, and he
says he'll wish the poison not to work on himself, and not bother with
me, so that he doesn't have to marry me. Father, he says he'll come to my
funeral!"

"He's not invited," said her father. "A head, a head that grants
wishes—but Villasse is long gone. How in the hell do I catch up with

him? Don't worry, Laurette. Slow, you said? I'll have a horse saddled right away and get it back for you. But what if he wishes me dead?"

"I knew, *sniff*, you'd save me, Father."

"Why of course I will. A head that grants wishes—what a thing to own. Does it talk?" They were returning to the house now.

"Yes, it says horrible things. But you have to say the words on the box, first."

"And what else did it say? Everything's important."

"It—it said, I swear I remember it right—that it had to go back some-where, so hurry—"

❧

Once beyond the boundaries of La Roque-aux-Bois, Villasse pulled up his horse beneath the shade of a large tree, and opened up the box. Something was wrong with it, it seemed to shimmer in the afternoon light, and it was hard to read the words written above the catch. He'd barely begun to recite the formula when the voice of the mummy, all dry and rustling like dead leaves, said, "Too late."

"What do you mean, too late?"

"I am already returning. Sibille Artaud de La Roque owns me, and I am bound to her—"

"Come back! Don't you dare vanish! I need to make you have the poison vanish from my blood."

"Too bad, too late, good-bye—" And with that, Menander and his box both grew translucent and vanished right from between Villasse's hands. Frantic, Thibault Villasse turned his horse and spurred it to a gallop, back in the direction from which he had come. And all the while he pounded on the lathered beast, he thought, how long, how long did that Goddamned astrologer say it took before the poison began to work? Unspeakable suffering, he'd said, slow, he'd said. How slow? How many hours, days, weeks?

❧

Inside the farmhouse door, Hercule de La Roque and his second daugh-ter heard a terrified screaming coming from upstairs. At the sound, the Abbé, dozing over a book, sat up all at once. Suddenly, it seemed to

Sibille's father, from all directions, annoying women seemed to be swarming up to the girls' room, Clarette and her mother putting down their embroidery hoops and running upstairs, his wife and sister, coming from the kitchen, his other daughters, and Sibille, gawky and homely as ever beneath her finery, all responding to Isabelle's shrieks of distress. Hercule flung them aside and pushed into the room, where he saw his third useless little daughter in hysterics, while an open box containing a live, severed head seemed to be materializing in the center of the bed.

"Shut up, you little cretin, and make a wish," it was saying. "You can have anything you like. All it costs is your soul, but yours is as light as a feather, and hardly worth the trouble of keeping. Such a little sacrifice, and so many lovely things could be yours. Wouldn't you like a pony?" But Isabelle just howled.

"It's alive! And it's ugly-dirty! Mama!"

"That's it! That's the magic head!" cried Laurette.

"I know," said her father. But instead of grabbing up the box, he grabbed Sibille instead, turning her arm behind her, and twisting it in an iron grip. "At last, you stuck-up, sapless old maid, you're good for something. Wish for me, Sibille."

"Wha-what do you mean, Father?"

"I heard what it said. Do you think I want to lose *my* soul wishing? No, you do the wishing for me. First, I want a fortune and a palace on the Loire. Hurry now, or I swear, I'll break your arm!"

"But Father, the poison—" Laurette cried, her voice between a sob and a shriek.

"Later, later. First things first. Sibille, wish for me, my dutiful daughter. Take the curse on yourself."

"Father!" cried Sibille, her voice full of shock at his unnatural demand. "That's wicked! I won't!" She tried to pull away, but he pulled her harder, making her cry out in pain. "You can't make me!" she shrieked in despair.

"Oh, can't I? Think again, you thief of inheritances—wish yourself to Hell for me. Wish me back the fortune you stole from me. I would happily cut your throat for what you've done. It's justice." There was the sound of a gasp from the women in the room, as the Sieur de La Roque pulled his hunting knife and held it to Sibille's throat. "Who will stop me?" he cried, the sweat shining on his brow. "I tell you, I *deserve* these wishes—this thing is mine by right!" His eyes glittered with the madness born of greed. "And what good has she ever been to me, this scheming old maid? Useless, vicious, bad from birth— At last I've found a use for you— Wish for me, Sibille, wish, or you won't be wishing for anything in the future." No one dared move. Even Aunt Pauline, huge in the doorway, paused in horror. In the unnatural quiet of the crowded room, it was almost as if you could hear the sound of Sibille's heart breaking. Somehow, secretly, she had always thought that beneath his hard shell of cruelty and scorn, her father loved her. Now she had seen within his depths—and there was nothing. Nothing at all. As the castle of a life-time's illusions crumbled into dust, she began to weep. Everything was gone. There was nothing left, not love, not home, not family, not any-thing. Could Menander's hell cause any more pain than this? "By Agaba—*sniff*—" The magic words were scarcely audible beneath her sobs.

"And don't weasel-word it. Make it clear the palace is for me."

"I wish for you—*sniff*—to give to my father, Monsieur Hercule de La Roque—*sniff*—a very large fortune and—and—a palace on the Loire—"

"In the new style—in good repair—with an excellent hunting preserve—"

"In— in the n—new style—in good repair—with an excellent hunt-ing preserve—"

"Well, at last, Sibille," said Menander. "And what a job it was—one of my hardest in a thousand years. You really won't miss your soul much. Not that many people have them these days anyway. And most of the time, a person doesn't even feel it."

"Hercule, you unnatural monster. The sooner you are dead and buried, the better for your family," said Aunt Pauline, even paler be-neath her white powder than usual.

"But Father, the poison—" said Laurette. She was sweating in terror.

"Not just now; I want eternal youth, too," said her father, never loosening his grasp on Sibille or upon his knife. "Go ahead, Sibille, wish for me."

"So sorry," interrupted Menander. "I'm still working on the first wish."

"Well, just put it on a list and do the second," said Hercule de La Roque, his voice impatient.

"It doesn't work that way," said Menander. "First I have to figure out how to do it, then I set Fate in motion, and then I can do the next wish—"

"It ought to be easy. Aren't you magical enough to give me a simple palace?"

"Oh, I've given kingdoms in my time. And right now, I'm engaged in fuddling Philip of Spain's mind to delay the entire Imperial army from invading Paris. I do great things, I'll have you know."

"Well, then, hurry up, I want eternal youth, and then absolute pow-ers of command over all living creatures—why, once I have that, I think I'll keep you after all, Sibille. You can keep up the good work for me. At last, a dutiful daughter. Why, I'll be able to command the King, the Em-peror, even the Pope!"

"Not just yet, you greedy old man. I *told* you I have to finish thinking about the first wish. I can't do any more of them until I've got that one figured out. You'll just have to wait," said Menander.

"What's so hard, thinking about a castle with a hunting preserve?"

"It's not the palace, it's who it's for—"

"It's for me, you damned fool head! For me! Hercule, Seigneur de La Roque!"

"Well, not quite. It's for Sibille's father, as well as for you. Hard to give a palace to two people, especially when one of them's dead—"

"What do you mean?" asked Hercule de La Roque, letting go of Sibille's arm, his face suddenly deeply suspicious.

"I told you, I have to think about it . . ." said Menander the Deathless, closing his eyes.

"Wake up, wake up, you damned piece of rubbish—don't you dare close your eyes on me!" Hercule de La Roque, insane with fury and the sudden realization of what had happened, rushed to the bed, and grabbed the box to shake it. The head rolled out on the ground and he picked it up by the ear, which came off in his hand. To the shrieks of the women, he kicked the head, then stamped it flat. But even he drew back in horror, when, from the flattened mass, the head began to re-form it-self and said, "Can you *never* leave a man alone to *think*? I told you, don't bother me while I'm *busy*."

"Where's Sibille?" Hercule de La Roque cried, looking frantically around him. "Damned bitch! She's done this to me." But the women had all fled. Only his sister Pauline, a vast mountain of flesh, leaning on her walking stick, remained in the room.

"Well, Hercule, you seem to have done it again. What a stupid ques-tion to ask. If you'd done your own wishing, you might be sitting in a nice palace at this very moment. And in my opinion, this was all a waste—you've been soulless for at least three decades, by my calculation."

"Pauline, I knew there was a reason I despise you."

"Maybe if you keep Menander a long, long time, he will wake up," said Pauline, her voice sarcastic.

"I always thought that girl was none of my getting. But the birthday, the christening date—when I came home, I saw the proof—"

"I slept with the priest to get the church records changed, Hercule."

"You? Ugly?"

"I was beautiful then, if you care to remember, and married off in haste to a man I didn't love for the sake of money. The priest was hand-some, Hercule, and brilliant—and . . . and he absolved me—"

"You don't deserve absolution, Pauline."

"For one thing that I did, yes. And he said God would forgive me if I made amends."

"Amends, for what? For sleeping with him?"

"No, for betraying my best friend, because I, too, loved the man who chose *her*. You sneer? Don't dare. I was capable of great love, of great passion in those days—and you, our father—on account of your greed—it was all, all wasted—" Pauline shook her head at the memory, her strange, pallid face a mask of sorrow and regret.

"When they planned to run away and marry in secret, it was I who carried the notes between them. How poisoned I was with envy! That was the sin, Hercule. Envy. Her father blessed me when I betrayed their plans, and then slaughtered him like a dog. Dead! I never thought he would be dead! And me the cause—"

"If it's so, Pauline—then it's the only honest thing you've ever done—"

"My life has been poisoned by that deed, poisoned. I still wear an amulet containing a handkerchief dipped in his blood, and for many years I had his Book of Hours—"

"The book you gave Sibille! *That's* what that was! You despicable hag!"

"But I have bent my whole life to make up for it—a lifetime of regret—yes, I arranged to conceal the birthdate when you were away at war—I would have adopted her as a baby, if you'd let me—"

"She didn't *deserve* it—"

"But she is mine now, and I will spend everything I have to make her happy—"

"Pauline, you bitch—"

"You would have done anything to marry an heiress, wouldn't you? Even conspiracy and murder. You and Hélène's father stripped him and threw the body in the river that night. Don't tell me you didn't, because I know. But you didn't know you were taking leftovers."

"That damned old man—he lied, too. You all lied."

"The servants sold his clothes, you know. I found his books, his belt, the little amulet he used to wear at his neck. I used to read every day from his Book of Hours. How many tears I poured into that book! Selfishness, it is the worst crime—"

"Your deceit has cost me the chance of my lifetime—"

"You've had your chances, Hercule, and you've lost them. And I have mended what could be mended. And how it's worked out for you—ha! It's a joke—a cosmic joke—"

"You put a cuckoo's egg in my nest—I could kill you for that—"

"I think not, Hercule. The world will know if I die here, and my cousin, the Abbé, is very well connected indeed. To say nothing of the good priest who absolved me. He has risen high, Hercule—I do not think you want to know how high. Did you imagine I would ever accept your hospitality without witnesses?" As she turned and marched out of the room, her brother, bitter with rage, picked up the box with the head in it, and gave it a last hard shake.

"Go away, I'm busy," it said.

"Damn you," said Hercule de La Roque. "Are you too stupid to know that wish was for *me*—me, Hercule de La Roque?"

"That's not what the girl said—if you don't like it, go settle with her," replied the malicious, leathery little voice.

"Sibille," said Hercule de La Roque, his rage rising. "Yes, Sibille—I'll settle with her all right." Arteries throbbing, heat and fury staining his face deep crimson, he tore out of the room like a madman toward the stairs, deaf to the evil laughter of the thing in the box under his arm.

But halfway down the stairs, still clutching the magic coffer, he saw that someone was waiting for him at the foot, with sword drawn. The man's face was haggard and haunted, his clothes sweat-stained from the hard ride. It was Thibault Villasse.

"Hercule, give me that box," said Villasse. There was a desperate edge in his voice. Was the poison already at work? Already he thought he could feel a certain shooting pain—or was it burning? Had the sorcerer said it burned? Or was it the eyes? Something. There was no time. No time for explanations, for discussion. "Give it over, hurry!" repeated Villasse, his voice somewhat shriller.

"No. Never. It's mine," said the Sieur de La Roque, his fury redoubling. "I have unfinished business with Sibille. Now get out of my way, you peasant oaf."

"Beggar! How dare you stand in my way!" cried Villasse, his face distorted with rage. With a single motion, he lunged forward and cut down the Sieur de La Roque on his own staircase. As the box tumbled down ahead of the body, and blood ran in spurts from a severed artery, Villasse grabbed up the bloody trophy and ran to the door. His hands were shaking as he recited the magic words, and sweat poured down his forehead.

"By Agaba, Orthnet, Baal, Agares, Marbas, I adjure thee Almoazin, Membrots, Sulphae, Salamandrae. Open the Dark Door and heed me— Give me that which I desire. Remove the poison from my body."

"Don't bother me now, I'm thinking."

"Give me my wish, you damned thing," said Villasse, shaking the box.

"I *told* you, quit bothering me. I'm thinking. When I'm done thinking, I'll see about your wish. But right now, there's another one ahead of it.

A fortune and palace, for Sibille's father. Or maybe for this La Roque personage. You're just going to have to wait your turn."

"Quit talking, you devil, and give me what I've asked for!" cried Villasse, and so intent was he on the box that he did not see the burly farmhands who were quietly coming up behind him with ropes and pitchforks.

"Can't," said the head, and Villasse gave a cry as six men leapt on him at once.

"Tie him up!"

"Kill him!"

"No, don't touch him. Why should we pay? It's him that killed the master. Tie him up for the magistrate."

All that night, locked in a windowless granary, and waiting for the arrival of the *bailli*, Thibault Villasse tried, over and over again, to calculate which was the worst death, the one the law required, or the one that God's justice had decreed for him. And which, which one would come first?

Twenty

Hundreds of rush lights gleamed in the dark like glowing orange eyes. Lights on the staircase, where the maids were mopping up the worst of the blood, lights flickering in the *salle,* on tables and sideboards, while mother and Aunt Pauline washed and laid out fa- ther's body on a trestle table in the center of the room. And I, I wan- dered like a ghost through the darkened rooms, up and down the stairs, among the eyes that seemed always to be watching, watching. It was father's last gift—to leave me soulless. I could feel the empty coldness inside, where before warm voices spoke, argued, made poetry, and mar- veled over nature. Somewhere in the night I overheard Isabelle and Françoise ask the Abbé in tremulous voices if father's soul was in heaven, and heard Abbé Dufour cluck his tongue and say it was cer- tainly *somewhere,* but they must consult a higher spiritual authority than he. But mine, where was mine?

The next morning, the *bailli* and his servants came and took away Thibault Villasse, who had chaff all over his clothes and was for some reason too weak to walk. He had to be slung over a mule, muttering and talking to himself like a madman. Laurette had taken to her bed, out of shock I supposed, but mother and Auntie insisted she lie alone on a cot in mother's room instead of in the big bed we shared. They barred the door to Clarette and me, and when I saw them come out, Auntie was wearing a pair of heavy gloves and carrying something I couldn't see, and mother was carrying scissors.

"I do hope it's not catching," said Madam Montvert, with some fear in her voice.

"No," sighed mother. "It's not catching. Pray for my daughter, Madame; only another mother's heart can understand how I am suffering."

"You are very brave," said Madame Montvert. "When she is recovered and this dreadful war is over, I beg that you both come and visit me awhile in my own house, to help you through this time of tribulation and loss."

But it was when I passed the maids scrubbing the bloody spots off the brass banister the next day that the heavy, iron feeling that encased my body and heart broke open, and waves of shock and fear coursed down me, and I trembled, and wept, both for my loss and the fear that God would strike me dead on the spot for my terrible crime. I had brought the loathsome Menander to my father's house and caused his death.

"I've killed him, my own father, and it was all my fault. I am the wickedest, most unnatural person alive, and even my soul is gone." I wept, collapsing in tears at the foot of the dreadful staircase. Behind me, there was the sound of slow footsteps and the tap-tap of a cane.

"My dear," said Auntie, drawing me up and putting her arm around me. "It's time I told you something—you are not a parricide, not even close. And as for your soul, it is quite safe inside your body still."

"What do you mean? I've wished on Menander—my soul has been taken—father made me, and now he's dead—"

"Let's start at the beginning, my dear. Your true birthday has been concealed from you, as it was from my brother. You were born on that blessed eve, when no soul can be lost—"

"Christmas? Not February?" I said, stiff with shock. I began to count backward on my fingers—"

"Yes, Christmas at midnight, in the convent of Saint-Esprit that you love so, where my brother locked up his new, young wife while he was away at war—"

"But, but—" I stammered "—how?" Wasn't my father my father? Wasn't I the daughter of a hero of Pavia after all?

"It is obvious, dear. My brother is not your father. Your father—"
And here Aunt Pauline broke off, unable to speak, and looked away
from me while tears crept down her pale face.

"But was my father—a—a—gentlemen?" I could feel the *me* that I'd
made all these years, the warrior's daughter, the pallid poetic rose, vanishing, and it terrified me.

"Well, I suppose—if you count foreigners. Foreigners who are baptized, but are not of Christian descent—"

"What?"

"I'm afraid, dear, that knowing the truth, you must never tell. You
would live a terrible life, between two worlds, accepted in neither—But
your father was brilliant, beautiful, a scholar who could quote from all
sacred texts, who studied the secrets of anatomy, of astrology—I—I
mean, your mother—loved him beyond all description, and wanted to
make her life with him, no matter what the cost." Aunt Pauline's voice
sounded as if it came from one of the spirits that haunted her house.

"The bloody flux of the lungs—she had it, her brother had it, that is
what brought it all about. Her father sent them both south for the cure
with a celebrated physician, with me as her companion. The summer
nights—Montpellier, the city of learning—we sat on the roof beneath
the stars—yes, the roofs are flat there, not steep like here, to shed the
snow—and on the roof of the pharmacist's house next door were medical students, who sang in their own language, to the music of lutes.
Those were beautiful evenings, looking across the rooftops of the city,
all bathed in moonlight, and hearing strange music in the jasmine-
scented air—"

"But—how, I mean, why—um—"

"Her brother died there, and we had to leave at once to bring his
ashes home. But they, my dearest friend—and . . . and—he—had found
they could not do without each other. He wrote. She answered. He came
and sought her out—here, at your grandfather's house—they planned to
elope. But your mother's father found out their plans, and with the aid
of my brother, murdered him."

"I always knew I didn't fit," I said at last.

"I'm afraid you don't, my dear. But your mother loved you too much to leave you with the nuns, and I loved you too much to see you cast out, or left unprovided for. You were *his* child, and for all I know, the last of that family. I think I recall that he once said he was the last remaining child of his father. So you see, for all the love I once bore him, you must live, and marry Nicolas."

"So my father is not my father, but murdered my father?"

"Yes, I'm afraid so. So you see, you hardly can be said to have killed your father. Besides, it was my brother's greed that killed him. That and a certain wily selfishness that at last overreached itself—I believe that God Himself would consider you entirely free of blame in his death."

"But how did my grandfather find out the time of the elopement?"

"I—I don't know—I think he intercepted a letter . . ." said Auntie, and from her voice I knew I must never ask again.

How strange, how awful—father had killed my father. Mother had returned home the sole heiress. And father's reward for his part in the betrayal was marriage, lands, the lordship of La Roque-aux-Bois. Who couldn't intercept a letter, when such a fortune was to be gained? Gained and spent away like water. . . .

We moved on to Auntie's house in Orléans a week later, but mother insisted on remaining at the farm. We left her wafting from room to room, her eyes empty as if already dead, consoling her younger children, but in a strange, absent mood. It was as if, now that her years of purgatory had been lifted, very little remained of her true self. Years of punishment, of silent resentment, of mistrust, had worn away her soul, which had become as pallid and translucent as one of Auntie's ghosts.

Luckily, Madame Montvert and her daughter were not the type to see spirits, and they were cheered by being at last away from La Roque-aux-Bois and its dreadful deaths. They exclaimed over the barbaric luxury of Auntie's furniture, her velvet curtains, her silver, her strange antique gowns, several of which she decreed "absolutely perfect," to be remade for Clarette. And, of course, there was Cousin Matheline, whose husband was such a dear friend of Monsieur Montvert's that she simply *couldn't* stay away, "in spite of all the scandal, my dear. And it is simply *dreadful*—they say Villasse has lost his mind, and speaks nothing but rubbish about disembodied talking heads."

"Disembodied heads? Why, certainly he must be mad," said Aunt Pauline. "Do have another of these lovely little sugared almonds, my dear, and tell us all of yourself."

"Oh, you do know how I hate to talk about myself. But my little cultural afternoons have become a *fixture,* yes, a fixture in the life of refinement in this city. Guests of distinction—so many! Everyone has heard of my circle! Why only yesterday, a *very* distinguished gentleman—there shall be no names—*begged* me with tears in his eyes for an invitation. And, *dear* Clarette, I *insist* that you and your mother attend my next Tuesday—imagine! D'Estouville has succumbed to Cupid's arrows at last! What a *distinguished* match for you! And his uncle is such a favorite with the king! And Sibille, and all of you—if only I can *prevail* upon the Abbé to attend my next Tuesday and read the latest additions to his monograph on the life of the tortoise! The tragedy, the tragedy—it is on everyone's tongue—I am sure you are much too grief-stricken to read, Sibille, but if you could just make an *appearance*—"

And satisfy the curiosity and lust for scandal of all of your friends, I thought. Matheline, you never change. There is a reason everyone within ten miles craves to attend your *cénacle,* and it isn't *Observations on the Life of the Tortoise.* The Abbé bowed graciously in assent from his chair, and smiled that curious enigmatic smile he has, the one that makes me think he knows everything but just doesn't choose to speak about it.

"Why, how can you bear up under so much success?" asked Auntie.

"I try, I try—but you must understand sometimes I am so *drained*—luckily my dear, dear husband is a saint"—at this point Clarette and her mother looked meaningfully at each other, since they were well acquainted with the "saint" in question—"and so terribly generous with me—you must both come and see the darling little fabric samples he had sent from Paris—of course it will seem ordinary to you—Clarette, dear, that wonderful cut velvet you are wearing—but the *color,* the shades, they are the very latest! Of course, if Paris falls, it will be such a pity, they won't be able to send the fabric, such a hardship, when I am just *desperate* for something more up to date this winter—but my husband writes that something has just *paralyzed* the Imperial army—they stay in camp and haven't moved a *step* toward Paris from Saint-Quentin—it's been that way for *weeks* and nobody understands it—it's as if they're just *waiting* for the Duc de Guise to arrive from the south—they say that King Philip's mind has gone soft—"

Now it was my turn to look meaningfully at Auntie. Menander. Whatever he'd set in motion before that last wish seemed to be grinding on, like the wheel of Fate. We'd thought that perhaps he'd stop working on everything, and at night, when we heard him breathing and muttering to himself, "No, not that way—well, what about this way? No, not that either—" we'd sit up and speculate. This particular gateway to hell had been shut, and evil forces no longer worked through him—but the old ones were still liberated. Strange, strange. But who were we to understand the operations of the infernal?

After Matheline had swept away with the rustle of silk, surrounded by the cloud-like resonance of intense gossip only partially expressed, we all looked at one another as if we had thought the same thought at the same time. Abbé Dufour shook his head unbelievingly, Madame Montvert and her daughter turned to me, then we all looked at Aunt Pauline. It was she who said what we all were thinking. "My, my," she observed. "If Matheline ever suspected that Menander was more than a figment of Villasse's imagination, I have no doubt that she would have invited him as guest of honor."

✤

That autumn, as the whole city, crammed with refugees from Paris, waited breathlessly for the Duc de Guise to arrive from the south, I hardly noticed any of it. The new steward's oldest son arrived one afternoon from the farm with news that I must return at once: Laurette was dying. It was the same strange malady that had swept away Villasse in prison before the inquiry was even finished. It was an illness of hideous pain, convulsions, and open, oozing blisters everywhere. Without a moment's hesitation, I mounted the pillion on the heavy farm horse, and the steward's son and I rode double that late afternoon and into the night, hoping against hope that we would not be too late. How strange the trees looked that night, and how eerie the cries of owls. Our way was lit by a bright half-moon, sometimes obscured by dark clouds that scudded across it in the autumn wind. Eddies of leaves blew across the narrow, hard-packed road. Trees stretched barren arms into the black sky. At last the dark tower loomed above us, and the waiting steward, lantern in hand, opened the main gate. The farm had an eerie, haunted look that night. Old murder, dismal secrets, and grief had stained the very stones of the place, caught beneath the slate eaves, hung in the doors of the courtyard houses and granaries like shadows darker even than the night sky. How could I have ever been in such a place, and grown, and lived, and breathed?

"Demoiselle Sibille, it is so good you've come home. The priest is already here, and your sister has been asking for you," said old Marthe, who stood with a shawl over her nightdress, holding a single candle. I followed her up the stairs to where Laurette lay on the little bed in mother's room. Even in the candlelight, I could see how yellowish stuff from the open blisters had stained the sheets. Her hands, lying on the bedclothes, twitched and convulsed, and she moaned in pain. The fingers had turned black. Her face was bloated and distorted, and I saw mother, hovering over her, wipe away the blood that was oozing from her ears. Such a terrible death; it froze my heart to see. The death that Villasse planned for me. It served him right that he had been pricked with his own poison. But Laurette, charming, pretty, a bit spiteful, to be sure—certainly there was nothing she had done to merit such an end.

"Come closer," said mother. "She has been repeating your name over and over, so we called for you, though we were not sure you would get here in time."

"I am sure she wishes to beg your forgiveness and give you her dying blessing," said the priest. "It is at this time, when heaven is so near, that we make peace with the world we are leaving." I leaned over the bed, to catch her words.

"Sibille," she said. "This is all your fault. You left that brooch among your things to poison me. You are my murderer, and I curse you with the last breath I have in my body." I sprang back as if shot.

"The brooch was poisoned? How could that ever be? It was a gift from Philippe d'Estouville."

"Sh, sh!" said mother, her eyes wide with horror. But Laurette's voice was rising, her face was swelling with a strange flush, and her body was shaking with the unnatural rage that precedes some kinds of convulsions.

"Philippe! My Philippe! You stole him from me with silk dresses and money! My money, my inheritance that Aunt Pauline should have given to me! I know everything now!" She tried to grab at the stuff of my dress, to pull me closer, but I pulled my hand away, stiff with horror. "She's *my* aunt, not yours! You never belonged here! You stole my place, my dowry, my everything! By what right did you save your face from the vitriol? Pah! I spit in it now! Poison! Poison of toad, that you poisoned me with! I spit poison on you! Suffer and die, you bastard!" Her eyes were rolling wildly as she heaved herself up, limbs convulsing, and spat bloody saliva at me, but missed.

"Mademoiselle, your immortal soul!" cried the priest, but Laurette's eyes had rolled up into her head, her neck was jerking, and her arms thrashing wildly.

"Father, it it not her soul speaking, it is the rage—she is delirious," whispered mother.

"I, I c—curse you—from—the—grave," she managed to choke out from her writhing mouth and near-paralyzed tongue.

"It's not my fault!" I cried out.

"No," whispered mother. "It's mine." And before my eyes I could see her shrink and shrivel and her face turn gray.

"Mother, never—"

"Pauline begged for you—she could never have children. But your father, poor stupid man, wanted to spite her, and I—I couldn't bear to give you up."

"Mother, is it a crime to love? It's not your fault."

But Laurette had lost the power of speech, and lay there choking and gasping.

"Madame, we must begin," said the priest, as he motioned everyone in the room to draw closer for the last rites. Laurette's breath came in rough gasps now, and she seemed insensible. By the time the last prayer was done, Laurette's breathing had ceased. Isabelle and Françoise, silent witnesses to this dreadful scene, retreated in shock to huddle together in the corner behind mother's bed.

The servants lit candles at the head and foot of the little cot, and turned back the sheets to strip and wash Laurette's body. The sheets were soaked with bloody sweat. "No, don't touch her," said mother. "I alone will wash the body." They brought a big brass bowl of water and set it beside the bed on the nightstand. They set out rags, a strip of linen to tie the jaw, a winding cloth. "No, Sibille, you must not touch her either. She is mine." She closed the staring eyes, and silently picked apart the single long, heavy braid into which Laurette's hair had been plaited for her illness. Tenderly, she began to comb out the matted blond curls.

"Mother, she cursed me, she said I poisoned her. I swear to you, I did no such thing."

"No," said mother wearily. "You did not, but the brooch was poisoned by Thibault Villasse and sent to you under a ruse." Her face was gray and grim as she stripped off Laurette's stained nightgown. "Take this and burn it," she said to her maid. As she began to wash my sister's bluish-gray limbs, she said, "It was beautiful. I do not understand why you never touched it yourself."

"I thought because it was from Philippe that it belonged by rights to Clarette, but then I thought if I gave it to her, she might think Philippe unfaithful, and me the cause. So I just kept it—but I didn't touch it—that would have been wrong." Mother sponged the corpse's dank, distorted face.

"So blue," she aid. "So cold." She was rebraiding Laurette's hair now, and laying it in great golden coils about her head. "My beautiful girl," she said. "My poor, beautiful girl."

"Mother—"

"You brought it here and my Laurette tried it on, and for that moment of vanity she is dead." Mother's voice held a deathly weariness. "Sibille, turn away from me and leave the room. Once I loved you, but now I cannot bear to see your face. I cannot love you anymore."

"Mother!" I cried, but she had turned herself away from me, toward the bluish, stark corpse of my sister. Hunched up like a ancient woman, she began to shake with sobs.

Icy cold, I passed through the open door like a ghost. Somehow, in some way, I knew that Menander was at the bottom of it all. His horrible secret malice, like an infection, had brought this all about. He was like a web that caught up all the hidden weakness and wickedness about him, and tied it together in one big lump. The gate of evil, Nostradamus had said. But Menander had not created it new—it had already been there for him to find.

As I stood at the head of the stairs, stunned, hardly able to move, clutching a little candlestick, the priest caught up with me. "Demoiselle, you must pray for them both," he said.

"My sister—my sister cursed me—" I repeated, over and over.

"And that is why you must pray for her," said the canny old man. "Only you can save her." The dark at the top of the stairs surrounded us; it seemed full of menace.

"What do you mean?" I said.

"I heard your answer, and I know that you are both honorable and honest. Only the living can pray for the dead. And when those who are wronged pray for the wicked, the foolish, the damned, they save them-selves, too." The evil in the dark seemed to retreat a little father into the corners.

"Is that true?" I asked, barely able to speak for the pain in my chest that seemed to stop up my throat.

"It is God's word. Pray, pray without fail."

"I shall," I said. "This moment, tonight, always." The dark seemed less impenetrable, the candle brighter.

"I know you will," he said. "And now, forgive me, I must attend to the lost souls in that room."

"Who is to blame? Who started it?" I asked. And my mind was crowded with the question. Was it Villasse, was it father, was it grand-father? Who started the greed, who started the vengeance? Who began the stuff that spread across the generations, leaving a trail of ruined lives behind it? I could tell by the priest's eyes, he knew what I meant.

"Those are the wrong questions," he answered, and his voice was soft. "The correct one is, who will be the one to stop it?"

That night, I did not sleep at all, and again and again as I paused in my prayers and my tears I looked up and said into the dark: *I will be the one to stop it.*

❊

"Sibille, Sibille! A letter from Philippe! He was wounded at Thionville and is recovering at Senlis. He's well, Sibille, and he's safe! He's lost the use of his right arm for absolutely months and months, so he can't go back to the front! And he writes that your brother is a hero! Oh, isn't my Philippe wonderful! He remembered us all in his letter!" Clarette had run to the door of Auntie's house to greet me with the news. Rumpled and despairing, I had been helped to dismount from Flora to Baptiste, who had been sent to bring me back from the farm. Clarette was flushed with joy. How can she be like this, I thought, when my heart feels like a stone?

"Clarette, I'm glad for you—"

"I know you're sad—it's only natural. I cried for days when I lost my baby sister. But now I am consoled to know that she's my guardian angel in heaven—just like your sister will be for you—" I looked at her sweet, uncomprehending, doughy face, and answered:

"You're right, that's a very consoling thought."

"And father has sent word that the Emperor's strange delay has allowed them to fortify the walls and ship in more arms—if only the Duc de Guise returns in time with his army, then Paris may well be saved, he says."

"That's wonderful, Clarette."

"But you'll be so happy, Sibille, he's sent word that he dispatches a courier next week for Genoa, and if you wish to send a letter to Nicolas in the packet—"

"Nicolas! Of course I do! I'll write today!"

"You see? I *knew* that would make you happier. Sibille, I would be so pleased if someday we could become sisters—I know I can never replace Laurette—"

And it's a good thing you can't, I thought. Nicolas—oh, if only he were here, everything would be all right. But then, as I entered the house arm in arm with Clarette, I had a stunning realization: Menander had lost his power. He hadn't had the strength to follow me to the farm! His box didn't always have that glossy shine, and if it got a scratch, it mended very slowly. And sometimes, though I had mistaken it for a trick of the light, his box seemed to grow translucent with the effort of thought. Yes, definitely, he was weakening. And with Menander useless, why, that was the greatest barrier to my marrying Nicolas! If there were only a way to bring Nicolas back from exile without risking his execution for illegal dueling. . . .

That evening after supper, I took a candle to my room and hunted among my things for paper and pen. I will write Nicolas a wonderful letter, I thought, with hints that only he can decipher about the fate of Menander. Rummaging in my writing desk, I saw that mingled with sheets of blank paper were several of my latest poetical efforts, three of which had been greatly praised in draft form by the ladies of the court.

I picked up my writing and looked it over. Admiring my poetry will repair me, I thought. After all these horrors, Art.... But instead of the usual warm feeling of satisfaction filling me from top to toe, I felt as if I were reading my work through some sort of uglifying spectacles. How formal, how frilly, how devoid of true feeling these poems were! They were mechanical creations, designed to flatter the tasteless, designed to flatter myself . . . Oh, God, look at this one on Death: "Robe of sable sorrow, cover me—" It had about as much feeling as a society lady might muster over the death of a pet squirrel. And here was one on the seasons, all full of mixed metaphors and shepherdesses named Phyllis. How awful! How could I have been so empty-headed and vain? How could I have understood so little of life? Miserable with failure and lost love, I put my head down on the blank paper I had laid out on the writing table and wept, making the sheet damp and unusable.

My letter. My letter to Nicolas. I had to make myself write. I took a dry sheet of paper, and dipped my quill in the ink bottle. But my head felt oddly throbbing, and I could hear the running of the blood in my ears as I set the first words at the top of the page. Nicolas's image rose in my mind. Everything in me, everything of me, was his and his only. "Beloved, the adored jailer of my heart," I wrote, but after that, I find it very hard to describe what happened. Words came up, blazoned in silver, from the depths of my shattered heart. They fell into place of their own will. Rhyme and meter flowed onto the paper as naturally as the pulsation of blood. I felt hot, a fever, then shook all over. The pen, the pen kept writing as if it were possessed. And from it flowed a poem—a poem such as I had never written before and may never write again. Agony and flame, on paper. The pain was like being disemboweled, the exhaustion that followed like death. I looked at what was written on the paper, unbelieving.

"I'm rather unbelieving, too. I didn't think you had it in you," said a disembodied voice. I saw, in the high corner near the ceiling, a pair of yellow eyes glowing. Around it, almost invisible, the dim shadow of raven wings, and here and there, little glittery things like sparks.

"I don't, Monsieur Anael," I replied, for I had recognized Nostradamus's familiar. "This was—too painful to repeat."

"It generally is. And you'll notice it can't be done to order. That's why court poetry is so shallow."

"Well, since my work is popular at court, why not continue being shallow?"

"Because you know the difference, now. And you are capable of far better things. It's too easy to please courtiers with shallow things—they don't frighten them."

"I—I can't—be what I was."

"And why should you? Myself, I like your dialogues. The last one you did was excellent—"

"But I can't—that was only—oh, I just had a thought." An idea was springing up in me like new, green life. "I *could* do another—what do you think of a dialogue set in Purgatory, between several lesser demons and the great sinners and courtesans of history? I'd model it on Cousin Matheline's dinner parties—they're Purgatory enough—"

"Oh, I like that!" said the Angel of History. "If there's any little historical details you'd like, I'd be delighted to furnish them—"

"Agreed!" I cried, newly encouraged, as I took out another sheet of paper. And that is how I not only wrote the only poem I have ever counted as good, and a very long letter to Nicolas, but also that very night began the first section of my *Cena,* or "The Dinner Party," which went through ten printings in the first six months. It is hard to say whether it or its successors were more popular, and they made my name, or rather, my pen name of "Chevalier de l'Aiguille," very famous, and not on a lie, either. But in a way, it was the last curse of Menander, because that night I had been given the gift of discernment of true art from false, which is the cruelest gift of all, especially for a poet.

❖

It was late on a January afternoon when a heavily bundled messenger appeared at the Porte du Temple, one of the fortified gates in the city walls of Paris. His sweating horse steamed in the cold air as he showed the seals on the letter he carried. After a moment's pause he rode off through the narrow streets in the direction of the Louvre, and the passersby clustered around the soldiers at the gate.

"What is it, what is it?" they cried, seeing the expression on their faces, hearing the shouts and exclamations.

"By God, the Duc de Guise has taken Calais! The English are driven into the sea!"

But the messenger did not hear the cheering; he was already halfway to Les Tournelles. Hundreds of candles were shining through the narrow windows of the Salle Pavé, and the faint sounds of music froze in the early winter dark as the messenger mounted the wide steps from the courtyard. There was a ball in progress, in celebration of the wedding of the Duc de Nevers's second son. The king was dancing, and as the long line of couples advanced in the pavane, he happened to turn his head toward the commotion at the door, and saw a dark-clad man coming toward him.

"What is it, Robertet?" he asked, stepping from the line. The music stopped.

"Your Majesty, the Duc de Guise has taken Calais," said the king's secretary. The words were no sooner spoken than they traveled through the room, setting off shouts of joy.

"Calais taken? How, when?"

"The English were completely unprepared. When the marshes froze, our forces moved the cannon across them into place and took the outlying forts. After two days of bombardment, we breached the walls, and yesterday the English commander surrendered the fortress—" The rest could hardly be heard for the babble, the shouts, the calls for toasts.

"Calais, the unconquerable—"

"Ha! Revenge for Saint-Quentin!"

"King Philip's English queen is a fool—they say the commander begged for reinforcements, and she wrote that there was no danger—"

"Women should not play at war—"

"Drive the goddams into the sea—"

The king waved his hand at the gallery, and the music began again—a trumpet fanfare, and with it came the cheers. Who could not rejoice that the last English stronghold in France had been taken? But the fiercest, the most immeasurable joy in the room was that of the Cardinal of Lorraine. His brother, Guise, had conquered. No longer could Montmorency delay the wedding of the Guise niece, Mary Queen of Scots, to the Dauphin. In conquering Calais, the Guises at last had conquered France. Mary would wed the Dauphin, the Dauphin would come to rule, and then Mary would rule the Dauphin, and her uncles would rule Mary. And after they controlled France and Scotland, they would reintroduce the Inquisition into England. . . .

✢

Under a gray sky, heavy with unborn snow, the King and the Dauphin, accompanied by high officials, priests, ranking officers, and a lengthy baggage train, rode out of the city gates and into the winter-bleak northern landscape toward Calais. There they would unfurl bright banners and make triumphal entry, reward the virtuous with lands and the right of ransom to the greater of the English prisoners, and cleanse the tainted cathedral, re-establishing the Catholic rite.

Back within the walls of Paris, inside Les Tournelles, Catherine de Medici had just finished dictating answers to a voluminous official correspondence.

"These petitions can wait until the king my husband's return," she said, as she finished reading several sealed documents, and handed them to Robertet. "But these others must be sent immediately." Her decisions were rapid, orderly, and her manner efficient. But there was no concealing the note of triumph in her voice. The king had left the management of the government in her hands until his return. Indeed, since her dramatic appearance in full mourning before the Parlement, and her successful and statesmanly appeal for funds, the king had granted her newfound respect, and consulted her on many matters of politics and diplomacy. As Robertet bowed backward out of her presence, she sent for her lady attendants to accompany her to the daily mass held in the chapel. After that would come dinner, served in a manner like clockwork, the *huissier de salle,* marching before *écuyer* bearing the *nef,* followed by the orderly parade of the maître d'hôtel, the officers of the pantry, the royal repast borne by retinues of officer-servers and pages of honor.

Formality, thought Catherine, as she knelt at mass, the women and lesser courtiers surrounding her. It is order and ritual that keep mankind under God, and under their king as well. This is the secret of continued rule—let no flaw be in the ritual, no disorder in the ceremony. Then all is well. Somehow her mind moved from the holy ritual in front of her, in which God was summoned to be present in the form of bread, to the unholy rituals of her little cabinet, where demonic forces were brought under her heel. There, too, order was necessary. The correct ritual had moved that malicious, useless Menander to act at last, and just look at the result: power, influence, all in the most natural way, and the Duchess of Valentinois steaming with annoyance as the petitioners streamed toward the queen, rather than herself.

A warm glow filled the homely queen's breast; the little bell was ringing at the altar. Thanks be to God for my victory, she thought, in a manner completely illogical, as the host was elevated. Indeed, now that she thought about it, it was probably God who had brought her this glorious personal triumph. Surely, good things were always from God, so therefore having a person as wise and sensible as herself gain the proper influence in matters of state was doubtless divine work. Now that God had shown himself to be on her side, perhaps she should abandon her consultations with that malignant little object, and devote herself to good works in her spare time, thus repurchasing her soul after this little detour. . . .

The glorious day poured on, through dinner, through audiences in the Galerie des Courges, and finally to the time of quiet conversation and reading among her ladies, who variously stitched at embroidery tambours, played at the *jeu de dames* or tric-trac, or devoted themselves to the perusal of worthy works. At last, outside, the dark clouds above the ornate rows of turrets opened, and began to let the first white flakes fall. But in the tapestry-hung room, a bright fire burned on the immense, ornate hearth. And in Catherine's heart, too, the glow continued. Seated on a cushioned bench, feet on a little stool, she looked up from her book to survey the room.

"What are you reading there?" asked the Duchess of Valentinois, her narrow white face peering over the queen's shoulder.

"A history of France," she answered, "and in it I see how often concubines have meddled in the affairs of kings." The duchess, silent and pale, withdrew to inspect the snowflakes flying against the windows in ever-increasing numbers. Her thin, ring-covered fingers tensed like claws. I was a fool, she thought. I urged this war on the king, on behalf of the Guises, and now look how I stand. They ride high, thanks to me, but already they are ungrateful. Why care for the mistress when the legitimate heir is theirs? What will happen when they at last control the affairs of state? How soon favors are forgotten, she thought, as she saw the queen look up from her book to converse a moment with the Duchesse de Guise. Such a delightful little moment, such smiles. "Concubine" the queen said. Look at them swarm after her. But when the king returns, they will see that I still rule.

❧

Such was the state of the winter roads that the Dauphin's wedding with the Queen of Scots had to be delayed until spring, when the King and Queen of Navarre could leave their little mountain kingdom to attend. And only when the winter seas had calmed could the commissioners appointed by the Scottish Parliament risk the dangerous ocean crossing. Alone, the crown of Scotland itself would not make the trip, for in spite of the King of France's request, the Scottish Parliament had refused to risk the precious object.

By mid-April, with the arrival of the commissioners, the long and complex arrangements to unite the two kingdoms had begun. First came the treaties brought by the Scottish Parliamentary commissioners: the sixteen-year-old Queen of Scots signed guarantees that Scotland would keep her ancient liberties, and that though she might be married to a French king, should she die without issue, the crown would revert to its Scottish heirs. Then came the secret contracts presented by her future father-in-law and her Guise uncles, and her pen scratched away just as happily, pledging the exact opposite: that the throne of Scotland would go to King Henri and his heirs forever, even if she should die without issue, pledging the entire revenue of Scotland to France, pledging that anything that she might grant to the Estates of Scotland that was prejudicial to the interests of the King of France would be invalid.

Scotland having been signed away in secret, the ceremonies contin-ued with the formal betrothal of the plain-faced little simpleton with the vain redheaded girl whose very footsteps he adored. Those who watched them sign the betrothal contract in the great hall of the Louvre, in the presence of the king and queen, the Papal Legate, and uncounted dignitaries of the church, saw in the two teenagers a pair of delightfully blank slates, just waiting to be written on by the ambitions of others. Such deliciously arrogant little fools they seemed, so easily misled by flattery, by professed friendship, and by backstairs malice. The courtier-wolves licked their lips in anticipation.

❧

It was early in the morning on the twenty-first of April. The first crowds and curiosity-seekers were beginning to swarm into the cobble-stone square before the Cathedral of Notre Dame. There at the edge of the square, a prosperous-looking man with a gray-streaked brown beard leaned down from a handsome black hackney to address two ladies in an open horse-litter.

"Well, my dears, feast your eyes; you will doubtless never see an-other such expensive wedding in your lifetimes." One of the ladies was an immense person in a headdress of strange design surmounted by a veil that was clearly intended to prevent any stray dangerous ray from the glowing orb above to touch her complexion. The other was tall and thin, her nose aquiline, her expression intelligent, but marked with some hidden sorry. Beside the litter, riding double behind a liveried valet, was a pale, dark-haired girl whose eyes were glowing with the romance of the whole thing. A wedding; what could be more beautiful? Before them, in the cathedral square, carpenters had built an arched platform and gallery, which was now being festooned with vine leaves. In front of the great door of the cathedral, workmen were setting up a canopy of blue velvet, spangled with gold fleur-de-lys and stamped with the arms of the new King of Scotland and his Queen.

"Father, must you speak always of expense?" said the dark-haired girl. "I'm sure the king does not even consider such things when it comes to a royal wedding."

"More puff and show; the king has been collecting money for this ever since he had to call the Estates General last January. Why, the bankers of Lyons have refused to advance him another sou; he had to force it out of the townsmen."

"A cheap wedding would mean he couldn't finance the war; then King Philip would redouble his efforts. Never economize on show, Sibille, remember that," said the large lady to her litter companion.

"I have rented a window right—up—there for the wedding procession," said the square-bearded man, pointing upward. "You'll have a perfect view."

"I wouldn't want to miss a thing," said the large lady, rearranging the folds of her veil. By the time they had reached their rented window, the crowd so filled the square that pikemen had to open a way to the canopy for the wedding parade.

❖

At last the watchers in the square could hear the blast of trumpets at the Bishop's palace announcing that the wedding procession had departed for the cathedral. Closer and closer came the sound of music and the cheering of the crowd, and finally the parade itself appeared. Musicians, dozens, no, more than that, all dressed in red and yellow led the way, first the drums and trumpeters, parting the crowd in the square, and then the hautbois, flageolets, viols, guitars, and zithers. The excitement in the crowd mounted with the appearance of a hundred gentlemen of the royal household, resplendent in satin-lined capes, heavy silk gowns, brocaded doublets, and loaded with adornments: gold chains, jeweled hat brooches and plumes, garters embroidered with precious metals, puffed and flared breeches made stiff with horsehair braid and embroidery. The growing mutter and murmur of the crowd grew: why, there's Vieilleville! There's Nevers! Are you sure? Just look at the size of that gold medallion! Then came the lords and princes of the church. Abbots, bishops, and archbishops walked before the cardinals: Bourbon, Lorraine, Guise, Sens, Meudon, and Lenoncourt, glorious in red silk, their red, cornered hats arousing awe. After that, Cardinal Trivulzio, Legate of the Holy See, walking slowly, grandly, preceded by two bearers carrying a great cross and heavy mace of solid gold.

"The Dauphin, there he is. That's the groom!" cried the watchers in the crowd. Faces crowded into the windows above the square to get a better look.

"Who's that with him? Look, it's the King of Navarre!"

Above the crowd, perched in the window, Madame Montvert got the first glimpse she had ever had of Henri II's first son and heir. "He looks awfully short for fourteen," she said.

"I'm sure he'll grow," said her husband. "They say he'll make a great king someday. I heard that Nostradamus himself predicted it."

"Oh, here is the bride! Just *look* at her gown!" said Clarette. "And that is the King! Just like his portrait on the coin!" Beneath the window, in the midst of the parted crowd held back by guards, Mary Queen of Scots walked to her wedding mass, between the King himself and her uncle, the hero of the hour, the Duc de Guise, conqueror of Calais, slayer of the English, savior of France. At the sight of them, the cheers, somewhat lackluster for the Dauphin, increased and grew to the strength of thunder. "Long live the king!" "Long live the Duke!" "Long live—long live—" And the bride, just sixteen, tall, rosy-white, what a beauty! "Long live—long live—" exclaimed the crowd. Her gown itself, a marvel to be told and retold by the fireside: made of cloth of silver, adorned with precious stones, and covered with a cape of violet velvet embroidered in gold. On her red-gold hair, a crown of gold, covered with pearls, diamonds, rubies, sapphires, and emeralds, and at its center a great carbuncle valued at five hundred thousand crowns. "Long live— long live—" Behind her, the Queen of France, the Queen of Navarre. "Long live the three queens! Long live—long live—"

At the door of the cathedral, King Henri took from his finger a ring, which he handed to the Cardinal who would perform the service, and the wedding was solemnized beneath the velvet-and-gold canopy, before the church door. As the newly wedded bride and groom and the bridal party entered the cathedral for mass, the heralds outside the cathedral flung gold and silver coins into the crowd, shouting, "Largesse! Largesse!"

Watching the scramble beneath the window, as the bodies in the cathedral square below crushed one another, screaming and grabbing for the money, Monsieur Montvert observed, "I much prefer a window for these occasions. One never knows what will happen when such a great crowd is assembled in one place." And with that, he sent for the dinner he had arranged, cold capon and duck, sliced ham, three kinds of wine, and a variety of sweet jams.

"Scramble outside, scramble inside; it's always best to stay apart," said Madame Tournet, cutting herself another slice of ham.

"True, true," said Monsieur Montvert, stroking his beard. "But so often one is drawn in in spite of oneself. It's a way they have of doing it—they like to keep us busy. I suppose they think it's safer that way." And no one in the room knew if he meant the wars, the new struggle for influence, or something else entirely.

❧

Six months later, in the midst of negotiations with the King of Spain for peace, Queen Mary of England, defeated, dropsical, and barren, lay dying. Lying in her great bed of state, surrounded by doctors, priests, and weeping waiting women, she gasped away her life bit by bit, until at last, before the final prayer for her salvation, she spoke something so faint her doctor had to lean over her to hear it. "Open my heart when I am dead," she said, "and you will find 'Calais' written on it."

When the messengers from England finally arrived at the Louvre, King Henri himself went to his teenaged daughter-in-law to inform her that she was now the legitimate Queen of England.

The King-Dauphin, heir to the throne of France, and the Queen-Dauphiness, his bride, quartered the arms of England with their own, in anticipation of taking over the English throne.

Far away in the Escorial, the news at last reached King Philip of Spain that his old, barren English wife was dead. Sitting down at the great desk from which he ruled one half the world, he wrote something, then sealed it. The next day, ambassadors rode out toward Paris. The word they carried was this: King Philip of Spain proposed to seal the peace with France by wedding little Elisabeth Valois, the King of France's fourteen-year-old daughter.

❧

"It is positively indecent, the way they look at each other," said Monsieur Damville, looking at the bride and groom seated on the dais at the head of the main table. Up and down the great hall of the Hôtel Montvert, servants scurried to renew the wine, and carry a parade of ever new and more exotic dishes to the long tables filled with guests. Married women in their headdresses, men wearing their best hats, the air bright with chatter and music from the gallery: it was a wedding feast to remember, although, as the higher-ranking guests said, rather pointedly, rather a bit excessive for a man of dubious family, especially when so many of the finest families had gone bankrupt in the late war.

"Yes, marriages should never be made for love," said his dinner companion, "which hardly lasts a week after the ceremony. They should be made for the advantage of the two families, which is permanent." The bride, so small, dark haired, and pink cheeked, was cutting up meat for the groom, whose right arm was in a black silk sling.

"I myself would have refused the invitation, if I had not heard that the Sieur de Vieilleville himself was coming." The guest surveyed the heavy silver on the long tables, the fabulously furnished room, the rare paintings, the gilded paneling, the festoons of garlands hung everywhere, and tightened his nostrils as if he smelled something bad.

"His uncle—these days even the best blood must pay homage to the bankers," said his companion, spearing a *pomme dorée,* a spicy meatball gilded with saffron and marigold, on the point of his knife.

"I hear that when the dowry was raised to two hundred thousand crowns, the father gave his blessing." His table companion paused in the consumption of a pheasant's wing to wash it down with the wine contained in a heavy silver goblet they shared.

"That, and the favors and titles the king himself is bestowing on the bankers—"

"Biragues, Gondi, where will it stop?"

"Not until the interest on the war debt is paid—and then, of course, there will be the celebration of the weddings that secure the peace—no, these are wicked times, when bankers are made gentlemen faster than maggots turn into flies."

"Still, you must admit this love match meets the requirements of a proper marriage: d'Estouville repairs his fortunes, and this Montvert fellow is tied even closer to the throne."

"It's still obscene. Look how he's beaming at her. He's given out that all his heroism at Thionville was inspired by her—how preposterous; she wasn't even his mistress. How can you wear the colors of a banker's daughter? Ah, another wedding toast—yes, let's drink—long life and good fortune!" And with a joyful shout, the guests raised their glasses again.

As the guests jostled into the bedroom, to see the bride and groom bedded and bear witness to the consummation of the marriage, the bride's mother could be seen conferring with a tall, somewhat mournful-faced young lady in deep black.

"Oh, my dear, it will be my greatest happiness to see my Nicolas as well settled as this," said the older woman. The younger one sighed.

"I don't see how it can ever be done," she said.

"Never underestimate my dear Monsieur Montvert's cleverness," said the older woman, her voice contented. "With his new connections, he has hope of negotiating a pardon for Nicolas so that he can return. A little money here and there, you know—the peace negotiations go well, and the latest gossip is that there will soon be a royal wedding. Monsieur Montvert's latest expectation is that there may be a general amnesty declared if the Princess Elisabeth marries the Spanish king. He plans to approach him then. But don't ever let him know I told you; he does love surprises. And since, well, that—um—well, that little *thing* in the box seems to no longer be a problem, he no longer has the slightest doubt about the fitness of your marriage. You know, my dear, that my husband has grown to esteem you and your aunt most greatly—"

Those who stood near saw the most amazing transformation of the younger woman's face. Color returned to her cheeks, and the radiance that surrounded her was almost palpable.

Twenty-one

It is part of the sleight of hand of kings that lets a bad peace treaty be disguised with an excellent party. And what a party this one would be: a double wedding, conducted in sequence amidst grand public festivity, in which the king's daughter would wed the old enemy, the King of Spain, by proxy, and the king's old-maid sister would be married to the Duke of Savoy. For the grand affair laborers, weavers, painters, carpenters, worked day and night to convert the entire city of Paris into a reception hall. Procession routes were hung with banners, treasures were brought out of storage to ornament the cathedral, and when the lists at the Louvre and even at Les Tournelles were deemed too small for the great crowd of dignitaries and guests, the wide rue St.-Antoine, which ran before the palace of Les Tournelles, was converted into the lists for the wedding tourney. An elaborate grandstand was erected in front of the palace for the great ladies and distinguished guests, and every window with a view on the street reserved and rented out—some even twice, by the more unscrupulous sort of landlord. Day after day of music, masking, public feasting, sport, balls, gifts of liveries, who could not be happy on such a great occasion? And happiest of all were the Italian bankers, who had floated a loan at high interest for all this partying, because the kingdom had been brought to near bankruptcy by the late war with the Empire and peace meant their loans might be repaid.

In the rooms on the rue de la Cerisée, Scipion de Montvert was consuming little cakes from a silver tray and discussing the return on investment on certain little funds that had been entrusted to him by Pauline Tournet.

"Doubled, my dears, doubled. It is an investment I would have made for my own dear mother, were she still alive. The only question is whether you want to reinvest, diversify, or take your profits now." Several large, expensive new paintings, religious in nature, stared down from the wall behind them. Madame Tournet, in a fit of redecorating brought on by increased prosperity, had added gilded fringes to everything in the room that was not mobile.

"How long do we have, dear Monsieur de Montvert?"

"The ship departs next month, but there is still time to invest in the cargo—I do not advise putting everything into it, however—"

"Yes indeed," said Aunt Pauline with a shrewd chuckle. "There's always the risk of pirates."

"And I've a treat for you both—I've rented a room exactly opposite the grandstand, with two excellent wide windows. I would be honored if you and your niece would join me and my little family to view the jousting. My new son-in-law will be serving as his uncle's squire. It's a great honor, you know." Montvert looked deeply pleased with himself. "And who knows, Demoiselle Sibille, you may find inspiration for one of your little poetic offerings that are so popular with the court ladies."

"Why, we'll be delighted to accept," said Madame Tournet. "Sibille needs to distract herself from yearning after Nicolas."

"Be brave, dear, love will find a way. I've already made approaches to the king's maître d'hôtel concerning the possibility of buying him a pardon—but it's delicate, you understand. And in the meanwhile, he is at last learning a trade. Someday, I hope he will be joining me in business."

"I'd leave to be with him in a heartbeat, if it were not for the queen," said Sibille, who had not touched the little cakes. "I would follow him to the ends of the earth barefoot. Couldn't you help me escape?"

"You can hardly join him if you and all the rest of us are dead. You see, if that odious little thing in the box keeps following you, the only thing that protects you from those who want that box is the queen, and the only thing that protects you from the queen is the box, and her fear that you might wish on it yourself. Let us hope that she never finds out it is too occupied to put into motion any more of its malicious schemes. The moment she knows it's not working anymore—then you're in even worse trouble. The best way of hiding her past involvement with the demonic is—well—not healthy for you, I'm afraid. Florentines, my dear, are a vengeful lot, and conceal their secrets well—believe me on that, since I am one myself."

"What a mind you have, Monsieur de Montvert—it is like a well-oiled clock. You overlook nothing. Won't you have another cake?" Auntie gestured to the tray.

"Ah, these are delicious," said Montvert, helping himself to another. "You must have one, my dear, so you won't wither away. You must keep up the strength of your mind. You are in a delicate position, you know, and only your mind will get you out of it. To think, even I, a blundering father, once misunderstood your ties to the court." He paused to consume the last cake, then brushed away the crumbs that had fallen on the bosom of his gown. "But delighted as I was to find you both virtuous and of noble lineage, you must admit that the true impediment to your marriage is far more vexing and complex than the ordinary sort. First, you possessed an accursed box; a definite drawback in a daughter-in-law. I feared lest you could never rid yourself of its diabolical influence. Now that you can rid yourself of the box, the fact that you know the queen's secrets puts you in greater danger than ever. Unless, of course you keep the box, which inspires fear, as well as the most astonishing urge in certain parties to shed themselves of their souls. However, if you keep it, you are in constant danger of being attacked by those who desire the box. A quandary—one more complex than Menander's, I fear. I find it difficult to imagine a way out, unless you flee somewhere beyond the reach of the queen's agents, burying the box in some unknown spot en route. But then, are we absolutely sure that it has lost its ability to follow you? A problem, a problem—we must wait for the workings of Fate to show us the way."

❖

"Queen of Spain, yes, Queen of Spain! My dearest wish is being fulfilled, exactly as I desired. 'All my children thrones,' I said, and how
perfect that she should become queen at exactly the same age that I
was sent into France." Through the days of balls, masques, and festivities that followed the wedding, Catherine de Medici clutched to her,
gloated over, and glorified the memory that would forever be engraved
in her heart: Elisabeth at the heart of the great cathedral, in a gown stiff
with jewels, as the heavy Imperial Crown of Spain was lowered onto
her narrow little head. At her side, King Philip's proxy, the Duke of
Alva, with his long, wispy goatee, his lace ruff stiff against his cold, narrow face, and surrounding her, the finest flower of French nobility, lin-
eages so old they were lost in the dust of time, deferring to her little girl,
her Elisabeth, as she was proclaimed Queen of Spain. Queen of the
greatest empire in history. Queen of two continents, of two worlds, of
east and west. *That* to the Duchess of Valentinois and her insults. *That*
to years of feigned friendship. *Your* daughter must marry beneath the
Princes of the Blood. *My* daughter is made a queen-empress.

"It is fate, Majesty. Thanks to you, the House of Valois is destined to
progress from glory to glory." As a maid pulled tight the laces of Catherine's corset, Madame Gondi fetched the gold-embroidered petticoats
from the locked armoire, and Madame d'Alamanni the jeweled overdress that the queen would wear to the evening's masque. Tomorrow
there would be the last and greatest event before Elisabeth departed for
Toledo: the Joust of the Three Queens. And then—and then—Elisabeth
would be gone.

"What risks, I have taken, and what cares—and all in secret! It is a
sacrifice, you know, a mother's sacrifice. Already I regret my Elisabeth's
company. She is so clever in her observation, so accomplished for only
fourteen. My mainstay, my delight—but queens must live differently
from anyone else—" Catherine sighed. Of all her children, it was Elisabeth who was her true companion, her favorite girl. Alone of all of
them, she was not marred, not twisted, not simpleminded, but bright
eyed and olive skinned, her intelligence quick, her manner tactful but
sprightly. What pains she had taken to raise her through a sickly child-

hood. And what a rare thing, how precious, how worthy was her daughter-treasure! But now they would be queens together. Forever, Elisabeth would sit at Catherine's right hand when they met, exactly as they would at the Tournament of the Three Queens that would crown the wedding festivities on the morrow. And, secretly, the worm of delight twisted in Catherine's innards; on her left hand would be the Queen of Scotland, her snippy daughter-in-law, or Queen-Dauphiness, as she was now called. Queen of a shabby half-island, with years to wait, petulant and spoiled, for Catherine's seat of honor, while *Elisabeth*, her Elisabeth, was Queen of *Spain*, and the greatest Empire of earth. Ah, sit and whisper all you want, Queen Marie, about "tradesman's daughters," today—*my* daughter is Queen of *Spain!*

A page in silk livery wandered through the array of ladies, maids, petticoats, and jewel boxes. Eagerly, the queen turned toward the lanky little twelve-year-old, the ungainly scion of a great house, so eagerly, in fact, that the attendant pinning her ruff had great difficulty in avoiding scratching her. "What said the king my husband when I sent him my colors to wear in the joust tomorrow?"

"Your Majesty," croaked the page, his newly changing voice alternating from low to high out of pure nerves, "his majesty the king said—he— would be wearing the colors of—the Duchess of Valentinois."

"Thank you," said the queen, as cold as ice. Inside her, the joy and glory turned into a stone, a tombstone, heavy and hard. The Duchess of Valentinois, poisoning the very moment of her glory. How much longer, how much, would she have to wait for the fulfillment of her other wish?

❖

In the royal stables at Les Tournelles, an army of smiths, stable hands, and boys had been at work from sunup to sundown for the past week. The roar of the lion in the menagerie and the cries of peacocks in the park were mingled with the clang and clatter of horseshoeing and of tournament armor being adjusted, with the cries of servants demanding that others make way as one of the huge, vicious jousting stallions was brought through the stables to his stall. Then there was the braiding, the brushing, the polishing, the trimming, the hoof gilding—all the primping and brushing that make a nobleman's jousting steed glisten in the sun like polished metal. Carts of oats, boys with buckets of water, saddlers with new bridles glittering with silver trim crossed paths and made way, for the stables were very crowded. Some of the guests had shipped in their own horses for the tourney. All had brought their own equipment, and their men and gear had to be stowed somewhere.

"Will the king be riding Le Victorieux?" a stable hand asked the master of the king's horse.

"No bays or chestnuts. He will be all in black and white, in honor of the Duchess of Valentinois, and he wants a black horse. The one the Duke of Savoy brought, Le Malheureux. Down there in the last stall. And Le Defiant kept in readiness."

A boy brought the big Turkish stallion, a gift from the king's future brother-in-law, from his stall and tied him between two posts. As two stable hands brushed the huge black stallion to a high gloss, the man who had asked the question applied himself to the delicate task of gild-ing each of the stallion's immense hoofs. As he worked, he whistled softly to himself. He'd get a good view, the next day, although it was only from the ground.

❧

That night, Catherine de Medici, Queen of France, amateur sorceress, dabbler in magic, woke up screaming. It was late, late, and in the shad-owy halls of the Louvre, the sputtering torches had burned almost to stubs. One of the archers stationed on the stair landing beneath the queen's apartments thought he might have heard something, but it could have been a cat, or perhaps some curious night breeze. The queen's sheets were tangled and sweat-damp, and it seemed to her that she had suddenly fallen from a great height. Terror lurked in the high corners of the brocade canopy of her bed, and in her ears she heard the dusty, metallic laughter of a thing dead and rotted for centuries. In her imagi-nation, the thing was hiding somewhere in the room, somewhere in its box, laughing at her. "Your heart's wish is granted, great queen. Time will show you the truth," said the mummified thing, in a voice that rus-tled like dead leaves. And the vision, the vision that had waked her could not be banished from her mind: her husband, the king, lying stark and dead in a pool of blood, his eye a dreadful bleeding socket, his mouth agape in some last expression of horror and surprise.

"Not this, not this, oh, God, this is not what I wanted," she said, or whispered, or thought—she could not tell.

"Oh, all this and more," said the rustling, sinister voice. "I have taken away the influence of Diane de Poitiers, Duchess of Valentinois, forever, just as you wished."

"What is wrong, Your Majesty?" asked the maid who slept on the truckle bed, wrapping the sheet about her naked body and hurrying to open the heavy bed curtains. Inside, she saw the queen, her face a mask of horror, her eyes staring at something invisible somewhere near the top of the bedposts. What the queen was seeing was letters of fire, which blazed and seared her heart, her entrails:

"The young lion will conquer the old
in single combat—"

Single combat. Not combat in war, but combat against one person. The king jousts tomorrow. Let it not be with a man who bears a lion on his shield. Ah, let it not be. Holy Virgin Mother, forgive me, protect, save—

"Too late," whispered the thing.

The maid saw that the queen's lips were moving in prayer. Silently, she closed the bed curtains and withdrew. But she could not sleep anymore that night.

✤

The day was fine and clear, and joyful crowds crammed every available window and rooftop on the rue St.-Antoine, where the brightly painted barriers for the lists had been set up and freshly strewed dirt raked, thick and even, over the rutted cobblestones beneath. From every turret of Les Tournelles, the ornate palace of the turrets, newly embroidered silk banners fluttered. The ladies' stand, canopied and hung with tapestry, was brilliant with color, and in the very center, at the place of greatest honor, sat the three queens, each more glittering than the next. Only one person was sour and angry, and he concealed it beneath a mask even deeper than the one with which the pale, round-faced Queen of France concealed her fear. This angry man, who sat in the grandstand reserved for foreign dignitaries and princes of the church, was the English ambassador. He had noticed that every banner, the embroidery on every herald's sleeve, the arms of the Queen-Dauphiness displayed hanging from the grandstand railing next to the arms of the Queen of France and the arms of the Queen of Spain, in short, every French royal coat of arms on display, had been quartered with the arms of England. No clearer declaration of war to the death between Mary, Catholic Queen of Scots, Dauphiness of France, and Elisabeth, the young Protestant Queen of England could have been made. But to the French, it was all part of the glory of the day. The inevitable triumph of the Catholic alliance was but part of God's great plan for France. What right had the ambassador of the bastard daughter of a divorced king to complain?

Tight-lipped, white knuckled, the troll-faced little Queen of France heard the heralds' trumpets announce the arrival of the king in the lists. The note she had sent him; had he received it? I have had a dream, it said. Do not joust today. Remember the words of Luc Guaric, and of Nostradamus. This is the forty-first year.

The king, a black-and-white surcoat of the ancient style over his glittering black, gold-engraved tournament armor, paused at the end of the list, leaning down from the high jousting saddle on Le Malheureux's back to take up the note.

"Superstition," he said, crumpling up the note and throwing it away. "What does she take me for, a fool? A king does not withdraw once he has announced his intention." Then he said firmly to the little page, "Tell the queen my wife that I will joust today, and that I shall have the victory." His squire handed up his lance, and he couched it. He was a beautiful horseman, handsomely mounted, and as he rode out to show himself, his plumes flying and armor glittering, it gratified him to hear the crowd's awed sound. I am not old yet, he thought. I have not put on *that* much weight. I can still show men in their twenties a thing or two. He lowered his gold-barred visor, then at the signal, spurred the black stallion forward. The two horsemen met with a crash; the king's lance shattered, his opponent was unhorsed. Cheers and applause. The King of France was still king of chivalry. Could Philip of Spain, that bleary-

eyed old man, do as well? In the stands, he saw Diane fluttering her
white handkerchief at him. His wife, pallid and stout, did not even smile
at his triumph. How many years more would he be saddled with this
stolid, superstitious little Italian merchant's daughter?

Again, the sound of trumpets, and again, the triumph. Let the Duke
of Alva return to his master, that old man who hides in his palaces, and
tell him that King Henry of France is a master of chivalry, still powerful
on the field of honor. Le Malheureux was stained with sweat now, and
the long black-and-white embroidered saddlecloth clung damply to his
flanks. The third and last encounter; his own captain of the Scottish
guard. Only twenty-eight years old; this was a conquest worthy of him!

When Montgomery was announced, and rode forward in the lists,
the queen's lips turned white. The younger man, mounted on a handsome bay from the royal stables, was carrying on his left arm a shield
painted with his coat of arms: most prominent, to her eyes, as if painted
in fire, was a red lion. The young lion, the thought hummed through her
brain. Here is death. One last encounter, then the three courses required
by the rules of the tournament were fulfilled. Mary, Queen of Heaven,
she prayed silently as the two heavily armed knights clattered down the
lists toward each other. They met with a thunderous crash; Montgomery sat firm, the king reeled, then recovered. He had lost—a stirrup.
There was a gasp, then shouts from the women about her, from the windows, from the crowd on the ground. But she sat, iron faced, and could
feel her heart begin to pump blood once again. Her prayers had been answered. The king had survived. Now tonight he would dance, he would
dine, he would bid farewell to his daughter. All was well. The time of
danger was past; sixty-nine years, Nostradamus had said. The kingdom
would recover from this backbreaking, fruitless lost war. It would knit
up the religious division that was splitting it apart and become the
greatest kingdom in all of Catholic Christendom. France would take England, conquer heresy, serve God, and become mighty. Then, to her horror, she saw her husband had not dismounted at the far end of the lists.

As several attendants rubbed the sweat from his horse, King Henry
accepted a drink of water, then handed down the empty cup.

"I lost a stirrup," he said. "Montgomery made me lose a stirrup; I
want to match myself against him again."

The Sire de Vieilleville, fully armed and mounted for the next joust with Montgomery responded. "Sire, you have acquitted yourself with honor, and mine is the next match. Don't ride again."

But the king, grumbling and enraged, thought of the disgrace of losing a stirrup before the Duke of Alva. "Move aside," he said, "I want to ride again against Montgomery; this time I will defeat him."

From a distance, the queen saw the two armored figures conferring on horseback. She turned to her daughter. "The king, your father, wishes to ride a fourth course." The slight, fourteenyearold girl looked at her, not understanding. Three pages stood behind the queens, to be at their hand for any little service. The queen sent the fastest of them to run to the end of the lists with a message.

The long pause had unnerved the crowd. The king's three courses were over. What was happening? A nervous muttering started up, and when the king heard it, it set him more firmly in his resolve. "Send a message to Montgomery that the king will have the next encounter," he said. "I insist on having satisfaction." Vieilleville looked long and hard at his sovereign.

"Your Majesty, for the three nights past I have been troubled with evil dreams. Do not, I beg you, run this next encounter. Here am I; honor has been served. Let me encounter Montgomery for your sake." Two little pages ran up, one of them in Montgomery's livery, one in the queen's.

"What says Montgomery?" said the king.

"Your Majesty, he says honor is served, and begs not to be asked to ride against you again," said the boy.

"Tell him to make ready," said the king. "It is my command." He looked at the second page, and raised his dark eyebrows. His long face looked disdainful. "What says my wife the queen this time?"

"Your Majesty, the queen begs you for love of her not to engage Montgomery again."

All decked out in his mistress's colors, he looked down, and said with unconscious irony, "Tell her that it is precisely because of love of her that I will run this next course," and lowered the gilded bars of his visor. His squire, shaken by strange demand, checked the buckles on his armor, the fastening on the visor. They seemed still sound. At the king's command, the trumpets sounded, and the king, refreshed, rode toward the lists again. As he passed, a little boy ran from the crowd:

"Sire, do not joust," he called after him, but the king did not hear.

With the thunder of heavy hooves, the two armed horses and their armed riders rushed down the lists at full gallop. The king's lance missed its target, and Montgomery's hit the king's canted jousting shield slightly above the center. It shattered with a crash and the long, sharp tip broke away. But in the very moment that the lance shattered, it slid upward, and Montgomery, in a moment of stunned paralysis, did not fling the stump away swiftly enough. Too late. The splintered stump of the lance glanced upward off the angled jousting shield hitting the king's visor, which flew open.

The crowd saw the king reel in the saddle, then slide slowly toward the ground. There was a collective gasp, and cries. "The King has fallen!" Before the king's attendants surrounded him to remove his armor, Catherine saw, from the stands, the vision of her nightmare: the king's face, covered with blood that flowed, flowed unquenchably, from his right eye, from which the huge splinters of the broken lance protruded hideously.

✢

High up in a window in a rented room on the rue St.-Antoine, a tall, angular young lady held her hand to her mouth and gasped in shock. Another young lady turned suddenly, rolled up her eyes and fainted into the lap of her mother. Aunt Pauline and Montvert the banker looked at each other with shrewd eyes.

"This changes everything," said Auntie.

"I'll send for Nicolas at once. The new regime won't be interested in the pursuit of bathhouse duelists."

"But if anyone suspects this is Menander's doing, Sibille is in great danger."

"Exactly. But it's not only anyone—it's the queen."

"While the king lives, all hope will be on him."

"And if he dies, there will be a required period of forty-days' mourning when she will be sequestered. Both give us time. They can marry in se-cret, and Nicolas can take her out of the kingdom. I hope that Sibille is not as averse to sunshine as you are, Madame."

"They say Italy is very healthful in this season," said Auntie. And even though the others were right in the room with them, they were so shocked by what they had seen that they did not hear a word.

It was the Old Constable himself, mended and freed with the peace, and the great Guise, victor of Calais, who carried the king into Les Tournelles. "I want to walk," he whispered at the foot of the great stair-case, but several more lords of the court had to support him. Behind him came a group of notables carrying the weakling heir, who had fainted. An evil sign, said those who witnessed the eerie procession into the palace. That night they sealed Les Tournelles, and Montgomery, the young lion, packed his belongings in haste and fled the country.

Lying in the great, draped bed, the king passed between fainting and waking, night and day mingled into a blur of surgeries, of dignitaries whispering in corridors, of papers presented for a feeble signature. "Per-haps he will recover; the surgeons say the wound is not mortal," said the queen to Madame d'Alamanni, as she left the sickbed for an hour or two of sleep. But her froggy little eyes, wide with horror and guilt, told another story.

"I myself heard Maître Paré's assistant say that if it has not pene-trated the brain, he will only lose the eye," replied her companion.

"And there is no fever," said the queen. "With no fever, surely he will recover." Already, she had seen the Guises, tall and arrogant, mov-ing in and out of the chambers where her sickly, simpleton son was be-ing consoled by his redheaded, vain, ambitious little wife. She did not need prophetic dreams to show her the pattern of the future, should her husband not rise from his sickbed. As she walked the corridors during the surgeries, wringing her hands, her heart was frozen with imaginings and phantasms. On the third day, she rallied when the great Vesalius, servant of the King of Spain and the finest anatomist in the known world, arrived, and the king called for musicians, and vowed to make a pilgrimage on his recovery. She remembered she had not eaten, and took a little wine and boiled fowl, then slept upright in a chair by the king's bed that night, lulled into sleep by his regular breathing.

But on the fourth day the fever began to rise, and no treatment could stop it.

❧

Outside the sealed gates of Les Tournelles, Diane de Poitiers, Duchess of Valentinois, was turned away like a beggar.

"Queen's orders," said the guard, as the duchess, her eyes red-rimmed, her face pallid and tense, fled to her ornate, gilded litter. Attendants drew the curtains, and as the guard watched the two white-draped black hackneys bear away their swaying, sealed burden, he thought: how could the king have seen anything in *her*? She's older than my grandmother, and as wrinkled as a prune.

In the reception hall of her luxurious Paris mansion, the Duchess of Valentinois paced up and down on the heavy Turkish carpet, blind to the passage of time. Anyone who had been near Les Tournelles, unworthy persons, pages, gossips, those who in past years would not have been allowed to set foot within her gates, were welcomed and shown in.

"Does the king live? Will the king recover?" she repeated over and over, her face taut and haunted.

On the fourth night, she awoke with a shriek from her opium-induced sleep, and demanded that the woman who attended her go immediately to the city archers and have the fortune-teller Simeoni arrested, but the woman took it for a hallucination, and poured the duchess another dose of sleeping medicine.

That morning, when the duchess held her *levée,* she noticed many familiar faces from the highest aristocracy were absent. Her courtyard was devoid of petitioners, her open table at noon without guests. Frantic, she sent a message by courier to the head of the family that owed her so many favors, but the Guises sent her a cold little note, letting her know that they were a family accustomed to dealing with legitimate rulers, not with former mistresses.

"But he lives; he still lives," she said. "By God, I will not be treated like this while he draws breath." Yet with each passing hour, it seemed that the abandoned duchess grew older and older looking. Lines deepened, and her white face took on a grayish tint. It was as if, as the king drifted toward death, the magic that had withheld her old age was fad-ing. She took up a hand mirror from her dressing table, and above her jeweled bodice and immaculate lace ruff, an ancient face stared back at her. A face—like—oh, God, that horrible mummy in the box. Dried up, decayed—no, it *was* that ghastly, vulgar thing. And as she stared in hor-ror, the thing in the mirror *winked* at her, with one of its peeling, leath-ery eyelids. With a cry, the duchess threw the mirror from her, and it shattered on the floor, sending glass shards everywhere. But no one heard the crash and came.

As the afternoon shadows grew longer, seated alone in her bedcham-ber, where an untouched meal lay on a tray by her bedside, she heard a timid knock on the door. A page, sent by the guard at the gate, had brought her a message sealed with the royal arms. Hurriedly, she tore it open. It was a letter addressed to "La Mère Poitiers"—old mother Poitiers, not the duchess, not dearest cousin, not anything. It was from the queen. It demanded the return of the crown jewels, of the funds of state, of the châteaux and gifts of the treasury and royal lands the king had showered on her. The queen desired Chenonceau, the white palace of light breezes and joyful celebrations, that lay like a wedding cake on the bank of the Cher. As cold and precise as a surgeon's knife was that letter, and it froze the duchess's vitals.

He must live, he must live, the duchess repeated over and over in her mind, as she knelt in the previously ornamental prie-dieu by her bed-side. And yet a whisper like dried leaves came to her ears: you wished that the queen will never have influence over him, and behold, she never will. I have fulfilled your heart's desire.

❖

In the cellars of Les Tournelles, four heavily shackled criminals were brought to a hastily erected headsman's block.

"Not now, not now, for God's sake," shrieked one of them, when he saw the masked executioner leaning on his axe.

"*In nomine patris, filio, et spiritu sanctu,*" intoned the priest who had ac-companied them, finishing the prayer with the sign of the cross. The dank, stony room smelled of mice and mildew.

"Orders. The surgeons want your heads," said the executioner. "You are condemned anyway. What does it matter if it's now or later?"

In the next room, beneath the heavy stone vaulting, the greatest sur, geons in the known world waited. As they heard the last of four dull *thunk* sounds, they nodded to one another and tied their heavy leather aprons over their doublets; the heads were ready. Freshness was essen, tial; the experimental material must be in a condition as close to the king's own head as possible. On a long oak table were laid the splin, tered remnants of the fatal lance, and several sets of dissecting tools. The surgeons looked up as the door opened, and two of the execu, tioner's assistants came in with a tub, awash in blood, containing the four heads.

The celebrated Vesalius himself lifted the first head out by the hair and laid it on the table. The other surgeons, like Vesalius, stripped to their doublets, their shirtsleeves rolled up, positioned the head while Ambroise Paré, the king's own surgeon, the brilliant battlefield sur, geon who had saved The Scar, who had invented the ligature of arter, ies, who had revolutionized the treatment of gunshot wounds, picked up the shattered lance. With a single sure blow, he drove the splintered weapon into the right eye at exactly the angle that it had entered the king's. Vesalius picked up the scalpel and laid open the skull.

Grave, bearded heads clustered around the table as the skull was opened.

"—here, the lesser wing of the sphenoid—"

"—the length, is it the same?"

"—there is no question. The lance has penetrated to the brain—"

"—the deeper splinter that remains in the king's eye socket, can it be removed without fatal bleeding?"

"—if it is not, the poison cannot drain from the wound—"

"—brain poisoning—"

"—a fresh infusion of blood—"

"—another surgery—"

By the time that the fourth head was dissected, the surgeons had planned the remaining treatment of the king's wound. And they knew that no matter what they did, it would prove mortal.

✤

On the tenth day, the king briefly recovered consciousness, and called the Dauphin to him. "My son," he said, "you are going to be without your father, but not without his blessing. I pray to God that you will be more fortunate than I have been." The wretched, sickly boy fainted, and recovering in his chamber, began to weep: "My God, how can I live if my father dies?" And though even the mighty Cardinal of Lorraine himself offered consolation, for that brief moment, the simpleminded boy had seen the dim mists of the future open, and knew that nothing could save him, not his pretty new wife, not his clever uncles-in-law, not his brooding mother. Death had looked down at him through that opening, and turned his decayed little spine to water.

That night, as the king's breath rasped in and out, the surgeons conferred on a last, desperate measure: they would trepan the skull. But when they removed the bandages, so much pus spilled from the eye socket that they knew no operation of which they were capable could save the king's brain. They rebandaged the fevered head, and sent word to the priests to come and administer the last rites.

✤

It was the custom of the widowed queens of France to wear white, but sealed in her rooms, Catherine de Medici ordered mourning clothes of black, like the widow of a lesser house, like the garments of an Italian courtier. The brilliant gold embroideries, the lush, bright velvets, the dappled silks were sent away, laden over the arms of her waiting women, and workmen came to drape her apartments in the Louvre, her furniture, her windows, in black. Wandering about the darkened rooms, her face swollen with weeping, kneeling at her prie-dieu unable to fix her eyes on her prayer book, sitting up at night in the dark, agonized thoughts came to the queen. One night, she woke her attendants to tell them that her coat of arms must be changed. The next day, when they hoped she had forgotten, she sent for a scholar from the College of Arms and banished the rainbow, which old King Francis himself had given her, and herself sketched a stump of a broken lance in a cartouche and beneath it the motto, *Lacrimae hinc, hinc dolor,* "Here are tears, here is sorrow."

But in the perpetual gloom of her black-draped chambers, so dark that they must be lit in daytime with candles, the queen heard a rustling, as if of rotted grave clothes, and hidden laughter that sounded like stones falling into a crypt. And then came the voice that made her insides twist with pain and her head throb as if it would burst: Great queen, the duchess will never again have his heart. See how I have fulfilled your heart's desire?

But Catherine was a Medici, and made of hard stuff. She whispered into the shadows: You have not won yet. I shall seek greater magic. I shall defeat you.

Oh, great queen, what a worthy opponent you are. Not in a thousand years have I met such a one. But before you think you have saved yourself, remember your other wishes.

"My children!" gasped the queen.

Why, yes, your children. Remember what you wished? That the Queen of Scots should no longer influence your son—

"No, no!"

Oh, but I am not done—and you wished that they all have thrones. Just see how I have arranged to fulfill your greatest desire of all.

Molten steel poured into the queen's body and grew hard. The ladies who answered the ringing of the little silver bell she took up thought they saw something in the corner of the room that looked like a statue, a ghost, a demon, but one that still held the shape of the queen.

"Madame Gondi," said the granite thing in the corner, "have a courier take the fastest horse in the king's stable and take this letter to Salon de Provence, to the house of Nostradamus. Tell him that I would have him come to Chaumont, and there I will meet him." And as Madame Gondi disappeared, she spoke to Madame d'Alamanni. "Madame, how stands it with the court, and with my son, the king?"

"Your Majesty, your son has fallen ill, but he has given orders that Constable Montmorency and Marshall St.-André shall have the honor of standing guard over the king's body for the forty days of mourning."

"No one but the Guises could have told him this. So now, in other words, the Guises now rule unchallenged."

"Yes, Majesty."

"And by the end of forty days, with the Constable and the Marshall unable to stir from the catafalque, there will be nothing and no one left to hinder them."

"Majesty, they but hold power during your hours of grief."

"My hours of grief are over. I wish you to call the King's Treasurer, so I may find out where the accounts of the kingdom stand. I heard the late king, my husband, say that the soldiers have not been paid these three years."

"But, Majesty—"

"No buts. That is the stuff of insurrection. And I wish to know if the Lutherans have begun to show their faces, now that a child rules. Bring me their pamphlets; I want to know what they are saying, they and their treacherous preachers. If they speak a word against me, they are to be caught and hanged. And—oh, yes, send for the Demoiselle de La Roque. I would have her come to Chaumont, where I will confer with her in private. Send a guard to make sure she does not change her mind. There is a sacrifice she must make for the good of the throne. But—tell her—tell her that—the queen has a special—reward—for her for all her services."

❧

That very evening, a fast courier from Genoa pulled an exhausted Turk-ish barb into the courtyard of the banking establishment of Fabris and Monteverdi at Lyons. Dropping his packet of messages with the eldest of the Fabris brothers, he paused only long enough to take a brief meal and change horses, then rode off into the dark. The moon was half full, enough to light the road, and despite the fact that he carried nothing of value, the dark-clad courier was armed with an Italian rapier, a long dag-ger, a hidden misericord, an arquebus and a string of powder charges around his neck. Nicolas's face was gaunt with fatigue, and he had gone unshaven for the last two weeks, but his eyes were determined. His fa-ther, his graceless, hard-hearted old father, had shown his human side at last. In a letter sent from Paris, he had forgiven him everything, had given him permission to marry, and had told him that if he did not has-ten, the treachery of the great would lay the love of his life in her grave.

Twenty-two

eath to the sorcerer!" Above the screaming crowd in the Place de Grève, the robed figure impaled on the tall stake was scarcely visible.

"Death to Nostradamus!" Men and women in clogs and rough clothes scrambled to throw more straw on the faggots.

"Burn the wizard who killed the king!"

"Au feu, au feu!" A man set a burning brand into the straw, where it smoldered a moment, then shot up a narrow tongue of flame. At the edge of the square near the ornate grilles of the front gate of the Hôtel de Ville, a half-dozen archers in broad helmets and metal-studded cuirasses lounged with their arms folded.

"Who is Nostradamus?" said one of them.

"Didn't you hear? A wizard who cast a death-spell on the king." The flames had caught on the hem of the gown, and a heavy smoke obscured the rest of the figure.

"Who was he working for?"

"They say the agents of the English queen—" There was a cheer as the flames suddenly exploded through the straw-filled effigy, and it dissolved in a fierce blaze.

"I take it he escaped."

"They've hunted for him everywhere, but he's gone. So they had to take it out on something—"

"Ha! If he ever shows his face in Paris again, he'll get a warm welcome, that's for sure!"

"All sorcerers should burn. Burn here, then burn in Hell."

"Well, Anael," said Nostradamus, who was watching the scene in the waters of his divining bowl, "if I had ever planned to visit that wretched city again, I certainly wouldn't now." Even at midnight, the day's heat was still close in the attic room of the house in Salon, and Nostradamus, his face streaming sweat, was regretting the heavy gown beneath his diviner's robe. In the candlelight, the brass of his armillary sphere glinted dully, and Anael was scarcely visible except as a sort of dark vapor.

"They aren't terribly logical," remarked the dark figure. "Predicting the future isn't the same as causing it."

"Parisians. Dreadful people. Poor pay, threats of the Inquisition, and now they burn me in effigy. Did I ever tell you about that inn at the sign of Saint-Michel? The sheets were dirty, and they overcharged for that despicable vinegar they called wine—"

"A hundred times, Michel. You're getting old and grouchy. What's worse, you're getting so forgetful you repeat your grouches."

"Me? Never! My mind's as sharp as a whole boxful of new needles. But I'm certainly not going to travel again. My dyspepsia, to say nothing of the ingratitude of folk like *that*—"

"I wouldn't count on that if I were you, Michel," said the Angel of Past and Future History.

❖

Now I remember the exact day very well, because it was the day I went to the printer's with the final draft of my new dialogue, the *Cena,* which was not exactly my typical elevated style, but what I was, if not what I craved to be. If they don't like it, well, it's just too bad, I thought. As I set down the manuscript, the printer brought out for my examination the page proofs of the tastefully black-bordered edition of my forthcoming collection of fashionable poems of grief, entitled *The Garden of Sorrows,* to be distributed only in the most exclusive court circles. Holding true work and false at the very same moment, and hearing the printer praise both equally, set me into a meditation on hypocrisy, which led me to an idea for another *Dialogue,* and so distracted me that I walked beneath a ladder, which always brings bad luck.

When I stepped into our *salle* on my return, I noticed that something had gone dreadfully wrong. Aunt Pauline, as white as one of her ghosts, her eyes sunk in deep circles, sat unmoving on her big, cushioned chair. Beside her stood the Abbé, more shriveled than usual, his face agitated. Around them stood six heavily armed archers in the queen-mother's livery.

"What is this?" I asked.

"Her majesty, the queen-mother, wishes to consult you, and orders that you bring with you the box of which you have custody." It had come. My heart sank into my shoes.

"But—but her majesty is not resident in Paris," I said.

"She wants you at Chaumont, and we are sent to see that you arrive safely," replied the captain of the archers.

"I—I'll need to pack a few things," I said.

"You'll want for nothing there. You are not to pack, but to come directly. Is this the box, this one just sitting out here?" There sat Menander, in his usual place on the sideboard, making the soft, busy, almost inaudible humming sound that he did almost all the time, now that he was totally engaged in thought. You useless, troublesome box full of ill fortune, I thought. This is where it ends. When she finds you are useless, she'll decide I know too many secrets—and I haven't got the fear of you to protect me any more. But I swear, Menander, I won't let you win. Something, I'll think of something. . . .

As we clattered through the city gates, I looked at the grim-faced men who surrounded me and tried to engage them in conversation. But they didn't answer, and one of them, younger than the others, looked away. Under orders, I thought. They're afraid I'll talk my way out of this. As we rode south into the rolling autumnal countryside, where the first yellow leaves were beginning to show among the green, it became clearer and clearer that nothing good was awaiting me at the queen's isolated château, so far from my relatives and friends, and any hope of help.

❧

It was already past dark, and the night watch was in the street, when Madame Tournet sent Baptiste, armed with a cutlass, to answer a frantic banging on her door.

"Madame Tournet, it's me, Nicolas," came the cry through the door, and Auntie heaved herself up out of bed, clad only in her nightcap, and allowed her maid to drape her in an immense *robe de chambre* and light a candle for her. As she entered the *salle,* she saw Nicolas and his father, wrapped in heavy cloaks, and carrying lanterns, standing in the doorway.

"Come in, come in and sit down," she said, and the bobbing candles of servants moved here and there in the dark, as chairs were drawn up and a bottle of wine and cups fetched from the sideboard.

"Where is your niece?" asked the old man. "My son arrived only this evening. A priest is waiting at the chapel of St.-Jacques de la Boucherie, and we will see her married this very night and out of the country at dawn, before the queen-mother's spies ever suspect what has happened."

"I sent a boy to your house less than an hour ago. Didn't you get my message?" said Auntie. "They've come and taken her away."

"She's gone?" said Nicolas, his eyes full of despair. "Where, for God's sake, did they tell you?"

"To Chaumont-sur-Loire," said Aunt Pauline. "Under heavy guard."

"A dreadful place," said Scipion Montvert. "They say the queen-mother keeps a ghastly tower full of magic enchantments at Chaumont, where she casts spells with the aid of the diviners and sorcerers she gathers there."

"A bad omen, that wicked castle. It's clear to me that the queen's mourning has at last turned to rage and vengeance. And where should this vengeance fall? Not on herself, for using black magic, but upon the head of Menander, or even on Sibille, for owning it. There is no doubt in my mind that she has laid plans to destroy the head of Menander the Undying."

"And with it my Sibille," said Nicolas, his face horrified. "I'll go, I'll go this very moment—"

"Even for a Montvert, the gates of Paris won't open before dawn," said Madame Tournet. "I beg you both to stay here the night. I—I need the company."

After they had convinced Nicolas that he must sleep, the old banker sat up with Auntie while the candles burned themselves flat, drinking bottle after bottle of wine.

"My only son, you understand—" said the old man.

"I've looked out for her since she was born—" said Auntie.

"If I let him go, or make him stay—either way I lose him," said the old banker, holding his head in his hands. "Love, it's a disaster—"

"It's more orderly the proper way, the arranged way," agreed Auntie. But in her mind she was imagining her father standing over her as she signed the marriage contract with the man she could never love.

"One should marry first, the right way, and then learn to love," said the banker, but in his heart rose the image of a brown-faced, dark-eyed girl at a certain fountain in Florence, filling her pitcher. Carefully, quickly, he erased the image and replaced it with the narrow, sickly visage of his wife, an heiress of good family, a prize, his father's choice. His father was right, of course. His father had always been right. That is how fathers are.

"Yes, that is the way it should be," said Auntie, pouring another cupful of wine. But in Montvert's place, she was seeing a joyful, beautiful young man, playing the lute on a flat southern rooftop with his friends. Two pallid girls and a sickly boy, come for a cure at the spa, sat on the rooftop nearby, listening to the music beneath the stars. Oh, what a feeling in her heart at the memory. How much I loved him. But not for me, her soul whispered. At least Hélène had love that once. But I, never. It was my fate.

Then she saw him, the one whose heart she'd craved, lying in a pool of his own blood at the foot of a ladder, and heard again the screaming, and saw again the men going through his clothes, and discarding the book, and the old man taking up the love letter that had brought the boy there, and tearing it to pieces in his rage. The blood, the blood everywhere. The old man smeared the blood across Hélène's face as he beat her, he dipped his hands again and again in crimson and smeared it on her as he tore at her clothes, her dead brother's doublet and shirt. And she howled, her hair all bloody, her mouth like the wound from which had flowed her young lover's life. What matter the old man had promised the unseen watcher he wouldn't hurt them? He'd lied, and she had seen what she had seen. The memory squeezed Auntie's heart like a vise. Death and love. It's come full circle. "Love's a curse," she said.

But the old banker didn't answer. He'd fallen asleep, dead drunk, his head thrown back in the chair. As he started to snore, Aunt Pauline noticed that a random tear glittered on his unshaven face. Carefully, she arranged his cloak over his bulky form, and staggered off to bed, where she dreamed all night of blood.

✣

In the dark, the waiting dockmen could hear the sound of oars over the water, as the two torches mounted on the bow of the approaching boat gleamed in the black night like two orange eyes. A sliver of new moon shone above, as shifting black clouds hid, then revealed, patches of stars. The Loire, black water between black banks, picked up the flickering orange lights, which seemed to spread like oil on the dark surface. Behind the men on the dock, horses moved impatiently, their harness jingling softly, and the dark forms of a litter, of mounted men holding lanterns, could barely be made out.

"He's here," whispered a guard.

"About time. They said he'd be here this afternoon."

"The current is bad this time of year."

The boat thumped, then made a grinding sound against the dock, as a pair of strong men lifted a human bundle out of the stern.

"We're here, Maestro," said one of the men. "Put in a good word for me, will you?"

"With the queen-mother, or with the spirits?"

"With both, if you have a chance. Remember that my son wants his own boat." On the hill high above them, a white stone fortress with peak-roofed towers gleamed dully in the starlight.

"I hope she doesn't expect me to walk up there," said Nostradamus, standing on the dock and smoothing out his wrinkled gown the way a disturbed hen would preen her errant feathers. He took a tentative step or two, leaning heavily on his cane. "Oof! My gout! Worse than ever. I tell you, this is the last trip I take. Secret missions, indeed!" A half-dozen heavily armed guards piled out of the boat after Nostradamus.

"He's all yours," said their commanding officer to one of the horse-men on the dock. "Remember, the queen will have your ears if he's not in perfect shape. He can't walk more than ten feet, he requires two feather pillows, he doesn't eat anything fried, and won't drink wine less than five years old. Good luck."

The old doctor and a large, mysterious bundle were loaded into the waiting litter, and escorted by torch-bearing outriders, the litter began the ascent of the steep, winding road to the waiting castle. In the forest beyond, owls hooted. One of the guards crossed himself superstitiously. Who knew what demonic magic lay within the bundle of the fearful prophet of doom? Those were not owls, but Satan's minions, greeting their own.

✣

The queen-mother was up late in her chambers, sitting at her desk writing by candlelight. It was a letter to Madame de Humières, discussing the care of her darling baby Hercule during this latest of his infant ill-nesses. "—and I have been assured that there is a sure cure in inhaling the smoke from yew wood to dissolve the poisons in the lung combined with the laying on of a poultice of oil of lilies and lavender—" There was a knock at the door. One of the queen's ladies opened it and announced that Maître Nostredame had at last arrived.

The queen sent everyone outside to wait, where they clustered out-side the door, hoping to catch a word or two of the secrets being dis-cussed within the room. Gesturing silence, one of the ladies knelt and put her ear to the keyhole, but it was all in vain. The only word they caught was "Ruggieri" spoken indignantly by the old prophet.

"—true, I did consult him in equipping the Astrologer's Room in the tower—it has everything you could possibly want, Maestro—but you understand I couldn't trust him at all for something as delicate as this."

"Cosmo Ruggieri could not make a magic mirror if his life depended upon it," huffed Nostradamus.

"Even if he *could*," responded the queen-mother, "he would turn around and sell the information to every enemy I have. Besides, you know that I consider only you the true prophet."

"Apparently, Ruggieri's attempt having failed."

"How did you know that?" said the dumpy little woman in black.

"I divined it two days ago in the boat. And after I'd been harassed into this trip with the assurance that my prediction would be exclusive. My powers are a curse," he grumbled.

"I have to know," she said in a mysterious tone, breaking off as if she could say no more.

"Exactly what?" asked Nostradamus, pretending to be slightly deaf.

"I thought perhaps your powers might have informed you," responded the queen-mother, rather waspishly.

"Even if they did, I want the word from your mouth."

"Very well then, I want to know the future of the throne of France." You mean you want to know how long the Queen of Scots and the Guises will rule the roost, thought the old prophet.

"The magic mirror is a very delicate object," he said. "Luckily, I began the forty-two days of purification on the road, so we will be ready at the next full moon."

"You are dismissed," said the little woman in black. "Do tell my attendants to come back in when you leave. And remember, rich rewards shall be yours if you keep my trust."

I'd rather be assured of a decent bed tonight, grumped the old prophet to himself. You're more likely to keep your word on *that*. Maybe I should ask for a deposit, before I set up the mirror. After she sees what it predicts, I'm just likely to leave empty-handed. Hmm. How to do it subtly? Perhaps I'll tell her I need several pounds of rare herbs and spices for spell-casting. Something that could be resold for serious cash. I certainly don't want to have to borrow the money to go home this time.

❖

Nine hours after Nostradamus's arrival by night, Nicolas arrived at Chaumont in broad daylight. Seated on his little hackney, he paused to survey the château in front of him and let the full hopelessness of his mission sink in. Chaumont sat on the crest of a green hill above the Loire. Hemmed in by forest on the land side, it was shut in and somber, built in four wings arranged in a square, fully walled, a fortress having yet to be remodeled as a pleasure-palace in the new style. High, pointed slate roofs rose above white towers; the windows were narrow, and the only access was by means of a drawbridge. How, how, Nicolas puzzled, was he to get in? Dusty and disappointed, he reflected morosely on the difficulties of being a hero in these modern times. In ancient days, he might have ridden up in full armor, pounded on a shield that hung at the gate, and demanded to challenge the governor of the castle in a fair fight, thus releasing the damsel in distress from her evil captors. But he was clad in a leather jerkin and dusty short cloak, and mounted on a piebald hackney that resembled a knight's charger no more than he did a knight. Well, he said to himself, the era of chivalry may be coming to a close, but the era of mind is dawning; after all, what's a brain for?

The drawbridge clearly was not pulled up until nighttime, and as he watched, he observed that all mounted men, armed men, and persons of rank were stopped and questioned. But in and out, almost as if invisible, wagons rumbled with grain and hay, old women with baskets of eggs on their heads, swineherds driving pigs, milkmaids with cows went unchallenged. The very thing, he thought, as he took his horse off to the village inn to stable it, and then hiked laboriously back up the hill. Ahead of him, an ox-wagon laden with wine casks was struggling on the rutted road. The proprietor of the casks had got out of the cart to help push from behind, while the boy driving the oxen cracked the whip over their backs, but could make no progress.

"Hey, fellow, let me help," called Nicolas, blessing all his stars that he was not in shining armor after all, and after a brief negotiation, shucked his telltale sword belt and cloak into the cart, and joined the vintner in disengaging the cart from the deep ruts. Couldn't be easier, he thought as they passed the guard without question and he retrieved his sword from among the casks. And before anyone had time to question him, he had dodged into the nearest doorway that opened onto the cobblestoned courtyard. Just walk as if you had business, he said to himself.

"Hey, fellow, where are you going?" said the captain of the archers, who was lounging on the staircase.

"Courier from Signor Gondi for her majesty, the queen-mother," he said, assuming a heavy Italian accent.

"Ha! The banker! Next time, bring my paycheck!" Pretending he didn't speak French very well, Nicolas nodded agreeably, the way foreigners do when they don't get a joke, and hurried up to the landing. An unpleasant thought had occurred to him. In all this great mass of rock, how was he to find where Sibille was hidden?

"Fellow, the queen-mother's apartments are that way," called the guard. With one hand, the guard indicated a vague direction Nicolas couldn't make out.

"Mille grazie," said Nicolas.

"Damned foreigners," said the guard, spitting on the stone steps.

Pretending that he knew where he was going, Nicolas followed the direction indicated by the hand until he was out of sight, then collared a page carrying a water pitcher, who told him that the queen had just left the astrologer's chamber. Astrologer's chamber, thought Nicolas. The very place that she'd put that dismal talking head of Sibille's. And where the head is, Sibille won't be far away. Hand on his sword hilt, he climbed the stairs of the turreted observatory that held the astrologer's chamber. Plunging through an open door, he found himself in a tall, brick-walled chamber where the last of the twilight filtered dimly through high, narrow windows. An athanor sat in a huge open hearth, there was a curtained bed in one corner, and a worktable against the wall, laden with books, bottles, and a human skull.

"Come in," said a voice from the shadows, and Nicolas made out the form of a long-bearded man of medium height standing in the shadows at the far side of the room. On a writing desk in front of him lay something flat and metallic; in front of the desk was a cage of live pigeons. The man was wearing the hat and gown of a doctor. The gown of Montpellier, not Paris. I know him, thought Nicolas. We've met. The man who saved Sibille's arm from the vitriol, and told me my astrological sign. Why is he here? "I've been expecting you," said the old man.

"Doctor Nostradamus," said Nicolas, "what are you doing here?"

"A secret mission," said the great prophet, stepping out of the shadows to greet Nicolas. "If you must know, I'm engaged in preparing a magic mirror, for which I expect to be paid far less than it's worth. So here I am, hauled off like a sack of barley in the middle of the night, and all because of a middle-aged lady's guilty conscience. It's not as if she ever asked *me* for advice when there was time to mend. Oh, no. Cosmo Ruggieri, Simeoni, Guaricus, any old quack that walked by her door— but not Nostradamus, who knew all along she should have kept her hands off the undead. So, why are *you* here?"

"I thought you'd know that already, too," said Nicolas.

"No, I just had a prophetic dream that you'd be standing here, all dusty, annoying me about something or other. State your business and be done."

"It must be Fate," said Nicolas, rather awed. "I've come to rescue Sibille Artaud de La Roque, the only woman I will ever love, who is being held here in secret. But I have no idea where she is. But you, a diviner, can obviously find her instantly."

"Hmp. The poetess. You expect *me* to find her? I should have known. People expect me to find everything they've misplaced," said the old doctor. "But tell me, what makes you think she'd be here?"

"It's that ghastly old mummified head she's stuck with," said Nicolas. "Her aunt Pauline says she thinks the queen has decided to get rid of it because it brought about the king's death. And once she gets rid of the head, she'll get rid of Sibille for knowing all about it." Impulsively, Nicolas knelt on one knee before the old man, and took off his hat, which he clutched to his heart. "Maestro, you have to help. I beg you to help. If anything happens to Sibille, I'll have to kill myself, and that would break my father's heart."

"And not yours, eh?" The old doctor chuckled. "Oh, you young men. When I was young, I was passionate, too—but for wisdom."

"I don't want any more wisdom than I've got. I just want Sibille. Help me, help me save her, Maestro!"

"Ah, my dear young man. Often in life we acquire more wisdom than we want. But, be that as it may—I see you are in a mood to draw your sword against the palace guard in an attempt to rescue the demoiselle, which would be quite fruitless and lead to your early demise. Therefore, put away your sword and rely on me. Tonight at midnight the queen returns for the reading she's ordered. I have a plan."

"A plan? Only a plan?"

"But it is a plan of Nostradamus, young man."

"Nicolas, please."

"Nicolas then. So, Nicolas, stay and help me. I'm much too stiff to do this all alone. I don't know what she had in mind, hauling me off like this. I could have sent her something by mail ..." The old doctor began to grumble as he opened the pigeon cage.

"What do you need done?" asked Nicolas.

"Well, first, rummage in that chest over there, I need a human tibia."

"A what?"

"A shinbone. And, if you're interested, I'll show you how to magne-tize a cat—"

❖

"I hate you, hate you, hate you. Just look what you've done now," I said to Menander's box, which sat on the floor in front of me, on a pile of rotten straw. The only illumination in the tiny, stone-walled room was a flickering candle in a cheap iron candlestick. Somewhere, a draft was entering the room and bringing air. But there wasn't even a window. Nor a chair, either, and the walls and floor oozing damp. My feet are cold and my bottom's going to sleep, sitting on the floor like this.

"Shut up, I'm thinking," said the thing in the box, and then it fell silent again. This must be the deepest cellar in the whole donjon of Chaumont, I thought. It must be a trick, locking me in here. Someone else has done this, not the queen. Someone who wants to own Menan-der, and that means I'm as good as dead. Who would even hear me scream, so deep down, behind such a heavy door? Then I thought about Nicolas, who wouldn't ever even know what had happened to me, and I burst into tears and sobbed a good long time. Why had I been given the gift of love, and from it, the flame of true art, if it was all meant to end like this? I had just about cried myself into exhaustion when I heard the jingle of keys, and the door opened inward. On the threshold stood a guard with a key ring and a blazing torch. Behind him came two guards and a huge, silent fellow in a leather apron, who was carrying a large sack. They filed into the little room without a word. Behind them came another guard with a torch, and then the queen herself stood before me.

She was all dressed in black, with a heavy veil over her face. The veil just didn't bode well.

"Mademoiselle de La Roque, the very least you can do is rise when your queen enters the chamber."

"I'm terribly sorry, but my joints are stiff, and my legs have gone to sleep," I said, making a show of a struggle, but not getting up. After all, if one is going to be killed, manners cease to take the preemininent place in one's consciousness.

"I'm sure you understand, this is a matter of state, not personal at all. Your poetry will live after you; I believe you will find that a consolation."

"I'd rather have children to live after me. What you have in mind is entirely unfair, I'm sure."

"I have come to destroy Menander, and while it is regrettable that you are attached to him, your presence at court is a sacrifice that I must be prepared to make."

The queen's voice sounded very nasty and cold, and I could hardly believe I'd ever thought her nice. Oh, Sibille, my Higher Self lectured me, you put your sweet and trusting faith in honey and falseness, and now you are doomed. Poor Nicolas will seek your tomb in vain, and be heartbroken forever. It's very poetic. But my Lower Self said to me, don't let her get off easily. Think! Think! Turn the knife of guilt in her bosom, and she may relent. "My blood will curse you forever," I said, but it didn't seem to bother her at all.

"I am already accursed," said the queen, "and it's all your fault for bringing me that evil, diabolical being in the box by your feet. You knew it would curse me. It is you that caused the king's death by sorcery."

"I hardly think so. After all, you wanted it, and if you hadn't sent for it, it never would have been attached to *me,* and I'd be happy drawing plants and writing poems in my father's house, at this very minute." Actually, I wouldn't be happy there at all, I thought, but there's no use letting *her* know that.

"That's what happens when women are not content with their lot, and go seeking after glory and favor," said the queen. "Let this be a lesson to you; a woman's crowning glory is service to her family. Everything that happened is your fault. You are fortunate that I am so merciful. The cup and flask—" She stretched out a hand to the man in the apron who had the big sack, and he took out a little flask and a metal cup, which he handed her. She filled it, and at a gesture, he took it and set it down beside me. "This is very quick," she said. "You may choose this, or the slower way. You have to understand, this room is very small, and I do not want blood splashed on my hem."

"What do you mean?" I cried, struggling to my feet.

"Oh, *now* you can get up. I always knew you were insolent. Yes, I'm sure you deserve this. Hold her while the box is sealed," she said. While I struggled against the guards, the man in the apron took a mallet and seven long steel spikes out of his bag, and drove them straight through Menander's box.

"Stop that," came a leathery little voice from inside. "You're interrupting my ratiocination."

"I assure you, you'll have perfect peace from now on, you malignant little thing," said the queen.

"What are you planning to do?" I cried.

"Why, lock the door and then brick up the doorway so that it is entirely invisible. These attendants, here, were chosen because they are dumb. No word will ever escape about your fate, or that of the dreadful magic with which you have destroyed the king. Both you and the Master of All Desires will be buried for eternity."

"Liar! I never did it! It's you who wished for it all—" I cried, and bit the guard who was holding me, trying to break free and run through the door before it was sealed forever. One of the silent guards grabbed me, and I bit and struggled while his huge hands held my arms tight. My dress tore as I broke away and thrust myself for a brief moment, halfway through the door. There was an annoyed cry from the queen as I snatched at her dress, only to be picked up as if I were a bundle of rags by one of the immense guards, then flung back against the rear wall of the dark little chamber. The door slammed, and I seem to recall that the queen said, "How dare you!" before the light from the torches vanished. I ached all over. The candle had overturned and gone out in the damp, and alone in the dark, I heard the awful sound of a key turning in the lock. I felt about the floor. The cup had spilled, too. How long does it take to starve to death in the dark? I wondered.

Outside the door, I could hear the rasping sound of mortar being smoothed. "Let me out, let me out! You don't understand! Menander can't answer wishes anymore. He's too preoccupied, don't you see? He's useless!" And faintly, through the heavy door, I heard the queen reply:

"But dear, don't *you* see? I don't want any living soul on this earth to know what my wishes have brought to pass. And you, only you, know what my desires were, and how they were answered."

"It's not *fair!*" I shouted at the sealed door.

"Nothing in life is fair," said the voice outside the door, fading away. And all I could hear was *rasp, clunk, rasp, clunk,* as the bricks were laid into place.

I won't give up, I won't give up, Nicolas needs me, I thought, feeling frantically along the floor for the candlestick. It had a handle, and a round rim, and a spike to hold the candle in place, and I had remembered something. The door opened inward. This was no prison, but a storeroom of some sort, some place that no one would think to look for a human being, a place that no one would miss when it was sealed up. The hinge pins of the door were on the inside. If I can pry them loose and get it down, I thought, I can use the candlestick to scrape loose the mortar before it dries. How long can it take? I pressed my ear against the door. I couldn't hear a thing. But then, there was a brick wall outside the door now. If there are guards posted, they'll hear. But then, if I can't hear them, they can't hear me, can they? Why hadn't I inspected the door more closely when I had light? What if the pins weren't there? What if they were too heavy and stiff to move? Terror-struck, my fingers as cold as ice, I began to feel along the edges of the door in the dark.

Twenty-three

he full moon shone all distorted through the heavy little green-glass circles that made up the window of the astrologer's chamber. With Nicolas's help, Nostradamus had made the chamber ready for the great prophecy the queen had commanded. The four sacred names had been written in the corners of the magic mirror, a rectangle of polished steel, with the blood of a male pigeon, and the mirror itself wrapped in a white linen cloth never before used. Nostradamus himself, with the charcoaled end of a cross, traced the double magic circle and the sacred symbols, while Nicolas tidied up, laid out the human bones, and caught and magnetized the cat, which lay completely stiff, but quite alive, along with the skull and the tibia along the rim of the circle. Outside, an owl hooted in the forest beyond the castle.

"She'll be here at midnight," said the old prophet. "I'm terribly sorry, but you need to be well away from the room when I call the spirits. We'll be in the magic circle, but you—"

"You will remember Sibille, won't you?" said Nicolas.

"How could I forget? You'll just have to trust me. You can watch outside the door, if you like. When you see her come out of the room, you come back, and I'll tell you how it went."

"Maestro," said Nicolas, doffing his hat again, and kneeling before the old sage, "if your plan saves my Sibille, I'll name my firstborn son after you."

My, my, thought Nostradamus, as he watched the young man leave, and to think they say the young have no manners anymore. Now that young fellow, he knows how to respect a prophet.

At five minutes before midnight, the dumpy little woman in black arrived at the door of the astrologer's chamber, and bade her attendants wait outside. The old doctor himself ushered her into the magic circle. He could feel the fine tremor that ran through her hand; her doughy face was sheet white.

"Where is the magic mirror?" she asked.

"There, on the mantelpiece, still wrapped in linen, Majesty," replied Nostradamus.

"H—how does it work?" asked the queen.

"It does not work by itself. We must invoke powerful forces. You had best be safe inside the magic circle." Her little pop eyes wide with superstitious awe, but her step determined, the queen entered the circle.

"I must know the fate of my sons, of the throne of France," said the queen.

"The power of the mirror is absolute in that respect," said Nostradamus, unveiling the steel rectangle that stood on the mantelpiece. And all the while he thought, you silly woman, you just couldn't resist, could you? You probably asked Menander to make your sons all kings, and now *I* have to deal with the mess you've made of it, and get away without being executed, too. Very well, awe and fear are my best protections. With a portentous gesture, he sprinkled an herb on the burning coals of a small brazier. A cloud of smoke with a curious scent arose.

"What's that?" said the queen. Hmph, thought Nostradamus, you're probably going to try this at home as soon as I've gone. Better do some chanting in Greek, Arabic, and Latin.

"It is saffron, the scent of which is particularly agreeable to the angel Anael, keeper of history past and future."

"The angel of Venus," whispered the queen. "I have him on my talisman." Nervously, she fingered the magic charm that hung around her neck.

"He is the door, the guardian of the secrets you seek," said Nostradamus, and he began to chant in several unknown tongues in a way that the queen did not dare to interrupt. At last, in the mix of terrifying supernatural tongues, she could make out French: "*O Roi éternel! O Ineffable! Daignez envoyer à votre serviteur très indigne votre ange Anael sur ce miroir—*" Ah, at last, he's calling Anael, she thought, and she trembled all over. How powerful, how dangerous was Nostradamus, who could call such mighty beings from the other world!

But the mirror, the mirror had begun to move, entirely without human agency. No longer did it tilt against the chimney, but stood bolt upright, as if being held by some invisible force. Then a shadow, a dark shadow that looked like an immense hand, seemed to lift it up, and tilt it as if to reflect some other, some unseen world beyond the tower room. And all around the mirror, she seemed to see strange, twinkling little lights, rolling and sparking against a midnight blue background. A face, was that a face near the high ceiling? An immense face, beautiful and frightening, staring at her with ancient, ancient yellow eyes. . . .

"Show us, O Anael, the fate of the throne of France," intoned Nostradamus.

The mirror had changed to reflect a black room, hung with strange tapestries the color of congealed blood. Into the room walked little François, shrunken inside his brand-new coronation robes, his right hand grasping the scepter of France, exactly as he had looked in the cathedral. Seventeen, and his nose was running.

"My son, the king," whispered Catherine de Medici. Solemnly, the boy made a single turn of the blood-draped room. "What does that mean?" she whispered.

"Shh!" said Nostradamus. A second phantom had appeared in the mirror. Her son Charles, hardly older than he was at that very moment, perhaps only ten, perhaps only a year from now, weighed down under the heavy crown of France, the scepter in his hand, the robes too large for his narrow little frame. Silently, in the polished steel, he began to make turns around the room. One, two, three, counted the queen, until she had counted fourteen, and then he vanished. Suddenly, the queen understood the terrible trick that Menander had played on her, the way in which she had been granted her heart's desire. As if in confirmation, a third phantom appeared in the mirror. A good-looking young man, foppish, wearing several diamond earrings. The crown looked like a piece of vulgar jewelry on his head. His eyes were narrow, his face malignant and scheming. Who was this? But her mother's heart knew him. Henri, her favorite, her beautiful baby, grown into such a man as this. With narrow little steps, his silk-shod feet began the circuit of the room. Fifteen times she counted, before the vision vanished. Menander, you monster, thought the queen. You made all my sons kings *of the same country*. All will die young. François will reign a year, then die. Then Charles will reign fourteen years—that means he will not live to see his thirtieth year. And Henri. Delightful, charming, lovely little Henri. Her heart felt like a stone, growing heavy, heavier. But where is Hercule? she thought. The next will be Hercule, or a grandchild. Yes, a grandchild. Show me that all my cares have not been in vain.

At first she did not recognize the figure in the mirror. Short and wiry, his step tough and springy, his face looked like no Valois. But that nose—there was something familiar about that big nose. The nose of old King Francis, or rather, of his sister, set in the face of—No! By God, it had to be—the son of the King of Navarre and that stuck-up, priggish little Protestant, Jeanne d'Albret! The Bourbons had taken the throne! "No!" cried the queen. "Never!"

"Can't you be *quiet*? said Nostradamus in a fierce whisper. "Now look what you've done. Forty-two days of purification, and you've spoiled the magic mirror."

It was true. The steel mirror was leaning against the chimney again, its base resting on the mantelpiece. It reflected only the plastered brick walls of the astrologer's chamber. The brazier was still sending smoke into the room, the moon had set, and the only light was from the array of burned-down candles of various sizes set out on the worktable, the nightstand, and the writing desk in the corner. Outside the dark, the impenetrable dark, seemed to veil the world in death and grief.

"I don't need to know any more than that," said the queen, her voice cold and distant. "There is only one thing I need to know, and that you cannot tell me."

"And what is that?"

"By what magic I can undo the work of that terrible head."

"Oh? What terrible head is that?" said Nostradamus, his voice sounding as innocent as a five-year-old girl's.

"Cosmo Ruggieri, may God damn his eyes, told me all my wishes could be achieved with the Undying Head of Menander the Magus."

"Ah, in my studies I have come across many mentions of this thing. Does it by any chance reside in a silver-gilt box with the curious figure of a rooster-headed god on the lid?"

"You know it," gasped the queen. "Help me, Maestro. Tell me, will I live long enough to undo its work?" Nostradamus took her measure with a single shrewd glance, and pretended to go into a trance over the last of the brazier smoke.

"O, Anael, a vision," he intoned. "Yes, yes,—I'm seeing something. Words of fire, written in the night sky."

"What words?" cried the queen.

"The queen's life will end exactly one day after that of the person who currently holds the head of Menander the Undying."

"Oh, that can't be, that simply can't!" cried the queen. "I've just buried it—I mean her—and if I open the tomb, then someone else may get the head and use it against me."

"Wha—where am I?" said Nostradamus, pretending to be groggy with his vision.

"I can't let that thing out, even if it costs my life. I've spiked it shut."

"Great queen, Majesty, worthy as the sacrifice you plan, I must tell you that in an ancient text—over here—I have a way of destroying the head's powers forever."

"But, but, it can't die." The queen's voice was frantic.

"Ah, it can't die, but it can be sent into a state where it no longer communicates with the living—"

"I can't read that book." Of course you can't, thought Nostradamus. Otherwise you'd know it's a formula for raining frogs.

"I'll write out the translation for you," said Nostradamus, who had taken the queen's measure. If Sibille had followed the instructions he'd sent along with the horoscope, the head was already permanently distracted. But he knew this queen. She was very fond of do-it-yourself magic, a fumbler, an amateur. If she could be convinced it was she who had neutralized the head, she might feel more generous toward Sibille, and live for a while with the distracting illusion that her powers were great enough to reverse the terrible fate she had set in motion. It can do nothing but good, thought Nostradamus to himself, as he copied out an entirely spurious, but very grand-sounding formula onto a piece of parchment.

"What are these little signs?" asked the queen, suddenly seeming in a great hurry.

"This + here is the sign of the cross, and this one here, the gesture of a circle, and this, the terrible three-headed beast. You make it like this—"

"Oh," said the queen, her gargoyle eyes even larger than before, as she realized she was being initiated into the very highest secrets of magic.

"Don't delay," said Nostradamus. "You must live. My powers have told me that only you can save the kingdom."

❧

Nostradamus was sweeping up all the powders and rubbing out the magic circle with a broom when Nicolas came in.

"Oh, there you are, young man. Could you pick up that tibia for me? My gout, you know. An old man like me shouldn't have to bend over." As Nicolas picked up the bone, the cat awoke with a howl, and ran away to hide under the bed, her tail as large and stiff as a bottlebrush.

"Where is Sibille? Have you saved her? Tell me where she is, and I'll hew a path to her with my sword." The old doctor looked at the younger man's anxious face, and beamed benignly.

"Don't worry about that young lady of yours. My powers tell me that the queen is going to look after her very well for the rest of her life."

Down the narrow stone steps hurried the torchbearer, two laborers with pickaxes, and the queen, her black silk dress rustling on the steps. Through the deepest wine cellar they passed, where dust stood heavy on the casks, down to blank place in the wall where new bricks masked what was once the entrance to a storeroom reserved for the very rarest vintages, the very choicest distillations. A brick had been poked from the top of the patch, and lay shattered on the stone floor. From behind the sealed wall, there came the diligent sound of scratching.

"Insolence, just plain insolence," said the queen, as she spied the broken brick in the torchlight. "Whatever did she think she'd do once she was outside and locked in the wine cellar? She could never have escaped me. A queen's will is sovereign." Then she gestured to the patch of new bricks. "Break it down," she said to the men with pickaxes.

When the battering and crashing ceased, the new section of wall lay in rubble, and the light of the torch revealed mad chaos and disorder in the little room. The door lay on the floor, covered with shattered bricks and powder, and in the corner, the dancing orange light played on the crazed, astonished face of a ragged, dust-streaked, frantic young woman. She had taken everything of metal, hairpins, bodice pins, ruff pins, to attack the wall. Her hair hung loose, a dusty brown mass, about her face, and the torn bodice of her overdress, once pinned to the corset, had fallen about her in ruins. Her hands, which had grown bloody in the struggle, she had wrapped in strips torn from her petticoat. In them she still held a fragment of the iron candlestick, which had broken apart at the weld with the rough treatment she had given it.

"My, you certainly do not look well," said the queen. "I hope you have not breathed too much brick dust. They say it is bad for the lungs."

"Being walled in is bad for the health, too," said the tall, bony young woman, her eyes bright with resentment, her hand still tight on the sharp fragment of candlestick.

"Why, darling child, don't you realize, this was just a little test I set you—yes, a test of—loyalty—" The queen's eyes slithered sideways as her brain sought for a more convincing lie.

"A *test*? You walled me in for a test?"

"Yes, I merely wanted to see whether you were *worthy*—oh, and please put down that sharp little thing and hand me that box in the corner. I have something I must do without delay."

"Worthy of what?" said Sibille, carefully reaching for the box without taking her eyes off the queen or putting down the candlestick fragment. Cautiously, gingerly, she handed Menander the Undying's battered, spiked box to the queen.

"I had in mind a reward—for silence—but first you, ah, needed to

understand my *power*—a great reward—I'll tell you in a minute. First
things first." The queen took a little piece of parchment and began to
read the oddest syllables over the box, all the while, making curious gestures, the sign of the cross, a circle, and yet another one, curiously obscene, to punctuate the speech. "There," she said with a sigh. "I've
sealed up his powers. Now for the test." Viciously, she rattled the box
back and forth.

"Quit bothering me, I'm thinking," came the leathery little voice from
inside.

"Wake up, wake up in there, you old mummy. I have a few dozen
wishes to make," said the queen.

"I can't be bothered with your wishes. Go away. I'm busy," said the
head in the box.

"Perfect," said the queen. "After centuries, I, Catherine de Medici,
have vanquished the accursed, undying head." She was so pleased with
herself that she did not notice the cynical, exasperated look cross
Sibille's face. Or perhaps she would have missed it anyway, there in the
dark, in the wee hours of the morning, with only the light of a single
torch to reveal it.

"When will you be done?" asked Sibille.

"My dear, your manners need much improvement," said the queen.
"Still, I am an understanding sovereign. And I had planned—let's
see—hmm, yes, that's come vacant—Beauvoir? It's quite well enough
situated—healthful air, a nice orchard as I recall. Fruit prolongs life—I
have a wonderful recipe for jellied crabapples that is excellent for
fevers—yes, I have been planning to make you, for past and future services to the crown, a baroness. Now, aren't you grateful and happy?"

"Oh, yes, Majesty, eternally grateful," said Sibille in a very cautious
voice.

"I'm so glad we understand each other, dear. Goodness, your hands
look just dreadful. I've a lovely little remedy for that—the purest olive
oil, first pressing only, with distillation of marigold, and a pinch, just a
pinch, mind you, of powdered mummy, which dear Doctor Fernel assures me is very powerfully renewing to the flesh—"

The woman's gone crazy, though Sibille. Play along with her, and
maybe you'll get out. "Oh, yes," she said. "I can hardly wait to try it."

"So splendid—I'll have some made up. But first, you'll be needing a new dress. That one is not fit to be seen in, let alone received by *me,* in your new estate. I'm sure the mistress of the wardrobe has just the thing. With a few alterations—oh, yes, and those feet—they must be disguised at all costs. However did you get such large feet? I must not have noticed before—"

Absolutely crazy, thought Sibille as she followed the queen up the narrow stairs. Her knees were still wobbling with the terror of death nearly missed, and her chest was heavy with the terror of the queen's unknown, mysterious purpose. Her mind's unhinged, it's all right, thought Sibille to herself, over and over. Surely, she's just insane, and it will all come out all right. She hasn't got anything worse in mind. No, she was just crazy for a while, and it's over. It must be the strain of widowhood. That, and having to defer to that snobbish little Queen of Scots. She never could stand her. Now, just so she doesn't change her mind about letting me go. The rest must be just lunatic ravings. Baroness, what talk. What is her real purpose? Why is she lulling me?

But by the time they had entered the queen's own chamber, and found the maid making up the fire in the cold light just before dawn, Sibille began to wonder whether it was all true. And as the queen herself directed the maid to make the necessary repairs to her person, she began to cheer up, and the tremor that had made her knees so weak began to fade away. Craziness in the great can be borne, so long as it is favorable to oneself, she thought, her breath coming back to her, and her blood beginning to thump through her heart again. Hmm, that could be made into a clever little aphorism, if I rephrased it right. Then perhaps I could work it into the *Dialogue.* What mythological setting would I place it in? It must be heavily disguised. I wonder if she still has a mind to sponsor my little cultural offerings—or perhaps I should arrange for a private printing. . . .

❖

The windows of the astrologer's chamber had been thrown open to allow the last of the smoke to dissipate, and now the rising sun stained the windowsill pink, and outside, newly awakened birds began to sing. Nostradamus and Nicolas sat side by side on the bed, and the old man watched the younger man wring his hands as he talked on and on in an anguished voice. The hours since the seance had dragged on like days, especially since the young man seemed bent on explaining the course of his entire life to the old doctor. Oof, I could never be a priest, thought Nostradamus. All those boring, ordinary confessions. They would make one yearn for scandal.

"—and then, after that, you see, my father at last gave his permission to marry, and I rode day and night from my cousin's household in Genoa, killing three horses and crippling two—"

"Hmm. Very fast," said Nostradamus, nodding.

"I've been learning the banking business, you see. I know you'll think that's lowly. I do myself, or, rather I did. I wanted distinction, and since I couldn't have a title, I thought perhaps scholarship—I tried several branches of learning—but did you know, bankers mingle every day with princes, and many obtain distinction. Look at the Gondis, look at the Biragues—they have reached the highest levels—it isn't impossible. And it requires a very shrewd mind—no great enterprise can be undertaken without money—it is the bankers, in the end, who decide whether there is war or peace, not rules—why, the last war—"

"My boy, let me impart to you the Secret of the Ages," said Nostradamus, interrupting the flow of narrative. "When I, as a young man, sought knowledge, after an unpleasant interlude which I do not care to discuss, I decided to discover the Secret of Happiness, which is the most important of all the Secrets—"

"Ah, um?" said Nicolas. Old man, they rattle on, and you have to pretend to listen. Respect, you see, it's important.

"The first secret is to find an excellent life partner. The second, is to take up a profession of interest, and the third is to do good wherever you find the opportunity presents itself."

"Maestro—ah, um, that's three secrets," observed Nicolas.

"In a larger sense, you'll find it's only one Secret, if you think about it, young man. Just one. That one is love."

"Love?" said Nicolas, perking up.

"Yes, love. For others, for the world, for wisdom, for what you do with your life—just love, but, as you see, rather broadly interpreted—"

"That, well, that's *definitely* a secret," said Nicolas, trying to be agreeable. The old doctor's gone a bit dotty, he thought. Too many late nights.

"Secret indeed, though you may shout it from the housetops," went on Nostradamus. "Though I shouldn't complain. A far greater prophet than I am tried to tell the world the same thing, and nobody listened to *Him,* either—"

But at this moment, the door to the astrologer's chamber was thrown open by a valet, who announced the Queen of France, and Nostradamus looked up to see a most pleasing sight, that validated all his trickery and made him feel very clever and smug, indeed. "Why, Nicolas, here is your ladylove come to find you, and looking very handsome, if I do say so myself," he said.

But Nicolas had already leapt up, his face transfigured with joy. With a cry, he and Sibille ran toward each other, and embraced, weeping, exclaiming over each other, and looking as if they could never see enough of each other's faces.

At the sight, the queen's face fell into a doughy mass, and an envious, evil glitter started up in her eye. Nostradamus, who missed nothing, bowed deeply to her.

"Great Queen," he said, "you will stand mighty in the annals of France, but even mightier in the secret annals of the occult, for with your fierce power, you have vanquished the unvanquishable." Inwardly, he sighed with relief as he saw the evil glitter vanish, and heard the queen's response.

"Mighty? Feared? A vanquisher?" she whispered, her doughy face distorted in sudden grief. "All that I craved in my life was for my husband, the king, to love me, and that creature in the box stole away all hope forever."

"Hope is not gone, Majesty," said Nostradamus, although he knew that for her, it was. "While you live and labor, there is hope. God's eye sees all."

"God? Where was God when the visor slipped?" she said, and as Nostradamus watched her, he had the most curious feeling, as if he were hearing some transformation within her barren, ruined heart. Black guilt and bitterest envy, fired by vengeance and rage, were working an alchemy in the secret chambers of her soul; there a vile substance was brewing and bubbling and changing, rising like poisonous smoke. And as he watched her aura, he saw a horrible sight, but being a philosopher of the highest order, his face never lost its calm and objective demeanor. What he saw was this: a writhing, rubbery bundle, like a larva struggling to metamorphose, like a venomous serpent's egg throbbing with internal life yet to be born, and then he saw it tear open, and something huge, pulsating, scaly, and swaying rise and surround the dumpy little figure in black.

Menander's last gift, thought the prophet, and his blood turned to ice within him, and the hair rose on the back of his neck. He has created this monster and laid her in the heart of history, and the evil deeds she will do will spread through time and space like the ripples in a pond, lapping on alien shores that never even knew that she drew breath on the earth. He saw the streets of Paris heaped with the bodies of men, women, and children; gory-faced madmen with knives and swords, loosed at her command, running wildly among the corpses, and the Seine itself flowing red with blood.

I think I need to go home, Nostradamus said to himself. My little house looks better than ever to me now. He drew a deep breath as he inspected the room. Sibille and Nicolas, the valets and attendants, all seemed oblivious to what he had seen. And then the queen said, "You will all be seated at places of honor at my table this very day," and everyone beamed at this joyful outcome, and only he heard the serpent's hiss behind her words. He looked at Sibille and Nicolas, who were still holding hands, and thought: they are clever enough to look after themselves—especially since I have convinced the serpent-mother that her life depends on Sibille's continued well-being. It is enough. I need to go home.

That night, after Sibille and Nicolas had departed, laden with gifts, mounted on the queen's own horses, and escorted by two armed guards charged with seeing that not a hair on their heads was harmed on the road to Paris, Nostradamus sat up late in the astrologer's chamber. The fire in the athanor had gone out, and the room seemed chilly and empty. A single candle leapt and bobbed before him, as he sat at the desk, turning over the pages of an ancient text that he didn't really have the heart to read.

"Michel?" said a voice.

"Oh, Anael, you're back. I'm cold, I'm sad, my gouty foot hurts, and I miss my family. It's a long way home, and I don't see any good coming to the country. The civil war of religion—I've failed. It's coming. The only question is when. God help us all."

"Actually, Michel, depending on how you count them, there will be six civil wars of religion."

"You didn't need to say that."

"I only came back after today's little seance to let you know that I have made a decision," said Anael, looking pleased with himself. His midnight blue frame filled the entire height of the tall room, and the twinkling lights were whirling and bouncing inside him with some hidden pleasure.

"You're going to keep the serpent-queen from taking power," said Nostradamus.

"Oh, heavens, no—I can't do that. It's already right there in the history cupboard. When that froggy son of hers dies, she'll pack the Scottish Queen back off to Scotland and move into her other little boy's room. She'll run him like a puppet for years, until he dies in an agony of remorse for all the evil he's done at her command."

"Anael, you're just plain nasty. I'm not in a mood to hear these things."

"I am *not* nasty," said Anael, drawing himself up and ruffling his shining raven's wings. "I'll have you know I'm very thoughtful and considerate. Not only do I put up with *you,* but I've made my great decision: I'm going to help that poor bony girl get into the history business. It will be a kindness all around. Her poetry—with one notable exception—makes my back crawl. And she won't give it up until she's sure of something better."

"Ugh, that floral tribute to the ladies of the court. Did you know she sent me a copy? All tied up in a pink ribbon. That slimy Madame Gondi as a white lilac, and Madam d'Elbène as a lily-of-the-valley—oof, the abominations. Too many to count—" Nostradamus shuddered.

"But the ladies just ate it up, you must admit. It looks well on its way to setting off a storm of even more revolting imitation. So you see—by assisting her to write history, and give up those horrid little poetic offerings that are so copied, I'll be saving the literature of France from de-cades, maybe centuries, of similar horrors. Now isn't that a fine thing? What's improving civil and political history compared to improving the history of a great literature? I'd much rather dabble in worthy, higher, spiritual sorts of histories." Anael preened himself and beamed down on the weary old doctor.

"Anael, you make me crazy," said Nostradamus. "I suppose that's part of the curse."

"Oh, no," said Anael, all happy and inflated with his new idea, "it's just your temperament. You poor mortals grow old and sour so quickly, where I—I am in the very dawn of my existence." He stretched out his wings until they were fully extended, then his bare, blue arms and smoky hands. His long, blue torso rippled and little whirling lights in-side danced and spun anew. Anael was indeed very beautiful, and quite conscious of it.

"So history is kept by a creature who is not only a bad housekeeper, but an irresponsible infant—"

"Michel, I refuse to speak to you in this mood," said the angel. "Go home and have your wife cook you a proper meal, or I simply will not be able to abide your company, curse or no curse."

"They don't use enough garlic here," Nostradamus grumbled. But Anael had vanished.

Epilogue

It was a summer night so hot even the crickets couldn't go to sleep and the stars vibrated with the heat. The stones of the streets of Salon breathed heat back up into the dark, southern sky. In Nostradamus's garden, the fountain splashed beneath the dark shadows of trees. The shutters of the bedrooms were open to let in whatever feeble night breeze decided to make its appearance. But high, high, in the top of the house, the shutters were latched closed, and the flickering glow of a candle could be seen between the cracks. Once again, the great prophet was summoning the ghosts of the future.

Beneath his white linen diviner's robe, the old magician wore only his undershirt, and even in that, he was sweating mightily. But he had not neglected his doctor's hat, nor his ring with the seven mystical sym-bols, nor the medal on a ribbon that he had received from the Queen of France for his extraordinary services, for even spirits require a certain level of formality at least in outward appearance. Dampening his laurel wand, he set the waters in motion, repeating the sacred words until he felt the familiar shadow rise behind him.

"So, Nostradamus, you can't resist. I would think you would weary of knowing the future," said the voice of Anael, whose invisible pres-ence now vibrated in the closed, muggy room.

"O Spirit, show me a vision of the wonders of the distant future," intoned the old prophet, as he stirred the waters in his brass divining bowl with his wand. As the waters stilled, he peered down to see a magical city, with sparkling towers and low, paneled houses with turned up roofs, stretching down to a blue-watered harbor full of immense, sail-less boats. The streets were filled with curiously dressed people, and covered coaches that moved about without horses. He couldn't read the street signs, which were in no alphabet he had ever seen.

"This isn't France," he said, enchanted with what he saw.

"Be glad," said the spirit, and Nostradamus saw a man pause and look up. High above the city, a sort of silver goose, drifting alone almost beyond view, glinted in the blue sky. What could that be? thought the prophet.

At that moment a huge and instantaneous fire swallowed the entire city so that the horrified seer saw nothing but a flash and then red, red, until he thought he had been blinded. Blinking his eyes, he saw an immense, billowing cloud rise above the city, as the goose—a winged carriage?—flew off. As the cloud cleared, he saw nothing but blackness, ruin, and scattered fires where the city had been.

"Anael, what was that?" Nostradamus could feel his voice stick in his throat.

"There are two," said Anael. "They also poison the wind."

"Two," whispered Nostradamus, and his hand shook as he scratched across the page with his quill pen:

Near the harbor and in two cities
Will be two scourges never before witnessed....

A huge weight crushed the old prophet's chest, his bones hurt, and he could hardly breathe as he pulled his gaze from the still-shifting waters.

"What's it all *about*," he cried in despair. "What's it all *for*?"

"How should *I* know?" said Anael. "I only look after it, I don't make it. I'm considerably older and cleverer than you, and I still haven't figured it out." The spirit had begun to form up in the room, although he was still quite translucent, and the little twinkling things inside him were all drooping and still, with some unmentionable sorrow.

"I thought, perhaps, He might have told you."

"He doesn't think like we do, Michel. You'll have to leave it at that."

"Then show me something cheerful, Anael, my heart is breaking."

"Oh, stir up your dish, Michel, I have just the thing. I've been saving it right on top for you." Anael's upper half vanished, and there was a rattling and a rummaging sound in the large, invisible armoire. Then silence, and Anael reappeared, looking smug. As the ripples stilled in the bowl, a rich hall appeared, all hung with garlands, and filled with strangers in fine dress. Who was that great, gaudy woman at the head table, beaming with pleasure, sharing a big silver cup with the curled-up little man in the gown and hat of an abbé? Yes, it just had to be—

"Why, it's a wedding," said Nostradamus, peering into the water. "It must be a very close vision in time—I can hear the music. And a *branle*— quite a lively one—a new tune I don't recognize. I can feel my toes just tapping. Did you know how well I could dance when I was young?"

"I'm rather fond of dancing myself."

"Spirits dance?"

"Yes, but not often. We have to be careful. It shakes the universe, you know."

"Why look, here's the bride. Goodness, it's Sibille, getting married at last. Hmph. Yes. To Nicolas, as it ought to be. And just look at her dance! There she goes—the leap and turn—heavens, that girl has big feet!"

"That fellow who's holding her waist doesn't seem to notice."

"They never do, when they're in love," said the old prophet. "Tell me, whatever happened to Menander the Undying?"

"You'll have to quit tapping your foot if you want me to show you," said Anael.

"I'm *not* tapping it," said the old doctor, suddenly remembering his dignity.

"Have it your way, but just take a look at *this*—"

Nostradamus peered at the bowl, but couldn't make sense of the image. Village people in festival dress, a holiday, a gathering of some sort— ah, a fair—there were the vendors, he could hear the cries of a woman selling pies from a tray—and a crowd. Oh, a dancing bear. Quite a good one, really—not moth-eaten looking at all, the way so many are. I'm fond of dancing bears, he thought, but what has this to do with Menander?

Now four monks, carrying a big wooden box on poles were pushing through the crowd. "Repent! Repent! The Kingdom of God is at hand!" shouted the monk who walked before them, ringing a little handbell.

"View the relic," he could hear the monks carrying the box shout. "View the sacred relic; only a small offering and you may kiss the box." Even before they had entered the shabby little canvas pavilion and shut the flap, people were crowding around the box, trying to touch it, trying to kiss it without paying.

A line had formed in front of the pavilion flap. Peasants in their Sunday clothes, cripples, women in wooden shoes carrying sick infants. A monk with a charity box was taking offerings almost faster than he could talk. "The head of John the Baptist, the one, the true, the only—all others are false—" he was saying.

"Anael," said Nostradamus, "those don't look like monks at all. That one there, I swear he's got a brand on his hand. See how he's smeared it with something?"

Inside the tent, on top of the wooden ark in which it had been carried, stood a battered, tarnished silver-gilt box, wide open, lit by two candles in tin holders, one placed on each side.

"I've seen better on pikes in the city hall square," a big man in wooden shoes was saying. "How do I know this isn't just some criminal's head?"

"It's *alive*," said the monk in attendance. And at that, the eyelids flickered, and a groaning sound issued from the mummified head. At this, the crowd in the tent pulled back, horrified.

"Why doesn't it speak?"

"The immortal head of John the Baptist is deep in holy contemplation. Come closer, good people, it blesses, it cures, it elevates—tell your friends."

"Anael," said Nostradamus, "did you know that Menander had his own *religion* when he was alive? And look at him now—"

"So did John the Baptist—"

"It's *entirely* different, and you know it," snapped the old doctor.

"I can *walk*, I can *walk*!" cried a man, ostentatiously throwing down his crutch. Outside, the monk taking cash cried, "A miracle! A miracle!

Hurry, hurry inside—it blesses! It heals!" Inside the tent, the crutch was being hung up. In back of the tent, the miraculously healed man was accepting payment from one of the monks.

"And not a peep out of Menander all this time. She must have done it—asked him for the impossible wish—" said Nostradamus. "I take no little pride in putting that monstrous thing out of business."

"*In* business is more like it," observed Anael, with a cheerful grin. But Nostradamus had collapsed back on his wooden stool with a sigh.

"It's clear to me," said the old man, "that getting rid of Menander didn't save the world at all."

"I thought I'd explained it to you, Michel. History works like a river—"

"What you mean is, humanity doesn't need sorcery to spoil the world. They can do it all by themselves," observed Nostradamus.

"Exactly. I couldn't have put it better myself," said the Spirit of History.